DEAD SET ON YOU

A Novel

LEXI ALEXANDER

Books should be disposed of and recycled according to local requirements.
All paper materials used are FSC compliant.

This is a work of fiction. All of the names, characters, organizations, places, and events portrayed in this novel are either products of the author's imagination or are used fictitiously. Any resemblance to real or actual events, locales, or persons, living or dead, is entirely coincidental.

Published in the United States by Alcove Press, an imprint of The Quick Brown Fox & Company LLC.

Alcove Press and its logo are trademarks of The Quick Brown Fox & Company LLC.

Library of Congress Catalog-in-Publication data available upon request.

ISBN (hardcover): 979-8-89242-404-2
ISBN (paperback): 979-8-89242-405-9
ISBN (ebook): 979-8-89242-406-6

Cover illustration by Mallory Heyer

Printed in the United States.

www.alcovepress.com

Alcove Press
34 West 27th St., 10th Floor
New York, NY 10001

First Edition: December 2025

The authorized representative in the EU for product safety and compliance is eucomply OÜPärnu mnt 139b-14, 11317 Tallinn, Estonia, hello@eucompliancepartner.com, +33757690241

10 9 8 7 6 5 4 3 2 1

For Julian and Luca — may your dreams be wild,
your bucket lists long, and your hearts all in.

FIVE YEARS BEFORE

The night of my thirteenth birthday, I wrote the first of now fifty-two items on my bucket list. Today, I planned on crossing off #17: *Get my first big job by 22*, which came right before *Buy my first apartment by 25* and somewhere after *Kiss someone who makes my knees weak* (still pending).

Most people my age were still figuring themselves out, but I didn't have that kind of luxury. I had lists that needed checking and timelines to stick to, and nothing—not love, natural disasters or other catastrophic events—was going to stop me. But delays? Those were harder to avoid. For instance, the blizzard currently rolling through Chicago.

It's why I was twelve minutes late to my first day at my "first big job"—half frozen and wholly mortified. This wasn't how I'd imagined my first day as a marketing assistant in one of Chicago's top marketing firms, working for the best in the business. I wasn't entirely sure they hadn't made a mistake hiring me to begin with. I hadn't gone to a fancy school or been mentored by anyone with a corner office. I'd just . . . worked. Hard. Relentlessly. Like my life depended on it.

And today, it did.

This is it, I reminded myself as I shuffled across the lobby of Lakeview Towers. Despite the snowstorm, the building bustled with people—my kind of people. People with dreams and aspirations, who didn't let a few snowflakes get in the way.

I deserve to be here.

I repeated the phrase the entire forty-seven seconds it took for an elevator to arrive, and then once more as I filed into the elevator after a group of people, most wrapped up in parkas and scarves. Me, though? I teetered on high heels and wore a Calvin Klein dress I'd gotten at Ross Dress for Less because not even snowmageddon was enough to keep me from making an impression. But it had been enough to make me late.

Stomach churning, I practiced my apology speech the entire way up to the thirty-eighth floor, and by the time I arrived at the entrance to Media Lab's lobby, I was convinced I had a fighting chance. Maybe. I just needed to get in the same room as my new boss.

Briefly, I stalled outside the glass doors, my reflection frowning back at me. The brisk wind had tousled my light-brown hair, which I'd carefully styled that morning, and my olive eyes were bright against my newly wind-chapped cheeks. My tote—heavy with my snow boots and the three library books I was absolutely going to return tonight because I couldn't afford late fees—made my body curve awkwardly to one side. I was serving *unprepared assistant* as opposed to *boss bitch.*

I'd have to change that.

I sucked in a deep breath, straightened my posture, and marched inside, shaking off my nerves like I hadn't just spent the last hour in a spiral of doom. Fake it until you make it.

I approached a shiny receptionist desk with a shiny assistant tucked behind a shiny computer.

"Good morning! I'm here for Dana Casper. I'm Ev—"

"She's with her nine o'clock." The curly-haired assistant—iPhone dangling in her manicured hand—didn't even glance up. "You can wait there." She gestured to the sitting area in the lobby, her eyes never leaving her very important scrolling.

I blinked.

"Um . . . but can you tell her that I'm here? It's my first day, and of course I didn't mean to be late. I left an entire two hours early, but I forgot my—"

Liv Houston, per her nameplate, continued to scroll. I could have been invisible for all she cared.

I clamped my lips together, my pulse pounding with indecision.

I figured I had two choices: wait in the lobby to get fired or do something about it, like I'd always done. And if there was one thing I knew, it was that life loved throwing punches. I'd been dodging and countering them since birth, and I wasn't backing down now, not when my job hung in the balance.

I was Evie flipping Pope.

I was going to—

"Evie?"

The male voice startled me so hard I yipped, snapping my head over my shoulder and clutching my twenty-pound tote to my chest.

"What in—" I stalled, and gawked.

A beautiful man stood—or rather, towered—a few feet away, looking the way you'd expect an executive at Media Lab to look, like they'd been plucked from the average masses because their DNA was superior in all ways: brains, bone structure, and boardroom swagger.

And him? He could have spawned them.

Dark hair, warm brown eyes, and sun-kissed skin that had no business existing in the terrible Chicago winter. A baby-blue dress shirt stretched over lean, toned muscles, broad enough to wrap me snuggly against his chest and strong enough to hoist me up against a desk and *oh God, no.*

Heat flared up my chest, my neck, my face as my thoughts derailed into no-go territory because sure, I had my lists, but damn if I wasn't lonely.

"You *are* Evie?" He smiled politely as I stared like an idiot.

"Ah, yes," I managed, voice too high-pitched. "Evie Pope."

I prayed for a quick death.

"Rafael Vela, but most people call me Raf." His grin stretched and curved, and—*oh Mamma Mia*—a dimple said hello as his hand reached for mine, engulfed it, warmed it, made me fixate on it.

"Hi, Raf," I said, still gripping his hand and knowing very much I needed to let go. My social skills were playing a game of hide-and-seek, and someone needed to find them.

Release! I commanded my fingers to disengage from his, to allow the blood to recirculate before I killed him, before I even had a chance to know who he was, what he did, and did he do it well?

Face flushing, I dropped my hand from his with an abrupt jerk, only to send my bag tumbling to the ground, half of its contents clattering and sliding across the marble floor.

And that's all I needed to snap out of it.

The cold must have iced my brain, because I was *failing* on the most important day of my life, and I couldn't afford failure. I'd be kicked out of my basement apartment if I failed. I'd have to continue working double shifts at Pauline's. I'd have to . . .

Nope. I needed to get my shit together.

Shaking off my fantasy-adjacent stupor, I sank to the ground, mumbling an apology as I reached for *Jane Eyre*, which had slid up against Raf's shoe.

He crouched beside me. "It happens all the time," Rafael said, picking up the book—part of bucket list item #16 (*read the classics*)—and handing it to me.

"People making fools of themselves?" I asked, taking the book, careful to keep our fingers from touching again and making me stupid. I tried not to dwell on his nearness or his scent as I stuffed the book into the bag, atop my boots, not bothering to organize things.

"Yep. Special magnets in the floor. To get shit to fall and break the proverbial ice." He knocked on the marble floor, face serious.

Oh God. He was attractive *and* funny. I was possibly in trouble.

"Hmmm. I'm afraid I only came prepared for icebreaker questions." I kept my features serious too. "My dream superpower. Most petrifying memory. That kind of stuff."

His lips twitched as he held out *Anna Karenina*. "We have that too. A list of a hundred icebreaker questions we go through, right after the tour."

"I didn't know about a tour." I tried to recall the numerous emails I'd received, printed, and highlighted to ensure I hadn't missed a detail.

"Standard first-day procedure. Tour. Meet and greets. Soul-baring icebreakers," Rafael added, reaching for my planner. It was open to this week's spread: color coded, overly ambitious, and ripe for the reading. I snatched it before he could get a closer look and shoved it into the bag.

"Carl's out today on account of the storm," he continued, unfazed. "So the role of tour guide falls to me. I apologize in advance for not knowing nearly as much as Carl about the history of the building or its intricate plumbing system. I've only been here six months, but I promise—cross my heart and hope to die—that I'll try my best to make it bearable."

I blinked, unsure I'd heard him correctly—the part about being a recent employee and the part about . . . "Cross your heart?"

"I have nieces. You get sworn to secrecy. Often. May as well call me Homeland Security." Rafael winked conspiratorially.

"Some drawbacks, though. The nail polish. That shit doesn't come off." He waggled long, tanned fingers, and while my lady bits urged me to fixate on the veins snaking up along his arms and disappearing beneath his shirt sleeve, I forced my eyes to the purple sparkles glimmering on his neatly trimmed nails. "Comes with the territory."

"World's best uncle?" I hoisted the tote onto my shoulder, and we stood at the same time, his back to Liv the Assistant, who scanned Rafael's backside like a Instagram feed.

"World's *only* uncle," he offered, those hands reaching toward me.

My breath hitched, stuttered, and came to a full halt.

"May I?" Rafael gestured to the bag.

I stalled long enough to mentally shake myself, ready to say no, to tell him that I had it. But the mental shake shook out another thought—a new, shiny, impossible thought. What Evie did I want to be at Media Lab (if I didn't get fired)? The Evie who made lists and plans and tried to keep life as controlled as possible because there was always another shoe that would drop?

Or Evie 2.0? Who was going to live a little. Who was going to make friends. And maybe, possibly, open up and accept help without thinking it was going to bite her in the ass.

"Yeah, sure, that would be great," I finally said, allowing myself to smile as I let him take the bag.

Rafael lifted it onto his shoulder as if it weighed nothing. And maybe it was my imagination, but something about handing him the bag made me feel a little lighter on the inside too. Because for the first time in a long time, maybe—just maybe—my fate was changing.

I added ten new items to my bucket list that night.

CHAPTER ONE
(UNDOUBTEDLY) THE MOST IMPORTANT NIGHT

What I can't fix with a ten-mile run, I fix with checklists and ABBA. Which is why fifteen minutes before the most important night of my career begins, I'm sitting in a private booth at the Aviary, one of Chicago's finest dining venues and my go-to for client dinners. "The Winner Takes It All" plays on my AirPods while I mentally run through the "Pitch-Perfect" Checklist I prepared between my morning run and breakfast.

Three more items stand between me and winning the account that could lead to the promotion I've busted my marathon-toned tush for years to win. Three items and I cross the finish line.

1. *Share new marketing numbers—during appetizers*
2. *Deliver final pitch—before dessert*
3. *Keep Rafael in line—all courses*

Most account managers would be anxious about the client dinner itself—the final step in a months-long process of wooing the CEO of OhLaLove, an online dating platform. Instead, it's sitting across from Rafael Vela that has me wanting to *run, checklist, repeat* before dinner is even ordered.

Five years of working with him have taught me that I should plan for all possible scenarios when it comes to Rafael. Including ones where he swaps out my carefully detailed pitch slides for inspirational Disney quotes or ones where he says we're on the same team—friends, even—and then steals the account we spent a year prepping for. No warning, no explanation, no consequences.

It's the reason item #3 is on the list tonight—and why it's been at the top of all checklists for the last six months. Because when our boss insisted Rafael and I work together on winning the multimillion-dollar, multiyear account, I had no choice but to *suck it up, buttercup* for 182 of the longest days of my life (even if you count the years I lived out of a basement room with mice as roommates and a steady diet of ramen and canned tuna).

So, of course, I said yes to the opportunity. The alternative meant showing the boss I couldn't handle a challenge, which wasn't an option, not when she dangled a long-awaited-for promotion at the end of it . . . for both Rafael and me.

As lead account managers, it's the two of us in line for director of marketing. Refusing to work with him would have been a lot like gift wrapping the promotion for Rafael. And he's had enough handed to him. Accounts. Clients. Discounts to major sporting events.

Tonight, my future rides on winning OhLaLove's business—and winning the business means keeping Rafael from messing things up for us. For me. Again.

I've made it six months working behind enemy lines, watching Rafael like he's a human land mine, triple-checking shared files for signs of sabotage, and keeping *my* pitch notes password-protected. Every team meeting, every strategy session, I've been one suspicious eyebrow twitch away from hacking his Outlook—just to make sure history won't repeat itself. I've spent more time prepping backup plans than actual plans.

So what's another few hours?

Enough to make my syncope kick in, that's what.

I imagine fainting into a bowl of boeuf bourguignon, and my stomach churns like a walrus on laxatives. It wouldn't be the first time he's made me faint during a client meeting (a long story that involves scissors and a supply closet), but I swore it was going to be the last.

Because I'm Evie Pope, and I'm in control.

One Mamma Mia.

Two Mamma Mia.

Taking several Rafael-expunging breaths, I straighten and smooth out my black Ted Baker dress, the one I chose specifically for tonight. It's sleek, professional, and the perfect dash of feminine. *Dress for the job you want,* and I've been doing it since my first internship, when I'd use any savings I could scrape together to buy business wear from thrift stores. My first work dress is still hanging in my closet—a reminder that *eventually,* the effort pays off. *Eventually* is a dinner and three checklist items away.

It's just the one item, really, and he's late, even though his apartment is conveniently located across the street from the restaurant (my one mark against the Aviary).

Casting a quick glance toward the restaurant entrance, I reach for one of the three wineglasses and stare down into the burgundy liquid. I don't usually drink before the client arrives, but the longer Rafael hangs out rent-free in my mind, the more I'm tempted to chug straight from the bottle.

One sip.

I bring the glass to my lips as a low, familiar chuckle floats over the din of chatter and dinnerware. I pause and listen.

Rafael's deep, husky voice is a discernible rumble from the rest. Annoyance flares, momentarily dousing my anxiousness. I don't look. I don't have to. No doubt he's taking his time joking with the hostess, talking about the latest sports stats with the valet, and getting Chef to share a secret recipe because Rafael also "dabbles in cooking."

With a sigh, I set down the glass, pop out my AirPods, and shove them into my purse as Rafael appears across the restaurant.

Tall and broad, he's impossible to miss as he saunters over, walking alongside the hostess, who's staring at him like he's dessert. Can't really blame her—it's part of the Vela effect. All of it is: the signature navy dress shirt, sleeves rolled up to reveal tanned arms, and dark slacks that hug his thighs. The way he runs a hand through his dark-chestnut waves as if to tame them and then casually tucks it back into his pocket. The scruff he sometimes sports is gone, and in its place is a jawline that demands attention. His dark bedroom eyes focus on the hostess as he stops and leans in to say something. She laughs, nudging him playfully, her hand lingering on his arm.

I roll my eyes the moment Rafael's gaze shifts and snags on mine.

It's too late to look away, and despite months—*years*—of conditioning myself not to care what Rafael Vela thinks, my cheeks heat at having been caught.

He smirks wickedly, his full lips pulling to one side, and his dimple—his weapon of mass destruction—makes an appearance. Melts my embarrassment into something else entirely.

Hating my body's traitorous reactions, I glare at him until he reaches the table and slides into his seat, dismissing the hostess with another knee-buckling smile.

"Hey," he says, his warm voice making me sit straighter.

"Hi." I avoid—and *deeply* resent—my body's insurrection to the enemy's nearness. "You're late."

"Had a long commute." Rafael's smile turns more devilish.

I know he's baiting me, and because I'm a consummate professional who absolutely will not lose her calm in the final stretch of this race, I bite my tongue and hold his gaze. Rafael's eyes don't stray from mine as his fingers snake around the stem of his glass and lift it, swirling the red wine before he takes a whiff.

I think his lips twitch as he brings the crystal to his mouth, downs a big gulp, and smacks his lips. "Not bad."

I blink. "We're at the Aviary, not Olive Garden, *Rafael.*"

"It's hard to tell with the lights so low, *Evie.*"

"You're ridiculous."

"I think the word you're looking for is *rakish.*" Rafael winks, draping an arm on the back of the chair, scanning me in a way that coaxes another heat wave to the surface (much like the onset of a terminal fever).

"Far from it," I scoff, starting to think it's ice-cold water, not wine, I need to make it through tonight.

I wouldn't have had this problem if I'd found a way to keep him from coming, not that I didn't try. Often and with bribes. I even offered him guest passes to the country club he's been trying to get into for years, but he's so far down the wait list, he has better chances working there as a cart attendant. Dangling that exclusive carrot was about as effective as the thirty emails I sent our boss, begging her to let me do this solo. None of it worked. So here he is, going for the promotion he wants as badly as I do.

Am I worried he'll get it? Maybe. A little bit.

Not only is he good at his job (not that I'd ever admit it out loud, not even on my deathbed), but everyone at Media Lab adores him. He's got pull, like gravity—effortless, inevitable. It's infuriating. It's also what made him my friend once—for almost three years after I joined. We were two junior associates then, tackling impossible deadlines and our boss's endless expectations. He used to save me from vending machine lunches, and I used to cover for him when he ran late. We had each other's backs.

Until he didn't.

Until he made a decision I never saw coming and stopped being someone I could trust.

Since then, staying in the running for the promotion has been a balancing act. While I've worked hard to prove myself to Media

Lab's mostly male ecosystem, I've also sprinted like hell to keep up with Rafael, because losing this promotion isn't just about righting a two-year-old wrong. It's about not falling *back*. Back to hunger, homelessness, and all the *lessness*es I've clawed my way out from.

It's been the marathon with no finish line, and if I'm being honest, I don't know how much more running I have left in me. I've passed too many stops and too many people along the way. Sometimes I wonder if there's a point when it's too late to stop.

I told myself thirty was the finish line. Land the promotion (and its financial security) and then I'd stop running. Then I'd start checking off all the other things I've put off—like the ninety-two items on my bucket list, a real vacation, maybe even a relationship not built on sabotage and sarcasm. Life.

An uneasy, familiar feeling lodges low in my belly, famished for my attention. I shove it aside before it can crawl into the space between my ribs and make itself at home.

"Hey. You feeling okay?" Rafael's voice whips me back to the table. The smirk I've come to associate with his usual smugness is gone, replaced by a different look. A look I've seen on him lately and not yet deciphered. Probably because he hasn't pulled anything nefarious today. No fake calendar invites. No last-minute deck edits. No classic Vela sabotage. Yet.

The silence—that look—makes me nervous.

Because he could be waiting for the perfect moment to wrangle this account—the promotion—from me, and tonight could be it.

"No need to stress, E. You can do this with your eyes closed," he adds, voice low. Almost soft.

"I'm—I know," I snap, surprised and confused. *Did he just compliment me?*

I search his unfairly handsome face. I know every Vela tactic in the book—and none work on me.

"You're so tense, I figured you needed a reminder."

"I'm perfectly fine," I say too quickly.

"You're going to snap the glass in two." His gaze flicks to my hand.

I loosen my hold. "I'm. Fine."

"You should be more than fine," he says.

The suspicion sinks in as Rafael leans forward, features turning conspiratorial, and his scent—aftershave and sandalwood—envelops us. "All we have to do is show Cyril a good time, and it's in the bag."

"It's in the bag? Who says that?" I ask, leaning away from him and his stupidly distracting scent with an annoyed groan. I need to stay on my A game and not let whatever he's doing throw me off. "In fact, it would be really helpful if you didn't talk. Not that you even needed to come tonight."

"And let you have all the fun?"

"*Fun*?" I almost choke. "This isn't one of your mom-and-pop accounts you can joke your way through. Everything is on the line." Our boss's approval. A sizable commission. A chance to slow down. "Do you even—"

"Bonsoir!" Cyril's accented voice interrupts before I can ensure Rafael gets it.

We stand to greet Cyril—kisses on each cheek—before we settle into our seats. Rafael in front of me. Cyril to my left. The wineglass within sipping distance.

"You look lovely tonight, Evie," Cyril says, undoing the buttons of his jacket.

"Thank you." I offer him a strained smile. Rafael's appears on demand.

"You too, Raf," Cyril adds, slapping Rafael on the shoulder. My gut cinches at their familiarity—their bromance, which budded on day one—but I keep my features smooth and friendly, focusing on Cyril, a picture of French elegance with styled blond hair and a neat beard. His eyes, like the sky on a cloudless day, are always assessing and calculating and doing none of the things Rafael's dark-brown eyes do.

Anxiety returning tenfold, I silently pray Cyril goes for the wine quickly so I can follow suit, calm my nerves, and get to Pitch-Perfect Checklist item #1 before #3 has a chance to compromise things.

The server arrives before any wine sipping happens.

I order on the table's behalf as Cyril and Rafael ease into friendly conversation. Rafael is Cyril's favorite, even if I'm the one who scoured the internet and dabbled in some light social media stalking of the CEO, learning as much as I could about him, his business, France, and anything that could remotely impact the future of our working relationship. But Rafael? Rafael bothered with none of this, save for the parts tied to OhLaLove and the online dating market. Yet here they are—fast friends, chatting away about a soccer (football!) match, and I feel like I'm two steps behind.

I take a sip of my wine, then another, and breathe out—*one Mamma Mia*. It's time to get control of things and cross the finish line. But I need Rafael to do that.

As if I've summoned him with my thoughts, Rafael looks at me. Cyril follows.

"Sorry—Raf and I could talk about football all night," Cyril says with a chuckle.

I force a smile. "No need to apologize. Rafael is our in-house sports expert. He must have mentioned he played at Loyola," I say, not missing the surprise in Rafael's eyes. Keep your potential clients close and your enemies closer.

"I might have mentioned it once or twice," Rafael says, his gaze lingering on me—knowing exactly how many times he's talked about Loyola and what it's meant to him, to his family. I look away.

Cyril twists the stem of his wineglass. "But knowing you, Evie, you've probably got a list of things to discuss so we can get to the numbers you mentioned in your email."

I laugh, breezy and brittle, as his implication hits me in the solar plexus. But checklist item #1 is at the top of the menu, and I need to do what I came here to do: close the deal.

Shooting one last *Behave or else* look toward my nemesis, I set my palms on the table, take a deep breath, and start the last pitch.

As I run through it—between sips of wine and nibbles of appetizers—Rafael chimes in, without interrupting or attempting to steal the show. In fact, each time he offers input, he looks to me to confirm it, and I have to mask my surprise the first time it happens. The second time, I'm prepared, and it's like passing a baton in a relay, one he made no time to rehearse for despite my repeated attempts to role-play the dinner. Even so, the conversation runs smoothly. We navigate through some of Cyril's tougher questions, steer around budget-focused topics, and race through to the end of our pitch.

While I don't trust a moment of Rafael's performance, I nearly squeal in relief. A grin slips out instead—and Rafael sees it. Winks at me. Makes my pulse spike.

I immediately sober, take another sip of wine, and turn to Cyril, eager for his response.

"Nothing less than I expected," Cyril says, his features inscrutable as he leans back, relaxing.

I realize I'm barely breathing as I wait for him to say more, to tell us if Media Lab won his business, if I'm one step closer to getting the promotion.

Brow furrowing, Cyril turns his attention to Rafael, like he's about to fire off a volley of questions.

Am I bothered he trusts Rafael to have the answers? A little bit. Am I fine with Rafael answering if it means getting the business? Yes, I have to be.

Cyril's frown deepens. "You know, it's been months of hearing about that tequila, Raf, and I've never had it. I think it's about time."

I blink, unsure if I've heard him correctly. *Tequila*? Now I'm the one frowning as I drag my shocked gaze from Cyril to Rafael, who shrugs nonchalantly.

"I doubt they have it here, but they have good options," Rafael says, summoning the server with a wave and ignoring me completely.

"Rafael." I almost grind my teeth into a powder saying his name.

"Evie." There's a dare in his tone, and it makes me resent Cyril's presence, because it's the only thing keeping my mouth shut.

I watch in disbelief as Rafael orders tequila shots as if the last hour and a half never happened. As if he's not about to shatter the last thread holding my nerves together—and our boss's very explicit two-drink rule.

By the time tequila arrives and Cyril slides a glass in front of me, I'm doing breathing acrobatics to "Mamma Mia" as I stare down at the golden liquid, feeling uneasy, nauseous, and on the verge of a first-degree felony.

Of course this was his plan all along. Wait for me to let my guard down, then take one reckless, salt-rimmed swing at the entire evening. Because he knows this about me. He knows exactly what tequila does to my system, my pulse, my control. Knows it short-circuits my focus—and that I'll spiral before I ever take a sip.

"Evie doesn't drink tequila," Rafael says, and my head snaps toward him. I don't know if it's another trick or his version of *Keep your enemies close—and memorize their weaknesses.*

"It's not my favorite," I say tightly, glaring at my nemesis.

Cyril chuckles. "Oh, non, Evie. Life is simply too short for you not to enjoy it a little." *Winning his business is what's going to help me enjoy life a little.*

Rafael holds my gaze, the dare ever present. His plan clear as day.

I bet he thinks I'll bail, so he can be the "fun" one who charms the client, wins the account, and takes the victory to Media Lab.

Beside him, Cyril watches me with curious amusement. Their energy presses an internal button I can't deactivate. I wrap my hand around the shot glass and down it in one gulp.

The liquor burns a path down my throat, and I fight a coughing fit as it settles low in my belly.

Cyril chuckles, but Rafael doesn't join. I flash Rafael a tight smile—the kind that says *Nice try.*

And it unravels from there.

Two shots in and a third on the table, I'm feeling warm, watery, and struggling to remember my checklist. There's something on it about keeping Rafael in check, but I'm barely keeping myself in check.

My fury spikes, even through the tequila haze. He's throwing me off my game, ignoring the plan, and I need to take control before Rafael sabotages the account and my promotion.

I clear my throat, squaring my shoulders.

Rafael catches my gaze and shakes his head. *Not yet.*

My returning glare tells him to shove it.

"Cyril—" I start.

"Maybe we get some dessert?" Rafael cuts in.

"Or maybe we—"

"Get another bottle?"

Cyril looks between the two of us, his lips parted. But then his phone buzzes.

"I have to get this," he says, his accent more pronounced. "Désolé."

"Go ahead," I say, biding my time as he stands and moves out of earshot. Then I pounce. "Are you insane?" I hiss, leaning across the table.

Rafael leans in too. "Insanity is relative, E."

I swallow a low growl, hating his light tone and the casual nickname.

"You're going to screw this up." Anger clips my words. I can't even fathom the idea of Rafael ruining our chances now. All those months. All that work. All the plans I've put on hold.

Anxiety sweeps through me like a wave, and I check it immediately. "I get that rules have never been your thing, but we can't lose the account," I say—to him, to myself.

"It's all going to work out," he says with so much Vela-brand certainty, it makes my fingers curl into the tablecloth. Of *course* he thinks it'll work out. For him.

I swallow past the burn in my throat. "Try taking this seriously for once," I hiss. "Because we can't lose this one. I worked too hard."

I aim for stern, but the tequila ruins it. Too many of my emotions bleed through those few words, and it takes too long to mask them.

Rafael's gaze softens—another one of his tactics—and when his fingers twitch, they brush mine, heat singing through me. "I wasn't going to—"

I jerk my hand away.

"I don't need excuses, Rafael. I need you to do what we came here to do," I say hotly.

Before he can attempt to Vela his way through this, Cyril appears in my periphery. I push away from the table, breathing through my nose, ignoring Rafael's phantom touch on my skin.

I rub my hand against my leg, keeping my focus on Cyril, who doesn't take his seat.

"I apologize, but I have a family emergency. My car is already waiting," he says.

As one, Rafael and I stand.

"I'm sorry to hear that," I say, my stomach knotting.

"Merci, Evie," Cyril says, buttoning his suit jacket. "Before I go, I want to share that you are very good as a team. I know it took many months of work to get to know OhLaLove and what we're aiming to do, and your preparation and pitch were very compelling." The dip in his voice hints at an incoming *but*, the kind that sidetracks careers, and I have the insane urge to slap my hand over his mouth and keep him from speaking it into existence.

Instead, I curl my hand into a fist and do *not* look at Rafael. If I do, I will break.

"Which is why I look forward to seeing what's next, working with Media Lab," Cyril adds. I blink in shock. Cyril smiles. "I'll have my team coordinate next steps in the morning, and we'll see where this goes. Who doesn't want to help people fall in love?"

Rafael chuckles. I suck in a surprised breath.

OhLaLove is mine. Ours.

Relief should crash over me, but all I feel is *not that*. Because Rafael did this his way. Not mine. Not the way we planned it from start to finish. And of course—*of course*—it worked.

Goodbyes are a blur.

By the time Cyril is gone and the bill is settled, my blood is boiling, my ire no longer containable.

Steps outside the restaurant, I spin on Rafael, finger wagging in his direction. "You couldn't turn it off for *one* single night, could you? Couldn't follow a plan?"

He flinches in surprise. "Evie, we won." He says it like that's supposed to fix everything—him bromancing it with Cyril and completely ignoring the carefully laid out plan I emailed him no less than ten times. Well, not completely. He followed it long enough to trick me.

"Oh, *we* won?" I repeat, voice pitching with barely restrained anger.

"Why are you upset?" He tilts his head, eyebrows pulling together.

Ohmygod—why am I upset?

I bark out a harsh laugh and look up at the sky, needing somewhere to direct my fury other than at his stupidly symmetrical face. The tequila makes me dizzy. "You think this was only about winning?"

"I mean . . . yeah?" His confusion deepens. "That's our job."

"To be Rafael Vela!" I throw my hands in the air. "Do you ever think about anyone but yourself? Do you ever follow through on plans—ones that are agreed upon? Or even attempt to keep your word?"

Rafael brows furrow. "Help me out here, E. We won. That was the goal. Sometimes plans are shit and you have to pivot." He shakes his head. "Cyril didn't want to discuss the account tonight. Didn't you see that?"

"Oh, did you find that out on some secret golf outing? Or was it a weekend tennis match?" My chest heaves with the effort of keeping it together. "Typical Rafael."

He rolls his shoulders, digging his hands into his pockets, and shakes his head. "No—there wasn't some special outing. I was simply *listening* to him."

"Like you *listened* to Art Betton?" I snap, hating the mere mention of the last account we collaborated on, nearly three years into my time at Media Lab. We'd planned then too. For almost a year, working side by side, until his knife slid gently into my back and he took the account from me. "God," I breathe. "I don't know why I even expected something different this time around."

The truth slips out, unchecked, because I drank one too many drinks.

"This is nothing like—"

"It's exactly like before. The same old Raffy Taffy, coming in with his sweet words and stupid smiles, expecting people to simply fall head over heels for you . . . because you're *you*," I say, gesturing at all of him. I sound unhinged, but I don't care. "You hijacked the meeting—tequila and all. Winged it like you always do, and it worked because it *always* works out for you." *Like it will with the promotion.* I don't say this, but I know it in my core. Cyril will sing his praises to Media Lab. Rafael will get the promotion. And Evie? I'll get to try harder next time.

"I—that's not what I was doing."

I huff out an angry laugh. "Nice try, bucko." I close the distance between us, jabbing a finger into his chest. "You can't fool me. I see right through you." *Jab.* "And I know every. Single. One. Of. Your. Weaknesses." A poke for each word.

Rafael has the nerve to lift a brow. "Is that right, E?"

"Every single one." I drop my finger. "And I'm going to make sure Dana and the other vice presidents know them too before they make a decision for their new director."

His expression shifts. "You're assuming they haven't?"

My heart lurches. "They haven't," I say with feigned confidence, swallowing past the lump in my throat. His eyes tell me something that makes my knees weak. That maybe—*somehow*—they made an early decision and the promotion is his.

I can't catch my breath.

I retreat a step and then another. I can't be around him a second longer.

"Actually, they—"

"Don't." I shake my head. One more step.

"But you don't even know what I have to say."

I make a strangled noise that's part growl, part primal scream. "Have you thought that maybe I don't give a damn about what you have to say?"

A look some would call hurt flashes in his eyes. Another ridiculous trick.

I can't look at him another second.

I turn sharply and walk away.

It's late and humid. My hair's sticking to the back of my neck, and my heart's pummeling my rib cage. I dig my phone out from my purse to call an Uber because I want to be far from Rafael.

"Evie!" Rafael calls, his voice following me when he should be going to his apartment—the one in the *other* direction.

"Leave me alone!" I increase my pace, balancing on Jimmy Choo heels.

"Can you stop for a second? I need to tell you something!" As if I'd give him the pleasure of telling me he's won.

I flip him off, something I've never done before. It's oh-so-liberating it makes me smile.

Whatever else he's saying is swept up in the cacophony of cars and the city—and doesn't matter. Because I'm going to make Cyril my new BFF and get that promotion, even if it means learning French and watching every soccer game in the history of soccer (football).

Rafael shouts my name, but I only increase my pace to get away from him. He doesn't get a chance to fool me again. Never again.

A car horn blares. Someone shouts a warning.

I look up. A bright light blinds me . . . and it goes dark.

CHAPTER TWO
THE DAY AFTER

Rafael was the second-worst part of the most important client dinner of my entire career. Passing out at the end of it was the first.

One moment he's inciting feelings that make anesthetic-free root canals seem more bearable, and the next I'm blacking out at the corner of Chicago and Wells. That's what I get for thinking I can keep my syncope in check long enough to get through the evening with him. Silly me.

I'm not sure how long I've been out, but my blood is on a slow simmer as I return to consciousness. With a quiet groan, I blink my eyes open, massaging my temples and fighting off grogginess as the room comes into focus.

Despite feeling like roadkill, I'm prepared for his smug face—because me fainting in the middle of Chitown is the closest he's come to winning a new tally in this war of ours (despite his best efforts).

But it's not his face I'm staring at as my vision clears, nor is it the gilded ceiling of the Aviary.

Oh God.

Morning light—hazy and nausea inducing—floods my senses, and I think I'm going to be sick. I shut my eyes, taking deep, deep breaths, and wait for the nausea to subside before I attempt to try again.

I squint my eyes open. Slowly the room shifts and solidifies around me. One. Terrifying. Element. At. A. Time.

The camel-colored leather sofa beneath me. The stone coffee table in front of me, laden with books and a half-empty pizza box. An unnecessarily large TV hovering over a marble fireplace. And there—directly above the liquor cart—is a framed poster of the *Publicity Today* cover, from last year, when he and I tied for its Emerging Game Changer of the Year award. Rafael is sitting in an armchair wearing a dark-gray suit, and I'm standing beside him wearing a crimson Oscar de la Renta gown that accentuates curves I don't actually have. When I found out I'd be the one to stand in the photo, I almost popped a seam on the one-size-too-small dress. It's why there's the shadow of a smile on my ruby-red lips. Even if we had tied for the award, *I* was the one standing a head above his in the photo. Naturally, I considered myself the victor.

But now I'm the one waking up in Rafael's apartment after screwing up possibly one of the most important nights of my career . . . possibly my entire life.

Who's the winner now?

A fresh wave of nausea makes it hard to think about the answer. The throbbing at the base of my skull makes it even harder. I swallow another groan and wish the world would gobble me up whole and spit me out approximately six months ago when I should've dug my heeled feet in and told our boss I wasn't going to work with him. *Wishing is for optimists.* So is hoping I didn't somehow give Rafael another reason to think he's got the promotion *in the bag.*

The pressure inside my chest might crack my ribs, and it's enough to make me double over and clutch my middle. I need to breathe, relax, and pretend like I'm not living out a nightmare.

The alternative is giving in to my extremely ill-timed condition and fainting. Again.

One Mamma Mia.

It could have been worse, I remind myself, hoping it'll calm me.

Two Mamma Mia.

His smirk in the poster taunts me.

Three. Mamma. Mia. My breathing has morphed into a harsh wheezing.

I'm in his *apartment.*

No breathing exercise will make this any less petrifying, because I'm on Rafael's sofa, wearing yesterday's clothes, without any recollection of the rest of last night.

This time when I groan, it cuts through the silence of his loft. I hold my breath for the span of a few seconds, readying myself for Rafael to pop out of wherever he's hiding and for whatever gloating he has planned. I imagine his knowing smirk and the glint in his eyes as he recounts the rest of the evening, and I haven't even had my coffee. Screw syncope.

I listen for a second. Then three more.

When he doesn't manifest from one of the rooms, I breathe a *quiet* sigh of relief. With slow, painfully *quiet* movements, I shift my body, perching on the edge of the sofa. I scan my surroundings for my things, mainly my purse and my phone. Whatever happened last night, my phone will have some answers. Texts? *Possibly.* Photos? *Dear God, I hope not.*

The Jell-O–like feeling in my limbs spreads as I search the area around me. Beneath and behind the couch. Beneath and atop the coffee table. No sign of my Prada shoulder bag.

Anxiety pokes holes at my resolve the more this entire situation clicks into place. Passing out on a crowded street. Surrounded by strangers. At Rafael's mercy. And I don't remember any of it.

Hands shaking, I press my palms together to keep them still.

Get a hold of yourself.

I close my eyes and take a steadying breath.

I'm Evie flipping Pope.

I breathe in.

I'm in control.

I breathe out.

A flash of sitting at the restaurant cuts through the mental fog.

Anger—the kind I usually experience in stress dreams where I show up to work in only my running shoes and Rafael taunts me from the break room—buzzes through me as details from last night click into place, one puzzle piece at a time.

The two of us and Cyril having dinner at the Aviary, the final step in our courtship of OhLaLove. Dinner. Drinks. Business talk. I do two of those things well, but drinking? It's not one of them. It dulls my edge and breaks Dana's Doctrine.

Our boss, Dana Casper, vice president of Media Lab and unflinching purveyor of corporate discipline, has three rules when it comes to client meetings: No drinking (more than two drinks). No gambling. No funny business (up for interpretation, but it isn't rocket science—if it sounds like a bad idea, it probably is).

Dana came up through the ranks during a different time, and she's dead set on making sure we don't have to stoop to old-school tactics to win business. I like rules as much as checklists (a lot), but Rafael? He went for the tequila, and I played along because the account was—*is*—everything.

And now I may have screwed it up because Rafael knows exactly what buttons to press to make me explode, and last night he smashed all of them. One by one. Until I actually passed out.

Was Cyril somehow still around when it happened? Did I sabotage the account because I let Rafael get to me? Did he bring me here because he thought he was helping?

The thought of Rafael thinking I *needed* him makes me shoot off the sofa—too fast.

The room spins. My knees buckle. And I almost topple over.

Somehow I'm still in my heels, because, of course, he didn't have the decency to remove my shoes or cover me with a blanket like a halfway-evolved human.

Not that I should have expected anything decent. It's Rafael we're talking about.

What *did* I expect?

That he'd hail a cab or call Gemma?

As my best friend, she would've been more than happy to take me home. As a junior associate on his team, Gemma is always a phone call away.

A man with basic reasoning skills would have called her. He's not that man.

I swallow a growl.

I'm going to make him pay.

Right after I pull my thoughts together and make a plan. Right after I find my phone and prepare my speech—because sure, I may have fainted, but he's the one who tipped me over the edge.

Keeping my movements quiet and my wrath in (temporary) check, I slip off my black pumps, tuck them under one arm, and start across his loft, scanning for my purse. The backstabbing jerk probably hid it to make me suffer this morning.

Illegal-adjacent ideas of payback moving solidly into felony territory, I pad across the hardwood floor from the living room to the dining room overlooking the city.

Dazzling morning light streams through the floor-to-ceiling windows, which open to downtown Chicago. The glossy facades of skyscrapers gleam back. Beyond them, Lake Michigan sparkles. I can make out the Aviary . . . and the corner where I passed out. People and cars move through their morning, business as usual.

And I'm here—temporarily out of office. No phone. No way to check my emails and see what I missed. I can imagine at least a couple of emails and several Teams messages asking for a follow-up on last night's meeting, and I haven't even responded. Because I *can't*.

So much for being a game changer.

Last night, I messed up the game.

That's what I get for thinking I could sit across from Rafael long enough to make it through dinner, win an account, and secure a promotion.

The need to get out of here has me feeling like I could crawl out of my skin. I scan as I go, desperate to escape the enemy's den. If this were any other time, I'd scour through Rafael's things, I'd take notes, and I'd use them to my advantage.

That day isn't today.

I make a mental note in big, bold red letters to *never* agree to work with Rafael on any account, no matter how big or life-changing. Ever.

A deep, low groan rumbles from the dark bedroom to my right, the one with its French doors pulled open.

I squeak in surprise.

I freeze.

Rafael.

Like a deer in headlights, I stand there, lip caught between my teeth and lungs forgetting their one job.

I should keep moving, forget about the purse and get out of here.

I stall, willing my nerves to calm.

It's Rafael we're talking about. And honestly? He's the one who should be afraid.

With pumps under one arm, I prop the other hand on my hip and decide to wait.

Whatever nonsense excuse he'll have for how I ended up here, I'll be ready. Tip-top fighting shape. Evie vs. Rafael.

If he thinks that me fainting is somehow his ticket to the promotion, he has no idea how much I've sacrificed to get this far . . . and how much I'm willing to sacrifice to stay here.

The mental image of me sprawled across a sidewalk makes my face flush with embarrassment.

Okay, maybe I fainted, but he was the one who compromised the account by breaking Dana's rules. That's my leverage. My ticket to my own office.

Dana won't find it *charming* when she hears about how he went rogue—ordering tequila shots after she explicitly told us to play nice, stick to the plan, and "work our magic" (whatever that meant) to win over Cyril and OhLaLove.

Rafael reveres Dana almost as much as I do, and he'll want to avoid that conversation. Maybe he'll even be *reasonable* for once and take himself out of the running for the promotion. And if he doesn't? I'll take care of telling Dana for him. I'd enjoy it. Might even toast to it—with tequila, even.

This could be it—my chance to finally land the director promotion and prove that I am, in fact, the better fit. The better leader. The one who stuck to the rules and plans and didn't crack under pressure, not once in five years. Not that it should have ever been a contest.

But with Rafael, it always is. Has been since the moment our friendship turned into this. Maybe even from that first day, when I let myself think that I could trust him, that my luck was turning.

If it weren't for Rafael's uncanny ability to charm people, especially Dana, it never would have taken this long for her and the other Media Lab executives to see that I'm better prepared to take the lead. And now I might have my leverage to take the lead.

This extremely mortifying (yet increasingly favorable) situation might be my chance to fully turn the tide in my direction. It has only taken the last twenty-nine years to get here.

From inside the too-dark bedroom, Rafael's feet hit the floor.

And just like that, my game plan clicks into place.

A sense of giddy calm settles over me as I slide my feet back into the pumps, smooth down my dress, and toss my hair over my shoulder.

I wait outside his bedroom door.

First, a low groan. Then footsteps thudding against the wood floor.

A jolt of adrenaline kicks in.

A tiny part of me second-guesses confronting him when I'm the one missing details from last night.

But no.

I'm in control.

I think of the Evie Pope on the cover of *Publicity Today*—sharp, confident, on the precipice of having it all . . . if not for the man with the challenging gazes and taunting smirks waking up in the other room. How many times have I worked my ass off only to have him swoop in and win accounts by simply *being*? Too many. He once turned a ten-minute coffee chat with a client into a six-figure retainer—*after* I'd spent a month building a pitch deck. Then there was the DeLuca campaign, for which I build an entire strategy from scratch. He cracked one joke about charcuterie boards, and suddenly he was the client's first choice for lead on the project.

And there's the Art Betton account. Which I refuse to think about, because I'm not giving Rafael the satisfaction of seeing me unhinged. Not today, at least.

I breathe out the rest of my doubt and smooth my features into my business-as-usual face.

And then he emerges from the shadows of his room, barefoot and shirtless. Gray sweatpants hang low on his hips. His hair is a wild chestnut mess, and he's rubbing sleep from his eyes.

The part of me genetically programmed to appreciate the male physique notices the lean, tanned muscles of his chest, the sugar skull tattoo wrapping around his left bicep, and the subtle way his muscles ripple as he moves.

My gaze drifts lower . . . and I drag it out of the trenches. This is Rafael Vela.

Rival. Thief. The one standing between me and my promotion.

I focus on all the parts *above* his neck and take in a steadying breath.

Game time.

"I can't wait to hear how you're going to explain your way out of this one," I chirp, folding my arms across my chest and arching a freshly threaded brow.

His head snaps up, his eyes widening, and he mutters one of only a handful of Spanish phrases I know. "Dios mío."

CHAPTER THREE
THE DAY AFTER, PART II

"Not even God is going to get you out of this," I say, feeling smug.

I can almost picture my new office, the one waiting for its new director and some fresh wall decor. With the promotion, I could justify the cost of the prints I saw in a gallery a few weeks ago *and* cross item #78 off my bucket list.

It's really hard not to smile, but I need to focus on the present moment: Being pissed at Rafael. Getting much-needed answers about last night. And reminding him that while he may have won a few battles, I'm certainly winning the war.

"You can start by telling me where I can find my purse."

Rafael doesn't answer.

He scrubs a hand down his face. Blinks once. Twice. Opens his mouth. Closes it.

"This isn't possible," he mutters.

"It's the first thought I had waking up here." I tap my heel impatiently. "Purse, Rafael?"

He shakes his head, mumbling to himself—and he smacks the side of his face.

I jolt.

He smacks his other cheek.

I blink at him. "Are you having a stroke?"

Rafael stares. Pales. And gives my plan pause.

If he's experiencing a medical episode, he'd better have a list of emergency contacts on hand. I wince at the knowledge that my emergency contacts are a long-gone great-aunt and a dad I never met. Rafael, on the other hand? His family once rented an entire hotel for a family reunion. He should be set on that front.

"I'm not taking you to the hospital," I add, suddenly half tempted to leave this for another time. I'm great at a lot of things, but I don't do well with blood and unconscious people (not even if it were Rafael).

My stomach folding on itself, I force my thoughts from a comatose Rafael to something better—to me sitting in my new office. Being his boss. Attaining something I've worked so long and hard for.

I stand my ground, even though he might be in immediate need of a doctor.

Rafael looks . . . *different.* His skin lacks its usual luster, his shoulders slump slightly, and his stubble? That definitely wasn't there last night.

The stress of the last weeks—months—must have gotten to him too. I know I've lost sleep over the OhLaLove account, over the promotion, over all things Rafael-touched.

Still, he looks tired. Like, *really* tired.

Did he even sleep? Or was he contemplating ways to make this more petrifying for me?

I imagine him taking Sharpie markers to my face, and the urge to find a reflective surface is overpowering.

"This is impossible," he says finally. "I'm losing it."

"The only thing you're losing is the OhLaLove account," I point out, eager to get the conversation on track. "Which, by the way, we can agree is now solely mine."

"OhLaLove?" Rafael's brows pull together like it's not fully registering.

"You know—the account you nearly tanked by going off script and channeling your inner frat boy?" I narrow my eyes. "Seriously, what's wrong with you?"

He doesn't answer. Just steps closer.

I fight the urge to retreat and maintain my power stance.

Rafael keeps advancing until he's within touching distance.

He's somewhere around six feet tall, and even though my heels address some of the height gap, I have to tilt my head to meet his gaze head-on. But his height doesn't intimidate me. Not one bit.

My lips twitch at the same time as his.

"I need to stop drinking," he says, rubbing a hand down his scruffy jaw.

"It's a little late for that revelation," I counter.

Flecks of honey glimmer in the dark brown of his irises. I've never been this close to him without my blood pressure spiking—which is clearly responsible for the heat climbing up my chest.

I swallow it down and lean closer into his space. "You should have thought about your drinking before you ordered tequila shots because you thought I couldn't handle it." I smirk. "Joke's on you. I handled your shots just fine. I feel like new." My pounding head would disagree.

His eyes scan my face. "But you seem so real," he murmurs.

Rafael's arm darts out.

I duck away before his hand can make contact.

"What the hell are you doing?" I gape at him.

Silence.

Rafael prowls forward a step.

I retreat. Once. Twice.

We do this absurd little dance until my butt is almost up against the edge of the dining table. I throw my arms out to stop his advance before we start climbing over the table.

"Enough!" I snap. "Are you on something?"

Rafael stalls, shaking his head. "I must be. It's the only explanation."

"I'll also need an explanation," I add. "And I'm *dying* to hear what it is . . ."

He scrubs a hand down his face, mutters unintelligible words in Spanish.

Outside, an ambulance siren blares. Inside, the AC hums through the exposed industrial vents above us.

Seconds tick away. Rafael just . . . stands there.

I imagine another email dinging in my inbox, and my irritation flares.

"While I'd love nothing more than to have a staring contest before I've had my coffee, I'll pass," I say. "You knew the rules, and you broke them. That was completely unprofessional!" I pause as more of the night comes back. Him and Cyril bro-bonding. Me trying to keep up. Him breaking the rules and me having to pay for it. Rage makes me want to tackle him.

Rafael doesn't respond. He's so still I wonder if he's about to give in to whatever ailment has got him looking like he's seen a ghost. Before he does, I need to say my part, get my purse, and maybe (if he doesn't piss me off some more) call an ambulance.

"Here's the deal," I start. "Tell Dana you don't want the promotion, and I won't say a peep to her about last night. I won't even tell Gemma about it. It'll be our little secret."

His brow furrows like he's not fully on board.

I thrust out my hand, ready to shake on it.

He looks from it to me.

The furrow deepens with an emotion I can't fully pinpoint. Doubt? Confusion? Indigestion? All three?

Or maybe he doesn't trust me.

The feeling is mutual.

Sighing with impatience, I add, "Do you want to sign on it? I can understand if you might be reluctant to trust me. We can draft a pseudo-NDA and seal the deal."

I glance over my shoulder, scanning the table for a pen and paper.

A mountain of books, magazines, and a half-full tequila bottle stare back at me. My stomach churns at the sight of the bottle, but I silently thank it for giving me the leverage I need against Rafael.

Inwardly, I celebrate with a little victory dance before deciding pen and paper are pointless amid the chaos that is his dining room table. So maybe we type one up instead.

When I turn to Rafael, his brow is still furrowed with confusion. It makes me want to roll my eyes and smooth the stupid crease between his brows. *As if.*

"You can pretend this is baffling all you want, but the rules about client meetings are crystal clear." I wag a finger in his direction. "And no exceptions."

"You're not real." His voice is raspy and low.

I swallow the urge to groan. "Unfortunately for you, I'm very real."

To prove my point, I step forward, closing the sliver of space between us, and jab his shoulder.

Only I don't.

My finger moves through—*through!*—him, emerging on the other side, like cutting through warm honey.

With a sharp gasp, I yank my hand back as if I've touched a live wire. I cradle it against my chest, staring at my fingers as panic sweeps in, sharp and furious.

Rafael makes a soft noise, and I snap my gaze to his face.

His eyes are wide with shock, but his lips are pressed tight, his jaw set.

"What the hell?" I breathe, shocked and unmoored—like someone's shattered my autographed ABBA vinyls.

Rafael sucks in an uneven breath. "I told you," he murmurs. "You're a figment of my imagination."

"You wish," I say, a little too breathlessly.

The panic tightens around my chest, unrelenting, as my mind replays the moment over and over, needing an explanation and logic.

I stare at my hands.

This doesn't make any sense.

"There's—" My voice wavers. I force steel into it. "Whatever you've done . . . . fix it."

Rafael's laugh is breathless. Shaky. "I so desperately wish I could," he says before he brushes past me, ready to walk away.

No way he's leaving without an explanation.

I reach out for him, for his shoulder.

And my fingers glide through his skin, like a boat cutting through water. I gasp or shriek—I can't be sure which.

Rafael keeps walking.

"Oh God. What's happening?" My hands. I stare at them as if I'm seeing them for the first time, but they look the same. I wiggle my fingers. They respond. Whatever is happening, it's Rafael's fault.

I fold my fingers into fists and tuck them behind me, where I can't see them. "Rafael!"

"You're not here, E. I've conjured you up." Rafael doesn't even turn around as he keeps walking.

"The only thing you need to conjure up is an explanation," I add. "Several, in fact!"

Heart beating erratically, I march after him.

And trip over my legs.

My heels—they don't make a sound.

The hardwood floor should be echoing with each of my stomps. But nothing.

I take a deep, deep breath.

I'm sure there's a logical reason for it—for all of this—and Rafael's going to provide it.

Despite the deafening roar of my pulse, I follow him and plant myself on the other side of the butcher-block island bisecting his kitchen.

I glare at Rafael's back.

"Did you hear me?" I snap.

Not bothering to look my way, Rafael digs through a cabinet, picking through a row of medicine bottles. He chooses one of several orange tubes as he mutters beneath his breath, something about hallucinations.

"I'm not a hallucination," I say through gritted teeth.

"Damn pills." Rafael tosses the tube into the trash beneath his sink. Then another and another. One bounces dramatically off the edge and clatters to the floor. When he's done, he braces himself against the counter and stares up at the ceiling like he's waiting for divine confirmation that he hasn't lost his mind. "I'm done with them, I swear."

Reluctantly, I follow his gaze upward to the wrought iron fixture overhead.

It's clear he's likely on something . . . and maybe I am too? Maybe I woke up in the middle of night and took one of his experimental mood-stabilizing, alpha-complex man-pills by mistake?

I imagine the cocktail I *might* have ingested. *BroZen Ultra: For men who want clarity, focus, and abs without trying.*

Oh God.

I press the heels of my palm into my eyes and take a deep breath.

This could be worse.

I took some pills I shouldn't have taken, and now I'm experiencing a series of strange symptoms.

Nothing more.

They'll flush right out of my body in no time. And then? I'm going to kill him.

I blink my eyes open.

Compelled by a jolt of fury, I march up to him and plant my hands on my hips. "Why didn't you take me home after I passed out?" The words aren't as steady as they sound in my head.

He offers no answer.

"Is it because you're not capable of making *sound* decisions?"

Rafael groans. "Even as my hallucination, you're a smartass."

"Call me a hallucination one more time, and I'll do everything in my power to make you wish you never stepped foot into Media Lab." I tilt my head to meet his incredulous gaze. "You'll be lucky to work in the mail room when I tell Dana how terribly you've messed this up."

Dana's face—sharp angles, shrewd eyes, and straight nose—flashes to mind. She'll put Rafael in his place, and if I'm lucky enough, she'll terminate him when she hears about him breaking her rules and then bringing me here to top off my humiliation.

"You might have had a fighting chance before last night," I say, cool and clipped, "but you can kiss your golden-boy status goodbye."

The speech I've been perfecting in my head for years practically writes itself. *Almost five years ago, Rafael Vela pretended to be my friend. He fooled me for three years, long enough to learn my strategies, clock my weaknesses, and store away anything he could one day wield against me. We worked side by side for months to prepare a major client pitch. Long nights. Research-filled conference rooms. More coffee than sleep. And when the work was done? He convinced Dana that he could handle the account solo—and cut me out.*

It tanked my shot at a loan and an apartment, pushed back my bucket list timeline, and confirmed the one rule I've followed since: Never trust Rafael Vela.

Some would argue he used his sweet talking and his six-month seniority over me to make it happen. That it wasn't personal—just business.

I'd never admit it, but it *was* personal. Almost too much so . . .

Since then? He's been leaning on half-baked tactics, trying to win by throwing me off-balance. Too bad for him. I know his game.

"Last night?" he asks.

I fight the urge to roll my eyes. "I don't have time for games, Raffy Taffy. You thought I'd just let you take the win this time. Head down. No fighting back." I want to cackle with unhinged joy or rage, or maybe it's a side effect of whatever mystery man-pills I may or may not have taken. "But this promotion's mine," I add. "No matter how much you want to fight it."

"Promotion? Are you—" Rafael's jaw works in frustration. "And now I'm talking to myself."

"I don't say this lightly, but I'm concerned about you."

"How do I make it go away?" His gaze moves back to the ceiling.

"Go see someone, like normal people."

"That's not a terrible idea." He pushes away from the counter. "I'll call Dr. Diaz."

"You're not going anywhere," I snap, my tone sharper than I intend. But the edge is a mask—a lame cover for a waver I hate myself for.

Because the truth is, I need him. To explain what the hell is happening. To stop pretending like I don't exist. To tell me what kind of absurd, overpriced pills I may have ingested.

Because, right now, I don't have all the answers, and needing him—*Rafael*—unearths feelings I never fully managed to bury. Just shoved into a box, taped shut, and labeled DO NOT REOPEN.

"Rafael!"

He stops midstep. His chest ripples with a deep breath. "Evie."

Briefly, Rafael's eyes connect with mine.

I swallow past the burn of emotions in my throat. "Tell me what happened."

He doesn't respond.

I'd have paid money for Rafael to be this quiet any other time.

And now? I have to beg him to say *something.*

Even though it physically pains me, I force myself to say it. "Please."

His jaw clenches. I see the telltale flutter of muscles in his right cheek—his tell, the one that means he's angry or frustrated. My go-to instinct is to press his buttons, poke the bear. But I need answers more than I need to get under his skin.

"Please," I repeat, this time harder.

He rolls his shoulders and takes a deep breath, like this conversation is physically paining *him.* "You can't be here, because you were in an accident." His voice is strained, each word deliberate. "You're unconscious. In a coma . . . at Northwestern Memorial," he continues, raking a frustrated hand through his hair. "That's why you can't be here, and that's why I shouldn't be talking to a hallucination."

CHAPTER FOUR
(IMPOSSIBLY STILL) THE DAY AFTER

A strangled laugh bubbles out of me. "Okay, I see what you're doing here," I say, any illusion of him wanting to do this the easy way gone. "But I'm not in the mood for your games today."

It's one thing for him to reorganize my desk every time I'm out on a work trip or to send a sympathy bouquet to Jane-from-HR on her wedding day on my behalf. But this? Orchestrating this entire situation where he acts like he's lost his mind? Makes *me* feel like I've lost my mind? This is a new level of low in Evie vs. Rafael, and I'm not going there right now.

Having had enough, I march past him, shoulders thrown back, toward the door.

"I hope your résumé is up-to-date," I toss over my shoulder, already envisioning a considerably more stress-free, Rafael-less Media Lab—and it puts a pep in my step to know I'm almost there.

But . . . I can't just walk out. Not yet.

Because the pounding in my head is nothing compared to the chaos whirring in my brain—the weird things my hands are doing, the maybe-pills, the utterly ridiculous story about me being in a coma. This entire morning feels like one long fever dream wrapped in a bad prank, and walking out without answers feels a lot like letting him win. And Rafael doesn't get to win anything. Not on my watch.

Despite my need to be far, *far* away from him, I slow my pace to give him a chance to come to his senses, to beg me for forgiveness, to bribe me with a month's worth of coffee runs, to grovel at the toes of my leather pumps, and to admit that yes, in fact, he has backstabbed me to get ahead, and yes, he's now staging some unhinged reality-bending performances to make me question my sanity.

That and he broke the rules—and used my fainting spells against me at last night's dinner (another hiccup in the *keep your enemies close* experiment).

I halt, shy of reaching the door, and give him another second to fix things.

He's as silent as a corpse.

No excuses. No explanations. No apologies.

Frustration curls my hands into fists, and my throat clogs with all the things I want to say—*have* to say—before I go.

If this is the end of Rafael Vela's tenure at Media Lab—if this is the moment our war comes to an end—I need something resembling closure. I need him to admit he's spent the last two years making things harder for me. That he manipulated me into friendship only to weaponize everything he's ever learned about me, from scheduling team-building events that involved hand-eye coordination (knowing I break into hives at the phrase "trust fall") to submitting petty facility requests under my name until they stopped responding to real ones. And let's not forget the time he sweet-talked Dana into assigning my best friend Gemma to his team (though there have been perks to having someone on the inside).

I know it's wishful thinking to want him to admit it.

Still, I turn on my heel and level him a look that's withered account execs and vendors who couldn't hold up their end of a project.

He doesn't so much as flinch.

In fact, some would say he looks sad. But I know better than to fall for those puppy-dog eyes. He's trying to Vela me. *As if.*

"This is all your fault," I point out.

His throat bobs. "Don't you think I know—"

A loud rap shakes the door.

I nearly jump out of my skin.

Rafael looks past me to the door but doesn't move.

Three more impatient knocks.

I'm close enough I could reach over and pull open the door. But what if I miss? What if my hand grasps the air again?

Anxiety prickles up my spine.

More knocking. Harder. Impatient.

I jerk my head at the door. "Aren't you going to answer?"

Rafael appears to think about it. Rolling his shoulders, he takes reluctant steps down the hallway, eyes on me the entire time. With nowhere for me to go, I press myself close to the wall and glare at him as he approaches, like a snail moving uphill.

"You're infuriating," I hiss at him when he slows beside me.

"Ditto." He wrenches the door open.

A woman—her brunette hair pulled into a messy bun and a Harry Styles tee tucked into ripped jean shorts—stands on the other side, fist hovering midair. She drops it at her side, her scowl matching my own.

"Oh, this should be good," I mutter, smiling for the first time all morning. She doesn't so much as look at me. Neither does Rafael.

"I never thought I'd have to come back *here*, but I forgot my phone last night," she huffs, her furious energy like that of a malfunctioning pressure cooker. "It happens when you're kicked out."

My mouth almost drops.

Rafael sighs. "It wasn't like that, Victoria."

"Victoria?" Her voice turns shrill. "My name's *Violet*, you douchecanoe." She shoves past him, bumps his shoulder, and stomps into the apartment.

"Wait—" I stare after her. "She was here? Last night? With me asleep on the sofa?" Nausea pushes into my throat. A brand-new set of horrifying what-ifs flood my brain, shoving everything else out. Did he have a woman over while I drooled on his sofa? Did they . . . *hook up*? Is he that insatiable?

Ignoring me like it's become his personal Olympic sport, Rafael follows Violet with the enthusiasm of an inmate on death row. I trail after him, desperately needing answers about last night because the plot holes are more confusing than assembling IKEA furniture *with* instructions.

"Explain," I command.

"Please, go away," Rafael mutters, rubbing the back of his neck. Violet halts her mission of pulling out sofa cushions to turn toward Rafael with a withering glare. Finally, a woman who gets it.

"Go *away*?" Violet almost shrieks. She chucks the cushion in his direction.

"Not you." Rafael holds up his hands as if to soothe her. Violet's face pinches with a mixture of distaste and confusion. I think I hear her call him *asshat*—and make a mental note of her insults—before she reluctantly resumes her search.

"Your manners are atrocious," I tell him as she lobs another cushion to the ground, cursing men and dating apps as she goes. But I get it. *Hell hath no fury* and whatnot. Rafael has incited similar feelings innumerable times (present moment included).

"How do you explain this?" I gesture in her general direction. "Or is she a hallucination too?"

Rafael pivots his body away from me.

I follow, circling into his line of sight. "Really? Are you five?"

Rafael's jaw clenches so hard the muscle in his cheek jerks, but he continues to say nothing, watching as Violet upends his living room.

"Whatever happened last night—and spare me the details—something tells me it didn't go according to plan." I jab a thumb toward Violet, who's moved to the coffee table, tossing magazines and books aside with fury and purpose. "Not what I would call a satisfied customer." A book hits the ground with a pronounced thunk.

Rafael doesn't react.

"While I'd love nothing more than to leave you at the mercy of a woman who might loathe you more than I do, I'm not going anywhere until you tell me exactly what happened after I fainted," I say, positioning myself solidly in front of Rafael.

I make myself tall. He steps to the side. I follow. Another book slams onto the wood floor. Nothing from Rafael except a throbbing vein along the column of his throat.

"Silent treatment? Really? You think that's going to help you?" I cross my arms. "You screwed up big-time—and I'm not talking about your late-night guest." Another thunk. "I probably have a hundred emails waiting for me, so I'll keep this brief. If you thought bringing me here was some kind of twisted favor, you were wrong on so many levels, and now it's my leverage." I let that sink in. "Unless you had plans to break several HR rules on your way out."

His jaw clenches.

Fine. We can play.

"That's on top of breaking one of Dana's rules," I add. "Which means you've basically rolled out the red carpet for Media Lab's newest director: me." Still nothing. "Dana won't be so lenient when she finds out. *If* she finds out . . ." I trail off, hoping the emphasis on the *if* will make him see things my way. "It's a win-win. I keep last night and this morning between us, and you keep your job. All you have to do is *not* get in the way of my promotion. You know—like you should have done two years ago."

Rafael doesn't look intrigued. He doesn't look at me at all.

Guess he wants to do things the hard way.

I close the distance between us, making it impossible for him to look anywhere but at me. "All right then, it's your funeral, Raffy Taffy."

"Enough!" Rafael snaps, hands thrown into the air, startling the panic out of me.

Violet gasps.

"Why won't you leave me alone?" He closes his eyes and presses the heels of his palms into them with an anguished groan.

I tilt my head, examining him. Something is off.

I've never seen Rafael lose his cool like this, no matter how many times I had his work badge deactivated or his dry cleaning canceled. I'd never admit it, but it throws me off. Because I thought I had him figured out.

"What the hell?" Violet squeaks, her eyes saucers. She's clearly never seen this side of him either. Hasn't seen *any* side of him, apparently.

"Yes, Raffy Taffy. What the hell?" I add.

"Dios, why me?" Rafael looks up at his ceiling again.

Violet grabs a magazine from the table and begins to inch forward, eyeing the hallway behind us.

I'm not sure which of them needs more help.

"You know what . . ." she starts, holding the magazine across her chest like a shield. "I don't need my phone."

"Don't—" Rafael says, cutting off her escape route. "I'm not yelling at you." He smiles, as if to show he's to be trusted.

A part of me can't help but enjoy his discomfort. Violet stalls. Her freckled face is tense and her hands shaky around the magazine. Like she might actually be afraid of him. I should let this play out, but she shouldn't be giving herself a panic attack on his account. Despite his many shortcomings, Rafael wouldn't harm a spider.

"His bark is louder than his bite," I offer, feeling icky about defending Rafael. But crazier things have happened today. "If anyone should be afraid, it's him."

"*Fuck.*" Rafael's cheek throbs.

Violet hesitates, her eyes darting between Rafael and the door. "I don't even use my phone," she says, her laugh watery.

"Please, I wasn't . . . I haven't slept well," Rafael says, his hand scrubbing down his face. "I'm not myself. Not last night. Not now."

"I . . . just . . . would really like to go." Her eyes finally move from Rafael to me. She takes a tentative step forward, eyeing the distance to her escape. I step aside and gesture for her to keep moving. She stalls halfway down the hallway, her lip between her teeth.

"Do you have this effect on all women?" I glare at Rafael.

His nostrils flare.

"It's both shocking and unsurprising."

"Please, stop."

"Maybe *you* should stop."

"What will it take to make you go away?" he asks icily.

My chest caves at his meanness, making me angry. With him. With myself.

"What's that supposed to mean?" I plant my hands on my hips, glaring at Rafael.

"It means get the hell out of here already!" Rafael snaps, whipping his head in my direction. His chest heaves with frustrated breaths, and his eyes burn with misplaced anger.

To my left, Violet whimpers. I want to tell her I've got this handled, but she rushes forward, like a linebacker locked on a target. Me.

Instinct takes over—and I brace for impact, hands covering my head and my chest. I suck in a breath, ready.

The impact never comes.

Because she runs right *through* me.

A sharp gasp tears from my throat. I feel like I've slipped beneath the surface of a frozen lake, and I'm struggling to breathe. To stand. To grasp for the surface.

Shivering, I double over, taking in deep, deep breaths.

I can't pass out. Not again.

Arms coiled around my middle, like they can keep me together, I drop to the floor. "*Ohmammamia*," I whisper. I'm not so sure it's Rafael's meds making me loopy.

Pressure builds inside my chest, compressing my lungs, making breathing painful. Tears prick the backs of my eyes, burning my throat and threatening to spill.

Oh God.

"Hey." Rafael's rough voice draws my attention to him. He's hovering near me, his face a mix of disbelief and exhaustion. But something else is there too (something that could be confused for genuine concern). I can't process him when I'm barely handling myself.

"What's happening?" I whisper, hating the plea in my voice. Nothing makes sense—waking up here, my hands doing crazy things, and Violet going *through* me.

What is happening? What is happening?

Cold burns through me. A beeping noise sharpens and intensifies, burrowing into my head.

I press my hands around my ears, close my eyes, and gasp for air.

Full-blown panic attack mode.

In front of Rafael.

Breathe, I command myself.

I can't faint again. I can't let him see me at my worst.

One Mamma Mia.

A traitorous tear slips out.

Two Mamma Mia.

I don't know how many breaths it takes for me to finally inhale without feeling like I'm drowning. But I feel steady enough to open my eyes and face Rafael.

Only it's not him I'm looking at.

It's me. And I'm lying in a hospital bed.

CHAPTER FIVE
SEVEN DAYS LATER

I wheeze in shock.

The body in the hospital bed is connected to so many wires and monitors it looks like a science experiment gone wrong, but worse—because that's undeniably *me.*

My face is a couple of shades darker than white, cheeks slightly flushed. My hair, usually styled into glossy brown waves, lies limp and dull against the pillow. I could pass for a corpse—would pass for one if not for the machines saying otherwise. The beeping monitors. The almost imperceptible rise and fall of my chest—*her* chest. Because that . . . can't be me.

You've been in a coma for a week. Rafael's voice is in my head.

No. *No.*

He can't be right. He almost never is.

My chest tightens, like it's trying to reject the very thought. This is impossible.

I can't be here and there. *Can I?*

Nope.

Rafael was messing with me. It's his thing.

But—

The body in the bed looks so much like me.

Propelled by inexplicable curiosity, I inch closer to the bed. My breaths hitch with each step until I don't breathe at all. Because now, up close, I can't deny it. The same pert nose and full lips, the beauty mark beneath the right eye, the faint scar above my wrist from a stupid dare that had me attempting to climb a fence into a cemetery at midnight and cutting myself open. I fainted right after and almost bled out.

Even if I dismiss the face, the scar, and all the physical signs it's me on the bed, it's hard to ignore the wristband—the plastic bracelet, snug around my wrist:

EVIE POPE. DOB: 11/02/96

Final, irrefutable proof.

I suck in another breath, willing my lungs to expand.

It's wildly, *wildly* impossible, but the evidence is becoming undeniable. And if that's me lying on the bed, then who is *this* version of me? The one who woke up in Rafael's apartment? The one who spiraled into a panic attack and somehow ended up here?

Lifting my hands to eye level, I recognize my fingers as my own. The scar is visible against my wrist. The nails are manicured and polished blush pink. My legs are mine, too, toned from hours of running and riding my Peloton. A smattering of beauty marks dots the pale skin.

I check the door before I quickly cup my breasts. They're definitely mine. Small, but not too tiny. Round and pushed up by a bra.

I glance around the room for a reflective surface. Nothing glimmers back, so I sneak into the gray-beige bathroom to the side of the room. Holding my breath, I face the square mirror above the sink. Only no one looks back.

I squeak in shock, blinking several times. *It's not possible.*

I wave at the mirror. Nothing stirs.

I inch up to it, almost pressing my nose against it. The room behind me is the only thing in the reflection.

Somehow, I'm here, but I'm *not*.

I spin toward the bed and the body hooked up to machines and tubes. I look at her, and she blurs. Morphs into my sister Annie. Like the last—and final—time I saw her. Pale and small and . . . lifeless.

Throat burning, I blink the image away. Annie's been gone so long now.

And that's me. *Me.*

Panic lands a roundhouse kick to my gut, and I stumble.

Oh God.

Rafael may have been right.

I'm in a coma.

Unmoving.

Half dead.

This is impossible. Not the *you'll never escape your past* impossible. The *not ever* impossible.

A whimper chokes out of me as full-body tremors roll through me.

This can't be happening.

I gasp for air that doesn't seem to want to go into my lungs, emitting sounds I've only heard in documentaries about whale songs.

Is this happening?

I can't make sense of what *this* is, but it's inexplicable. A mental breakdown. A nightmare. A glitch in the matrix.

My sobs evolve to wheezing.

I shouldn't cry. Crying solves nothing, and I need to solve this.

Taking a steadying breath, I start to pace the length of the room, humming through sobs. I make it through half of ABBA's greatest hits (and lots of sniffles and snot) by the time I feel brave enough to look at the bed again. That unmoving body is mine. Once so full of life and possibilities—a bucket list of them.

The waterworks start again. Worse than before.

The last time I cried was two years ago, and I'd never admit it to him, but it involved Rafael, a supply closet, and a flask I discovered hidden between reams of printer paper. I haven't cried since, not unless I was getting emotional over a documentary about endangered animals or climate change.

I most certainly don't cry when it comes to me. Because one: it's pointless. And two: I don't believe in feeling sorry for myself—not when being logical and making checklists are so much more effective for solving problems and moving forward.

Only *nothing* is logical about being in a coma when I was just *here*. More specifically, at the Aviary, on the verge of a long-worked-for promotion and slowing down. In the middle of training for my fifth marathon and checking one of the more attainable items off my bucket list. I ate salads for lunch, and I exercised like it was my religion. I saw a therapist and meditated, even if I couldn't ever quite manage to get my head quiet. I couldn't have simply slipped into a coma. Right?

I press a hand to the base of my head, where the throbbing intensifies, and I sniff back another round of tears, fighting for control over my emotions.

I need to focus on facts. On the parts of the puzzle I *do* have. The Aviary. The dinner. Rafael.

The pieces click together so fast my stomach drops and my blood pressure spikes.

I didn't *slip* into a coma. Maybe someone *put* me into one. And only one person could have pulled that off. The same person who was with me the last night I remember being . . . in my body. The same person who's made it his life's mission to drive me insane.

What if he somehow drove me out of my body? Long enough to snag a promotion? The idea is as ridiculous as me being in two places at once. Yet here I am. Or *there* I am.

If Rafael were here, I would—

"Dios mío." Rafael's voice makes me jolt with a squeak.

I spin on him so fast I forget I'm a snotty mess.

Rafael stands a few feet away from me, wearing The Sweatpants and a tee that hides but not-so-subtly silhouettes the abs beneath. He hovers in the doorway, staring at me with wide eyes.

He's staring. Right. At. Me.

"You can see me," I blurt with a hoarse voice. Feeling like a wet sock, I sniffle and straighten, smoothing down the dress and tossing my hair over my shoulder, as if that could mask that I'm currently the antithesis of Evie Pope.

Rafael blinks, looking past me. I falter.

Maybe I imagined it all—him talking to me, responding, seeing me.

Maybe I've tricked myself into believing he could because the alternative is too terrifying.

Because he's staring straight *through* me. Like I'm not here.

Needing confirmation, I ignore the tempest of uncertainty inside me and take a small step toward him, tears drying and hands shaky—exactly how one should approach their sworn enemy.

But I need him to acknowledge me.

"Rafael," I say, my voice cracking slightly. "You can see me, right?"

Rafael doesn't react. As still as my body in that hospital bed behind me.

Maybe the apartment thing was a fluke—*my* hallucination. I need to know.

I inch closer.

His hand moves to the doorknob.

"Rafael!" The desperation in my voice startles me, and I clamp my lips together.

Rafael stills. His gaze lifts from the body in the bed—*my* body—to me.

Relief is short and not so sweet (because *hey, I'm in a coma, everybody*), but I think I have Rafael's attention. And I need to play my cards right because he *can* see me, which means he can finally explain things: what really happened at the Aviary . . . and every question I've been dying to ask all morning . . . and right now.

I clear my throat. "Why are you here?"

The question is out of my mouth before I can answer it myself. *To see me at my weakest? To possibly shave off my eyebrows and snap a photo of me?*

"I wish I knew," Rafael says, shaking his head. The door groans as he leans against it with a heavy sigh, considering me in a way that leaves me feeling like I should add another layer of clothes.

I scowl. "Nice try."

"Nice try? What is it I'm—" Rafael stops abruptly. "I'm talking to a hallucination. Again."

"I'm not a hallucination," I repeat for the thousandth time. I also mentally kick myself. My tone isn't communicating that I need something from him, and I don't want to scare him away. Yet. "I promise."

Rafael's cheek twitches, but he stays. Long enough for me to take action and address the two things that need checking off before he makes a getaway:

1. *Prove I'm not a figment of his imagination (he wishes)*
2. *Get answers*

"I'll prove it to you," I say. Rafael's brow lifts, and it's all the dare I need to dig for something his hallucination wouldn't know, something his imagination wouldn't fathom me capable of doing. "Would your hallucination admit that I purposely lost the Culture Jar so I could be the one to bring in breakfast the morning of your meeting with Nova Kare?"

As the confession takes root, Rafael's face morphs. Surprise, then horror. I'd savor the moment if it weren't for my predicament. Culture Jar is Dana's attempt to create team cohesion and build a collaborative culture. Whenever a team member exemplifies Media Lab's values, their name is tossed into a jar. At the end of each month, the person with the fewest tickets buys breakfast for the team.

The day before the Nova Kare meeting, I pulled most of my tickets from the jar and bought the best damn breakfast for the team, including Rafael's favorite: the Belgian Malted Bacon Waffle—a heart attack in the making—from Mama Scott's Cafe. Heavy on the bacon, light on the Dulcolax. Rafael spent most of his morning in the restroom, and I was the only one to pitch my ideas to Dana and get the go-ahead to take lead on the medical device account.

Payback is a bitch, and Rafael had pissed her off one too many times.

"You didn't . . ." he starts, his jaw clenching.

"Or . . ." I continue, undeterred, looking past his shoulder to the sign near the door. "If I was a hallucination, I couldn't know something else that you didn't, right?" I can tell he's still catching up on the Dulcolax incident, but I continue regardless. "Like the name of the nurse on duty?"

Rafael's dark brows meet over his straight nose, but he only shrugs.

I know he's resisting, so I push forward. "Well, it's Cassi S." I gesture to the sign over his shoulder, and his gaze reluctantly follows.

"I must have seen it subconsciously," he mutters.

"Oh? Did you grow eyes in the back of your head?"

"No. Only a smartass alter-conscious thing which eerily resembles Evie." His eyes shift to the physical Evie, lying unmoving on the bed, and his gaze changes. Softens. I'm not sure what to make of that, so I look too.

So much for not being vulnerable in front of Rafael. No makeup. No designer dress and pumps. Simply Evie. Flaws and all. *Flaws.*

"Okay!" Feeling a surge of hope, I spin to face him. "Would your subconscious know that I have a birthmark shaped like a wing?"

Rafael opens his mouth, then clamps it closed, as if he's running through his catalog of All Things Evie, but the birthmark is nowhere he'd *ever* have access to or knowledge of. Until now.

"Or that it's on my right thigh?"

He shifts uncertainly from one foot to the other, but I can't lose his focus, not yet.

"Well, it's there," I say, reaching for the blanket covering my thighs. My hand slides through the polyester material like it's sifting through frigid sand. I come away with nothing. Disappointment stabs through me, but I fix my features before I turn to Rafael.

He hovers by the door like a brooding Horseman of the Apocalypse.

I beckon him with a finger. "I'm going to need you to look."

"No fucking way."

"Get over here," I demand, breathing through my impatience. Rafael doesn't budge, and I swear the man can infuriate me by simply *being.* I take a step toward him and plant my hands on my hips. "I swear I will haunt you for the rest of my days. I won't let you sleep. I won't let you eat. I won't let you have another peaceful date in your life." So much for doing this the nice way.

With each threat, the pulsing in his cheek intensifies. Rafael has moved from level-four angry to level-nine pissed, but he can't even begin to fathom the variety of pissed I'm experiencing at the moment. "Now get your ass over here, lift the damn blanket, and look!"

Infuriatingly, he doesn't listen. He gapes at me like I've asked him to help move a dead body.

Fury propels me forward.

Rafael moves too.

He casts another glance toward the ceiling, shoves from the door, and slowly approaches, grumbling too low for me to hear. He stops beside the bed, close enough I can see the beauty mark beneath his left ear or run my palm over the scruff on his chin. *As if.*

"I'll be supervising, of course," I say, gesturing to physical me.

Rafael throws me a scorching look. "How do you manage to make me do the craziest shit?"

I roll my eyes at that ridiculous assessment, because it's him who makes me participate in *crazy.* "No higher than the thigh."

Rafael inhales. His gaze fixes on the gown, but he doesn't do or say anything.

Beeping and hissing fill the silence.

Impatience trills through me.

Before I detail more ways I'll make his life miserable even as a plasma whatever-I-am, Rafael reaches across the bed. I swear his hand trembles as he lifts the blue-and-white hospital blanket aside, and I find myself holding my breath, prepared for the worst. Horrendous scars. Missing limbs. Overgrown toenails. But when he removes the blanket, the hospital gown covers my thighs, grazing the tops of my knees.

I exhale, relieved I still have two legs with no disfigurement to speak of.

Rafael stalls again, pushing air out through his nose. A shadow of doubt flits across his features.

"Rafael," I urge, needing him to get this over with already. "The gown."

His eyes collide with mine. "Your bossiness might be enough to convince me you aren't a hallucination."

"Then lift the damn gown."

"I will."

"Before I decompose."

"You're morbid."

"Realistic," I correct. "Do it already."

Rafael presses his lips together, working his jaw, and then, ever so slowly, his hand moves from the blanket to the hospital gown. I hold my breath, cringing at the reality that my legs haven't been shaved for as long as I've been here.

With the speed of a three-toed sloth, he begins to lift the gown, muttering beneath his breath as he goes. When we can almost see the top of my thigh, the door to the room swings open.

CHAPTER SIX

SEVEN DAYS AFTER, PART II

Rafael drops the gown and digs his hands into his pockets. Neither he nor I so much as breathe.

A doctor, her gray hair chopped into a stylish pixie cut, stands in the doorway to the room. Her dark eyes widen behind thick-rimmed glasses as her eyes dart between Rafael and my partly uncovered body on the bed.

"Hello," she says, her voice slightly accented. "What are you doing here?"

"Dr. Wagner," Rafael starts, shaking off his temporary shock with an apologetic smile. "I was . . . I thought it was warm in here . . . and her cheeks were a little flushed." He gestures to the body, shrugging innocently. He's transformed from a Horseman of the Apocalypse to an angel at the pearly gates. "I apologize if I've overstepped."

The doctor's frown smooths out into a kind smile. "It is normal for her to appear that way, Rafael."

My jaw drops in surprise. "She knows you?"

Ever the gentleman, Rafael ignores me.

"How have you been?" The doctor lets the door slide closed behind her and ambles into the room, circling to the other side of the bed. She wears a striped dress beneath her lab coat and holds an iPad.

"You've been here before?" I lean close to his ear, shock making my voice squeak. Rafael flinches but doesn't look my way. His silence is an answer that only piques my curiosity.

Why *is* Rafael here? Why does he know this doctor? Why is she so quick to ignore he's in a patient's room without the patient's written, explicit permission? The last one's an exaggeration, given my condition, but . . . *how* does Rafael get a pass?

I know the answer to this question too.

For all the reasons he gets them all the time. He can be friendly and charming. He wields an irresistible dimple and bedroom eyes. I can think of several reasons others have let him off the hook, so it shouldn't surprise me that *this* doctor is any less susceptible to the Vela effect.

"I've had better days, Doc," he says, his eyes flicking to me for a nanosecond.

"It's a difficult situation," she says with sympathy. Features serious, she swipes across the iPad and looks up at the monitors beside the bed. I squint at the information—mostly numbers—but none of it means anything.

"What *is* the situation?" I focus on my silent nemesis. "Besides the fact that I'm unresponsive in that bed, wearing that awful thing they have the nerve to call a *gown*."

Rafael groans beneath his breath, rubbing his scruffy jaw. This close, I don't think I've ever seen him in this much disarray, not even that one other time I actually lost the Culture Jar and had to personally deliver a get-well basket from the team (no Dulcolax involved). It was the first time in years I'd stepped foot in his apartment. While there wasn't any late-night client pitch prep, I did get to see Rafael out of his element. The flu had taken him out for an entire week, long enough for me to step in, nail one of his pitches, and even recruit someone—Dana wouldn't let me get Gemma—from his team.

"You can always talk to me, Rafael. Tell me how you're doing." Dr. Wagner continues swiping across her iPad. I can't help but scoff. Rafael is fine. It's me we should all be worried about.

"Ask her about the . . . whatever she's doing," I say, craning my neck so I can see her notes.

"No." Rafael turns his body so that his shoulder blocks me.

"Excuse me?" The doctor looks up from her device, leveling a questioning gaze at him.

"Um. I'm fine." He clears his throat. "Just wondering about how Evie's doing. Any changes?"

Finally.

I focus on the doctor, whose eyebrows knit over her prominent nose. "I'm sorry to say this, but there hasn't been much of a change, not since the other day you checked in," she says.

"The other day?" I narrow my eyes in suspicion. "How often have you been here? More importantly, *why*?"

"I understand." Rafael pretends I'm not here.

"Well, *I* don't understand," I hiss, positioning myself so I can peek over his shoulder. "So explain, Raffy Taffy." His nostrils flare, but that's all I get. Annoyance makes me lean in so close I could bite his ear. *If* I were into that kind of stuff. "I'm not going to stop until you explain."

"*God!*" Rafael snaps, startling the doctor. She eyes him warily over the rims of her glasses.

"You're doing a stellar job of scaring off women. I'm surprised I ever thought the contrary," I say, a little bit comforted by his discomfort.

"Not all of them." He glares pointedly at me. Dr. Wagner follows his line of sight, her brow quirking in question. "Oh, I wasn't talk—" he starts, then stretches his neck from side to side and heaves a deep sigh. "Actually, I think I'm having some sort of . . . hallucination."

I snort beside him, unsurprised he's resorting to this excuse. Again.

The doctor appears thoughtful as she sets the iPad on the tray table beside her and gives him her full attention.

"What kind of hallucination?"

"The kind where I see things that aren't here?"

"That's the definition of a hallucination," I insert.

"More specifically, one that looks and acts like Evie but like one hundred times more . . . irritating." The way he rolls his *r*'s is irritating.

"Ah," Dr. Wagner says, removing her glasses and tucking them into a pocket. "And is this Evie here now?"

"Yes! I'm here!" I shout, startling Rafael, who jerks in surprise.

He shuffles a step away from me. "What happens if I say yes?"

Dr. Wagner chuckles. "I won't have you taken out of here in a straitjacket, if that's what you're thinking."

"Should have happened long ago." I scan my archnemesis—his rumbled hair, his thigh-hugging sweatpants, the somewhat crazed look in his eyes. I'm surprised she hasn't called up the psych ward already.

"What does the hallucination tell you?"

"Mostly nonsense. Wants to prove she *isn't* a hallucination."

"Nonsense?" I squeak.

Rafael continues, "It's incessant. Since this morning."

"Hmm. And why do you think you're seeing her now?"

He shrugs. "No clue, but I'd like for it to stop. It's driving me *crazy*."

I sidle back into his personal space. "You haven't begun to understand the meaning of crazy."

"Are you drinking?" Dr. Wagner asks—a little too nicely, in my humble opinion.

"Ask the bottles of wine and tequila in his loft," I add.

"No!" He's a little too passionate for someone who isn't lying. "Um. Not more than usual."

"Usual for who?" It's too bad the doctor can't hear me, because I'd tell her I've seen him take tequila shots like he's discovered the fountain of youth.

Dr. Wagner seems genuinely worried. "As a doctor, I will advise that you cut out all alcohol and any other recreational pastimes. Get some rest. Find some time to integrate physical activity into your routine—it's a good, healthy distraction."

"Dr. Wagner, I'm not on drugs," Rafael assures her, rubbing one of his arms in discomfort.

"*Noooo.* Just the loads of pills in your cabinet," I say.

He grumbles beneath his breath, which doesn't sit well with me; neither does the doctor's misplaced concern. While I'm the one in need of help, the doctor stares at him like he's a three-legged puppy.

"I didn't mean it that way. Sometimes pills can have strange side effects," Dr. Wagner continues, taking the iPad from the table and circling around the bed to Rafael. "But if you're not taking anything, a good week of rest will help. Do you have a pharmacy?"

"Yes."

"Your primary physician can write a script for sleeping pills."

"No, that's not necessary, Doc. I have those already."

She reaches out a hand and rests it on his shoulder. "I know this is tough for you. It's hard to see loved ones suffering, but we are doing everything possible for Evie right now. Our goal is to keep her stable and allow her brain time to heal." Her voice softens. "However, the more time that passes, you have to prepare yourself for the possibility that she might not make it."

Loved ones? *Not make it*? "Mamma Mia," I breathe, feeling like oxygen's suddenly the scarcest element in the world.

"You already know this, Rafael, but what you're doing is helping. Spending time with those in a coma, sharing memories and talking to them, can make a difference." Dr. Wagner squeezes his shoulder. "As long as she's *here*, there's hope."

I'm here, but I don't feel hope. I feel the opposite of hope—*desperation*. Like someone has tossed me off the top of the Willis Tower and I'm tumbling through air. I grasp for something to steady myself. My hand goes through the bed frame and wall.

Anxiety makes my chest cave and my legs weak. Sound fades. The room blurs. The ground gives.

Far away, Rafael is having a conversation with the doctor. If I didn't know any better, I'd think he was concerned, but that would be absurd.

Feeling like I might finish dying right now, I drop into the pleather chair—and stay there. Sitting is allowed. I try to grasp the seat. My hand moves through it. Touching is still a no-go. Apparently, the afterlife has arbitrary physics and a messed-up sense of humor—and I'm the butt of some cosmic joke.

I want to cry. I *don't.*

Instead, I push the air out and press play on the mental jukebox, humming "Dancing Queen," a tune that's Swedish disco, sparkly despair, and an urgent need to escape. The opening notes sound like a battle between a car alarm and a bagpipe. But what do I care?

I keep going and going. Even when Rafael throws me a look—half pain, half prayer—as if he's begging the universe to make it stop. I glare back and sing louder.

He visibly stiffens before turning back to the doctor, and I feel slightly better. I continue, belting out a few more tragically projected lines that have Rafael rubbing the back of his neck before the doctor leaves.

And I'm left alone with the bane of my existence.

"You're a very convincing hallucination," Rafael says.

I snap my head in his direction. "You're a very convincing asshole," I fire back, managing to sound more stable than I feel. Sniffing back tears, I stand too quickly and stumble forward.

Rafael's hands shoot out—but they pass through me. The sensation is warm, like sunshine on a summer day.

We both jerk back in surprise.

Rafael looks down at his hands like he's realizing he has ten fingers for the first time. "What just happened?"

I rub my arm, trying to shake off the strange sensation. "I told you I wasn't a hallucination."

"Then what are you?"

I grasp for the quickest response. "A . . . spirit," I say. It takes effort not to make it sound like a question.

Rafael lifts a brow. "A spirit?"

"Evie's spirit."

His gaze flicks over me. "The resemblance—and attitude—are pretty spot-on."

"As is my patience." I hold his gaze, my tone sharper now.

"Let's say I believe you and you *are* Evie's spirit," he says. "What the hell do you want with me?"

Good question. One I'm completely unprepared for.

I look from him to my body.

I consider the facts I've turned over all morning—waking up in his apartment, on his sofa, wearing last night's clothes, with my last memory being the OhLaLove dinner.

My earlier theory might still be true, but I need to check one more item off the checklist. "Tell me about last night. About the accident," I say, turning back to Rafael.

The shadow of a smile vanishes.

CHAPTER SEVEN

SEVEN DAYS AFTER (BECAUSE IT'S TAKING A MINUTE FOR IT TO SINK IN)

A car knocked me into a coma.

"After the meeting with Cyril, we left the restaurant," Rafael says, his eyes distant and his voice almost a whisper. "A car veered onto the sidewalk near the intersection and clipped you. The impact threw you across the street." His throat bobs. "You sustained a head injury. Trauma."

It takes effort to keep my face blank. To not crumble. Hearing the details—how I wound up *here*—isn't easy, not even the second time around. I don't typically need things repeated to me like I'm a toddler, but this isn't typical. Far from it.

"And the driver kept going?" My voice is tight, strained with the effort of keeping my emotions in check.

"Yes. Until the cops caught him. He'd been drinking."

I swallow past the rush of panic. Someone made a reckless choice . . . "And now I'm . . . here."

A barely-there inhale before he says, "Yes."

Standing in Dr. Wagner's vacated spot, I stare down at my body and rub the base of my head, the source of my injury. A dull throb of pain, but otherwise? Nothing. Nothing except the sharp ache of having everything snatched from me. The years of running to escape my past, to provide for myself, to finally reach a point where I could ease into a different pace. All of that . . . for *nothing*?

No. Nope. I won't accept the possibility. *Ctrl-Alt-Delete.*

I step away from the bed and pace my side of the room, chewing a nail—a habit I try my best to conceal but can't bring myself to care about because I'm-in-a-coma-and-does-it-even-matter. Still, I shoot Rafael a glance, but he's not even looking at me.

Gaze distant, he's sitting rigidly in the pleather chair, head propped on his knuckles. I don't dwell on whatever's eating him because I have enough to worry about.

"And what, they couldn't do anything when they arrived?" I gesture to my body—the one connected to machines. "Like CPR? Or aren't there defibrillators for this exact situation?"

Rafael peers up at me through his tousled hair. "Your heart's fine."

I touch the place over my chest. It's thunderous and erratic and not so fine at all. "So they didn't even try?"

"They did everything they could when you got here." His voice is low, rough. "They had the best doctors—they *still have* the best doctors—taking care of you. They acted fast. Ran tests. Stabilized you. But . . . the swelling in your brain—" His hands press against his thighs, rubbing absently. "They had to induce the coma. To protect your brain and give your body time to heal."

His voice catches, barely. But I hear it. I *feel* it. And for a second, it throws me. Because Rafael doesn't care, not about me—and if he's worried now . . .

I look away, back to *me*—the body in the bed. It's been an entire week with little change, the doctor said. No movement. No sign of waking up. Just a terrifying, ticking silence.

"Wake up," I whisper to myself—half plea, half command.

Panic claws up my throat, sharp and sudden, but I force it back down, where it belongs. Vulnerability is dangerous, especially in front of Rafael. I square my shoulders and turn on him, reaching for the familiar and the safe: deflection, suspicion, control. "And what about you? Where were you?" I lift my chin. "Giving my head another thunk? Making sure the deed was done?"

Rafael's brows shoot up into his forehead. "What? You don't think I had something to do with this?" His tone is incredulous, offended. "Believe it or not, Evie, I'm not willing to maim someone to get an account."

"Because you can charm them to death?"

His eyes blaze. "Because I . . ." He clamps his lips together.

"Because you . . . *what*?" I cross my arm, expecting a Vela-esque response. *I don't need to try hard. I'm loved by all. I walk through life without a care because everyone wants to be my friend. My colleague. My client.*

"Because it's not important. It's work," Rafael says, pushing from his chair. "That's all it is."

I stare at him. I know he's lying.

Media Lab has been almost as important to Rafael as it's been to me, not that he could understand what it means to me.

Back when we were "friends," Rafael didn't even know if Media Lab was for him. He joked about starting a YouTube channel called Tacos and Tequila Tuesdays (but Every Day), launching a sports merch line, and even getting his pilot's license. One foot in and one foot out. But the longer we worked together, the more the "one foot out" stepped *in*. The more he started—pretended—to care. About the work, and because I was stupid enough to believe it, about me. And then he turned his charm and ambition into a weapon, stole an account we built side by side, and cut down my trust, our friendship.

Still, we came up through the ranks together, never much further ahead than the other—not for lack of trying on my part.

We each have our own teams now and manage several accounts. Even our cubes are shoved across from each other's, a cruel joke brought about by the age of "collaborative" workspaces.

Somehow he's made everyone a friend along the way, and I . . . well, I've made myself indispensable—with Dana, with leadership, with my clients. I built a reputation rooted in reliability and results so I could be someone they needed because I needed Media Lab more. The money. The stability. The means to keep myself from falling back into the poverty and chaos (and mother) I spent my life attempting to outrun.

So it's more than just *work*. For both of us.

Rafael steps toward the door.

"Where are you going?" I cut him off, slipping between him and the door to block his exit. The truth is terrible and hard to face, but I need him to stay. I need him to help me weave together the rest of how I got here so I can figure out how to get out of here. This hospital. That bed. And that gown.

I make myself tall, hating that I've tossed my shoes aside. His brow lifts in a way that tells me I'm ridiculous to even try because he can walk through me, of course. "Rafael."

"Evie." His stern tone matches mine.

We've been here before. Needing something from the other but not quite asking for it. Call it rivalry. Call it pride. A mix of the two has always drawn the line in the sand between us. Dana once joked that he and I could dominate the industry if we put our talents together. I scoffed. Rafael laughed. And not once did I think I'd be the one to shift the stalemate by backing down from a challenge, or worse yet, asking for help.

"One more question." I clutch my hands behind my back, waiting to see if he'll stay. When he doesn't stomp through me, I continue, "Why are you the only one who can see me?"

"No clue."

I narrow my eyes. "You can tell me, you know . . ."

"Tell you what?"

"If you had something to do with this." And there it is—a chance for him to tell the truth.

Rafael grumbles like he's the one peeing through tubes and brushes past me. Too fast, he tugs the door wide open and slips into the hallway. A nurse almost crashes into him as she hurries down the corridor, but his hands shoot out and grip her arms.

"I'm sorry," he mumbles with a reassuring smile. The young nurse blushes. Rafael ensures she's steady on her feet before he drops his hands and rushes down the muted-beige hallway, past hospital staff clad in various shades of blue and turquoise, patients in wheelchairs, and visitors hidden behind flowers and gift baskets.

"Hey!" I hurry after him, ducking and weaving between people who can't see me. I'm almost on his heels. "Rafael! You can't blame me for thinking it. It's the only reasonable explanation." And by reasonable, I mean I can't accept the alternative—that this was a freakish twist of fate. Because Annie ended up in a hospital too. Annie slipped into a coma. And Annie never woke up.

The same thing happening to me isn't comprehensible. I was careful and calculated. I planned. I ran. I did everything I was supposed to do—but not everything I needed to.

I can't be done yet.

I was supposed to do more.

I owed—*owe*—it to Annie . . . and our bucket list.

Rafael keeps walking away, too fast for someone with an obsession with carbs.

"Admit it!" I command.

Rafael's long strides have me scrambling to catch up. He doesn't look back, doesn't so much as acknowledge my presence.

I quicken my step. "Raffy Taffy!"

The telltale cheek muscle pulses. Likely because I've hit too close to home. Touched the proverbial nerve. I just need to prod until he breaks.

"The truth shall set you free!"

Rafael growls as he heads toward an elevator, which is already packed with two nurses chatting over Starbucks cups, a young doctor on his phone, and an older couple holding hands. He abruptly changes direction and marches past the elevator toward a stairwell beneath an EXIT sign. I rush through the door before it closes, trailing him as he clambers down the stairs at a quick clip.

I flail after him, half running, half floating. "Rafael!"

"Leave me alone!" he shouts, his voice echoing up and down the concrete stairwell.

Typical Rafael. "Making things harder than they have to be."

Rafael halts.

I barrel into him—through him—and warmth washes through me. Rafael inhales sharply, rubbing his arms, making me wonder what he felt. Warmth? Cold? Who cares?

I scowl at him, clutching my chest. "What is wrong with you?" I huff.

"I make things *harder*?" Rafael's tone is low and accusatory.

I inject self-indignation into my tone. "You're the one who won't stay and talk!"

"You don't want me to *talk*. You want me to admit I had something to do with this." He gestures to me—or rather, the floaty mess that used to have a pulse.

While the run down the stairs hasn't winded me, it's the glowering that hits me square in the chest. I ignore it. Pretend to be unfazed.

"Isn't confession part of your Catholic upbringing?"

"Chingado." He grumbles the word, throwing his hands up as he storms down the stairs again.

I rush to keep pace with him.

The level-eight ire pulsing along the column of his tanned neck tells me I'm treading down a path that's not going to lead to answers, which are what I need.

If this were any other situation, I would keep pushing his buttons. It's not often that I get under Rafael's skin without some elaborate plan, but I need to get him from level-eight on-the-verge-of-explosion to level-two on-the-verge-of-explanation.

Shifting to troubleshooting mode, I draw in a deep breath, determined to steer things back on track. I'm Evie Pope. I'm an expert at taking complex problems and solving them. Like Rafael's inability to answer my questions.

"Okay. So let's say you didn't do this," I start. Rafael mutters and continues to hurtle down the stairs. "Okay, okay—you *didn't* do this." I lie easily, chasing after him.

Rafael doesn't stop.

He reaches the bottom of the stairwell and opens a door beneath an EXIT sign. Eye-watering light swamps the stairwell, and then the door begins to shut. In my face.

"Hey!" I yelp, walking through it. The sensation of moving through the metal door is like treading through frigid water. "Rafael!"

Undeterred, Rafael storms halfway across the packed parking lot, weaving through parked cars with surprising agility.

"Can you wait?" I run after him, my dress hindering my movements.

"Can you be a normal human?"

"Apparently, the 'normal human' ship has sailed." I hop over an overturned cup of Dollop coffee.

"That's not what I meant!"

"What *did* you mean?" I huff, easing into a power walk as Rafael barely breaks a sweat. It takes several more steps for me to catch up.

Rafael shoots a glare in my direction. The intensity in it makes my stomach flutter. "You don't know when to turn it off."

Something in my chest shifts uncomfortably. "I think I've been turned off," I scoff.

"Your body—maybe," Rafael says. "But your desire to reach some imagined goalpost clearly hasn't turned off. Evie, you're in a fucking coma, yet you're here, asking me if I'm the one who put you there because you're more worried about me having the upper hand than you are putting your own shit aside to ask yourself why."

"I did ask why."

"Did you?" He arches a thick brow.

I nod, still without an answer.

"Then *why*?"

I open my mouth to answer.

Of course I want to know *why*. Why do people drink and drive? Why did the accident happen on the most important night of my career? Why is Rafael the only one who can see me? I've thought about the *why*s all morning. Just haven't found an answer yet.

"Evie." Rafael halts.

I almost crash into him but manage to stop, close enough I can track the trickle of sweat along the length of his neck. Whispers of silver in his chestnut curls.

"You're asking the wrong *why*," he says.

There must be something happening in this alter-form that's making me heat at the intensity in his gaze. It's like he can see me and *into* me. I'm convinced of it. I'm irritated by it.

I take a step back, needing some space. "Which *why* should I be asking?" I prop a hand on my hip, curious to hear what Rafael Vela has to say.

His features smooth out, the anger-slash-frustration erased from his face in one blink. We might be back to we-have-answers level two. I hold my breath, but Rafael shakes his head.

"For someone so smart, you make me wonder if I know you at all," he says.

I want to argue. No one knows *all* of me. Not Gemma or Dana. Not any of my exes. Least of all him. Opening up to people means opening up to hurt, and hurt's been trailing me since I could walk.

Since the nights I lay in bed, curled around Annie, whispering silly stories to distract her from the pain in her stomach—the kind we later learned was her blood sugar crashing. Since the nights our mother left us alone for hours, heels clicking unsteadily across the floor as she left with her boyfriend-of-the-month. Since the times I called 911 from our neighbor's house because our mother wasn't around, because she never would, because she said Annie was "being dramatic."

So, yes, allowing someone in takes a lot. And I once had let Rafael in. Stupidly.

I push the memories—the past—away. "Explain."

Rafael leans in with those big, all-consuming eyes, as if he purposely wants to disarm me further. Joke's on him, though. It'll take more than three thousand pounds of car to make me succumb to his tricks, so I arch a brow in challenge.

"If I woke up as a spirit stuck outside my body, the question I'd ask is *why*?"

"Oh" is all I manage.

CHAPTER EIGHT
SEVEN DAYS AFTER (STILL IN A COMA, THANKS FOR ASKING)

We sit in Rafael's truck—one he bought after his third promotion. I'm surprised it's not been keyed by the countless Violets he's no doubt left brokenhearted over the years. I've imagined taking a key to his overpriced, gas-guzzling baby a time or two, but I have *some* boundaries when it comes to our rivalry.

"Thought of anything?" His question cuts through the quiet hum of the AC.

Palms out, I reach for the vents but feel nothing. None of the cold air. None of the sun's warmth. Apparently, afterlife physics means I can walk through walls but not enjoy central air. Figures.

But none of this stops the chaos happening *inside*, where everything's a hot, confusing mess with zero explanation—no *why* for my predicament and definitely no *why* for Rafael's question.

Because I don't know why spirit me would have been separated from physical me without me actually moving on to wherever it is spirits go next. *Heaven,* Great-Aunt Julia would have said while she was alive. *It's where we all go when God calls us home.*

Wherever you are, Great-Aunt Julia, my invite must have gotten lost in the mail. If there was an invite at all. The last time I stepped into a church was on the second-worst day of my life, and it's been fifteen years since.

So, if why I haven't moved on is a matter of missing church and learning some big lesson, I'm probably stuck here for a while. I shudder at the thought of haunting the world forever . . . but that can't be my ever after, right? I mean, I don't go to church, but I'm not an entirely terrible person. Did I pay someone to move Rafael's truck to another parking structure three months ago? Sure. Did I enjoy his five-hour-long search? Also, sure. But that can't be why I'm here, can it?

I've tried to balance my more questionable actions with *good*. I rarely lie. I almost never curse. I've never stolen, despite having been homeless for months at a time. I've fostered dogs and mentored girls. I would never admit this to Rafael, but I once bought all the Girl Scout cookies he brought in to work (okay, I did it twice—I don't lie—because his nieces are very, very cute).

None of this leads to *why* I'm stuck here.

Great-Aunt Julia would pat my head and tell me to pray on it. I think I might be a little late to the prayer party, given I'm *this*.

"Since when do you bite your nails?" Rafael asks. I feel his gaze.

Despite not caring what he thinks, I drop my hand from my lips into my lap, curling my fingers into a fist. "It's a habit I picked up postmortem," I offer with a sharp smile.

"You're *not* dead."

"Halfway there."

"You don't know that," he insists.

I let him have that one because my ghostly expertise is still loading, because I don't know much of anything at this point. Nothing that makes logical sense, at least. Great-Aunt Julia thought we all went to heaven, but the sweet woman was clearly wrong.

"I think I have an explanation," I offer, leaning on the only spiritual knowledge I ever learned.

"Explain."

"It's the only thing that makes sense," I offer as preamble, shifting so I can face him fully.

My dress hikes up my thigh, and I dig my fingers into my palm to keep from tugging it back into place. An hour ago, I was asking him to feel me up, so showing him a little skin shouldn't bother me, but it does. All things Rafael Vela get under my skin . . . which leads me to my explanation.

"Hell. I'm in hell."

Rafael doesn't so much as blink. "What?"

"This is hell." I gesture to his truck, to the outside. I don't point to him, because that would be too on-the-nose. If I haven't made it to Great-Aunt Julia's heaven, then this must be the alternative. I've died, and Rafael is my perpetual punishment (because I clearly didn't buy *enough* cookies).

"Let me get this straight," he says, leaning his back into his seat and leveling a narrowed gaze at me. "You think you're in hell, and I'm the only one who can see you?"

"Yes . . . minus the burning fires." I mime flames with my fingers.

Rafael pinches the bridge of his nose and lets out a deep, frustrated sigh that makes me bristle. "If this is your hell, then why am *I* the one who can see *you*?"

He's the devil is a plausible explanation, but one that might result in him going back up to the hospital room to finish the deed (if my current theory is off the mark). I imagine his tanned finger wrapping around my pale neck and squeezing.

Shaking the image from my mind, I clear my throat. "Maybe you're dead too?" I say tightly, momentarily petrified by the thought of being stuck in perpetuity together.

He mutters a string of Spanish. Another heavy sigh. A dark look. "Being on the other end of this, I understand if this is traumatic for you," he starts, speaking to me like a child who needs to be talked to slowly. "But I can tell you for certain, this isn't hell."

I swallow a knot of annoyance. "Oh, is that right? Who died and made you an expert on all things heaven-and-hell?"

"For one, lots of people." Rafael holds up one finger, the tip of it bearing a white scar. "And two, you'd probably have to be *dead* to be in hell." Another finger pops up beside the first.

My annoyance flares.

And because I need answers, I focus on his words instead of his tone or his fingers. I consider my comatose body, kept alive by medical equipment. *Alive.* He has a point. Not that I'll admit it.

"All right. What's your theory?" I ask. "About what's happening?"

Rafael rolls his shoulders and takes another deep breath. "That I've taken too many meds."

I snort.

Rafael's eyes snap to mine.

"What?" I scowl.

"The flesh-and-bone Evie Pope never made such sounds," he muses, tapping his finger against the steering wheel.

"I can assure you I'm one and the same." Give or take some bones. "You don't believe me?" I push, needing an answer.

Rafael does what he's done all morning—and not *once* in years—and ignores me as he reaches for the center console and presses a button. The screen lights up; the truck purrs to life. My nerves short-circuit.

A different kind of distress—some would call it a phobia—kicks in as he shifts the truck into drive. I grind my teeth against the rush of anxiety. *Breathe.*

Hands pressed against each other, I count through four *Mamma Mia*s and direct my thoughts from the moving vehicle to something more productive than giving in to my fear. Like my situation and dissecting the *why* on my own because he's not been helpful.

Although I hate to admit it, Rafael might be right. This may not be my hell, and it's most certainly not Great-Aunt Julia's heaven. Arriving at either of those places would mean it's game over for me, but I'm still here. Which means it's not *over* over, only like a little bit over. And what if that means I still have a chance to *go back* instead of moving forward or upward or whichever direction I'm destined to go? What if I can find a way to get this ghost me into the hospital bed me? The thought makes me jerk up and gasp, "*Ohmygod*."

"Are you seeing the light?" Rafael's voice makes my ears perk in his direction.

Scowling, I slowly twist to face him. He watches me with amusement while the truck idles at a stoplight. "You're infuriating," I say.

"I think you mentioned that in the *Publicity Today* interview."

"Ha. I told them you were *incorrigible*."

"Was that before or after you told them you'd mentored me?"

I felt quite proud when that bit of information made it into the final published interview. I remember the day Rafael read it. Sipping my coffee, I watched from my desk as he scanned the piece. His eyebrows danced as he read about how I'd taught him a lot of what he knew, and I experienced a giddiness only he could make me feel. Only *torturing him* made me feel.

A satisfied smirk tugs at my lips, so I quickly fix my face into a scowl. "Were it not for all of *my* work on the Betton account, you wouldn't have gotten that promotion before me."

Rafael tenses, amusement fading. "If you say so."

He gives me nothing to fight against—just the maddening silence from this morning. I attempt to push the memory of our first major account back into where I store all rage-inducing memories, but the hurt is still there. Achy and all-consuming, if I let it. Almost three years of friendship, of thinking we were in it together, that we had each other's backs. Rafael helped me think like *one of the guys*, and I helped him pursue accounts like *someone with an actual plan*. I took up golfing (Rafael's idea) and, for a short—unfortunately unforgettable—time, smoking cigars (my idea). He took up organizing projects in folders and even used a planner—for two weeks. He challenged me to stop overthinking and go for it, and I challenged him to talk less and observe more. He made me see the benefits of networking, and I helped him see the benefits of really knowing what our bosses wanted. And along the way, we spent countless hours together and he became someone who was more than a colleague—a friend. Until he had me cut from the Betton account. Because after almost a year of prep, he decided he didn't need a colead.

So, when I relied on him implicitly, he took it away—not only the account, but also the sizable commission and the stability that would have come with it. The opportunity to move from the rat-infested basement I was renting to somewhere less hazardous. The chance to work fewer hours and maybe, finally, catch my breath. I cried into a tub of ice cream that night . . . and came back the next morning, ready to play the game his way. I haven't looked back since.

Always forward. Until now, that is.

Because the only way forward might be by going back . . . and using him to help me.

"I understand that this will probably go against your Evie instincts, but I'm hoping you can help me," I blurt as Rafael steers the truck onto Lake Shore Drive.

A black SUV allows him to merge onto the busy road, and Rafael accelerates with ease. Momentarily frozen by terror, I grasp the edge of the seat, but my hand moves through it. I swallow a frustrated sigh and curl my hands into one another, savoring the solidity of the grip. Of course my hands are useless, but my ghost ass stays planted just fine. I'd ask questions, but the universe isn't exactly playing Team Evie.

The thing is, not a lot scares me—I *was* raised by a narcissist—but there's something about being in a vehicle with someone else in charge of what happens, of how fast and where we go, that makes me feel unmoored. Helpless. A little sick.

I force myself to steady my breathing.

Rafael doesn't miss any of it. To my shock, the truck slows. "Evie instincts?"

"You know—the knee-jerk inclination to thwart me and take things from me?" The words slip through my lips. His jaw clamps down and flexes, and I inwardly kick myself.

"You have an interesting way of asking for help," he says, his hands tightening around the steering wheel as he navigates the truck between lanes and cars. Even if he's not speeding, my breathing hitches. If I didn't die by a car the night outside the Aviary, perhaps this ride will be it.

My heart pitches against my ribs, and I press my hand against my chest. Distantly, I think I hear the beeping of monitors. Feel a dull throbbing at the base of my skull. Sounds fade. The road blurs.

"Hey." His voice pulls me to the present moment. "I was kidding about going toward the light."

I blink and straighten. "It was so tempting," I say airily, shaking off a panic attack—and potential fainting.

The truck stops at a red light, and I relax long enough to remember I need something from him, something I won't get playing Evie vs. Rafael. I need a better tactic. Like seeing Rafael as a client, not an opponent. Someone to win over.

While it pains me to ask him for help, he might be my only option.

"As I was saying . . ." I start.

The light turns green, and Rafael accelerates, following behind another car too closely for my liking. "Maybe you . . ."

My voice falters. I can't look at the road. This is the point where physical me would be barfing into a bag. Ghost me battles waves of nausea. "You might feel inclined to help me," I manage through clenched teeth.

We turn onto Michigan Ave., the truck finally slowing. I force air into my lungs.

"What can I help with?" Rafael asks.

Watching the road. Not getting us killed. "Getting me back into my body, preferably," I say, but I can't bring myself to look at him . .. and it has nothing to do with the traffic and everything to do with my situation.

I never ask for help, least of all from Rafael. The last time he "helped," it left me with low-key PTSD—and a deep mistrust of all things male, dimpled, and Vela. How do I convince him to help when I haven't convinced myself?

"I know this is a little—*a lot*—surreal, but you're the only one who can see me. As you might imagine, it makes my options very limited." I attempt to keep my voice level and detached, even as I'm feeling walls crumple around me. Feeling bits of Evie Pope become exposed to the one person I've built them to keep out.

"And you want *my* help?" He sounds surprised and unsure, and we might be feeling the same things.

"Uh-huh." I barely hear myself.

I feel Rafael's eyes on me, but I can't look at him. He'll see right through me.

"You don't want my help," he says.

Don't I know it.

The truck rolls through the city. The sun's bright against a clear-blue summer sky. Buildings stretch tall above the city. People buzz past, their cell phones plastered to their ears. Tourists huddle around a busking duo. The world is so achingly alive, and the desire to stay in it is crushing. Rafael's silence more so.

"I really *need* it." Needs trump wants.

Another stretch of silence—and it's enough to get me to look. His features reveal nothing. No stretching of his toned muscles or smiling into dimple territory. Not even a sign of the tic in his cheek.

"I mean it," I add, feeling like I need to try harder. Still nothing.

Okay, he's playing tough ball. I've played tough ball since the day my mother disappeared for a week, leaving Annie and me to fend for ourselves. We were nine and seven years old. Annie took care of the both of us, even though she was the one who needed taking care of—already getting sick more often, already carrying more than any kid should. Somehow we didn't fall apart or starve. We danced and sang and wished on shooting stars. We would move to the big city—Chicago, because Great-Aunt Julia brought us here once—and buy the prettiest dresses. Annie would become a singer, and I would be a dancer. We'd make our biggest dreams possible.

I need to do whatever I can to keep that dream alive. I owe it to Annie to fight.

I have one bargaining chip left, and it's the most important, the one I've been busting my ass for years to earn and then protect from Rafael. And if I hesitate—remotely give the decision a second thought—I'll talk myself out of it, backtrack to ground zero, where there aren't other answers or options.

Taking a steadying breath, I say, "If you help me get back into my body, I'll drop out of the running for the director role. I won't fight you for it. I'll tell Dana it's all yours." I swallow. "Well deserved, even." Even though the words burn my throat, my voice is clear and firm. Everything I've worked for in exchange for another chance at life.

But these are the types of deals you make when you're in hell and dealing with the devil.

CHAPTER NINE
SEVEN DAYS AFTER (YES, STILL)

I offered to drop out of the race, and he hasn't said anything.

That's how it typically goes. I trick myself into thinking I know him—that little he does can shock me—yet here I am, baffled. It makes me wonder if I miscalculated by offering him the promotion, the job I've raced like hell toward. Scraping and clawing for more accounts. Working more hours. Taking more meetings. Focusing on little else. Because racing forward meant never having to go back. This job—the promotions along the way—meant freedom from the constant shadow of poverty, hunger, and desperation and a guarantee that I could feel secure enough to get to my other goals.

And now I'm pulling myself out of the race.

The accident pulled me out of it, I remind myself.

No matter how long I've fought to move forward—checking off lists and keeping my eye on the next promotion—I've been whipped backward so hard my soul's popped out of my body. Literally.

My chest is about to combust as I marinate in the loaded silence, waiting for him to give me *something.* I pick at my nails, tempted to chew on them. The glossy polish doesn't budge. The best shellac manicure and pedicure this side of Chicago. I go every two weeks, like clockwork. Part of the Evie Pope package. Look where that's got me.

"We're here," Rafael says at last. His response isn't the answer I expected. It's not an answer at all. Which means he doesn't want the deal. Which means I'm on my own.

And I'm fine with this. *Completely* fine. So fine I can't even meet his gaze, so I stare straight ahead and nod.

He shifts in his seat, the leather squealing beneath him. "Evie."

Rafael. If I speak, he'll know he's affected me. I won't give him the satisfaction.

Beside me, he sighs, opens the door, and slips out of the truck—and I deflate like a popped tire.

I shouldn't be so affected by his lack of a response, but if Rafael doesn't help, how do I fix myself? What if I can never go back?

I'm on the verge of dry heaving, but the door opens. I grit my teeth together and suck in a pocket of air, ignoring Rafael as he leans into the truck. Keeping my gaze fixed on the dashboard, I look inward for a ghostly power to take me far, *far* away. Not heaven or hell far, but somewhere I can come up with another plan, one that doesn't require his help. Because who needs him anyway?

"Stevie," he says.

I whip toward him so fast, Rafael flinches. "What did you say?" I ask, blinking and breathing fast. The name—the one I haven't used in almost a decade—makes me exchange grief for anger faster than I switch out of my pumps at the end of the workday.

"That's your name, isn't it?" His tone is even and unperturbed, but a familiar spark has entered his gaze, and it makes me want to hurtle myself at him.

"No, it's not." I narrow my eyes, daring him to continue.

A brow rises in question. "Stevie Popovici. That doesn't jingle a bell?"

I balk. "You . . . couldn't know . . ." No one knows my real name, the one I discarded along with my old life. Yet he's throwing it around like it's written on my forehead.

If I were a little more certain this isn't all some final "heaven or hell" test, I'd give him a slice of hell. I'd tell him that he's lucky he's handsome and charming because if he weren't, everyone would actually see beneath the facade to the double-crossing jerk beneath. I'd admit I'm not sorry about the laxative incident or the parking ticket or that Gemma only pretends to like him because she's a junior associate on his team. And I'd make him wish he'd never heard my name—*either* of them.

I realize I've floated out of the truck, advancing on him, hands balled at my side. Rafael concedes a step, then another. We're in a parking garage, and he cuts through two empty parking spaces before he backs into a minivan and halts.

Somewhere my heart's slamming into my rib cage, and my breaths pump out of me, short and rapid. "I'm going to haunt you and your children and your children's children if you ever so much as speak that name to another living soul again," I warn, jabbing a finger at his chest.

Surprise flits across his gaze. I'm the one who's a ghost-thing, but I can see right through him, and his soul is scared.

"Your grandmother doesn't have enough prayers to save you from the kind of torment I can inflict." My voice becomes deadly quiet. "I'll be there at every turn."

I've been a spirit all of twelve hours and don't have a clue about my paranormal abilities, but I'll find a way to pull it off. If nothing else, Rafael knows my relentless determination. I wasn't one of *Chicago Business Journal*'s "Thirty Under Thirty" for nothing.

"I'll never speak a word of it," Rafael says, holding up three fingers.

I frown, not following. "What's that supposed to mean?"

"Scout's honor."

"If you say so. But don't test me on this," I warn, injecting years of resentment into my gaze before I spin and walk away.

Fighting to get my breathing and emotions under control, I grind out a few *Mamma Mia*s through anger-blurred vision.

The underground garage—painted in shades of green—comes into focus.

Emerald Heights. *Home.*

"How did you—" I start to ask, but bite my tongue. Literally. Asking the guy who has intimate knowledge of my birthmark and real name how he remembered my address from a single drop-off years ago feels like the least of my concerns.

I ignore his "What?" and speed-walk to the elevator, back straight and brain buzzing with questions. I ask none of them.

I slow at the elevator and reach for the buttons before curling my fingers into a fist. Right. *Useless ghost hands.*

I consider taking the stairs up to my floor. Eight flights. Time to think and figure this out on my own. Or—I could wait for him. For answers.

Footsteps sound behind me.

I cross my arms and fix my gaze on the elevator doors. A flyer informs residents that dues are increasing in the winter. Another mentions a Fourth of July celebration on the rooftop in a few weeks. Neither of which I might be here for.

Rafael reaches past me and jabs the up-arrow button before his hands slip into his pockets. I angle my head away so he's no longer in my periphery.

Rafael sighs. "That first day? I passed by your desk after lunch. Your paperwork was out—a photocopy of an old ID," he says quietly. "I figured it was easier to shove it back into the folder before I walked away. If Media Lab does anything better than marketing, it's gossip. And since you started the job under another name, maybe you didn't want that out there. For the longest time, I figured you were KGB."

I roll my eyes at that last part. But I don't respond, because I expected something sneaky or nefarious, not *this*.

That first morning—running late and battling the snowstorm—is forever seared into my core memories. My anxiety made me sloppy. I accidentally grabbed *all* of my paperwork, including some I hadn't used since before college, before I legally changed my name. And I never even realized I'd left it out for public consumption.

And Rafael's known. This entire time.

That same afternoon, he was setting me at ease—telling me about the HR manager who napped in the janitor's closet and the accounts payable specialist who snuck toilet paper home in his trench coat. His office intel, peppered with jokes, made me lower my guard—maybe he *did* think I was KGB. Part of some elaborate plan to glean his own intel and store it for a rainy day.

Today's more of a storm, so it doesn't surprise me that he's whipped this morsel of information from his ammunition belt.

But he's kept it to himself for so long. *That* surprises me.

The elevator dings and the doors peel apart, revealing a lone occupant.

"Hi." Charlene Baker, the lawyer who lives on the floor above mine, smiles at us. She steps forward, clad in her signature black pumps and YSL handbag. As one of the youngest Black attorneys in Chicago, Charlene is one person who I know has worked harder to earn her spot than even I have. We don't get drinks on the weekends, but we grab the occasional coffee and chat in the elevator as our work schedules allow (not often).

I wave.

"Hey," Rafael says beside me, and I remember that she can't see me. It's him she's looking at with bright hazel eyes. I look from her to him and back to her when a second ticks by. Charlene's grin is all straight teeth. Friendly. Inviting.

They know each other.

"Nice to see you back," she says, slipping out of the elevator as Rafael steps into it. He keeps the doors from closing with an outstretched hand. She stalls; so does he. I look between the two of them, a little bit confused, which seems to be the flavor of the day for me.

They *definitely* know each other, and I'm not sure how I missed this. It makes sense, though. She's a lawyer. He's a troublemaker.

"Char, I'm sorry I didn't call after . . ." Rafael starts.

Charlene stops him with an upheld hand. "Please, don't apologize."

"No, I *am* sorry." Rafael offers an apologetic smile, which toes dimple territory.

She answers with a shake of her head, but something familiar lingers beneath the brightness. Something that makes my breath catch. Something I *know*.

A glimmer of loneliness.

In a blink, it's gone, and . . . *ohmygod*, Charlene is into him.

I look between the two of them, speechless.

"Seriously, I should be apologizing," she assures him with another megawatt smile. "I should've known there was someone else."

The elevator doors push against his hand. "Still feel like a jerk," he says, dropping his hand and stepping into the elevator.

"Don't."

"You should."

Charlene and I respond at once, and his eyes dart to mine. I glare back, hoping I'm communicating that he's an asshole extraordinaire. *Assholedinaire.*

"Door's about to close," Rafael says.

Charlene laughs softly. "I know how doors work, Raf."

"I know *you* do." Rafael winks at her. "Bye, Char."

The doors begin to slide shut.

"See you around." Charlene waves at him before she turns and walks to her car. I stare after her. I wouldn't have thought someone like her would be into someone like *him*, someone who doesn't even bother to learn the names of all the someones he's into. Charlene can do way, way better, but she's clearly been Vela'd.

I have so many questions, but mostly I want to hurt him.

"Rafael." I turn toward the elevator—the one that's gone up without me, with the man who's most likely broken my neighbor's heart. Of course he'd leave *me* down here.

The elevator dings.

The doors slide open again.

Rafael leans against the back wall, hands tucked into his pants. "Coming?"

I march into the elevator, ensuring I keep the farthest distance from him. The doors close, but the lift doesn't move, not until Rafael's arm brushes past mine and punches the floor number. *Eight*.

My nerves flare as I brace for the worst. What if I plummet through the floor? Or short-circuit the entire system with my ghost vibes? But nothing happens. The elevator moves. The floor stays solid. The cables don't snap. I breathe—or seethe—for oh-so-many reasons, but I bite my tongue. It's none of my business if Charlene wants to hook up with Rafael. I only wish she'd asked me first, because I know more about Rafael than he knows about himself. His cholesterol-loaded diet. His proclivity for jaywalking and absentminded humming of Disney tunes. The way he stretches when he's sitting and standing and doing nothing that remotely resembles physical activity.

"What's going through your Rafael-consumed mind?"

I snort at his question, feeling my neck and cheeks heat. I'm glad he can't see my reflection in the elevator doors. "It's not Rafael consumed, thank you very much."

"So you weren't thinking about me?"

"Not for one second."

Rafael hums as the elevator lurches to a stop at my floor, and luckily for me, I don't have to wait for the doors to open to get out. I almost fly across the hall in my attempt to get into my apartment, to be around my things, to feel a little more like flesh-and-bone Evie after the dumpster fire morning I've had—*am* having.

When I reach apartment 821, I don't slow as I float through the door and the rush of cold.

Rafael's faint command to *wait* is muffled—and ignored—as I take a deep breath and soak it in.

Pale-pink and beige tones. Velvet and leather. Soft and feminine. My apartment is a carefully curated reflection of me—years of effort arranged into something calm, intentional, *mine*. Art prints. My favorite books dog-eared and overread. A collection of records I once spent hours alphabetizing. Nothing is out of place. I have Cristina to thank for that. She's been cleaning my apartment—and feeding me—since I hired her three years ago. And somehow, despite my week-long absence, everything looks untouched. Even the fresh daisies in the vase on my dining table. Like I never left at all, like I'm about to walk in at any moment.

The feeling is dizzying—disorienting. I take a breath. I *am* here.

My fingers ghost along the white quartz countertops as I move through my kitchen. A cookbook—one I've attempted (and mostly failed) to use—sits on a metal stand. Crystal wineglasses hang above a distressed-wood wine rack. The floor-to-ceiling window beside the dining area overlooks a park where most of my neighbors walk their dogs and hold playdates for their kids. And if I ever get to bucket list item #48, I'll have a picnic there on a date.

If. If. If.

*If*s and bucket lists aside, I find my bedroom.

My king bed—draped in a white down comforter and matching quilted pillows—is exactly as I left it. Inviting. Familiar. Not connected to hospital monitors.

I hesitate, halfway expecting to fall through it like everything else I've tried to hold on to.

But I don't.

I land.

Solid. Still. Somehow spared by ghost logic I don't understand. I sigh, my gaze drifting to my nightstand for the picture of Annie, Great-Aunt Julia, and me on our first and only trip to Chicago. We're smiling at the camera, standing on Navy Pier. The best day ever. My favorite photo.

Sighing, I close my eyes, willing the tension I'm feeling to pull a disappearing act. According to Rafael, it's been a week since the accident, but somehow it feels like a lifetime since I've been here.

"Do you know the meaning of *wait*?" Rafael asks from the doorway.

I snap my eyes open.

He's leaning against the doorframe, hands tucked into his pockets, looking every bit as broody as he did this morning.

I immediately sit up. "How did you get in?"

Rafael dangles a key, the spare I leave for Cristina.

"Should have guessed you got to Cristina too," I mutter.

His brow lifts. "Got to her?"

I don't elaborate, because I'm trying to protect my microscopic bubble of joy before he pops it with his brooding and questions.

"Forget about it." I slide off the bed and head toward my walk-in closet, the one that leads to the master bath. The one with my clothes and shoes and purses organized by color. Whites, purples, and grays.

Behind me, Rafael exhales. "I met Cristina at the hospital. She told me about her car situation—unintentionally—and I offered to drive her the other day until she got her car back. Helped her bring up her cleaning supplies. Nothing nefarious."

I keep my back to him, glad he can't see my face pinch. Because I'm momentarily feeling like a jerk for assuming the worst. It's hard *not* to.

"Evie." His tone makes my muscles tense.

"Rafael." I glance over my shoulder.

He's moved. He's closer, standing in the doorway to the closet, jaw set and eyes devoid of their usual warmth.

A warning bell goes off. "What is it?"

"I can't be here."

"Then why did you bring us here?"

"To drop you off."

"Drop me off?" My stomach performs a somersault. "What do you mean?"

He drags his hand through his hair. "I mean, I don't know about all this. My head's a mess. This past week has been . . . rough."

"Sleep more, drink less?" I offer, aiming for some lightness. *Needing* it.

"Wish it were so simple." No smirk. No amusement. Not even a flicker of it. And when Rafael looks down at his hands, I feel a new stab of panic. "But I can't help you."

"No." I shake my head, panic taking hold. "You can't back out. You made a deal."

"There was no deal."

Even though it's the truth, his words are like a roundhouse kick to my ribs. "You can't just . . ." I start but stop myself. Because he *can*. He can leave. He can say no. He owes me nothing.

"Listen, I woke up this morning, and the last thing I expected to find was her—*your*—spirit in my apartment, and while you seem so fucking real, you're not." He exhales sharply. "You're not Evie. The things back at the hospital—that's my brain messing with me." He blows out another rough, uneven breath. "I can't explain what's happening, but this isn't real. None of it."

I'm not sure if I should laugh or cry. The one person I need to help me happens to be the one person who hates me. Worse yet? For a moment there, I thought he would.

Dumb Evie.

I should know better.

I swallow, forcing my voice to steady. "Get out," I say, so quietly I think he doesn't hear me.

But his face—his *goddamn* face that's fooled so many—does this stupid thing where it softens and twists my memories to day one. To the Rafael from that first day at Media Lab. The one who tricked me into believing he cared. It's not an act I'll believe today . . . or ever again.

"Get the hell out of my apartment." My voice is sharp and cold, and I think he flinches. Part of his act. "Now," I add.

Rafael lingers, long enough I want to shout at him to go and never come back, but then he turns and leaves. The door clicks shut behind him, and the tears fall.

CHAPTER TEN
EIGHT DAYS AFTER

A cell phone buzzes, and I immediately reach for my nightstand. It's most likely Dana asking for the updated budget on the See-Side account, and I haven't even had my coffee. My hand grasps for the nightstand, for my phone. I grab at air and jolt up in panic.

It's always on the nightstand.

I blink through the grogginess. My vision clears—and my stomach drops.

I'm not in my comfortable, linen bed. In fact, I'm in the place that's the exact opposite of *comfort*: hell.

His apartment closes in on me as all of yesterday—each petrifying piece of it—clicks into place, and the urge to wail is almost overpowering.

One. Mamma. Mia.

Maybe the ghost stuff was a dream.

I glance down at myself, at my hands that look so *human*. Taking a deep (almost hopeful) breath, I reach for the *Food & Wine* magazine resting atop his coffee table. My hand moves straight through it, through the table, like slicing through ice . . . with no resistance.

The air whooshes out of me.

Ghost powers: still intact. Nightmare status: officially confirmed.

Curling my fingers into my palm, I dig my nails in, needing to feel something besides the dread spreading through me like a swarm of angry termites, devouring everything in their path. So much like the morning after Annie died.

Two Mamma Mia.

Waking up in a world without my sister was worse than not waking up at all. At least, that's what fourteen-year-old Stevie Popovici thought.

Three Mamma Mia.

But twenty-nine-year-old Evie Pope hasn't lost anything. Not yet.

A phone buzzes and rattles against the wood floor beneath the sofa. It could be mine or Violet's—one of hundreds in a graveyard of phones beneath his sofa. It wouldn't surprise me.

I don't bother checking. Phones are as useless to me as the man who refused to help me.

I glare at the poster above his TV. The ridiculous man smirks back. Who even prints posters of *themselves* and frames them like this? A vain, selfish, loyalty-optional human. That's who.

I stick my tongue out at the poster, displaying about as much maturity as the man in it. Must be something in the Vela-oxygenated air.

And it makes me want to deliver on my promise to haunt him and make his life hell.

I eye the door to his bedroom.

Why not?

Ire and determination fueling my movements, I shoot from the sofa and cut across the apartment, trying really hard to not question why I'm wearing the same heels from yesterday, ones I *wasn't* wearing when I fell asleep. Getting an explanation for that is about as likely as Rafael admitting he planned to backstab me from day one. That would require him to be decent and truthful.

Decent, truthful people don't deserve hauntings, but *this* one? Oh, he's got it coming.

A sense of wicked glee settles over me as I enter his dark bedroom. His king bed dominates the room, a shadowy monolith for nocturnal adventures I try desperately not to imagine. Rafael's nothing more than a shape sprawled atop it. He's sleeping like *he's* the one in a coma.

This might be the first time since waking up yesterday that I feel a sliver of something besides dread as I close in.

Flipping my hair over my face, I imagine I'm a ghost out of a horror movie and circle around the bed, arms raised above my head and teeth bared. I open my mouth to unleash a ghoulish moan.

But the shapes move. The shadows shift and settle. And I almost finish the process of dying.

Rafael is sprawled across his bed, sheets twisted around him—around his *bare and naked* body—leaving very little (*nothing* is little) to the imagination. I want to simultaneously look and look away as heat sweeps through me, flowing and ebbing. Rafael mumbles in his sleep and flips over. His backside says *Hey, girl.*

Ohmygod.

I squeak, half tripping over my legs as I scramble out of his bedroom.

Heart thundering against my ribs, I'm breathing like I've sprinted a 5K as impossibly vivid images of Rafael's toned chest and taut ass play through my mind like a movie reel of *abs, thighs, ass.*

I count the seconds—which feel like lifetimes—before I decide it's safe to get out of his apartment and leave the haunting for another time, like when hauntees are wearing lots and lots of layers.

Gaze averted, I slip past his bedroom, out the front door, and down the fifteen flights of stairs to his building. Outside, I suck in a deep breath of air, hold it for three seconds, and release. I repeat it several times, and each time I think of dirty diapers, spoiled eggs, and very old, saggy-skinned men.

Too-many breaths later, I finally collect myself.

So much for *doing* the haunting.

I doubt I'll ever recover.

I start to stalk down the street, avoiding tourists and locals, needing to channel my mental energy to more productive (and less disturbing) endeavors. A plan. A checklist. A way out of this situation.

A few blocks later, to-do items fall into place—the Revival Checklist:

1. *Find Gemma (as my best friend, she has to be able to see me)*
2. *Research cases similar to mine, figure out what's wrong with me*
3. *Consult with professionals*
4. *Use professional help to fix myself (defibrillators not off the table)*
5. *Make Rafael regret he ever met me*

Thirty minutes later I'm in Wicker Park, walking down Gemma's street. Her blue-brick duplex is within sight—and so is Gemma. My heart skips at the sight of my best friend, her red hair her signature feature. Gemma Quincy-Kaneko is the closest thing I have to a family.

We met as interns at a public relations firm. She was a badass former athlete with a personality to match, and I was her polar opposite. For one reason or another, she decided we were going to be best friends, and the rest is history. For the last decade, she's dragged me to bars and events. Taken me to meet her family. And introduced me to two of my exes and threatened to dismember one of them.

She showed me what family was supposed to be like. Was more motherly than my mother ever was.

When she moved to Media Lab two years ago, she became a buffer between Rafael and me. When she was transferred to his team, she became a source of intel. Not that it's helped. There isn't a formula for understanding Rafael.

Seeing Gemma sparks hope.

I run toward her, shouting her name. "Gemma!"

She doesn't turn.

I shout again, louder. Still nothing. I pick up my pace. As I close the distance, Gemma's husband, Oliver, joins her on the sidewalk, dragging a suitcase behind him. The trunk of the SUV pops open.

"*Gem!*" I'm jogging now, but neither of them turns. Not even as I wave my arms wildly and shout their names as if from the top of a mountain. Like a screaming banshee.

They don't turn.

Disappointment crashes through me as I slow to a stop, breath unsteady and pulse hammering. They're standing beside the driver's door, holding hands, oblivious to anything else—me included.

Ollie and Gemma met freshman year of college. He helped her get her grades to a passing level so she could keep her scholarship, and several late nights and study guides later, Gemma passed statistics and Ollie proposed. They were married a year later and have been inseparable since.

"Gem. Ollie," I say, looking between them. The urge to hug them is overpowering.

"Are you sure you don't want me to come?" Ollie asks.

"No. I'll be fine," Gemma says, pressing a kiss to his lips. She brushes his jet-black hair from his forehead before she retreats and slides into the car. "I'll call as soon as I get there."

"Where are you going?" I ask, needing to know.

She doesn't hear me. Not as she pulls on her seat belt and leans out the car window. Not as I get within inches of her face.

"Love you," Ollie says with a wave.

"Back at you." She blows him a kiss.

"Gem!" I'm desperate as the Jeep begins to pull away. I march alongside it, face practically glued to the window. "I'm here!" I shout, hoping like hell she'll hear me.

The car accelerates. I sprint after it—after Gem. But no matter how many marathons I've run, I can't keep up. Still, I try because I *need* her. The distance stretches between us, and I push harder, faster. No feet hitting concrete. No breath in my lungs. But somehow I'm moving, maybe floating. New afterlife physics rule: Where there's obsession, there's propulsion.

Halfway down the next block, something in me cracks. Not bone or breath—just the kind of hopelessness that hollows you out, that makes running pointless.

I stop and double over, eyes stinging and chest tight.

Gemma's leaving.

My best friend. My one shot at figuring this out.

I breathe through the tightness in my chest.

And like that, the first item on the Revival Checklist is null and void.

I don't bother looking toward Ollie as my breathing evens out. He's probably already inside their house, diving into another of his high-profile legal cases. And I'm out here in the middle of the street, feeling like reanimated roadkill.

* * *

Hours later I'm back in my apartment, surrounded by my things and humming ABBA's "Gimme! Gimme! Gimme!"

Time to regroup.

This morning was a setback, and I can do setbacks. They're temporary, even if this one seems a little more permanent. But

I've tackled tougher obstacles—like surviving the first sixteen years of my life.

All I need is a *new* new plan. One based on facts and logic.

Fact: I've been in a coma for a week, yet it was only yesterday I woke up in *Rafael*'s apartment.

Fact: *Rafael* was the last person I was with before the accident, and *he* is the only person who can see me.

Fact: While he can deny it all he wants, all roads lead to (a fully clothed and completely undesirable) *Rafael.*

I'd buy Culture Jar breakfasts for a year if he'd admit that he's tied to this situation. I'd give him my country club membership if he helped me out of it. And as much as it kills me (poor choice of words, given my present state), I need to go back to his loft and find a new way to get him on board. I'll need a far more compelling argument—a stronger negotiation tactic.

Nothing's coming to me right now, but it can't be too hard. I have years of knowledge on the man . . . who is currently sprawled across his bed like a fallen angel.

The thought comes from nowhere.

I douse it immediately.

His body is a weapon—like his dimple—and I should be prepared for him to wield it. Anytime. At all times. It's another tactic meant to—

The front door opens. I drop to all fours in fright and hide behind my sofa, like I'm the one who shouldn't be in my own apartment. Blood pressure spiking, I tune in.

"I made it." Cristina's muffled voice makes me slump in relief.

"Cristina!" I jolt to my feet and rush to her, feeling better than I've felt all morning. "I'm here," I say, waving.

Phone tucked between her shoulder and ear, Cristina closes the door and sets her bucket of cleaning supplies to one side as she changes out of her sneakers into her cleaning Crocs. Her dark hair, sprinkled with grays and whites, is secured in her usual tight bun, and she's wearing faded scrubs. I want to hug her.

"Cristina." I step in front of her. "Please, see me."

She picks up her cleaning supplies and walks past me, talking into the phone, "No, not the candy house." Cristina laughs, a warm, familiar sound that makes me ache. "Da. The pretty lady's house." The fondness in her voice means she's talking to one of her three granddaughters. It's usually the youngest who calls, the one who's seven and named for her grandmother. Their relationship makes me long for things I never had.

"No, puiu," she says, setting out her cleaning supplies. "She isn't home yet." Cristina's tone changes, softening. Her face turns sad, and now I know she's talking about me.

When she first started working for me, Cristina brought homemade treats. *The way we make them back home,* she said. I was reluctant to try the Romanian cornulețe—candied jelly wrapped in dough and powdered sugar. She watched me the way a bird watches her hatchlings feed. I didn't dare tell her I was training for a marathon. So I ate the dessert . . . and had another and another. I must have passed some unspoken test, because Cristina started showing up with treats every week. With stories about her homeland and family. With an easy disposition and smiles.

It didn't take long for me to look forward to the days our paths crossed, to consider her more than someone who makes a part of my life easier.

I never told her that.

Now the need to tell her scratches at the back of my throat.

I scramble to the other side of the counter. "I'm home. I'm here," I say, my voice desperate. Cristina doesn't respond. "*I'm right here!*" I shout, waving wildly.

She chatters as she walks.

I amble after her, across the kitchen and living room, down the hall, toward the linen closet.

"It is in God's hands." She switches to Romanian . . . and passes me without a glance.

I don't follow.

Instead, I slide to the ground and pull my knees to my chest, feeling more helpless than I've felt in the last decade. And that's saying a lot.

Stevie Popovici knew how to survive, because if Margot—my mother—taught me anything, it was this: how to figure things out with Annie. Our mother was too busy chasing attention to give it to her daughters, so prone to spending any income on herself that we became survivors.

Annie was only two years older than me, but she was my sister, my mom, my best friend. She was a wild spirit who had big dreams and an even bigger heart. With her around, nothing felt impossible or scary. Whatever our mother didn't provide, Annie found a way for us to get.

By the time I was six, Annie had taught me how to heat up canned spaghetti on the stove without burning myself. By my eighth birthday, we'd figured out which utility companies gave the longest grace periods before shutting off the lights. By the time I turned ten, we had a rotation of excuses for why I was always late getting to school, because most of the time we'd walk the entire way.

And by fourteen, I was standing alone, planning Annie's funeral.

We had no clue that she was diabetic at first. It started with dizzy spells, rapid weight loss, blurry vision—things Margot waved off, calling them "growing pains" or "attention grabs." It didn't help that she didn't trust doctors. One of her loser boyfriends had once said hospitals were for people too weak to fight, and Margot made it gospel. She said modern medicine was a scam, that pills were poison. So Annie didn't get the right treatment, but she didn't push Margot. And when it got worse, I begged, and we finally got insulin . . . because Great-Aunt Julia stepped in, offered to pay and care for Annie.

For a while, it worked. Until Margot found other uses for the money. She also liked the sympathy, the way people asked about her sick kid. She liked being seen and doted on. And when it mattered most, when Annie didn't get her insulin in time, her blood sugar dropped and she collapsed in our living room. Margot wasn't there. But the damage was.

By the time Annie made it to the hospital, it was already too late. The machines kept her going for a while, but she never woke up. Margot only showed up to sign paperwork. And at the funeral? Margot didn't cry. She sat rigidly beside me, offering no comfort.

I already hated her by then.

I cried for a week straight. Hating the four walls of the trailer home closing in on me. Hating the patch of daisies outside the door and how they reminded me of Annie. Hating the universe for taking her and leaving me behind because I wasn't half as good.

But I survived.

It took me two years to save up enough money to leave. Great-Aunt Julia's 1990 Honda Accord brought me to Chicago, where at sixteen, I worked odd jobs and put myself through school. I faked parents when I needed to. I gave out burner numbers when teachers asked for emergency contacts. I learned how to talk like I had a home to go to, a family who cared.

So I lived out of the Honda until I could pay the rent for a basement room, where I lived through the first years of college, alternating between working and studying. Seeking internships and scholarships and any *ship* that could help me pay the bills and move forward. Not once looking left or right or behind because forward was the only direction that meant survival. A way out.

And finally, when I'd scraped and clawed my way out of the darkness, I emerged as Evie Pope and kept doing what I'd always done. *Run.*

Straight into the afterlife.

You're not dead, I can almost hear Rafael's voice reminding me.

Releasing a shaky breath, I press the heels of my palms into my eye sockets. I haven't allowed myself to feel so Stevie in a long time.

A sharp pain radiates from my chest—from the place where something new grew after Annie died. Grief lodged itself between my ribs that day, an unshakable, throbbing, broken thing. An imagined appendage I never asked for. It's been aching quietly ever since. Thinking of Annie makes it sharper. Thinking that all that running led me right back to nothing makes it unbearable.

A deep, familiar voice makes my breath catch.

CHAPTER ELEVEN
EIGHT DAYS AFTER, PART II

Rafael is in my apartment.

I pump the brakes on my emotional tailspin and scuttle to the end of the hallway on all fours, ears perked toward the voices.

His voice is a low rumble.

I lean in a little more, curiosity replacing the ache in my chest, and peek around the corner.

He's leaning against the counter, wearing another form-fitting tee (because he clearly shops at Muscles N' More) and dark-wash jeans. Cristina, oblivious to the enemy in our midst, wipes down the windows, her back to him.

"Ah, we need to have faith," Cristina says, her tone comforting. As if *he* needs to be comforted. "And pray. I always say *Prayer is powerful.*"

"So does my grandmother."

"Grandmothers are smart like that," she says. Rafael nods and casts his gaze around. I duck before he can spot me, my heart thumping in my chest.

I'm not entirely sure why I'm the one hiding like I'm here to rob the place when it's Rafael who shouldn't be here. Unless he's here to admit he's somehow tied to my predicament and come to help put me back together. If there's some profuse apologizing in there, he'll definitely be on the right track.

Feeling much better, I shoot to my feet, smooth out the dress, and tousle my hair.

Game time.

I step from around the corner and almost crash into him. Rafael stops short of walking through me. His hands dart out to steady me, but they slip right through me, like mist.

We both jerk back.

I scowl, rubbing at my arms. "What the hell!"

"Evie," he says, like he's learning my name for the first time.

"Evie?" Cristina repeats from the kitchen.

"What are you doing here?" I arch a brow in suspicion. Without my stilettos, the effect is diminished, but missing a few inches has never held me back.

Rafael shifts. "I was just . . ."

"Hoping to gather some intel?" I finish for him.

He inhales deeply. "Yes, that's exactly what I'm doing. I'm here to ask Cristina about types of cleaning supplies so I can use them for my nefarious means."

"I wouldn't put it past you. The job's halfway done." I poke the bear.

He grumbles. "You're so . . ."

"Right?"

"Righteous."

"Rafael?" Cristina appears behind Rafael, her brow crinkling in concern. "Are you all right?"

"No, he's not," I answer on his behalf, hating that she can't hear me. "He hasn't been all right for a moment in his entire life." It's a bit of a lie. There were brief, brief moments of Rafael being an *all right* human (so brief they don't count).

"Yes," he responds, shifting from one leg to the other, the way he does when he's *not* all right. "Just . . . it's like she's here."

I roll my eyes. Cristina sighs, planting a hand on her hip. "I feel her too."

"You do?" Rafael and I ask at the same time.

Hope has me swooping around him and placing myself between them. I'm inches from her face, but she looks beyond me—through me—at Rafael.

"Yes, of course. I can still smell her perfume. Her books are the same way she left them. Some days I think I will hear her on the way to work. Always rushing to be on time but never leaving without saying good morning or asking about my girls." Cristina sighs. "She is truly an angel."

I stiffen at her choice of words.

"Yes," he says, and I can almost hear him want to add *and other things*, but he's smart—or scared—enough not to.

Cristina's arm darts out, cutting through the air so fast I barely get out of the way. I flatten my body as close to the wall as possible without touching it. Her hand falls onto Rafael's shoulder and squeezes.

"She will make it. I know it." Cristina smiles warmly.

"I hope so," he agrees.

"You shouldn't lie to good people, Raffy Taffy." I glare at him. Rafael tenses but doesn't look away from Cristina, who's wiping away a stray tear.

"I really should get back to work, Mr. Rafael. The vacuum that needs to be fixed is in the linen closet." She sniffs once and returns to the kitchen.

"Why are you here?" I plant my hands on my hips. "To make another woman cry?"

"To fix the vacuum." He stuffs his hands in his pockets. "And to help you."

"Sure you are," I snap, even though my breath catches. He's lying, I know it. I saw him do it to sweet Cristina.

Rafael mumbles a curse. "We can either argue or figure out what's happening with you," he says.

"Why?"

A muscle tics in his jaw. "Let's just say I'd prefer not to be haunted by Evie Pope's spirit for the rest of my existence."

"You'd throw in the towel before you're thirty-five."

"That's this year," he clarifies.

It's my turn to smirk. "Exactly."

Rafael throws a look up at the ceiling. "Dios! There will be no haunting, because I'm serious about helping you."

I almost laugh. I'd bet there's more than the promotion that's made him come back. There has to be something else fueling this, something beyond just assurance of future ghost-free dates and hauntless nights, something he's choosing to keep from me.

"What changed your mind?" I ask, watching him closely.

"Gemma."

I gape, hopeful and surprised. "You told her about me?"

"Nope, but she confirmed some things."

"Like?"

Rafael's lips twitch in a way that makes me nervous. "The location of a birthmark, among other things."

Oh.

I scan his face for the lie.

I consider pushing, but to what end? To loop back to square one?

So I let it drop.

"Okay, then, what's the catch?" I ask, playing along. Maybe it's not just about the promotion. Maybe there's more. The truth is, he's here, and he's the only one who can help. But whatever his reasons, in my experience there's always fine print. A hidden trap. A shoe waiting to drop.

"No catch," he says. "Only conditions."

* * *

"So, condition number one," Rafael says, leaning against the door of my guest bathroom. We're crammed inside, barely two feet between us and the shower at my back. "You don't disrupt when I'm interacting with other people. If I'm having a conversation and you chime in, it's going to look questionable—make me seem crazy—and I'd rather not have to explain myself."

I have to bite my tongue to keep from reminding Rafael that he *is*, in several ways, a little crazy. He buys the same socks so he doesn't have to sort them. He sits at least ten feet away from bodies of water, kiddie pools included. And he prefers pineapple on his pizza. I shudder at the thought.

"So, when we go back out there and I have to help Cristina fix the vacuum, not a peep. No back seat repairing," Rafael clarifies, his voice barely above a whisper. It's hard not to roll my eyes at the insinuation that I'd instruct him how to do it the correct way. I know *nothing* about vacuums.

"Okay," I agree. "Easy."

Rafael eyes me like he doesn't quite trust me before he digs his hands into his pockets, which tugs down his waistband, revealing a sliver of tanned waistline that says *Hello—remember me from this morning?*

A volcano of mortification erupts, making me wish we weren't packed together, separated by only a few feet of space. We haven't been this smushed together since The Elevator Incident one year ago, and the memory of those forty-five minutes is seared into my DNA forever.

It was the Mondayest Monday—a full twelve months into freezing him out—and I was ready to call it a day earlier than normal. As luck would have it, Rafael was the sole passenger on the North Elevator, and with no other choice (taking the stairs in stilettos wasn't an option), I got on, eager to get home before seven. Two floors into the ride, the elevator stalled. Two minutes later, disaster struck.

A small space, no AC, and mild claustrophobia were all it took to break me down. It started with pacing the elevator, moved to profuse sweating, and ended with me throwing up—all with him watching. It was one of the most mortifying days of my existence, and that has nothing to do with puking and everything to do with him lending me his backpack to do it in.

The memory makes my cheeks flush.

We're not in an elevator, and I'm not on the verge of puking. But we are packed together, and his nearness does *things* I can't rationalize.

"Okay—what else?" I ask, my tone impatient and annoyed.

"Condition number two—you stop insinuating I put you in a coma."

"Did you?"

Rafael groans, rubbing the back of his neck. "Would I be trying to help you if I had?"

"Maybe your Catholic guilt got to you?"

He mutters to himself, a mix of Spanish and frustration.

"About done?" I level a questioning look at him.

"Are you?" he parrots, his brows crinkling.

I answer with a shrug, but we both know I need him, which means I need to save my theories on his involvement for another day. One when I can pick them apart and analyze them.

"I won't make further accusations." I hold up three fingers, like he did yesterday, and try hard not to feel pleased with myself when he mumbles to himself again. "Anything else? My parking spot in front of Media Lab? Lifetime supply of free lunches? My firstborn?"

"Oh, have you penciled children into your five-year plan?"

I try not to react to his tone. "Nothing you should worry your twisted mind with," I say, feeling increasingly convinced that working together might not work at all. "And it's a ten-year plan, Rafael. It's—"

Two knocks rattle the door. We both startle.

"Mr. Rafael, are you okay in there?" Cristina's voice is muffled.

Rafael clears his throat, but his eyes never stray from mine. "Yes, all is good. Just . . . some indigestion. From breakfast."

"Indigestion?" Cristina repeats. "Oh no."

"Yes. Too much . . ."

"Alcohol," I provide when he delays too long.

"Gluten," he answers instead. The amount of pizza and burgers he eats would disagree.

Cristina is quiet for a moment, likely because she's probably also seen him tear into her desserts right after saying, "Come to Papa".

"Okay, Mr. Rafael. Can I get you something to help?"

"Um. No, no. I'll be right out." Rafael leans into the door and groans for dramatic effect. "As soon as it passes."

"Oh, poor dear," she adds. I roll my eyes at her concerned tone. "Please let me know if you need something."

"Yes, thank you." Rafael watches me with self-indulgent satisfaction. I glare back. We have a staring contest for the duration of time it takes Cristina's footsteps to fade.

"Poor *dear*?" I narrow my eyes in suspicion. "What have you done to Cristina?" Cristina, with her no-nonsense Romanian upbringing, should know better than to be Vela'd, but she's Play-Doh in his hands.

Rafael smirks knowingly, the dimple appearing (as if to show me *this is how I tricked her*), and he shrugs. "We bonded over mutual interests."

"Oh, yeah? Like what?"

"Wouldn't you like to know?"

I would, in fact, like to know what a sixty-something, kind, loving Romanian grandmother and a thirty-something, smooth-talking, backstabbing Mexican American bachelor have in common.

"Was it your mutual interest in women's gymnastics?" I ask, arching a brow in question and earning another dimple-baring smile. A rush of warmth surprises me. He said I wasn't in hell, but the lack of cold air and oxygen would disagree.

"You're funny, E. You should let your guard down more often." His words are a much-needed bucket of ice.

"My guards are intact, thank you very much, and don't call me that." I cross my arms, adding another barrier between us. "Any other conditions?"

Rafael, unbothered by my tone or glare, flattens a very male hand against the wall beside my head, his arm muscles cut as if chiseled from stone. The tattoo along his bicep peeks out from beneath his shirt sleeve, and I swear another minute in this bathroom is going to accomplish what the accident didn't.

I push air through my nose and force my eyes to stay on his face.

"Only one more." The signature, challenging gleam enters his eyes as he leans in, close enough my breath hitches.

"Okay. What?" I half whisper, half rasp, torn between my desire to put distance between us and my reluctance to concede a step. I make myself tall instead. "My firstborn?"

"Close." His full lips pull to one side. I have a strong feeling I'm not going to like whatever he's about to say. "Don't fall in love with me," he says, low and husky.

"Oh *Go-o-o-od*," I groan, covering my face with my hands. "You can't possibly be the only person in this entire world who can help me."

"Entire world? Maybe not. But your circle of closest confidants? Possibly." Humor accentuates his tone, as if this is some joke to him, and it mortifies me further. "Anyway, I thought you'd appreciate that last condition because you—"

I hold up a hand, refusing to look at him. "Stop, please. This is humiliating enough for me without having to waltz down memory lane." The stroll down Elevator Incident Lane was enough. But another memory of the earlier months at Media Lab tugs at me.

We were sitting through a late-night meeting, during which we had a similar conversation to the one we're having now. I outlined my very serious, very professional conditions for working together on a local grocer's account—our first shared client—one of which was that he wouldn't fall in love with me. It was meant as a joke. A line I'd seen in a movie or read in a book. Light and fun.

Only it wasn't entirely a joke.

A hopeful (mostly silly) part of me that was slowly learning to open up envisioned the possibility of our friendship evolving. Eventually. Because he was charming and easy to be around. He made me laugh and he'd figured out quite easily how to pull me out of my head, to stop me from overthinking, to get me to loosen up. He'd bring in oversized lunches because he'd always "accidentally" pack extra—usually things I liked. He'd doodle in the corners of my planners or leave ridiculous sticky notes on top of my files—like *This one's cursed. Burn it.*

So yes, there was a point—one infinitesimal, blink-and-you-miss-it moment in time—when I believed Rafael might be easy to love. How naive I was.

"I'm not trying to humiliate you," he says, the humor fading. A trick.

"You might be more convincing if I didn't know you."

Rafael's jaw works like he wants to say more, but he drops his hand from the wall. His demeanor shifts, turning serious. Almost like the distance between us has stretched by feet, and it doesn't have the relief-inducing effect I imagined.

"There's another thing. Not a condition, but . . ." He hesitates. I tense immediately. "Just a complication."

My pulse stutters. "Okay . . ."

I want to make a joke about the suspense killing me, but the sudden coolness in his gaze sends my anxiety into a sprint.

"They tried reducing your sedation last night."

My stomach hollows. "What?"

"They lowered the dosage—just a little—to see if your body would start to come back on its own. But . . . it didn't go well." He looks down at his hands. "Your vitals crashed. You were in distress. They had to sedate you again because it wasn't safe."

The words dig into me like claws.

"What . . . what does that mean?" I can't keep the panic from my voice.

His eyes connect with mine. Almost sad. "They said your body should've started waking up by now, but it hasn't." He swallows. "They'll try again in a few days, but if it doesn't work, they'll have to change course. Move you to a long-term facility because the hospital needs the bed."

"Long-term?" I breathe. "As in give-up-on-you storage."

"No! It's not like that," he says quickly. "But it's not ideal. It's farther. Less access. Gemma's pushing back, but it's only Gemma and a Julia Popovici who are legally allowed to visit you . . . based on your consent."

The words hit like a kick to the chest.

"Shit." It slips out on a breath. A very young, very naive version of Evie Pope signed a medical consent form almost a decade ago, adding only her best friend and her great-aunt.

Not that I would have added Rafael Vela to the list. Not in a million years.

"But *you* were at the hospital," I point out.

Rafael shifts from one leg to the other. "Yes."

"How?" His sudden aversion to eye contact piques my curiosity. "Rafael."

His head jerks up, his features suspiciously sheepish. "I know Dr. Wagner from before . . . and I told her we were together."

"Together?" I choke out, horrified. "Like *together* together?

He doesn't answer because his face says it all. "Technically, we are *together*. Every day. Longer than most couples who *are* together. I let her assume the rest," he says, offering a one-shoulder shrug.

The urge to tug out tufts of his unfairly thick hair is overwhelming, but I curl my fingers into my palm instead. "You are . . ."

". . . the only one who can help," he finishes, daring to offer a chaste smile. "It's also made it easier for others to come see you."

Grinding my teeth, I consider fighting this particular battle. But I know when the odds are stacked against me, and currently, their weight is pretty crushing.

I stretch onto my tiptoes and into his space. "This isn't the end of this discussion," I say.

"Wouldn't dream of it."

"Good." I hold his gaze a second longer. "So, we have what—a few days in the hospital and then you can't help me?"

"Until Gemma finds a way to modify the consent or keep you in the hospital, because that's the best place for you," he says. "Regardless, we'll figure it out."

Rafael says this like a promise, like he needs me to believe him . . . and I know I have to.

Because I can't start this by thinking we'll fail.

"Is that it, then? Are those all the conditions?" My voice comes out strong and steady, nothing like how I really feel. The desperation termites are swarming, fast and frantic.

Rafael holds my gaze like he's trying to see through me, but my guards are White House–level secure. "That's it," he finally says.

Despite the tightness in my chest, I take a deep breath, square my shoulders, and move to the last part of getting Rafael on board. I hold out my hand. "All right then, it's a deal?"

Rafael glances at my hand before pressing his palm to mine—flesh-and-bone hand ghosting against something not quite there. I can't feel him exactly, but I *feel.* An energy. A flicker of awareness that ripples through me, and it silences my thoughts.

I keep my features neutral as he says, "Deal." And like that, we become reluctant partners.

CHAPTER TWELVE
EIGHT DAYS (AND SOME CONDITIONS) AFTER

We're back in Rafael's apartment.

Because I'm not rushing to make a getaway, I notice things I didn't before. Bits of him lurk in every corner, like his mind exploded and ideas splattered all over. A half-painted canvas, paints and brushes and canisters tucked beneath it. A guitar case. Books and magazines about beers, wines, and spirits (the other, much more fun kind). And the most mysterious of all curiosities—three black crates stacked atop each other in a corner. Most likely the remains of scorned lovers and former rivals. *Conditions,* I remind myself.

I push the boxes from my mind and steal a glance at Rafael. We've hunkered down at his dining room table, and he's sitting inches away from me, munching on Cristina's desserts—his gluten sensitivity having flatlined—and staring at his laptop.

I'm gnawing through another fingernail as some distant clock ticks away the seconds until Dr. Wagner's team drop-kicks me to a long-term care facility, complete with vinyl recliners and sad linens.

What I should be doing is focusing on our task—on getting through the checklist, the one from this morning, now amended and self-dubbed Evie's Second-Chance Checklist. I've mentally crossed off Gemma's name, replacing it with Rafael's. Never thought I'd be working with Rafael again after the OhLaLove account. But here we are.

Attempting to tackle item #1 (researching similar cases), we've enlisted the help of Google to dive down the rabbit hole of *what* I am before we do anything else. Half a dozen tabs line the top of his browser, each more unhinged than the last.

"The obvious choice is . . . *ghost*." He slides his gaze to me. We're sitting beside each other, separated by inches of space and years of distrust, and I still can't believe he's the only one who can see me—and help me. "You're invisible, you walk through walls, and you're definitely haunting me. I'm going with ghost. Final answer." He gives me a smug look, like he nailed it.

"Boo," I deadpan.

"I am very scared." His lips pull to one side. I scowl, daring him to even go there.

I nod toward the screen. "What makes a ghost a *ghost*? There has to be a definition, maybe a . . ."

"Checklist?" His smile stretches. My scowl deepens. "There's criteria . . ."

"What. Does. It. Say?"

"Hold. On." He matches my staccato, but has the self-preservation to turn to the screen and read before I throttle him. With words, of course. "The Ghost Club experts say ghosts are tied to the places of their death . . . and they don't typically retain their consciousness."

"Next," I say, not hesitating. And before he can argue the point, I speed things along. "This option doesn't work for two reasons: One, I'm not dead. And two, while I'd much prefer to be unconscious while everything fixes itself, that's not the case. What else you got?"

"There are about four more tabs on ghosts—" He points to the screen.

"I'm not a ghost . . . because I'm not *dead*," I repeat, and point to the mouse. "Next . . ."

Rafael mutters to himself but clicks on another tab. I lean in, squinting. *Spirits.*

"'Spirits are the souls of humans who've passed on,'" I read aloud before Rafael even opens his mouth. "'Spirits retain consciousness and have been known to interact with others, should they choose.'" I pause, considering. While I'm *consciously* experiencing my worst nightmare, I've only been able to interact with one person—and as much as I'd like to haunt him for eternity, I definitely didn't choose Rafael.

"This has got to be it," Rafael points to the screen—specifically to a ghoulish figure looming over a bed like something out of *The Conjuring.* "Looks pretty spot-on."

I look up at Rafael's divine ceiling. "Are you sure this isn't hell?"

Rafael laughs. "It's a joke, E," he says. "You're *much* more intimidating."

I reach for something—a pen—and attempt to grab it. To stab him, obviously. But my fingers go right through it.

I swallow a growl. "Let's move on, unless you have an actual desire to join me on this side of life."

He has the good sense to sober, but the ghost of a smile lingers. "Okay, so it's a no to spirit—and definitely no to ghoul," he says, clicking through the search results a little too slowly for my taste. I resist the urge to lean into his space and nudge him out of the way, even though I'm itching to take control. Instead, I cross my arms and lean away. And wait.

He mutters to himself as he scans the pages.

"Yes! This!" His enthusiasm startles me. I immediately lean in.

"A crisis apparition?" I'd have to get closer to read the small font.

Rafael nods, pointing to the screen like he's uncovered a conspiracy theory. "'A crisis apparition is when a person who is very sick or dying—or very obviously in a crisis of similar proportions—telepathically communicates images of themselves to others who are living. Usually those with whom they have a close relationship.'" Rafael reads the exact definition from the *Encyclopedia of the Paranormal.*

Another dead end.

"It's certainly not that," I say, hand halfway to the mouse before I remember I can't toggle the mouse or move several times faster than Rafael, who's downed two cups of coffee since we've been here. I'd be running the wheels off my Peloton with that much caffeine in my system. Not Rafael. "Next."

Rafael doesn't click as he drags caffeine- and mischief-glazed eyes from the monitor to me. "I think it's the most reasonable," he says, his tone alight with humor.

"Says the expert on all things reasonable?" I raise an eyebrow.

"Why are you certain you're *not* an apparition?"

"For one, apparitions appear to . . ." I scan the page, narrowing on the exact reason I cannot be a crisis apparition. "*Loved* ones," I enunciate, hoping I won't have to spell it out.

His lips pull to one side, his dimple popping in to say hello. "Just because you don't want to admit it . . ."

I narrow my eyes. "Don't you dare finish that thought."

"No?" He leans back, stretching his arms over his head. "Because I was going to say . . ."

"Rafael." I glare, warning him to stop.

But him? He has the nerve to smile. "Evie."

"I can't do this," I groan, more to myself than him. Blood pressure simmering, I jump from the chair and turn my back to him because I *can't.* Because this is a joke to him while I'm here thinking this isn't like all the other times, thinking we can work like (incredibly reluctant) partners, (very tenuously) committed to one goal. But my plasma-for-a-brain clearly forgot that Rafael doesn't do serious or commitment or any form of those two concepts. I shouldn't be feeling hurt about it, but hey—more surprising things have happened these past twenty-four hours.

Needing to regroup, I circle to the other side of the table, my throat burning with an unexpected rush of emotions. *What am I? And why can't I keep it together?*

This is a job—a project. Nothing requiring feelings, I remind myself.

I face Rafael, feeling a little steadier. "I know this isn't ideal—helping me—but can you at least pretend to take this seriously? Pretend to care?"

The chair scrapes as Rafael stands and props his ridiculously manly hands on the table, leaning on his forearms. His features shift from amused to the same intense look from the Aviary, and my stomach churns at the possibility that he's going to end this deal right now. I steel myself.

"Look, I'm sorry, but I don't need to pretend to care," he says, serious and flat.

His words carve into my chest like a serrated scalpel.

"Oh. Okay," I breathe, swallowing past the sudden sting in my throat. *WTF, Evie?*

"No—that's not what I meant!" Rafael shakes his head, but it's too late to take it back—to unring the proverbial bell.

Throat burning (with the onset of strep or something), I wheel around and stare out the massive window. It's so bright out my eyes are starting to water.

Rafael's reflection appears in the window, his body angled toward me. I refuse to look his way.

"Listen, E. That didn't come out the right way," he says, his tone almost apologetic.

I pivot further away from him so he can't see my profile or my moment of weakness. "You don't need to explain yourself. I heard the message loud and clear," I say, hyperfocused on a woman walking several dogs on the sidewalk across the street. They drag her, tugging on their leashes, and she stumbles to keep up.

"I need you to look at me," Rafael says.

I stiffen, because I will do no such thing.

"Evie." His voice softens. "Please."

Sucking on the insides of my cheek, I slowly turn and meet his eyes, fully expecting humor, a challenge, or something equally destructive. But the openness in his gaze unnerves me more than any of those things. "Rafael."

"I was saying that I don't need to *pretend* to care, because I *do* care," he says. I want to roll my eyes. "And before you roll your eyes or say something to dismiss what I've said, I want you to hear it again."

That look—thc one that may be intended to kill me—is back, and it leaves me a little breathless.

"You listening?"

I nod, wishing I could disappear. For real this time. Fade into the ether, float into the cosmos, get yanked back into my body—literally anything but this.

"I *care* about what happens to you." His words rattle through me, caressing all the places I've sealed up to protect myself against hurt, ones he keeps finding. I want to rewind the last few minutes. Go back to his dumb jokes and infuriating smirks because that was familiar and easy, and this is not.

"Okay," I breathe.

His eyes trace my face as if to ensure that I get it (I don't). I mean, I do, but Rafael does this—he disarms people and makes them question their entire existence (or at least the last five years of it), and I am not—*not*—one of those people.

But I am someone who can play the same game . . . and lead him to believe otherwise.

"Got it," I say, my voice perfectly even. "Now, can we move on?"

Rafael watches me for another second, like he's got me under a microscope and can detect my lie. My pulse thrums in protest. I look away first, not waiting for an answer, and return to the table. I feel his gaze trail after me. I hold strong.

Resisting the Vela effect is like attempting to resist Earth's gravitational pull or a vampire's compulsion. It requires special preparation, and I have years of it.

"You sure you're fine?" Rafael asks, settling back in his seat.

"Not if you keep asking me," I mutter. "Now, where were we? Screaming banshees?"

Rafael's mouth quirks, another cookie in hand, and gestures toward the laptop. "Forget all that. Spirit or ghost—they all have something in common."

"Which is?"

"They're all tied to a place or a person, and—" He pops the cookie in his mouth and swallows, because he's a grown child with a sugar addiction. "Damn, those are good."

"Which is . . ." I try again, less patient.

"I think that might be tied to how we get you back. A person or a place." He shrugs. "Dr. Wagner said something that's kind of the same."

"The doctor from the hospital? Who up and forgot her HIPAA oath when you smiled at her?" I arch an eyebrow.

He frowns as if I've just told him I dip my fries in Frosties or something equally nonsensical. "Yes, that one. I've known her for a while. She treated my grandmother a few years back," he says.

Oh. "I'm sorry."

"Don't be. She's going to outlive us all." Rafael smiles to himself. "Anyway, Dr. Wagner said that in some coma cases, like yours, the voices of loved ones can sometimes help with recovery. Something about how hearing stories stored in long-term memory can help wake up the brain and speed up recovery."

I let the information sink in. Stories. Loved ones. Recovery.

My mind immediately runs through the list of people I can send to the hospital. For starters, Gemma. She has stories. Like the first (and last) time I got drunk. It was during our college internship. Tripoli and Sons' holiday karaoke party. I bayed my way through "Dancing Queen." Gemma chuckled and at times snorted—*snortled*—her way through it. There were videos. One made it to YouTube, all because of gin and Gemma's insistence.

Or my first-ever road trip, when we (very carefully) drove cross-country to Yosemite. I'd gotten food poisoning from a sketchy restaurant with an all-you-can-eat breakfast, and I couldn't make it to the bathroom on time. We pulled over in the woods, where I promptly contracted poison oak. Down *there*. The subsequent ER visit involved a Dr. McSteamy and lots of calamine lotion. Retelling that story might actually induce cardiac arrest.

There's a repertoire of Rafael stories she could choose from. Ones involving modified presentations and canceled appointments. Or the time I bought an exact, much-smaller replica of one of his suits and Gemma made the switch on dry cleaning day. I almost snorted my coffee when he walked into the office with a suit two sizes too small. Rafael skipped Friday doughnuts for the first time that week.

"So Gemma needs to go to the hospital is what you're saying," I say, more energized about this bit of information than anything else. "Call her."

Something flashes across his face, but I don't have time to dissect it.

"She's been there. Almost every day," he says. "It wasn't only her who came. Cristina and Dana came. Even Charlene."

The words sink in like stones, dragging something heavy down with them. It gets harder to keep the disappointment, the momentary sense of defeat, from my face. From my voice.

"So Dr. Wagner's method didn't work?" I clarify, trying my best to keep my voice flat.

Rafael clenches his jaw but nods.

"Then why tell me if it's pointless?"

"In case there's someone else." He leans in, just slightly. "Maybe someone we don't know about? A family member? A friend? A . . . boyfriend?"

My throat closes up.

I need to look away from him, because I don't want him to see it. The pressure expands, painfully pressing against my lungs. I have no other friends or loved ones. Acquaintances and work colleagues, yes, but no one else who would have stories to share. I hadn't had time for anyone else. And I most certainly had no time for boyfriends. Not that I didn't try.

There was Chip, who was a literature professor at the University of Chicago. We'd met at an alumni event, one I'd attended for networking. Chip was suave and sharp and could type a grammatically correct, well-punctuated sentence, even when texting. He and I lasted all of a semester, until I discovered he was the weekend extrovert to my introvert. He preferred cocktail lounges and whiskey, and I was more of a *stay in, drink tea, and work* kind of girl.

Then there was Theo, the sexy-AF French chef I'd met through Gemma and who, one night, over his signature coq au vin, declared he was moving back to Paris. He didn't ask me to go with him. But he did ask me to stay for dessert.

Most recently, I dated Trevor Rhodes, a professional basketball player, and while he'd been nothing but a gentleman on our dates, we both loved our jobs more than we'd ever liked each other. There simply wasn't space or time for a man. I had other priorities. Succeeding at work. Thwarting Rafael. Getting ahead.

"If it didn't work with Gemma, it won't work with anyone else," I tell Rafael, ensuring my tone communicates I don't want to talk about it further. "Did Dr. Wagner say anything else? Maybe something about other cases?" Yes. Other cases. "I can't be the only person who's ever been in a coma."

Rafael leans forward, his tanned hands splayed against the wood table. "Other cases . . ." he says, more to himself than me. His brows shoot up. "Shit! I can't believe I didn't think of it before."

"What?" I hedge, careful not to get too excited.

"I had an aunt in a coma."

"Oh." It's not what I expected, and I'm not sure what to say. "I'm . . . sorry to hear that. Did she . . . ?"

Rafael frowns. "She didn't die, E. She had a long life. Lives down in Florida. She has—"

"Rafael." I barely manage to keep my impatience in check. "The point?"

"The point is that she made it out of the coma, and I happen to know the person who made it happen." I arch an eyebrow, needing him to speed things along. He smiles. "My abuela."

CHAPTER THIRTEEN
NINE DAYS AFTER

Rafael's grandmother's house is a quaint redbrick bungalow in Melrose Park, surrounded by a tidy yard. A kid's bike leans against the side of the house, and boisterous voices echo from somewhere in the backyard. I stall in the driveaway, standing beside Rafael's car, which seems like a much more desirable option than his grandmother's house. It's saying a lot, given I'm still breathing through waves of nausea from the thirty-five-minute drive here.

"There are *people* here?" I ask in disbelief, my eyes boring into the back of Rafael's head.

Rafael halts at the door, crooking an eyebrow in question. "As opposed to goblins?"

"Very funny."

His gaze turns challenging. "Scared?"

Yes, a little bit. I can't face his family when I can barely handle *one* Vela. But it's not the number of Velas that's got me wishing I'd let him come on his own. It's the fact that I don't do *this*. I don't do families and whatever's happening to make them sound so *happy*.

"Petrified," I respond with sarcasm.

"You can't be—"

"Tío Raffi!" A voice shrieks from the other side of the screen door, which is whipped open. Tiny arms wrap around Rafael's waist, followed by tiny giggles. When he turns away, I catch sight of two pigtails and a hot-pink dress with purple unicorns. The little girl's body is protectively enveloped by his, and this is one of those moments where most women would be sampling their first name with *Vela.* Lucky for me, I'm not most women.

"Come on!" She tugs him through the screen door, and Rafael throws me one last gaze that says *She's terrifying, isn't she?* before he disappears inside after the mini-Vela. The screen door squeals shut, and he doesn't see me flipping him off.

This is *fine.*

Rafael can talk to his grandmother for me. It's not like I can do anything anyway. I'd probably be watching her ruffle Rafael's hair and stuff his cheeks full of churros. And while that sounds like a good time, I have no business going in there with his family, people who love and care for him when I barely trust him. It was stupid to even think—

"Coming?" Rafael's question startles me.

I half yelp as I whip toward him.

He's leaning against the screen door, smirking wide enough his dimple flashes, and I wonder what it'll take to finish the job already because *not* existing is starting to sound really, really good. "Or do you need more time to practice that rendition of 'Dancing Queen'?"

Embarrassment flushes my face.

I hadn't even realized I was singing. It's like I'm advancing through levels of mortification when it comes to all things Evie vs. Rafael, and I've unlocked a new level.

"I hate you, I hate you, I hate you," I mutter as I march up the stairs to where Rafael waits.

"Not sure you're getting the words to the song right, E," he says.

I swat at his head with a low growl. Rafael ducks, grinning his stupid grin, as I push past him into the house—

And stumble to a halt.

It's worse than I imagined.

Organized chaos surrounds me. Patterns and colors clash on almost every surface. Beautiful pottery fills the shelves. Woven rugs, decorated in intricate patterns, cover the ancient wood floors. Pictures line most of the walls, smiling faces staring back. Weddings. Birthdays. Visits to other countries. Pieces of moments lived everywhere.

I feel Rafael behind me. "Something out of an Evie Pope nightmare, right?" He chuckles, but beneath the light tone, I detect something else. He's expecting me to criticize the clash of colors and the clutter.

I won't give him the satisfaction. Also, I don't like to lie.

This is a *home*, and there isn't anything nightmarish about it.

"Not—"

"Raffi!" a woman's voice calls right as a smiling face pops into the hallway. The woman, somewhere in her mid-fifties, stares right at me. *Through me,* I remind myself. "You're here," she says.

Her chocolate-colored hair bobs as she walks straight for Rafael with outstretched arms. He leans into her, wraps her in his arms.

"My baby," she mutters, squeezing him around the waist. "You're late. Are all the clocks I've gotten you broken? Or have you been avoiding us?"

Mamma Mia—it's Rafael's *mother.* I've only ever seen a photo—a brief glimpse—because even when we were friends, talking about moms was never my comfort zone. I stare, trying to discern the similarities.

She's lithe and elegant. Seems sweet and decent.

I don't see it.

"I wouldn't dare avoid you," Rafael mumbles into her hair. "Are you trying to suffocate me?"

She pulls away, smiling widely—and oh, now I see it. A single dimple creases her cheek. "I wouldn't be so obvious if I was," she says with a wink. I can't help smiling as she hooks her arm through his and starts to drag him away.

Rafael looks over his shoulder and jerks his head for me to follow.

Of course I don't.

I retreat a step.

This was a big mistake. I shouldn't have come inside. Should have known better than to think Rafael intended anything but to unsettle me. What I should have done is stick to the checklist and advocate *professional* help.

What can his grandmother possibly do?

Kill me with kindness?

Feet stomp on the staircase to my right, startling me. The girl with the pigtails and unicorn dress storms down the stairs, construction paper and crayons in hand, and she zooms past me, humming a song that's vaguely familiar. Something about standing at the edge of the ocean. *Frozen*? *Tangled*? *Moana*!

Rafael hummed it a week straight, taunting me as he "brainstormed" across from me. I parried with ABBA, humming "The Winner Takes It All" until the songs induced nausea . . . and we were called into Dana's office to discuss appropriate work etiquette. Another level unlocked in Evie vs. Rafael.

Cringing at the memory, I turn to leave, determined to start walking home. I'm almost out the door . . . but a photo along the wall catches my eye.

Although I shouldn't, I give in to the temptation and inch toward it, curious for another little peek into Rafael's life.

When life gives you lemons, you make lemonade. When life throws you behind enemy lines, you gather intel, and if that means naked-baby photos, lucky you. Although *lucky* wasn't how I was feeling when I saw his naked tush. *Liar.*

Fanning my face, I lean and squint at the photo, needing to see a baby in diapers to get rid of the image of a man in bed-sheets. I focus on the photo of a kid. Rafael's toothless smile is discernible in a beach photo. In another, he's surrounded by three girls, and they're standing in front of a church. Here he's waving from a cherry-red Chevy Camaro . . . and here he's standing beside a handsome man dressed in a striped suit and sporting a thick mustache. It's like I'm looking at an older version of Rafael, and he doesn't wither up into a raisin like I imagined. Wishful thinking on my part.

The last photo on the wall features Rafael in a graduation cap and gown—Loyola University's colors. A group of people surround Rafael, each person's smile wider than the one before. Except that of the man I imagine is Rafael's father. Still, if pride were to be captured in a photo, it's in this one. So much happiness. So much love. So unlike my graduation.

I celebrated alone, sitting in the booth at Pauline's Diner, enjoying a slice of cheesecake (on the house). After which I went home and cried. Not because the day had been pathetically sad but because Annie wasn't there with me. I'd crossed bucket list item #3 (*Get a degree*) off the list, like I'd done with #1 (*Move to Chicago*). I was checking things off alone, even if we'd started the list together, and somewhere along the line, I'd stopped doing the things at all.

"Proof I graduated," Rafael says, startling me.

I freeze, hoping he can't see the welling of tears from my profile.

"From the school of assholedinaires?" I pretend to study the photo.

He huffs a laugh. "Close. Prelaw. To my father's dismay, however, I didn't follow through with the law school part." I don't miss the way he slightly tenses. I know from the way he barely speaks about his dad that there's more there. It was how I realized there was more to him than what he offered the world. There were breadcrumbs, and I hoarded them for a time. "That's Gloria." He points to a more-recent photo of his oldest sister. "And her three children. She's the closest to my mother, Louise, who just tried to smother me, so I'm sure you'd approve." He grins as he drags his finger across the photos. "This is Graciela—Gracie. She's finally pregnant, but she's had a hard time getting here." I should walk away—tell him to stop—but his guard is down (and I'll take the lemons and lemonade). His finger hovers over a young woman blowing a raspberry at the camera. She's older in this photo than in the one on his iPhone screen saver. "And here is the real baby of the family. Gianna. She's finishing her first year of law school at the University of Michigan." The pride in his voice makes my chest ache. "She's the one who's going to become an immigration lawyer and make up for all the ways I disappointed my dad."

While pride still lingers in his voice, his almost-smile hints at something else. A missing piece he won't talk about. From years of intel, I know Rafael Senior passed away shortly after things fell apart between Rafael and me. It was a short, aggressive fight with pancreatic cancer. Rafael was out of the office for twelve days after it happened. I remember The Dimple didn't make an appearance for another three months. Mostly, though, I remember missing Rafael's stupid jokes and relentless humming (I'll die before I tell him).

I find I'm curious to know more . . . and willing to spend a few more moments hearing what he'll share. For research, of course.

"We don't have to talk to my abuela if you don't want to," he says, digging his hands into his back pockets. The change in topics has me trying to remember why we're here to begin with. "I can do that on my own. I should have thought—"

"¿Con quién estás hablando?" We both jump as another Vela woman steps into the hallway. No taller than five feet, she commands attention. A gray braid over one shoulder, skin that's age loved and tan, and a kind smile kind beneath brown eyes.

"Abuela," Rafael starts, turning to speak to her. He switches from English to Spanish. She listens and nods before tucking her hands into her colorful apron and walking away.

The floor creaks.

I stare after her.

"She's waiting for me in her prayer room, but you don't have to do this if you don't want to," Rafael says. His sincere tone startles me. I hold his gaze, trying to see the trick.

I know Rafael isn't so great at following through on plans, so I can see why he'd give me the option to back out . . . or maybe he *doesn't* want me to go with him because he's got some reverse psychology at play. Like the one time he went on and on about Vinay Patel being an asshole who didn't turn in projects on time and bullied others, only for me to discover Rafael wanted Vinay on his team and thought I wouldn't take the time to actually do my research. As if I were some amateur. (Vinay works for me.)

I'm not falling for it.

We're sticking to the plan.

"Lead the way," I say, gesturing for him to go first—because never turn your back on a Vela.

Rafael stalls briefly before he follows after his grandmother to a room at the back of the house. His grandmother sits in the tiny room, which is just large enough for two wooden chairs and a shrine crowded with religious artifacts. Figurines. Crosses. More photos.

I halt in the doorway, the room already feeling too snug. Rafael looks at me as if to say *I gave you an option*. And I answer with a look that says *I got this, thank you very much.*

Rafael's grandmother gestures to the seat beside hers. "Come, sit with me."

Rafael obeys, the wood chair groaning beneath his weight. Even if his size seems to take up the entirety of the room, seems to dwarf her, she takes his hand in hers like you would a child's.

"I missed you, mi amor." She squeezes his hand. "Now tell me—how is your friend?"

Friend?

"She's . . ." His brow furrows when he sees me rolling my eyes. I expect him to say lost or crazy or scared (but then I'd have to hurt him). "The same."

"Between one place and another," she says. Her thumb rubs his hand in a comforting way.

Rafael nods. "Like Tía Sofia. It's why I'm here. I should have thought to ask before. How did she wake up? What helped her?"

His grandmother's gaze turns distant. "Those first days of Sofia's coma, I cried beside her bed night and day, not caring about anything else but bringing her back to me. She was so little, and there is nothing like the pain of losing a child." She shakes her head. "I hope you never have to experience that, mi amor, because you will give me great-grandchildren." Her tone is stern, but her smile belies her seriousness.

"Of course, Abuela," Rafael agrees. Exactly what the world needs. Mini-Rafaels.

Nodding, she continues, "It was the most difficult ten days of my life, and while the doctors did their jobs and their machines kept her alive, I believe it was something else—something much greater at work—that helped her."

My ears perk in anticipation.

"What was it?" he asks.

"Dios," she says. *God.* "Prayer, Rafael. Like I taught you since you were little. That is who I turned to then, and every time since. But you see, I was so sad and lost, I had forgotten for a while." She pats his hand. "Prayer is the easiest thing to do but the one we dismiss the most often. It is universal."

That's a lie.

I glance up to the ceiling, where Rafael so often seems to go for advice.

God, huh?

Anyone up there now?

Too bad I know the answer to that. Nope. Not for Annie and most certainly not for me. My heart squeezes in disappointment.

I feel Rafael's gaze on me, and I keep my features reaction-free.

"And it worked?" Rafael asks.

"The doctors believe it was their medicine, but in my heart, I know it was prayer," she says, her eyes on Rafael. "And if you wish, Padre Victor can meet with you—pray with you. He has better connections with the Big Guy." His grandmother smiles, pointing up at the ceiling, a hint of Rafael's ruefulness in the curve of her lips. "But prayer has to come from here." She moves her hand and taps over the place where Rafael's heart *should* be. "So don't lose faith."

"I won't," he answers.

Abuela smiles. "Now, I have a celebration to get to," she says. "We both do."

She stands with surprising agility, touches his cheek, and shuffles to the door. I move to the side, squeezing into the room before she marches through me.

She stops in the doorway and says, "Ella tiene suerte de tener a alguien como tú en su vida."

I can only pick up some of the words, *luck* and *life*, and I have neither. In fact, I'm feeling more frustrated than when we came here.

Rafael's eyes shift to me as his grandmother leaves.

"Celebration?" I ask, not yet prepared to talk about what she said.

He toes the carpet. "Elena's tenth birthday."

"Something you forgot to mention?"

"We can go. If you don't want to stay," he says, his gaze sincere in a way that takes wind from my proverbial sails. "We can call Padre Victor or—"

"No. Stay." I cut him off. I have some things to work out, and he may as well have a distraction instead of being mine.

Rafael disagrees with a shake of his head. "Evie—"

"I need a moment, so if you'd be a good *partner* and go be with your family, it would mean a lot," I say, leaving no room for argument. His mouth opens, but I cut him off. "*Please.*"

Rafael's lips close around words—a rebuttal, most likely. But he's wise enough to swallow whatever he was about to say and—too slowly—vacates the room.

Finally, I'm alone. Just me, my thoughts, and his grandmother's words. I can actually think now that he's gone and not looking at me in that way that makes me question if he's a descendant of Count Dracula.

Refocusing, I think about prayer, something I once believed in. Mostly because of Annie and Great-Aunt Julia, who took us to church. Annie loved the choir's singing, and I loved Annie and Julia, so I went. When Annie was gone, when there was no one who could bring her back—not even Great-Aunt Julia's God—I stopped praying.

Maybe it's time to start? Because what other option do I have? Not many. There isn't a road map for fixing me. For getting my second chance. For checking things off my bucket list. For doing all the things I've put off.

So, when there isn't a clear answer, you try *all* the possible answers.

A grandmother's prayers or sacrificial offerings—I need to do whatever it takes.

I haven't quit a single thing in my life.

I won't start now.

CHAPTER FOURTEEN
NINE DAYS AFTER, PART II

There are things you learn when you spend years beside someone, then across from them, but always within several feet of each other.

You learn about their habits and their quirks. Their likes and dislikes. In many ways, you sometimes know more about your coworkers than you know about your loved ones. Add intention—and subterfuge—and you know more than you'd probably like to know about a person. Take, for instance, that I know Rafael has nine levels of anger and gets a pain in his knee when it rains. Would I ever confess to having this knowledge? No. Not even on my deathbed.

Which is why meeting his family and learning more about this other side of him is alluring. It's the reason I seek out Rafael instead of heading far, far away from here. That, or deeply embedded vampiric compulsion leads me to the backyard, where at least ten people crowd around an outdoor table. Spanglish and laughter mingle with music from a radio. Rafael's grandmother commands the grill with metal tongs in hand while his mother entertains two little girls—Elena and her sister Emma of the Girl Scout cookies—and their dolls. He stands between a dark-skinned man and his sister Gracie, who absently rubs her belly. The man says something, and Rafael throws back his head and laughs, deep, low, and full of joy.

The sound makes me stall, makes me swallow past a rush of warmth in my chest.

I'm sick, I remind myself. Almost dead. It's why I'm feeling this way.

Still, I take preemptive steps to safely distance myself from Rafael and his family, circling to the back of the yard, where a lone swing sways beneath an elm tree. I press close to the tree and watch.

Rafael pulls away from his sister. His gaze connects with mine, and the warmth rushes up and down and everywhere at once. I look away, suddenly fascinated by the tire swing, and will my fever to subside. Dirty diapers. Really spoiled eggs. Old, saggy . . .

A squeal has me turning back to the Velas.

Rafael has an arm around his mother, and she leans into him, dwarfed in his embrace—like one of those staged photos that come with photo frames, only this is real. I've imagined this, the coven of Velas he returns to each night, many times. But I never came close to guessing that Rafael Vela came from . . . *this*.

Love. Laughter. Togetherness.

Everything I've been deprived of. Everything I've been starving for.

And now I'm a ravenous person staring at a feast I can't have.

Or maybe . . . *won't* have?

Because if we don't figure out a way to get me back into my body soon, I don't need a doctor to tell me my chances of going back are more brittle than my chewed-through nails. The thought stabs at the hollow spot grief has carved out in me—sharper than anything I've felt in a while.

I breathe past the pressure burning my throat, searching for the words of an ABBA song.

"Swing me!" a voice trills, drawing my attention away from the lyrics of "Super Trouper." Rafael is walking toward the swing, Elena's tiny hand tucked in his. He lifts her onto the swing, not even wasting a breath with the effort. She kicks her legs as he gives her a push, groaning dramatically.

"What did you do? Eat a hippo?" he asks.

She giggles, a soft tinkling noise. "Just the hot dog!"

"Those Chicago dogs, huh?" he huffs, smiling at me over the top of her head. I hold his gaze for exactly the length of one swing because the fondness in his gaze (the one directed at Elena) makes my chest squeeze, but this time it's not the usual ache—it's something else. Something that wasn't there before the coma, something that makes me wonder what it would be like to know this side of Rafael, whose smile reaches into dimple territory and who laughs with his entire being. Who hugs like it's the last goodbye or a long-awaited hello. Who tries food when it's shoved into his face without thinking it's been laced with Dulcolax. Who makes your chest feel too full and too fluttery with a gaze.

Easy.

The answer surprises me. I tear my eyes away, fighting the blush blossoming in my chest. I massage the place between my breasts to ease the fullness. Someone must be sitting on my body in the hospital room. It would explain these new symptoms.

"I'm going to have to go home soon, tornadita," he says. The nickname makes me wonder if they have more in common than DNA.

"Aww," she pouts, swinging her bare feet. "Why?"

He gives her another push. "I have some business to take care of."

"Mama says you're not working anymore."

"Your mama talks too much," Rafael says, deepening his voice to mock sternness, which only earns another giggle. "Now, go wash up for dinner!"

She hops off with a squeal and darts across the yard, her younger sister chasing after her. Rafael stuffs his hands into his back pockets and hangs behind. "I'll be quick."

"You and food? Quick?" I roll my eyes. "Sure."

"One serving only." He pats his belly—which is mostly muscle—and winks. Another wave of warmth flushes through me because I'm nothing but plasma that's clearly lost its ability to process normal emotions.

Lucky for me, he's already walking toward his family.

I can't help but watch the Velas as they move in coordinated synchrony, passing around plates loaded with food. Toasting with wine and tequila.

I lean in to listen, but there's too much chatter and lots of it in Spanish. It's what I get for never getting to bucket list item #8 in all these years: *Learn Spanish*. Would have helped. Especially behind enemy lines.

Rafael looks this way, flashing a smile.

My brain glitches, and I skip a breath (or several). I need to make myself scarce. I shouldn't be here, for lots of reasons. Mostly, they don't need my Evie energy around them, not on his niece's birthday, not around his sister who's hoping for a baby, and certainly not around his grandmother with the prayers tucked into her heart.

* * *

I decide to wait for Rafael in the front yard, watching fireflies dance in the dark. Crickets chirp. A breeze makes the leaves sing. And oh, what I wouldn't do to feel it.

Even pray.

I peer up at the clear sky. *If you're up there, send help.*

It's not God who shows up.

I feel Rafael before I hear him.

"Hey," he says from the doorway. The wood creaks beneath his weight as he joins me on the stairs. "Everything okay? You disappeared."

"Part of my ghostly prowess," I say, my gaze wandering in his direction. Somehow Rafael looks better now than he did this morning—and it does the opposite of convincing me he isn't a vampire. The charm. The Vela-ing. The ability to do things to my blood. The theory has merit.

Rafael grins, leaning his elbows on his arms. "We can be a little much," he says, watching the fireflies. The breeze catches his hair, musses it and moves on. "Sorry."

I'm glad it's too dark for him to see my shock. Must be the way he says sorry, or the fact that he's said it at all, that stuns me. Are there countless things—stealing my yogurts, in addition to my accounts—that he could apologize for? Yes, certainly. But for this? For taking me to see his grandmother, bringing me into his home and around his family, to help me?

"Don't apologize. I was . . . unprepared," I say, unable to look away even though I want to disappear. It's hard to be honest with your enemy. It's much harder to apologize. "I'm the one who's sorry."

Rafael scans my face.

I've never apologized, not once in all these years.

"It's okay. I know it's all a lot to process," he says, without a trace of sarcasm. Like he's also testing out the *reluctant partners* thing to see how it works.

Feeling strange without our weapons at each other's throats, I shake my head. "You have no idea, Raffy Taffy . . . or is it *Raffi* now?"

A grin splits one side of his face, and The Dimple makes a brief cameo. "Only if you want me to inform the Oak Ridge Country Club there isn't a Mr. Pope."

I gawk at him, mouth open. "You know about that?"

"You basically stole my spot."

I bite the insides of my cheeks to keep from giving myself away. I may have pulled some strings at the ORCC and had Rafael Vela's name swapped to Thomas and Evie Pope. I don't care much for golfing, but the number of CEOs and business owners at the club were enough to make the membership—and its steep cost—worth it. Taking Rafael's spot was the incentive I needed.

"Your name disappeared from the wait list," I say innocently.

"Like my truck disappeared from my parking spot?"

"I plead the Fifth."

"Can't say I haven't entertained repainting your apartment while you're away."

I press a hand against my heart. "You wouldn't dare."

His gaze turns positively wicked. "Rafael wouldn't dare. Raffi is a different beast."

"I'm surprised you're still single."

"Who says I am?"

I ignore the challenge in his eyes and the ridiculous tightening in my chest, and I hold up one finger. "For one, your atrocious driving skills." Another finger pops up. "Your irrational obsession with carbs." Then another. "The Violets of the world."

"Only *one* Violet." Rafael pointedly waggles one finger. "And you forgot *attempted murder*."

A snortle croaks out of me before I can stop it. We both freeze. Rafael stares at me as if I've sprouted horns.

I clear my throat, refusing to acknowledge the last few seconds. "I didn't forget. Just trying to abide by your conditions, that's all." I shrug. "The third one is proving *especially* difficult," I drawl, giving Rafael a chance to forget he made me laugh and a chance to remember The Conditions™.

He leans back, resting his elbows on the stairs, mouth curling into a sly grin. "I am lovable, aren't I?"

"In the way serial killers are lovable . . ."

Rafael barks a low, rumbling laugh that has me smiling too. I catch myself and immediately press my lips together.

I shift my gaze to my hands and remind myself we've gotten off track. *Way* off track. "If your grandmother is correct about priests and prayers, I have no clue where to start," I admit.

"Luckily for you, I have a few connections," Rafael says. "A priest, a rabbi, maybe a couple monks."

"All of them?" I try not to break out in a sweat.

"Nothing but the best for Evie Pope."

I roll my eyes, despite the lack of sarcasm in his voice. "You're making it hard not to think you didn't have something to do with my untimely demise."

"One: You haven't demised. And two—"

"Conditions! I didn't forget."

"Have to make sure. Head injury and all." Rafael looks sidelong at me, face too serious to be actually serious, and I bite my cheek against another smile.

"I'm still obsessed with rules, thank you very much."

"Oh, good. Otherwise, we'd be in real trouble."

It's hard to know what to make of this new *thing* between us. So I say nothing.

We're quiet, long enough the crickets and breeze fill the silence. I know we should be going, but there's something about this moment that makes me feel like the *old* us, that makes me want to draw it out a little longer. Learn more about him. Make the most of his guards being down.

"Did you spend a lot of time here as a kid?" I dare.

He's close enough I could lean in and our shoulders would brush.

I lean the other way.

"Most evenings. We lived two streets away. Me and the girls would walk here after school. Abuela would cook for us while my mom took care of other stuff. Carting us to sports and activities, grocery shopping, chores, whatever was needed."

"And your dad?" I shouldn't go there, but I can't help myself.

Rafael clasps his hands together. "He worked a lot, built up his business from a young age and made it his life because a lot of people depended on him. It was important to be counted on—relied on—and that meant having direction and stability to him." I could relate to that part. I don't say anything. "From a young age, I knew he was counting on me to shoulder that burden. We had to, as the men of the family. I was going to go to law school and take over the family business, and he was going to slow down and take more trips with my mom. But when it came to it, I couldn't do it." He shrugs, looking down at his hands. "I didn't know what I wanted to do, not for a long time, but I knew I had to *like* what I was doing. He didn't agree. He also thought college would change my mind about law, and it didn't. It made me realize it wasn't for me, that no matter how much I wanted it to be different, none of his dreams were mine. I let him down." The way he says those four words makes my breath catch.

"No, you didn't," I say, surprising myself . . . and him. His gaze meets mine. I freeze, holding my breath, desperately wanting to kick myself for interrupting him.

His chuckle sounds forced. "You and my mom share the same opinion, but I know my dad. He had his entire life mapped out—and I couldn't even be counted on to continue what he started. How was I going to provide for a family? Be someone others could count on to be there? And by the time I had a better sense of what I wanted to do with my life, he was . . . gone."

Rafael's honesty is a battering ram, and it leaves me at a loss. The vulnerability in his gaze makes me want to course-correct this moment and say something more in line with what one mortal enemy would say to the other. Only I don't.

"I think you're wrong," I start. "For one, maybe you needed some more time to figure things out, but you're always there for your family. If listening in on your family calls over the years taught me anything, it's that they adore you and count on you. And two—if you needed to prove to your dad that you had direction, you should have brought him to Media Lab. Don't take this as a compliment, but you've done okay for yourself. I'm sure he knew it too—he just didn't say it. Sometimes men can be obtuse and difficult . . . and not know how to communicate when it really matters."

A look flits over Rafael's features and leaves him looking at me in a way that makes me feel like I've undressed.

I bite my lips to keep more words from spilling out.

He clears his throat. "I . . . we need to make a pit stop," he says, holding up a paper bag I didn't notice before. "Some left-overs to drop off."

Oh.

The abrupt change of topic has a dowsing effect. It recalibrates things. Reminds me that we are *not* friends or allies.

I swallow. "Sure," I say, pushing to my feet. I should thank him for the reminder.

Without looking at him, I head for his truck, feeling like a stupid fool.

We take our seats, the leftovers safely in the back seat, a manila envelope shoved between his seat and the center console. I look from the folder to Rafael, who starts the engine, reverses, and doesn't say anything as he steers his truck down the street. Like he's thinking about how I tried to pry into parts of his life I had no right prying into. Like I made an enormous mistake that could potentially break our deal.

I shouldn't have gone into the backyard. I should have left and . . . prayed. I glance out the window, up to the handful of stars in the dark sky.

If you're not going to bring me back, at least split the ground open wide enough to swallow me whole.

The road doesn't crack apart.

Rafael doesn't fill the silence either.

Please?

Minutes pass. No act of God occurs.

I take a deep breath, determined to fix this. "What's in the envelope?" I point to it. "Hush money?"

Rafael's hand twitches on the steering wheel. "Something like that," he says, but offers nothing else. Just more silence.

It doesn't take a social science expert to know I ruined whatever fragile truce was between us, and it makes me feel helpless—even *more* helpless.

I'm open to fully transitioning to ghost mode at this point! I close my eyes and send the thought into the prayer-verse.

I wait.

"I've been thinking." Rafael startles me from fantasies of disappearing.

"Wish I could make a note in my planner," I say, my tone betraying my relief as opposed to sarcasm.

"I bet that old thing misses you." His tone hints at amusement, like he might be edging back into Evie vs. Rafael territory, like maybe this prayer thing has merit.

"Some of us like organization. I know it's a foreign concept," I quip, trying to do my part in getting us back to familiar ground. "And do you plan on telling me your bright idea anytime this century?"

Rafael is quiet a second too long for comfort, so I look at him. He meets my gaze, his face creasing with a smile. "Doesn't look like you're seeing Operation Ghostbuster in the same light as me."

I gape at him. "*That's* what you were thinking about?"

"Too on-the-nose?"

"How are you in marketing?"

"Good looks. Great sense of humor. Impeccable persuasion skills."

I groan at his smug grin. "You're ridiculous."

"Remarkable, you mean?"

"No. I mean ridiculous. Absurd. Ludicrous."

The grin doesn't slip. "Since you're the word expert, why don't you name it?"

"It doesn't need a name!"

"Every great mission needs a name, E." His eyes slide to mine. It takes willpower (and mostly pride) not to squeal at him to look at the road. Because spirit me may survive a crash, but flesh-and-bone Rafael? He wouldn't make it, and despite my best efforts, I need him.

"One-letter nicknames work only for really close friends." I gesture to the road. "Who keep their eyes on the road."

He glances at me a second too long for comfort, and the queasiness I've attempted to keep at bay spreads into my chest and throat.

Can ghosts puke?

I imagine Rafael's reaction to me throwing up all over his shiny truck. Some of the queasiness eases at the thought of him having to clean the leather and chrome. Tears would be involved for certain. How's that for a mission?

"I'm keeping them." Rafael returns his focus to the road. "Both names."

"Of course you are," I mutter. If this all falls apart and I don't make it back, I make a mental note to extend my haunting to at least three Vela generations, because that's exactly what he deserves.

Only I really *need* this to work, for us to be on the same page and try whatever idea we come across, however kooky.

It's what I tell myself when I say, "What about a medium? What if we tried that?" The words tumble out in a strangled rush because I'm embarrassed to suggest it. "If I'm a spirit or ghost or whatever, then a medium would be able to help. Or so I've heard." The moment the words are out, I want to shove them back in. *Bad idea.*

"Not a bad idea," Rafael says. His phone dings, lighting up, but he doesn't even glance at it. "I'm surprised I didn't think of it."

I scan his face for a smirk or a hint he's joking. I detect nothing. "You're . . . being serious?"

He flicks a gaze my way. "Yeah, I said we'd try everything—and that's a good idea."

"Oh," I say, trying not let on that I'm stupidly relieved that he didn't tell me it's a dumb idea. Because I would tell me it's a dumb idea. Because I don't actually think *sane* people can speak to ghosts.

I keep my reservations to myself, turning my attention to our surroundings, deciding it's easier to focus on anything but the fact that Rafael Vela, of all people, is taking this more seriously than I am. That he may actually be sticking to a plan.

We're on the outskirts of downtown, where the buildings aren't so tightly packed together. Several restaurants here. A few bars there. A smattering of coffee shops. We turn down an alley, garden lights strung along the length of it. He pulls the truck to a stop right beside a back-alley door.

A massive, leather-clad man, looking like the love child of Sasquatch and Tony Soprano, leans against it, cigarette between his lips. His dark gaze cuts to us and creases into a menacing scowl.

"Where are we?" I mask the swell of uneasiness with a glare.

"Our pit stop." Rafael reaches for the leftovers, then grabs the envelope.

"Which is what? An underground fighting ring?"

Rafael chuckles. "Only on weekends." He opens the door and slides out of the truck.

"Hang on . . . you expect me to wait here? With *him*?" I gesture to the behemoth of a man.

Rafael doesn't seem fazed. "I won't be long. And if anyone bothers you . . ." He leans in, his smile positively wicked. "Just say boo." He winks and closes the door before I can curse him with a lifetime of incontinence and unsatisfied lovers.

CHAPTER FIFTEEN

NINE DAYS (AND AN ALMOST RUINED PARTNERSHIP) AFTER

He left me here.

I squint, watching as Rafael approaches the man, who tosses his cigarette so they can shake hands and pat each other on the back. I don't know why I'm surprised that Rafael's friendly with shady types. I should be surprised they're not sharing a smoke.

The man opens the door, and Rafael disappears inside, the door shutting with a bang that makes me startle. Sasquatch Soprano resumes his post beside the door, lights another cigarette, and blows out the smoke directly toward the truck.

On instinct, I duck. My heart hammers. When I peek over the dash, he's staring at his phone, distracted—my cue to move.

I rush out of the truck and race past him, into the building, ignoring the unnatural sensation of moving through metal and concrete. Whatever Rafael thinks is so important that we have to pause our mission of figuring *me* out, I should know. Especially if it involves manila envelopes and hush money.

The hallway is dimly lit, faint music playing from somewhere up ahead. I follow it. Closed doors line the hallway, but one of them is cracked. Tentatively, I peek inside.

An empty industrial kitchen greets me. Stainless steel appliances gleam pristine and unused. Boxes of condiments line the steel shelves. A massive metal counter cuts down the middle like an operating table.

Ohmygod.

We've stopped at a restaurant.

Furious, I bolt out of the kitchen, determined to find Rafael and have a long discussion about priorities. Starting with their definition. And how stopping for a snack after he *just* ate isn't one of them.

I stomp down the hallway, where doors lead into a sleek, moody restaurant.

Exposed brick and metal pipes stretch across a black ceiling. Plush leather chairs curve around tables and booths. A massive white skeleton—a bony finger held up to its mouth—is painted onto the farthest wall above the words *La Clandestina Taco & Tequila Bar.*

The logo is vaguely familiar, but my gaze snags on the expansive bar at the center of the restaurant. Or rather, the man leaning against it, his back to me.

It's bad enough he needed a taco, but a drink too?

Anger propels me forward.

"It wasn't the only thing." A female voice has me digging in my heels.

A woman stands opposite Rafael, the bar separating them. She's tall, tanned, and has curves that make you want to take Pilates. A sleeve of tattoos covers one arm, and her dark curls swish as she shakes the envelope in a menacing way.

I find I'm intrigued.

"I was ready to kill you," she says.

Very intrigued.

Keeping out of Rafael's line of sight, I lean in.

"You can't do that to me." She swats his shoulder with the envelope before he can shield himself.

"I *said* I was sorry," he says, ducking when she tries to swat at him again. She switches to Spanish briefly, her voice sharp. Rafael tenses.

I can't help but wonder if he's lost his touch with the female species.

He holds up his hands in surrender. "It won't happen again."

"It better not." Her hazel eyes narrow.

"I promise." He flashes a smile, all charm.

There's a pause. A collectively held breath.

"Okay," she says, lowering the envelope.

And just like that, the tempest passes.

For a minute, I thought Rafael had met his match—someone immune to The Vela Effect™. But nope. Of course not. He has an arsenal. A lopsided grin. A clever quip. Stupidly deceiving puppy eyes. And *bam*—he's bending and twisting you to his will . . .

And—*ohmygod*—I'm thinking about his naked body and tangled bedsheets.

Diapers. Eggs. Octogenarians.

"How long do I have you for?" she asks, sliding the envelope beneath the bar. "There's some stuff I'd like your eyes on."

"No time, L."

Her face contorts with disappointment.

"Way to go, Raffy Taffy," I mutter. A knee-jerk reaction I kick myself for. *Conditions.*

Rafael's shoulders stiffen, but he doesn't glance my way.

"Right," she says, her movements tense as she starts to wipe the bar.

"I'm sorry, but I have a *problem* I need to take care of." Rafael projects his voice in my direction.

"A problem?" I squeak.

"Conditions." Rafael coughs into his shoulder.

"Conditions?" The woman stops midwipe.

Rafael scratches his chin. "Yes. The air conditioning in my apartment is down."

"Hmmm. Shit time for that to happen. It's like ninety degrees out there." She resumes cleaning the counter. Rafael shoots me a warning glare.

I return it and say, "You dropped off your super-secret Mafia payout. Let's go."

His jaw locks up, swallowing words I imagine he desperately wants to say.

"What are you looking at?" She sees him stare at nothing.

Rafael swiftly shifts his attention to her. "Nothing. Thought I heard something."

"Probably Owen. He's in and out all day. I told him I didn't need him around, but he insists on standing out there." She shakes her head. "Stubborn-ass men all around me."

Rafael chuckles. "I promise I'll be less stubborn once I deal with my *problem*." I don't appreciate the emphasis on the word. "And you might be able to help."

"With the AC shit?"

"No. My other problem."

She drops the rag and leans her elbows on the counter. "Something else broke?"

"Yes, like your ability to define *priorities*," I say, enjoying the way Rafael tenses. "And unless she has a solution for fixing me, we should go."

Rafael shifts his body away from me. "So, you remember that medium you were telling me about? Can you give me her address?"

"A medium? For you? Raffi, I don't think you can—"

"It's for a friend."

The woman appears to be considering the truth of his words, then says, "I'll text you the address and give her a heads-up." She digs into her fitted jeans and pulls out a phone. "When do you think you'll finally be ready to—"

"Soon." He cuts her off, his tone abrupt.

"I know it's tough for you, but I need you too." She sets the phone down and reaches over, despite his harsh tone. Her hand covers his, her thumb brushing his skin in an easy, familiar way. My breath catches. Something in my chest feels icky.

"I missed you," she says.

"She's your girlfriend?" The words fly out before I can stop them. My hand jumps to my mouth.

Rafael's head snaps in my direction, his expression shifting to one of horror. "Fuck no."

Her brows jump at the same time as his, only her horror is directed at him. "Who are you talking to?" she asks, narrowing her eyes.

"Um. Myself." His answer sounds more like a question. If this non-girlfriend knows him like I do, she can detect the lie from a mile away.

"It didn't *sound* like you were talking to yourself." She dips under the bar and emerges on the other side, beside him. Her eyes scan the restaurant. "Are you seeing something?"

Rafael chuckles like she's told him a joke. "Nothing more than what you'd get with good old twenty-twenty vision."

She doesn't return his smile. "Is that why you need a medium? Because you're seeing something that's not there?"

"Shit. I told you it's for a friend, Lupe," he says.

Lupe.

She has a name.

Lupe doesn't seem appeased. Her gaze is fixated on Rafael like she's about to dissect him.

"Anyway, I should get going. I'm tired." Rafael stretches his arms over his head and feigns a yawn. The movement hikes his shirt, revealing the waistband of his briefs and the strip of skin above it. I snap my gaze away, feeling several degrees warmer.

"*Tired*, huh? That must be why you're talking to yourself," she says, cutting off his escape.

"I think she might want to kill you," I whisper, because I'm not sure what she is to him, but *dangerous* is coming to mind.

"Sí," Rafael agrees. I'm not sure if he's talking to her or me.

She's close now, her eyes sharp and hawklike and not at all like the doe-eyed women he usually goes for. I don't know if I should be impressed or scared.

Lupe crosses her arms. "Are you drunk?"

"Surprisingly, no." The words slip out of my lips. Rafael repeats this. I groan beside him.

He shakes his head quickly. "No! I meant no. I haven't had a drink in . . . days."

"You're acting very strange, Raffi."

"Like I said, super tired. Should be getting home." He leans in, closing the distance between them. My chest feels suddenly too tight, but I can't look away—not as his arms wrap around her, his mouth moving toward her.

He kisses her.

On the cheek.

"I'll call you later, cuz."

Cuz?

They're cousins.

The tightness doesn't loosen up as I look between them. I'm not sure how I didn't see the similarities before. The same full lips. The intense eyes. The confident stance. Oblivious me.

Rafael steps around Lupe. I follow, torn between feeling a strange sense of relief but also concern because she has the same expression Rafael gets when he's up to something . . . and I've sat across from him long enough to feel uneasy.

He takes three steps.

"We don't lie to each other. Ever," Lupe says, voice cool.

Rafael halts. I keep walking until I'm beside him. "No lies needed if we go," I whisper, sensing things are about to take a bad turn if we don't.

"Who were you talking to?" Lupe asks.

"You *can* lie," I tell him. Because the alternative is telling the truth, and I'd rather spend a month in my former basement apartment than have another Vela involved. "So lie."

"I was reacting to the skeleton—the logo." Rafael gestures to the wall behind Lupe. "It seems off-center. Which is why I was like *fuck no*!"

Lupe doesn't even bother turning. "Skully is perfectly centered." Her tone is almost predatory. Even her lips press into the same firm line I've seen Rafael wear countless times. "The truth?"

"Let's go," I instruct, my tone edged with warning. Rafael's eyes flick to mine.

"Raffi?" Lupe hedges.

His gaze asks for something that makes my stomach twist. "Rafael," I warn. His jaw works. "Do *not* bring her into this."

"I can't lie to her, E." His shoulders sag.

"No, no, no." I whip around him, into his line of sight. "You can certainly lie!"

"It's too late," he says. "She's like a CIA-trained hound."

Lupe gasps. "Oh, chingado—are you on drugs? Because you know what happened when Abuela found out Mateo got—"

"No! No drugs."

"It could be," I interject. "Blame it on your pills or early-onset Alzheimer's. Even aliens, but stop this while you still can."

"It's too late," he says, sidestepping around me.

I follow, blocking his view again. "I'm not kidding about the haunting for eternity. Think of the mini-Rafaels. Do you want me around forever?"

There's a shift in his demeanor—another part of Rafael I don't have time to examine—and his lips press together. Hope sparks. Maybe I'm getting through. Maybe he can see how completely absurd it would be to bring his cousin into all this.

"What is it, Raffi?" Lupe's voice coaxes. "You can tell me."

I glance over my shoulder. She's so close . . . predatory.

"Don't do it," I warn again, holding my breath. His gaze drops to my face, lingers on each inch of my skin. I fight the warmth heating my cheeks and shake my head no.

"The thing is . . . I don't know how I can see her. I don't know if she's a spirit or something else, but it started a couple days ago. I thought I was hallucinating, but now I . . . I'm not sure. I don't know what the fuck is happening, but she's here. Right in front of me." He sighs deeply. "And she needs my help."

"*You* will need help when I'm done with you. The kind that requires years of exorcisms," I hiss, a rush of fury replacing the heat, making me want to dig my fingers into his hair and give him a shake. His eyes are far from fearful, like he's up to the challenge. Which only makes it worse—because he's clearly determined to bring Lupe into it. And yes, I'm tethered to the one guy I trust least, but looping in his cousin? That feels like a kind of surrender. Like I'm accepting I'm helpless on my own.

Lupe clears her throat, drawing our attention. "That's . . ."

"I know it sounds crazy," Rafael continues.

"Crazy is that night we ate shrooms and slept in Pepo's doghouse, but this is next-level shit." Lupe whistles low, then curses in Spanish. "I'm a spiritual person, Raffi. You know I believe in the spirit world, but—" She stills, hand going to her mouth. "Hang on. If she's a ghost, does that mean she's dead?" Her features soften. "Raffi, I'm—"

"No," he says. "She's not dead. Nothing's changed since the last time. Nothing but her being here, right now." His thumb points in my direction. She follows the movement to where I'm glowering. Her gaze is two feet to my left. "And I need to figure out how to get her back into her body."

Lupe's features contort from puzzled to concerned to curious. "Right there?"

Rafael nods. "She's not too thrilled about me sharing this, but I think we're past that point." Yep, and we've moved directly to my breaking point. "Like I said, it's crazy, and we're trying to figure it out. Why she's here . . . and how we can get her back into her body before . . ." His tone dips. My throat closes up. "It's why I went to see Abuela and why I want to know about that medium. We have to figure this out. Soon."

"And your extended family is going to help how?" I snap.

"I'm sorry." His attention turns to me, pleading. "But she might think of something I can't. One Vela is good, but two—that's basically a superpower."

"A superpower would be *listening*."

"Says the kettle?"

I narrow my eyes in fury. "I listen. To people who are *reasonable and sane*."

"You know you look like a crazy person talking to yourself like that?" Lupe eyes her cousin the way you'd watch someone streaking through church.

"Thank you!" I mutter. "He *is* crazy."

Rafael draws in a deep, impatient breath. "I'm not talking to myself. I'm talking to her." He gestures toward me. Lupe doesn't look convinced. He mumbles, scanning the room, and then his gaze snags on the paper bag from his grandmother's house. His eyes light up. "Okay! If you don't believe me, then let's try something. He points to the bag. "Open the bag, take the item on top, and show it to Evie. I'll turn around. She'll tell me what it is. I tell you. Easy proof."

"No," Lupe and I answer in unison.

"*Por favor*," he tacks on, his eyes pleading. I haven't once—not since that one time—fallen for this Vela trick. "For me."

I snort. *As if.*

While I'm stalwart in my decision, Lupe hesitates, her face creasing with indecision. She pushes out a big breath before she says, "All right, primo. I'm doing this because I love you." She twirls her pointer finger. "Turn around before I change my mind."

Shoulders relaxing, Rafael catches my gaze as he pivots his body toward me. The plea remains. I cross my arms over my chest to communicate that I will *not*, for any reason whatsoever, do this.

It's bad enough Rafael has witnessed some of my deepest, most personal parts—my birthmark, my severe amaxophobia, my poorly timed syncope. He's seen too much already. She doesn't need to be a part of it too.

Muttering to herself, Lupe takes the bag and opens it. "Hmmm." She pulls out a small box wrapped in pink construction paper. "How do I know you don't already know what's in here?"

Rafael sighs. "Don't pretend like you don't know how Elena is with her secret drawings."

Nodding her head in agreement, Lupe unwraps the box.

"I'm not doing this," I assure him, needing to get far, far away from Rafael Vela.

And how far is that?

I'm only going to end up where I started, because whatever—or whoever—made the executive decisions thought it would be fun to have me wake up on Rafael's sofa each morning. *Wherever you are, Great-Aunt Julia, it wouldn't kill you to help me out a little.*

"Evie," he says, his eyes locking onto mine.

"Rafael." I make sure my tone communicates I'm not allowing another Vela in on my misery.

His jaw clenches in frustration, but I don't waver.

Across from us, Lupe unwraps the box. Removes the lid. And pulls out a pink sheet of construction paper folded in four.

"Please." Rafael's soft tone kicks me in the chest—or whatever is swirling around inside there, undoing years of conditioning against him. Because somehow—impossibly—I find myself listening. Considering his request. And I hate it. "Would it be so bad to have her on our side?"

I glare at him, masking the chaos bubbling up inside. She's a Vela, and I don't need her. She can't even see me.

But . . . if I'm being rational and reasonable, he's right. Having someone else help might speed things along; maybe she'll think of things we haven't. Also, she doesn't make me feel like I'm glitching in the same way Rafael does.

It could work—as much as I hate to admit it.

I take a deep breath, steeling myself for potential smugness. "Fine. I'll bite, but this is it—the last Vela that comes into the mix."

He doesn't smirk or give me reason to think I've made a mistake. "She's not a Ve—" he starts.

"Rafael." I narrow my eyes in warning before turning my attention to the paper in Lupe's hands. As I squint the drawing into focus, my breath catches. "It's daisies. A field of them. And a . . . dog?" I frown, trying to make sense of the shapes.

Rafael repeats my words.

Lupe puts a hand to her forehead. "Híjole."

* * *

Lupe forbids us to leave.

She plants herself at a table—one beer for her, one for Rafael—and commands Rafael to *sit*. "Start talking," she says. "All of it."

Rafael throws a glance my way.

I hang back near the bar, arms crossed, equal parts impatient and curious, trying to ignore the pulsing that's started at the base of my head. Mostly, I hope we were right about bringing Lupe into this. Because right now? She's slowing us down.

Rafael starts with the condensed version: the coma, the hospital, the shortened timeline, me waking up in his apartment. Nothing about The Conditions™.

"So—you're the only one who can see her?" Lupe asks.

"Seems like it."

"Unfortunately."

We speak in unison. She only hears one of us. Rafael throws me a look. I smile sweetly.

"And what's the game plan? How are you guys fixing her?" Lupe scans the room as if to pinpoint my location. She looks over Rafael's shoulder. I'm standing behind her.

"We haven't gotten into the weeds—" Which is funny, because that is not Rafael's strong suit. "But . . . we have a name." I groan. "Operation Ghostbuster."

Lupe beams. "Love that!"

"We're not calling it that," I say, rubbing my temples. A dull *thump, thump, thump* agrees.

"E's not a fan," he says, cradling the beer bottle, "but I think it'll grow on her."

"It won't," I deadpan.

Rafael smirks. "You underestimate my abilities."

I look up at the ceiling. *Anyone?* Rafael's answering chuckle makes me wonder if he *deserves* a lifetime of Evie Pope trailing him.

"What did you try so far?" Lupe asks, placing her phone on the table.

"Abuela, for now, but we have some other ideas." Rafael finds my eyes. "The medium."

"Solid start, primo. But we need to think *bigger*." Lupe swipes across her phone. "Like . . . that psychic who predicted the Cubs win? She owes me a reading." She continues typing, pausing to look at Rafael. "And you remember when I dogsat for Gracie?" He nods. "Met a Reiki healer–slash–dog groomer. Haven't used them yet, but maybe we can get them to come to the hospital. That's what we need."

Rafael looks the way I feel—skeptical. "Lupe—"

Lupe's undeterred. "Chakra cleanses, moon water, salt circles, séances—and there's something called a water rebirth."

Rafael blinks. "A what?"

"It's when you dunk her body in water and hope her spirit gets the hint."

"Lovely. I probably need a good bath," I mumble.

Rafael's lips quirk. "Maybe that's plan B."

"Or Z," I add.

"There's this other lady on TikTok who reads past lives through teeth. Maybe there's—"

"An exorcism?" If we're going for crazy, then let's go.

"No," Rafael interrupts. He looks to Lupe—to me. "I think that we start with the sane options before we dive headfirst into the drownings and demons."

Is Rafael the practical one? My temples *thump, thump* to their own beat.

"I'm scheduling them all," Lupe says. "But we can start with the *obvious* ones."

Rafael downs the rest of his beer. "We're going to sort this out." He looks pointedly at me. "Whoever—whatever—it takes," he says, like he's making a promise. His voice low and sure. My breath hitches at the intensity in his gaze. It feels slightly more difficult to breathe. Maybe this is *it*?

Lupe follows Rafael's line of sight. "This will never not be weird."

"Tell me about it," I say to myself, trying to keep my face from showing how I feel.

"You have no clue," Rafael says. His phone buzzes on the table, catching his attention. He stiffens, then stands abruptly. "I have to take this."

The jarring shift in his demeanor throws me. Even Lupe looks surprised.

"It can't wait?" Lupe shouts after Rafael. He ignores her.

"Is that your sponsor for Tacos and Tequila Tuesdays?" I ask dryly as he passes me. He stumbles midstep, likely surprised I remember his ridiculous YouTube idea.

"Funny, E." Rafael disappears down the hallway. "Hey . . ."

I don't catch anything else as he answers his mystery call, but my curiosity tugs at me like a leash.

"Evie?" Lupe's voice startles me.

I turn to her. She's looking to my left—trying to find me. On instinct, I move closer.

"I need to say something before he comes back." Internal alarms go off. I brace myself. For what? I have no clue, but the sudden change in her tone sends a pang of panic through me. "Raffi's like the big brother I never had. Helped me get my life together after I screwed it up with partying and bad people—even while dealing with his own shit. Made sure I'd never have a reason to go back." Her gaze is distant, pensive. I didn't know. "Going through that makes me protective of him, so don't take this the wrong way, but I have mixed feelings about Raffi helping you." The words hit like a wrecking ball, harder than I expect.

What does that mean?

I wish I could ask.

"I'm helping *him* because I'd do anything for him," Lupe continues. "But honestly, he's told me a lot about you." I try not to cringe, thinking of the not-so-fun things that could have made the list. "I know I shouldn't be saying this. He'd probably kill me actually, but hell, it's about time you knew. Probably not a better time than now"—I brace myself—"but he is—"

"Wary of leaving his cousin on her own," Rafael interrupts. I yip, turning on him.

"What? I was just going to say that you told me Evie plans free time," Lupe says, her tone changing back to fun and light. Shrugging, she downs a swig of her beer. "Nothing to be ashamed of."

I gape at Rafael, who's glaring at his cousin. A silent exchange passes, and I'm convinced it might have nothing to do with scheduling free time and everything to do with some secret.

Rafael must feel my eyes burning into the side of his stupidly handsome face, because he turns to me. "Sorry?"

"What's wrong with time management, Raffy Taffy?" I ask, scanning his face for more. What did Lupe want to say? A secret that's making them both wage a staring war? And that call he left for?

He's definitely hiding something. *Secrets.*

"It's late," Rafael says, stretching like that settles it. "And we have a medium to see in the morning."

Translation: Subject closed. But my gut says otherwise—because all I can think is *secrets, secrets, secrets.*

And the worst part? I was starting to think I could trust him.

CHAPTER SIXTEEN
TEN DAYS AFTER

The next morning, I'm back in Rafael's loft, waking up on his sofa in the same clothes, same shoes, like I'm living some demented Groundhog Day. It doesn't help that I barely slept, the night a battlefield of anxiety, paranoia, and the occasional movement in the bedroom beside mine: Rafael's. Where he was likely undressing and performing his bedtime ritual, probably involving the hair locks of his exes and cologne-scented candles. Three hundred push-ups. A shot of tequila.

While he dozed, I spent hours alternating between obsessive overthinking and wishing away the throb inside my skull—a *thump, thump, thump* accompanied by a replay of the night, mainly the part with Lupe's almost-revelation.

And now I'm back on the sofa, staring up at the ceiling, wondering if I'll find any answers to my questions. Rafael seems to think answers often linger in the ceiling—and I have questions. If Lupe's almost-revelation is to be believed, it means Rafael might be hiding a secret. Something to do with me being here?

But I'd know if something *serious* was going on.

Rafael's an open book. Written in large-print font.

Right?

Thump, thump, thump.

The throbbing is the only answer I get.

I breathe through a wave of frustrated alarm when I hear Rafael in the dining room, his voice low and urgent but frustratingly unintelligible.

Secrets, secrets, secrets.

I shift on the sofa and catch a glimpse of him over the armrest. Wearing nothing but sweatpants, he's leaning against the table, talking on the phone . . . and possibly telling Dana all about how he's going to run the OhLaLove account with his newly expanded team.

The Evie who has known Rafael for entirely too long separates from the one who has spent the last three days with him, and they each prop themselves on a different shoulder.

Pre-Coma Evie: *He's tricking you. Can't you see? The smiles. The dimples. They're all part of the distraction. He thinks he can Vela you long enough to get comfortable with his new promotion* and *get his choice of account managers—you included.*

Coma Evie: *You offered him the promotion—remember? Also, Rafael wouldn't be focusing on his promotion when you're in a coma. Sure, he swapped out your sanitizer for hand soap and made you faint that one time, but he's not* evil. *Have you seen where he comes from? No one raised in that kind of family would do something like that.*

Pre-Coma Evie snorts. *That was part of the trick. The smoke and mirrors. "Look at my family—aren't they wonderful? Aren't they loving? How can I be anything but totally, completely harmless?" Don't you dare fall for it. If he thinks you'll just ignore the shadiness from last night, he's got another thing coming . . . and she's invisible and furious.*

Coma Evie rolls her eyes. *Oh, please! Rafael has a good heart. Deep, deep down, you know this. You know he wants to help you.*

He took you to his grandmother's house. He dragged his cousin into this. Whatever secret you think he's hiding, you're wrong.

Pre-Coma Evie: *Bullshit.*

Coma Evie: *Language.*

I groan, willing the Evies to shut up.

As if he has Evie sensors, he looks directly at me. I want to duck before he can detect the suspicion on me. It'll only make things more difficult—and we've only just made it to reluctant allies. As much as I don't like it, I need his help, and I have to keep the peace. I'm cool, calm, collected.

Smoothing down the same dress I've worn for three days, I join him in the dining room, where he's exchanged his phone for a mug of coffee. While his sweatpants hang low on his hips, the rest of him is bare and tanned and being used as a weapon of mass destruction in this round of Evie vs. Rafael.

I mentally kick Pre-Coma Evie and focus on his hairline when I say, "Sleep well?"

He watches me over the rim of his mug. "Fine. You?"

"Like the dead," I offer with a shrug and an overly bright smile.

His eyes narrow. "Why are you smiling like that?"

"Like what?"

"Like you've laced my coffee with cyanide."

I gasp, hand over chest. "Please. While I'd love company in this liminal hellscape, I'm not *that* desperate. I thought we were past that."

He glances into his mug, then brings it to his lips slowly. Cautiously.

I look at him as if to say *Really?*

"Are you okay?" He lowers the mug, regarding me. From head to pumps.

"Fa-*boo*-lous," I say. Too sweetly, because his brows dance in surprise. He seems unsettled. And maybe this is the way to go. Make him feel a little off-balance. If he's rattled, maybe he'll slip, and maybe I'll get to the bottom of whatever he might be hiding.

Pre-Coma Evie is running victory circles.

"Spit it out, E," he says, setting his mug aside. "What's wrong?"

"Besides the obvious?" I drag my hand along the wall—*through* it—for additional clarification.

"Not what I mean. What happened? You're acting weird." He narrows his eyes. "Was it a nightmare? Separation anxiety from your planner? What's making you all . . ." He waggles his fingers in my direction.

"Hilarious," I say, gesturing to the door. "Are we going anytime this year?"

Rafael's mouth opens—then shuts. Whatever he was about to say gets swallowed (along with other maybe-secrets). He swipes a black tee from the back of a chair—because he is *that* organized—and wiggles into it, his toned back stretching with the effort. The cotton clings to him like it missed him. I hate that I notice.

Still turned away, he pats down his pants, then sifts through the chaos on his dining room table.

"Take all the time you need." I stretch, feigning relaxation. "No rush whatsoever."

He throws a scowl over his shoulder. "We need keys."

"You left them by your meal for five." I offer, gesturing to the kitchen, where abandoned Indian takeout boxes have staged a coup on his countertop. Most are empty.

He smirks. "If I didn't know better, I'd say you were body shaming."

I'm ashamed of my thoughts as they relate to his body. "I wouldn't be so subtle."

He laughs—a low rumble—and grabs his keys.

I trail after him to the door, needing him to open it and lead the way. He slows, hand on the door handle. "Ready?"

"I'm absolutely *dying* to get this over with," I say. My smile returns. Suspicion enters his eyes.

He says nothing as we walk to the elevator, but I can feel him watching me. Waiting.

I turn to him abruptly. "You wouldn't be keeping anything from me, would you?"

His face crinkles in confusion. "There's plenty I'm keeping from you."

I roll my eyes. "Not what I meant."

"Then what do you mean?"

I debate whether to ask. About Lupe's something. About his call. About the promotion. About why he might be helping me if he's already gotten it.

The elevator dings, then opens.

I swallow my questions.

An older man, tortoiseshell glasses perched on his nose and newspaper under his arm, perks at the sight of Rafael. "Good morning, Raf!"

"Morning, Frankie." Rafael shakes Frankie's hand. The elevator doors close, and I'm shoved between the wall and Rafael. He's distracted by his neighbor's thoughts on the Bears' next season, which gives me time to assess. My gaze inches up the length of Rafael's neck, his jaw, his lips, and linger on his eyes, seeking any evidence of a secret.

See? Nothing suspicious there, Coma Evie says, triumphant. *But maybe don't stare like you're contemplating having him for dinner.*

Mortified, I drop my gaze to my knotted hands.

The elevator takes too long to stop.

When it does, I'm the first one out.

"Have a good day, Raf. It's nice to see you out and about again." Frankie waves with his newspaper.

"See you around!" Rafael says, following on my heels. I scramble into the truck, shivering as I pass through the metal. He joins me, watching me as he starts the engine.

"I promised I would help you, and that's what I'm doing," Rafael says, shifting in reverse. "Whatever alternate reality you've created where I'm the devil? It couldn't be farther from the truth."

The truck rolls backward, and panic rolls in my belly. I clamp my hands together. "I don't think you're the devil," I say, to distract myself.

He shoots me a look as we pull out of the parking garage. "Devil's son, then?"

I shrug, biting down against a grin. "A distant cousin."

Rafael chuckles, maybe calls me a smartass.

I'm focused on keeping calm. On distractions. Like the clogged street. People and cars. It's all familiar. Two turns and we're driving past a high-rise. I crane my neck, trying to see up to floor thirty-eight. Media Lab. I wonder if my things are still at my desk—or if Rafael has pushed his chaos across the threshold of the two. Or maybe he's already moved into the office reserved for the next marketing director.

Pre-Coma Evie tackles Coma Evie. *Of course he's already moved into the office. He's Rafael!*

Does he already have the promotion? Would Dana have given it to him without waiting to see what will happen with me? My stomach churns in response. I can't fathom it. My life *was* Media Lab. My distraction and refuge. A way out of being Stevie Popovici. The place where I reinvented myself after I left Michigan and never looked back. Except for that one night.

Before I started courses at Northeastern Illinois University, I drove to one of my favorite spots overlooking Lake Michigan. I took out an old phone and turned it on. It was the one thing I had from my old life, and not that I'd ever admit it, but each night before bed, I turned it on, held my breath, and waited. Not once was there a missed text or voicemail from my mother, Margot.

I'd waited for years for her to call—to care—but getting love from Margot was like trying to squeeze blood from a rock. As much as it hurt, I hurled the phone into the lake with a "Screw you, Mom!" and I moved on. The next day, I started investing my focus and energy into my future because I'd already given my past so much. The only thing—person—I took with me was Annie.

I became Evie Pope at Media Lab. Someone with a career and the means to provide for herself without relying on anyone else. It started with my one-year plans, which changed to five- and ten-year plans because there were always bigger and better opportunities ahead. Even more stability.

And then there was Rafael.

Rafael who knows I'm Stevie.

Rafael who makes me feel more unstable than anyone else I know.

Rafael who's helping me, despite everything.

See, you know I'm right! Coma Evie dusts herself off and flips off Pre-Coma Evie.

I sneak a peek to my left. The sun kisses his skin, giving him a faint glowing outline that screams Team Edward (cue that Cullen sparkle from *Twilight*). He's drumming his fingers against the wheel, anxious about something. I know this about him, just like I know about half a million other things.

He catches my gaze and frowns. "Plotting my demise?"

"No!" I snap my gaze to the road. A blush creeps into my cheeks, and I blame it—and these new symptoms—on my condition. The fullness. The inability to think clearly. "I'm just . . . nervous about this," I admit, quieter than I intend. I haven't let myself be vulnerable with him in a long time.

I feel his gaze on me.

"Me too," he says, his tone warm and honest, and I fear he's swapped one weapon for a much more dangerous one. Because beneath his tone is something else, something a lot like sadness.

It's not anything I've associated with Rafael before, save for when his dad passed. I've imagined it, sure. Multiple times across multiple scenarios. Only I didn't think it would somehow make me feel *not* happy.

He catches me staring again, and I manipulate my features into a scowl, gesturing at his hair. "What's happening up there?"

"Oh?" He rakes his long fingers through his hair, tousling it in different directions. I want to reach out and fix it. I want to throw myself out of his moving vehicle and see what happens. "Lupe keeps saying she can give me a trim."

"She's a hairdresser too?"

"There's little she's not good at." He grins. "Well, maybe except sticking to one thing. We're alike in that way. We'll get into one thing, invest our time and energy into it until something else comes along and becomes the new thing. It's how I ended up at Media Lab. The draw of new clients and projects. Some days it's working on marketing plans. Other days it's learning a new product."

"What you're saying is that all I had to do was make work boring and then you would have quit?"

Rafael's shoulder lifts in a shrug. "Doubt it."

"You underestimate *my* abilities." I use his words against him.

He smile slips. "Never. Not once in five years," he says, his tone suddenly serious. His words sear themselves into bits of me I didn't know existed. My chest. My belly. Lower still. I'm glad his eyes are on the road.

"Too bad I don't believe a word of it," I say. Face flushed, I sink into my seat and look out the window, turning my attention outside.

We continue along Michigan Avenue, passing Millennium Park. The Bean shines in the sunlight. Tourists already crowd the park, snapping photos and posting to their social media feeds. I remember wanting to soak up all of the city when I first moved here, and I took photos of almost every moment in my completion of bucket list item #1.

An architecture tour down the Chicago River. Dinner atop John Hancock Tower. A Cubs game. A slice of deep-dish pizza. Ice cream along the Riverwalk. I took my time learning the city and becoming a part of it. I'd come here for Annie, but I stayed for me.

As we pass the Wrigley Building, I feel a renewed desperation I haven't felt since waking up in Rafael's apartment. I want to stay and be a part of this. I want to feel the sun on my face when I run at sunset. I want to pick up breakfast at Dollop Coffee and dinner at Francesca's. I want to cross things off my bucket list. I want to stay.

Who cares if he's hiding something?

You do, both Evies say.

CHAPTER SEVENTEEN
TEN DAYS AFTER, PART II

Thirty minutes later we're standing outside a canary-yellow bungalow in Rosemont. A yard sign stuck into the lawn reads *Helene Flowers, Medium*. At least a handful of wind chimes tinkle softly along the awning of the white porch, on which several cats lounge. One's head perks up at the sound of the truck door closing. A shiver rattles down my spine.

"Looks legit," Rafael says, hands dug into his pockets.

"Do you frequent many mediums?" I feel none of the amusement in his eyes. My gut's telling me this is a bad idea, one that will only lead to disappointment.

Rafael offers me a one-shoulder shrug. "Here and there, as the ghosts come and go."

"*Ohmygod.*" Ignoring his soft chuckle, I march toward the stairs leading up to the veranda, anxiety spiking as I land on the first of the steps.

The cats, at least ten of them, doze, laze, and stretch in nooks of faded patio furniture or beneath it, and their eyes seem to simultaneously settle on me. One's tongue darts out as if to taunt me.

"Not a fan of cats?" Rafael's voice startles me.

I shoot him a dark glare Pre-Coma Evie would have been proud of. "I'm not *not* a fan."

He has the nerve to smile. "Who hurt you?"

An image of my mother makes me stumble. Bleached-blond hair, over-the-top makeup, and drugstore perfume. Boyfriends, booze, and Benji the cat, who got more attention than either of her daughters ever did. "Not a cat," I say, not missing the way his features shift with my tone.

Before he can use his compulsion abilities to see through me, I climb the stairs, trying my hardest to avoid every single feline I pass. The stairs creak and groan as Rafael follows. At the top, I step aside, giving him the space to knock.

Three raps break the silence. A cat meows. My unease grows. I know I had the idea, but we're about to meet with a *medium*, someone who makes money off people's grief by pretending to talk to their loved ones. I shouldn't have suggested this.

Rafael seems unbothered. Even when it takes several more knocks and almost an entire minute for the door to open.

A woman with dark-brown skin scans Rafael from behind oversized glasses. Her permed hair, like spun silver, is pinned in a bun atop her head, and her shoulders, draped in a burnt-orange satin robe, curve inward as she leans heavily on a bejeweled walking stick.

Rafael flashes her a smile like a badge. "Hi! Helene?"

"Yes?" Her mismatched eyes—one sea blue, one forest green—narrow as she peers at him.

"I apologize for dropping by so unexpectedly, but my cousin Lupe sent me your way. Said you could help with a reading." Even if he's much taller, broader, and more imposing than Helene, he comes across as sweet and harmless. "I don't mean to interrupt your day, and I wouldn't do it if it wasn't urgent."

I watch Helene, curious if she's going to allow herself to be Vela'd in her old age. She purses her red lips, and while I should be thrilled that she might say no—so we can skip this whole charade—I also know we need to try it. Desperate times, desperate measures.

"Smile wider," I instruct.

Rafael eyes me like he's discovered a new species.

I jerk my head to Helene. "For her."

His lips tug wider, slow and practiced. The Dimple pops out. Coma Evie feels faint.

Helene hums. "Lupe, you said? You know, I think she texted me." A southern twang softens her words. "And I have some time before I need to head out, young man. Come in." She beckons him inside, her bracelets singing alongside the wind chimes.

I feel the absurd urge to do a victory dance, because we're *in*. Rafael's still staring at me as if I'm on the cover of *Wildlife Magazine*, but I follow Helene into her house. And stumble to a stop.

"Oh, my . . ." I gasp. Rafael's shoulder brushes my invisible one, and the sensation—the warmth of him when it happens—doesn't make me want to pull away. I ignore my riotous reactions, because Helene's place is . . . *distracting*. It's as if every shade of yellow has been splattered on every surface. The walls. The upholstered furniture. Her wall art and ceramic cats. "I will never unsee this."

"Plenty for your home decor Pinterest board." Rafael nods thoughtfully. I snort, then cover my mouth with a hand. He responds with a wink that makes me skip a breath, and I categorize it as a new kind of vampire compulsion.

"Through here!" Helene declares, disappearing around a corner. I shake myself out of whatever he's done and follow after them to a sunroom at the back of the house, where more of Helene's interior design has me gawking. So. Much. Yellow.

"Sit, sit," Helene instructs, waving Rafael to one of two sunshine-yellow armchairs. She shoos an orange cat from a chaise before she settles into it with a sigh. Rafael drops into one of the fabric armchairs, sinking into the cushions.

I inch into the room—until a meow echoes from somewhere unseen. I dig my heels in. I can observe from here. Both Evies agree.

"All right, young man, let's start with the easy things. What's your name?" Helene rests her hands in her lap.

"Rafael Diego Vela," he says, his fingers drumming against the armrest.

"Lovely name," Helene says with a warm smile. "Now, tell me—what brings you here today? Is there a loved one who has passed?"

Even if I'm not one hundred percent on board with this idea, I feel a twinge of disappointment. I'm not a loved one, and I haven't passed. And if those are the conditions for Helene being able to help us—me—then we're not off to a great start.

"She hasn't passed," Rafael says.

Helene's forehead crinkles into a hundred creases. "Hmmm. I'm not sure I understand, Rafael."

"She's actually in a coma, but"—he rolls his shoulders, clears his throat—"I sense her . . . spirit. Can talk to her."

"Hmm . . . hmmm," Helene is not at all surprised by his confession. "And is she here now?"

"Yes." Rafael casts a quick glance my way. I try to mask my doubts about Helene's abilities, but shouldn't she know this? Feel my presence or aura?

"Hmmm." Helene hums as she closes her eyes.

A white kitten (more fluff than kitten) meows from beneath Rafael's armchair. I eye it warily. Rafael grins and reaches over, smoothly scooping her up and bringing her up to his face. He nuzzles her for a second, then three, before settling her onto his lap, where she stretches once and settles down for a nap. Rafael digs his fingers into her coat, tan fingers against white fur, and begins to massage her. The kitten mews. Helene hums.

And I want to slap myself for having been hypnotized by it all. The kittens are a distraction, I realize with no small amount of horror.

"I've seen enough. This was a bad idea," I admit, irritated with myself *and* the obviously pretend medium humming to herself. Rafael looks at me like I've suggested we shave the kitten.

"Can you tell me more about her?" Helene draws his attention back to her.

"Seriously, let's go." I attempt to steal it back.

"She's demanding, ambitious, stubborn," he says.

"Murderous," I add, glaring at him.

Helene makes a noise. Then her face sobers, her entire body tensing. "Oh, I'm getting something."

"It's a whiff of bullshit." I roll my eyes, retreating to the door. "You can't be buying this," I hiss, furious that he's not seeing the truth. He simply shrugs, and—*oh Mamma Mia*—I think he's being *Helene*'d. "You've got to be kidding me."

Helene taps her chest. "I'm getting an *eee* sound. Would this young lady's name start with an *eee*? Or is there an *eee* in her name?"

Rafael's brows shoot up in surprise. I roll my eyes because—lucky guess. "Yes," he responds.

She nods, encouraged. "Well, I'm also getting the sense that she's quiet and shy, but happy. Real bright smile she has."

I'm actually scowling like a ghoul. Rafael knows this. "Convinced now? It's complete bullshit. Let's go," I command, jerking my head toward the door.

But Rafael continues to sit there, because he's definitely been Helene'd. *And he doesn't want to help you,* Pre-Coma Evie taunts.

"Wait—there's more . . ." she says. Rafael leans in.

"I'm going to leave. Now." I have one foot out the door.

"She's younger. Maybe a teenager. She's gesturing to her heart and clasping her hands. The symbol for sister."

Rafael shakes his head. "Um. No. Not my sister. She's—"

"Oh!" Helene exclaims, her eyes popping open. I turn to leave. "Daisies! Do daisies mean something to you?"

Her words have a paralyzing effect. I stumble to a stop, my breath hitching and limbs going numb. Helene's staring at Rafael and I'm staring at her, feeling like she's knocked the breath out of me.

"Annie," I whisper.

"Annie?" Rafael's gaze shifts to mine.

My throat closes. I nod. "She's—was—my sister."

A beat of silence.

"I'm sorry. I didn't know." Rafael's voice softens in a way that makes my breath catch. Like he sees a fracture in me that no one—not even Gemma—has fully seen.

Of course he doesn't know. I don't talk about her. Annie is sacred.

"Ask her—ask her about Annie," I say—*beg*. I know it's stupid to believe anything Helene says, but if there's a chance it's Annie . . .

Rafael turns to Helene. "What else is she saying?"

"She's not saying anything, darlin'. She's smiling and spinning around, showing me her daisy dress."

"She's *here*?" I can't conceal the hope in my voice. I whip around—desperate to see Annie, more than I want anything else. But there's no flash of her bright-green eyes. No faded daisy dress. Not even a hint of her summer-and-sunshine scent.

Nothing.

Disappointment punches into my chest.

Helene continues, "It seems like dancing is important to her or to her loved ones. Nothing is ever really clear with these things."

Tears sting my eyes. Annie and I loved dancing. We found old records and made up our own dances. We watched *Mamma Mia!* so many times we ruined the DVD. We once even used one of our mother's boyfriend's cameras to film our own musical.

I smile at the memory. "Is she okay?" I say, my voice sounding like a frog's.

Rafael repeats the question for Helene, whose hand stills over her chest. "She's showing me some pain around her passing now."

My heart jerks in response. Endless nights and weeks and years. Feeling alone, gutted, and afraid.

"There was pain. There *is*," Rafael says, answering for me. As if he can see right through me. A part of me wants to know how he'll use this against me. Another part knows he never would.

"She's showing me she didn't feel pain, and she certainly doesn't want you to feel pain. She's showing me the symbol for moving on. She wants that for you." Helene's smile is kind. I breathe through my mouth to keep the tears from falling. "She's showing me she's with you always, and . . . she's doing this." Helene's hands clasp together and squeeze. "Hold on."

The air thins, and I'm sucked into a memory. *Hold on,* Annie whispers, voice barely audible. She's clammy, pale, and trying to smile. Her green eyes flicker to mine—scared but steady. I grab her hand. She squeezes back, weakly. My other hand scrambles for the phone, needing to call 911 again.

I remember feeling frantic—panicked. She was fading. Her body felt too small, even though she was taller than me. I held on to her with all of me. "Stay with me," I whispered. "Please."

That's how the paramedics found us—her head on my shoulder, my hand locked on her like it could anchor her to this world, to me.

Tears slide down my cheeks, too fast for me to mask them. Rafael is watching, but I detect no smirk. No judgment. "What else?" I ask, sniffing.

Rafael repeats my question.

"The holding-on is important to this person," Helene muses. "Maybe she's telling your friend to hang in there. I don't know the specific meaning of what spirits share—that's for their loved ones to piece tougher, and I hope it means something to you."

It does. It means *everything*.

How often did I stay awake, wondering if she was taken care of? More times than there are stars in the sky and raindrops in the ocean. All it took was getting separated from my body to get an answer. Helene—and Rafael—gave me a gift. My big sister's *okay*.

"I'm afraid I don't know." Helene's voice reminds me I've zoned out. I blink, focusing on the present. "If she's here with you, it means there's something keeping her from moving on."

They're talking about me.

"Perhaps you must start there," she continues, leaning on her cane.

"How do we get her to *not* move on?" Rafael asks, his voice quiet. There's something else there, something I can't pick apart.

Helene's smile turns pensive. "Darlin', I wish I had an answer for you. The world can be hard and cruel, and although it feels like centuries that my old body's been on this earth, this is the first I've heard of a spirit stuck in between for so long. But I wonder . . ." She taps a red nail against her chin.

Rafael leans forward. I hold my breath.

This could be it. Our answer.

"Maybe she has some unfinished business. Something she didn't get closure on or something she's not quite ready to let go. That might be what's going to bring her back," Helene says.

"Unfinished business," Rafael repeats, focused on me. Like he's asking me.

I take a deep breath to keep the rush of anxiousness at bay.

Everything is unfinished.

"Unfortunately, I'm running late for brunch with a special someone, and I'm going to be uncharacteristically inhospitable and send you on your way," Helene says. We both look to her. She leans on her cane as she pushes to her feet. "But you come back, and I'll be happy to see if I can learn a little more. I do hope you understand."

"Of course," Rafael says. "Thank you so much for your time." He unfolds himself from the chair and sets the kitten down in his place. She stretches, purrs and settles back to sleep.

"She'll certainly be happy to see you back." Helene gestures to the kitten.

"I'll bring treats next time," Rafael says as he digs into his pocket and tugs out his wallet. "Please let me know how much I owe you." He leafs through the bills.

Helene sets a hand atop his. "No need for that, young man, but if you can manage to get a hold of that wonderful tequila of Lupe's and set it aside for the next time, we're even."

"It's a deal. Thank you."

Helene pats his arm before she hobbles toward me, passing me without so much as a twitch in my direction.

Rafael slows to a stop beside me, his eyes assessing in that disconcerting way of his. "Ready?"

I'm not, but I nod. A part of me wants to remain here and recount everything Helene told me about Annie. Another part knows I have to push forward and figure out how I'm going to stay here. *Hold on,* Annie said.

I glance around the room one last time before I follow Rafael out of the house and onto the lawn, taking a deep, deep breath when the sun hits my face. It's my Annie ritual. Whenever life goes "pear shaped" (Great-Aunt Julia's phrase) and I need Annie, I find her in sunshine. *I miss you,* I tell her. *And I'm going to figure this out.*

I feel Rafael beside me. "Listen, I'm so sorry. I didn't know that would be so . . ." he starts.

I spin, facing him. "It was everything," I say truthfully. Surprise—and maybe doubt—lights his eyes. I wouldn't have known about Annie without his stubbornness to stay here, but I can see he needs some convincing. "I'm serious." I hold up three fingers.

Rafael's lips quirk. "I know what it's like to lose someone you love, E, and I'm sorry you had to experience it." His honesty rattles me. I blink, unsure of what to make of it, of whatever is happening between us. Showing each other these parts of ourselves. Almost like we're *friends.*

You're not friends, Pre-Coma Evie pipes up. That's right. We're just partners with one mission: I get back to my life. He gets my promotion.

"Thanks." I clear my throat. "So, what's next?"

Rafael's quiet for a moment. *Not-friends don't look at each other the way he's looking at you,* Coma Evie adds. I suck in a shaky breath, because he *is* looking at me like he wants to make sure I'm okay. It only intensifies the sensation of not having enough oxygen.

"Depends on what you're up for," he says at last.

"Short of animal sacrifices, just about anything." I slowly release the bubble of air, eager to be back on normal Evie vs. Rafael ground.

"Okay, does that include deer? Because they're overpopulating Illinois, Michigan—"

"Rafael," I warn. "No."

"Kidding!" He holds up his hands in defense. "I'd prefer you don't haunt my bloodline!"

It gets tougher to not smile. "Do you have ideas that don't involve murdering animals?"

"Actually, yes." He lifts his phone. "Lupe wants to meet us at the hospital."

My anxiety rebels, but I manage a nod.

CHAPTER EIGHTEEN
TEN DAYS (AND A MEDIUM) AFTER

I hate hospitals. I've hated them for the last fifteen years, and I'll hate them for another hundred. Sure, good things happen here, but I've only ever associated hospitals with *bad*. Loss. Pain. Grief. All those things combined—and I'm not immune to them when the doors of Northwestern Memorial shut behind us. My chest tightens. My hands turn clammy. And suddenly, the thought of passing out doesn't seem entirely unfavorable.

Beside me, Rafael's seemingly unbothered, hands tucked into his jeans and his *hey there* smile at the ready for anyone who'll gaze his way. He wields it often as we make our way through the bustling corridors of the hospital, and I'm not excluded from his list of victims.

"Hey. You're looking a little green," Rafael says, his smile slipping from charming into something worse: concern (much like the look he had at Helene's).

"Conditions," I remind him, wishing he'd keep his eyes off his *invisible* companion, because they're doing something that's not helping with the mash-up of emotions I'm feeling.

A questioning look creases his stupidly handsome face, but he must remember the conditions because he turns away, heading straight for an elevator. A pretty nurse walks out, ogling him like he's steak when all she's had is hospital food. Rafael misses this entirely as he slips inside the ridiculously small space, waiting for me to follow. I stand rigidly to one side. His eyes catch mine as he leans over, brushing past me to press the button to the ninth floor. The doors close. My stomach churns.

"Whatever's got you looking a lot more *ghost* than usual, I don't have a backpack to sacrifice this time, E. Even if I did, I'm not sure I'd lend you my new one. I'm strangely attached to it."

I wheel on him, mortified that he's thinking about The Elevator Incident. That he still has the backpack I got him to replace the other. "You're *very* funny."

"Part of the package." As if trying to prove his point, his very masculine hand flexes. The kind of hand that could probably loosen knots from your shoulders or lift you up against an elevator wall.

And *ohmygod*, someone put me out of my misery.

Burning, I peer at the elevator ceiling. "If you're listening, I'm ready to come back now."

Rafael chuckles. "Not sure that's how it works."

"How *does* it work?"

He shrugs as the elevator lurches to a stop. "I don't think the Big Guy appreciates all the sarcasm." I catch Rafael's smirk before he slips out the doors. I follow, staring fiery daggers at his broad (and arrogant) back.

He had this exact view when he stole the Betton account, Pre-Coma Evie pipes up from nowhere. *Think about* that *when you're ogling his backside.*

The thought is immediately sobering.

I haven't processed the Annie thing or the unfinished-business thing, yet one part of me can't stop ruminating on the Lupe thing that she was going to share. I know I should trust

Rafael on this, but the fact that I don't know the entire truth bugs me. The thought of him sabotaging me hurts.

"Now I know something's up. You look like you guzzled a bottle of Dulcolax," he says, slowing in front of room 922, the room with the other half of me.

I twist my lips into a smile that feels brittle. "Not a fan of hospitals and not a fan of"—*seeing myself tied up to tubes,* I want to say—"being so completely at your mercy in there."

Rafael smirks, rubbing his palms together. "Oh, the possibilities."

Imagine yourself with shaved eyebrows or a buzz cut. Lots of possibilities. Pre-Coma Evie is relentless.

"Centuries of haunting," I parry, my stomach dipping despite the confidence of my words.

"Then I'll do my best to stay away from your hair." He winks, pushing the door open.

I steel myself and slip into the room first.

The room hits like a punch—bleak and sterile, all harsh light and humming machines. It screams *You shouldn't be here.* My gaze snags on the bed—stiff white sheets, too-still body. *Me.* My stomach coils.

I shrink back some more at the sight of a man in a black cloak beside the bed.

But Rafael is at my back, blocking the door—the only reason I don't immediately evacuate.

"Finally!" Lupe's voice makes me jump. She greets Rafael with a bright smile that matches the energy of her RBG tee and ripped jeans—a jarring splash of color and energy in the room. *Secrets, secrets, secrets* is the mantra pounding in my head as I look to the stranger in the room. My potential solution.

The man's face is lined with age, like the rest of him. He seems kind and welcoming. Or maybe that's part of the gig. He hovers at my bedside, a silver cross dangling from his neck.

"Hola, Rafael," he says.

"Padre, thanks for coming on such short notice," Rafael says, reaching over to shake the priest's hand.

"Of course," he says. "Lupe tells me she is a close friend."

"Yes," Rafael responds without hesitation. I'd be surprised if it weren't for the walls closing in. My chest tightens, each breath shallow and sharp. I press my fingers to my temples, but the pressure mounts, doing nothing to quell the rising tide of nausea and dread.

I feel like I'm going to pass out.

I need to get out. Now.

I retreat a step. Then another. I feel the chill of the door as I back through it, catching Rafael's gaze. His face crinkles in confusion. I don't stall—I disappear before he can ask me what's wrong or, worse yet, to stay. The hospital blurs as I rush through the stairwell door. Down the stairs. Out the door.

Outside, I take deep breaths, clutching my stomach to steady myself.

I know I'm a coward, but I just can't do it. Being in that room makes it real, makes me feel like I'm suffocating, and that can't be good for making sure this works.

Pacing the parking lot, I glance up at the place where I imagine my room is located, where I've left Rafael and Lupe to pray for me because maybe their prayers are better than mine.

I move my gaze beyond the hospital, shielding my eyes from the bright sun. Annie wants me to hold on, so I'll try it all. I dig deep, imagining the prayers working their magic from somewhere up above. Calling to me. Urging my spirit back where it belongs. And me finally waking up, returning to my regularly scheduled programming.

I close my eyes and think about Helene's words—*unfinished business.*

That could mean anything.

I'm almost thirty and have spent the better part of two decades running. From my past. From my mother. From grief. It's mostly *all* unfinished business.

"So, what is it?" I shout up at the sky. "How do I get back?"

A siren wails in the distance. I wait.

And then—as if divine intervention meets lightbulb moment—it hits me.

My bucket list.

I almost squeal.

Yes, yes, yes! That's *it*. The bucket list. The numerous items that I've collected over the last fifteen years. Hopes and dreams and aspirations of things I wanted to accomplish but never found the time for because there was always something more important. And maybe the Big Guy (or Gal) thought I needed a wake-up call to focus on the *other* stuff.

Maybe focusing on the bucket list is what will bring me back, because it's the one constant that's kept me pushing forward.

Excitement flutters through me, so strong. I'm convinced I'm back in my body.

I blink my eyes open.

But I'm not looking up at the hospital room ceiling tiles. It's Rafael.

He's close enough I can see the sun reflected in his eyes. A flare of disappointment douses some of my excitement, but I check it because I'm onto something and I feel better than I've felt all morning.

"Are you okay?" he asks, hands tucked in pockets. He scans me in that disconcerting way of his.

I don't look away. "Sorry I couldn't stay."

"I wouldn't have even been able to come through the hospital doors." There's no sarcasm in his tone, and it might be more debilitating than the look on his face. Because he's trying to make me feel better when I just left him to deal with my mess.

"Still, I don't . . . I just . . . Thank you." I hate being so completely at a loss. More than that, I don't completely resent that he's taking the lead. That I'm trusting him with this.

"No need to thank me, E. I haven't even done anything," Rafael says. I want to contradict him, but I have a sense I'll lose. "Father V said to keep praying, and I say we keep trying other ways as well. Because we're going to figure this out." Rafael's determined tone catches me off guard.

"You're a really good liar," I deadpan.

Rafael shrugs. "Father V's sermons dissuade any sort of fibbing."

I snort before I can catch myself. "I choked."

"You, on the other hand," he drawls, "are a *really* talented liar."

"Like I said, you have a lot to learn."

"Ah—yes, my *mentor*." Rafael grins, and I can't help but smile at the memory of the *Publicity Today* interview where I said as much.

Rafael's phone buzzes, and he digs into his pocket to silence it. *Secrets, secrets, secrets,* Pre-Coma Evie chants. I need her to stop.

"Is that Dana?" The question escapes my lips before I overthink it.

Rafael blinks. "Um. No."

"Because you can take the call, especially if it's work."

"I know."

"Okay."

"Okay."

We have a minute-long staring contest. *He's hiding something,* Pre-Coma Evie nudges me, and I might never have another chance to get to the truth. If I'm ever going to ask him, it's now. "How's work?"

Rafael hesitates. "Fine."

"Really? Because I haven't seen you go to the office at all, and the other day? Your niece said you weren't working."

Pre-Coma Evie jumps with glee. *Go, Evie, go!* And I push forward. "Are you hiding something? Because you can tell me if you got the promotion."

Rafael doesn't mask his surprise. "No! Is that what you think I'm hiding?"

His tone suggests I should probably find another answer, but I answer honestly. "Yes."

Rafael sighs with frustration, then drags his hands through his hair. "I wasn't promoted. In fact, I haven't been to the office in almost two weeks." He looks at me like he's begging me to *read the large print, Evie*, but I don't know what I'm supposed to be figuring out. Almost two weeks—

That's . . .

"You haven't been back since the accident?"

He swallows, his throat bobbing. "No."

Oh Mamma Mia. He's been out of the race for as long as I have.

Whatever he's hiding might . . . it might not have anything to do with Media Lab.

Take that. Coma Evie jabs her finger into Pre-Coma Evie's chest. *He hasn't been back at work.*

And if he hasn't been at work, he's been elsewhere. *Planning your demise.* Pre-Coma Evie props her fists on her hips. *He wanted to make sure he wasn't distracted.*

I force both voices from my mind, because I need to think clearly and piece it together already. I replay the conversation. Rafael hasn't returned to Media Lab since the accident. *Blame it on guilt,* Pre-Coma Evie says. *Guilt can get to a person.*

Does he look like he's guilty? Coma Evie, the one who notices his hands and muscles, offers. *Plus, look at those eyes. If anything, he was traumatized and needed time off.*

Rafael looks neither guilty nor traumatized. He looks *good.* Whatever his reasons for taking time off, it has nothing to do with me. *Nothing.*

No matter how much Pre-Coma Evie would like to convince me otherwise, I don't think Rafael has some elaborate plan to beat me while I'm down.

I let the realization settle.

Something stirs in my chest—tight and unfamiliar, like I'm expanding too fast from the inside out. It presses against my ribs, making it hard to breathe. Rafael watches me, and I will my outside to appear less vulnerable than my inside. "Rafael?"

"Evie?" He holds my gaze.

"I think I figured out my unfinished business."

CHAPTER NINETEEN
TEN DAYS AFTER (LATER THAT DAY)

There are secrets, and there are things I wouldn't admit out loud, not even to myself.

Like WWRD—*What would Rafael do?* It's a question I've asked myself more times than I care to count—whenever I've been stuck or stumped. Because (for better or worse) Rafael always has a way out of situations. A half-assed solution. A witty response. Whatever it is, I've never seen Rafael fall apart under pressure. I both hate and admire that about him. While I'd never, *ever* admit to using him as a way to motivate myself, it has often helped.

And now, with time pressing so crushingly against my spirit—literal and figurative—and a bucket list that might be my way back into my body, I ask myself: *WWRD?*

Would he hand his nemesis his deepest, most secret dreams and wishes?

Would he put himself out there if it meant getting back to his life?

I think *yes.* Hell yes.

So I blame *WWRD* for bringing us to my apartment. More specifically, my kitchen, where Rafael's ordered himself a large deep-dish pizza and a bucket of wings. He's halfway through his second slice when he asks, "So? Plan on telling me your *why* anytime soon?"

No! Yes!

My stomach knots the more I think about telling him about the bucket list. He'll probably think it's silly or stupid—likely both. Or maybe that I'm wrong . . . because I don't know for *sure* that the bucket list is my unfinished business. It could have been the sun searing my brain cells and playing tricks on my mind, making me feel like I was onto something and . . .

"I can practically see the fumes coming out of your ears," Rafael says, stopping midchew. "Whatever's got you looking like you're trying to solve an episode of *Black Mirror*, get it out, E."

I think about chickening out, but *he* wouldn't.

I take a deep breath.

Time to WWRD.

I start. "Before I get to the details, I was wondering if our roles were reversed and you hadn't gotten to all the things you wanted to do and had a few days left to figure it out . . ."

Rafael goes still, making me wonder if the pizza has lodged itself in his throat. "You don't know that." His hard tone makes my chest feel too tight again. I press my hand to the place between my ribs, where the pressure is the strongest, and I'm wondering if it's a heart issue and not a head issue I've suffered.

"Well, I don't know anything for sure," I clarify, "But what I want to know is—what would Rafael do? In my place?" It feels strange to speak *WWRD* aloud when it's only been something I've kept to myself, but I can't take it back, nor do I want to. "If you were in my shoes, what would you be doing with the time you had left?"

Rafael sets the rest of the slice on a plate and leans forward, a faint smile playing on his lips. "If you must know what I'd be doing, I'd probably spend it at Abuela's house. The backyard, food for days, and the family going about their day." He shrugs. "Can't ask for more."

I can imagine it clearly, and I can't think of anything more fitting than being surrounded by loved ones. Like Gemma and Cristina. But if it comes to it, I don't know if I'd want them there with me at the very end. I remember what it was like to say goodbye to Annie. The ache that follows feels old, yet still sharp.

"That's how I'd do it because I'm completely lazy, and I can't be bothered to do more than the bare minimum," he adds, stretching his arms. "But you—you're doing the right things. In no time, we're going to figure this out so you can get to your planner and that list of things in the back."

I blink, shocked. "You snooped in my planner?"

"You tricked me into giving up doughnuts for a *month*."

Oh God. I don't know which is worse—him going through my planner or him thinking the two are remotely on equal playing fields. I laugh, surprising Rafael. Surprising myself. "You're . . ." I begin.

"Dashing?"

"Dastardly."

"I take it that means charming."

"If you're the devil."

"Which you've established when you insinuated you were in hell."

"Well, this most certainly isn't heaven," I quip. Secrets would be sacred in heaven, as would hopes and dreams and several items on my bucket list. That he's seen. *Visit Skopelos, Greece. Sleep under the stars.* Or #44, *Join the mile-high club* (one of two items added by Gemma).

And he's seen them all. I groan into my palms, thinking of him leafing through my planner, reading through the last five pages of items.

"I've seen it already, and there's no reason to work yourself up over it," Rafael says. "There's some good stuff in there. Get a tattoo? Volunteer at a theater? Date someone for longer than one year? You've covered lots of bases."

"I'm going to kill you," I growl, low in my throat.

He chews, swallows, then picks up a chicken wing and dips it into a container of ranch. "Speaking of which, how long *has* your longest relationship been?"

"Not sure how that's any of your business," I huff, pacing the floor of my dining room while he takes a bite of his wing. I hope he doesn't choke on a bone. "And it's off-topic."

"You asked me 'What would Rafael do?' And what I would do is answer this question." His eyes gleam with mischief, and it makes me wish I'd never had such an idiotic idea.

Note to self: *WWRD* works only in my head.

"How about this: You show me yours and I show you mine?" He waggles his dark brows, lips curled in a sly smile.

I level him with a look. "What—are we in high school?"

Rafael leans forward, his elbows braced on the marble countertop. "Is Evie Pope backing down from a challenge?" he goads, demonstrating what happens when someone has intimate knowledge of what makes you tick and go *boom*.

I shouldn't play along, but part of me is curious and the other part is comatose. Also, *WWRD?*

"Six months," I say, my words clipped.

Rafael's eyes bulge. "Who? Chip?"

My jaw literally drops. "You know about Chip?"

He nods. "And Theo . . . and the athlete . . ." With each name, my mouth gapes, but Rafael? He's in his zone. "Gotta love open-concept office space. And what kind of name is Chip?"

I've questioned it myself, but he doesn't need to know.

I lean forward, brow arched. "All right then, Raffy Taffy, what about you? How long were you a one-woman man? Two days? A week?"

He presses a hand to his chest. "Shit. Do you really think I'm a playboy or something?" He pretend-pouts, then holds up three fingers.

"Three hours?" I ask.

He chuckles. "Three *years*. You can add that to your list of All Things Rafael, por favor."

I'm almost speechless. "No."

"*Yes!*"

"With a human woman?"

Rafael scowls, but his lips twitch with the effort. Whatever he's about to say is going to be ridiculous. "Yes, a *human* woman. Phantom women weren't yet in the picture."

I roll my eyes, biting back a smile. "So, what happened?"

"There was an accident, and here you are."

A growl crawls up my throat. "With the girlfriend!"

"Last I heard, she was married with twins and a doting husband."

"Rafael."

"Okay, okay!" He holds up his hands in mock surrender. "She broke up with me."

"Let me guess—commitment issues?"

He scowls playfully, then sobers. "No—because I was distracted."

"By work?"

There's another shift in the muscles of his face, and I try to figure out what it means. His features smooth out too quickly for me to piece it together. "It was work related."

I watch him for a second longer, trying to draw out the entire truth, but he doesn't give me much more. "Intriguing."

"Which part?" He reaches for another chicken wing.

"Three years is a long time." I try to think back to when that would have been. I don't remember Rafael being in a long-term relationship while at Media Lab. In fact—before the betrayal—he didn't mention a girlfriend, and afterward, any morsel tied to his love life was a result of hearing it from others or having Gemma stalk his social media. For intel, of course.

"I was young and so was she. We grew apart." He shrugs as if he hasn't just offered me a glimpse into an entire chunk of his life during which he was involved with a woman—in a committed relationship. I have several hundred questions I want to ask and answers I want to tuck away for the futu—

A stab of panic pierces my interrogation bubble when I think about the future.

"What about you? What happened?" Rafael's question draws my attention back to him.

I try to form a response. Late nights and work-laden weekends. Promotions to chase. A rival to keep at bay. I consider lying to keep him from seeing how pathetic I am, but he's shown me his. I have no choice but to say, "Work."

"They must not have been worth it, then," he says casually.

I frown. "Explain."

He rests an arm over the back of the chair. "Believe it or not, I know a thing or two about you, and you would have found a way to pencil in someone worth your time."

My instinct when it comes to Rafael is to argue with everything he says. This time, I think about it first. Would I have made time for someone worth it? I think of Theo and his passion for cooking. Trevor and his dream to be in the NBA Hall of Fame. Chip and his ambition to one day be a published writer. And then it hits me: I chose men who were just as distracted as I was. Who wanted something more than we wanted each other.

I think Rafael is right.

He smiles knowingly.

I scowl. He knows too much, more than I give him credit for.

"So, are you going to tell me your unfinished business now?" he asks. The change is abrupt . . . and I know I can't put this off forever, not if we want time to test my theory.

"I think my bucket list—*the one you already know about*—might be tied to why I'm here," I say, needing to get through this part before I start thinking about all the items on there and chickening out. "There are things on there I never got to do . . ." Like all of them except five or so. "And maybe that's the *why* I'm here. I had planned to get to it, immediately after the . . ." Promotion. "OhLaLove stuff."

I've revealed more than I intended, and I feel the sudden urge to take it back and hide.

"What's first?" The earnestness in his tone matches the warmth in his gaze—heat that somehow travels the space between us and sets up camp in my cheeks and chest.

"Um." I yank my thoughts back to the bucket list. "Try caviar. Take professional dance lessons. Swim in the Pacific." I'm going through the easier items on the list, but the more I run through it, the less of it I realize I can do in this form. Like, almost none.

Panic severs upward, making me feel hot and cold. I clench my hands into fists and swallow.

"Hey—" Rafael's beside me. In front of me. His eyes scan me. "Whatever is going on in that head of yours, don't listen to it."

I nod, unable to talk.

"We'll tackle the list together. We'll get creative, whatever it takes to make it happen," he says, like he has front-row tickets to my deepest thoughts. I imagine Rafael doing things from the list. The number of water-related items he wouldn't attempt with a ten-foot pole.

"You might be afraid of half of the things on there," I say, some of the sharpness dulling at the thought of Rafael doing item #86: *Jet Skiing.*

"All the more reason for you to *want* to do them," he says, grinning in a way that makes me want to believe we can make this work.

"There will be water, and there will be dancing," I warn.

Rafael swallows, then pastes a courageous smile on his face. "As long as they're not happening at the same time, I might survive."

"And if you don't, I'm keeping things warm on this side," I say, patting the seat beside mine.

Despite the levity in my voice, he sobers a little. "You're not staying on that side, because someone is going to pray so hard you're going to wake up before they say *amen*, and if that doesn't work, I think you have skydiving on your list—maybe that'll pop your spirit immediately back into your body." He slaps his hands together and mimics an explosion. "Boom!"

I grin, some of his enthusiasm rubbing off on me despite one last thing I didn't yet ask. Because most things come at a price. "Okay . . . so what's this going to cost me?"

He leans forward, hands splayed against the table, his face suddenly so serious my breath catches.

His intensity paralyzes me, especially when it settles on my lips. "A kiss."

A breath puffs out of me as I die a little more. "A kiss?"

Rafael's dark eyes meet mine. "Yes." Heat burns through the synapses that ensure I'm breathing. "In the rain, of course."

I open my mouth to say something. Anything. He wants to kiss, in the rain. He's gone mad.

"In case you need someone to help you with the bucket list after we figure this out." There's a dare in his eyes.

And it clicks. Number 38. *Kiss in the rain.*

I can't tell if he's joking or serious, but I know I'm dangerously close to passing out.

He's toying with me.

Evie vs. Rafael.

I force a laugh that sounds like I'm choking. "I don't think I'll need help with that," I say, playing along. "But it's nice of you to offer, Raffy Taffy. I'm sure there's a fan club on standby."

His grin doesn't slip, but something in his eyes shifts. Like maybe it isn't a joke. Like maybe I'm missing something. "Well, then, I'm happy to help you with the Spanish lessons," he says.

I swallow, hating that I don't know if I turned down the promise of a future kiss.

CHAPTER TWENTY
ELEVEN DAYS AFTER

We don't immediately get to the bucket list, because a shaman is coming to my apartment.

Lupe found Doug on a website. Which possibly accounts for why he arrived ten minutes late, looking like the lone survivor of a postapocalyptic wasteland with his sun-bleached dreadlocks, wool poncho, cowboy boots, and a faded JanSport backpack. He's singing a country song as he sets candles around my living room while Rafael and Lupe crowd beside an armchair, close enough that I can hear them whispering (or rather, whisper-yelling).

"He doesn't look like a *shaman*," Rafael says, the muscle in his cheek vibrating with frustration. "Where did you find him?"

Lupe, dressed in jean shorts and a Barbie tee, shrugs. "Website. One with reviews."

"Did Doug score above a point-five?"

"*Three*-point-five, and most points were knocked off for . . . *odor*." Lupe lowers her voice saying the last part.

Rafael visibly cringes, then curses. "I should have done it myself."

"Don't judge a book by its cover, primo."

Doug pauses, throwing a thumbs-up in their direction. "Good energy, fam," he says. I can't help but laugh at his totally inaccurate assessment about what's happening on this side of my living room.

Rafael scowls at his cousin, but Lupe's unbothered, watching Doug as he finishes with the candles and lights up incense, coaxing the smoke with his hand.

"You sure that's allowed in a multi-residential building?" Rafael eyes the candles warily.

Lupe glares at him and tuts. "Allowances are made for religious folks."

"Religio—" Rafael cuts a gaze up to the ceiling and mutters a string of Spanish. Lupe elbows him in the ribs when Doug looks at them.

"All right, now the incense is burning . . . and we can get started," he says.

"How does this work, Doug?" Lupe gestures to the coffee table, where a makeshift shrine has been set up. A photo of me on my first day at Media Lab. My planner. My favorite sneakers. And a vinyl of ABBA's greatest hits.

Rafael finds my eyes and whispers, "I'm sorry—I didn't think she'd find some guy on Craigslist."

"I mean, it could be worse," I say as Doug scratches at his clumps of hair, which has been chopped to different lengths. "He could be naked."

Rafael's frown splits into a small smile. "I'll make Lupe get him out of here."

"No, you won't," Lupe says without sparing Rafael a glance.

"All right, fam, I will need silence." Doug's voice becomes quieter. Incense wafts into the air, and I wonder how long it will be until a smoke alarm goes off. "Come closer." Doug's looking at Rafael. The way his jaw twitches tells me he's moved from level-four my-blood-pressure-is-spiking to level-six someone-get-my-blood-pressure-pills.

Rafael reluctantly inches forward, his eyes connecting with mine. It's as if time slows, long enough for me to notice the flecks of gold in his dark irises, the fine wrinkles in the corners of his eyes and around his full lips, lips which were only inches from mine last night. I warm at the memory—how he wanted me to promise him a kiss and how utterly and irrefutably I regret not saying yes.

I watch him as he joins Lupe and Doug around the table, feeling thirsty for something I shouldn't want. Yet I can't help but wonder . . . what if I'd said yes? What if after this was all said and done—and we found a way to fix me—I asked for that kiss and it wasn't a joke? What if I had a chance to answer a question I only started asking?

"So, what's next? Do we hold hands and sing 'Kumbaya'?" Rafael asks. He earns a belly laugh from Doug.

"You're a funny man, my man, but there will be no singing," Doug says. "All I ask is that you keep silent as I attempt to connect with the energy around us and see if I can find hers."

Energy? Rafael mouths to Lupe, his eyes wide with irritation.

Lupe swats at his shoulder. "Shhhh!"

All eyes are on Doug. He's lit enough candles to hold a séance, which I suppose would be appropriate. If I were dead.

"Spirit of Evie . . ." Doug says, his eyes closed and hands crisscrossing over the table. "It is I, Doug, and I ask you to kindly give me a sign that you're still tied to this place." The room is quiet. "Don't be afraid."

Doug's lips move, and his face pinches in concentration.

Thump, thump, thump.

The incense makes my headache suddenly intense. A wave of nausea follows.

"I'm getting something, fam," Doug says, his eyes still closed.

Thump, thump, thump.

"Tell us," Lupe says, leaning in, almost as if she's buying it.

Doug shimmies and shakes invisible maracas. "She's a sassy one, this one." I think he means *skeptical.* "But I like a woman with a personality."

"All right, I think we've heard enough . . ." Rafael leans over to blow out a candle.

Lupe grabs his arm and tugs him back. "Stay."

"Hmmm. There's more," Doug mumbles. "She's a tough one to read. Sassy *and* stubborn."

"Are you sure you're not talking about Lupe?" Rafael glares at his cousin, who digs her fingers into his arm. "Ah! Mierda!"

"No, no, fam. This is different." Doug is oblivious to the bickering cousins. "There's some strong energy keeping me from fully accessing her energy." His face crinkles in confusion. "It's almost like there's another energy, something bigger and stronger. It's shared between two people in this room." Doug shakes his head. "It makes it tough for me to full access hers."

"When you say *shared* energy, do you mean cousin-to-cousin stuff?" Lupe asks. Rafael tries to pull away, but she digs her fingers in. He winces and stays put.

Doug frowns. "Could be . . . but it's almost like this energy is giving me romantic vibes. That's not to say—different strokes for different folks, fam, so if you're into—"

"No!" both Rafael and Lupe shout, startling Doug and me.

"Sorry, fam, didn't mean to offend," Doug says, turning back to the shrine. "It's crazy. This energy is almost all-consuming in its intensity, and it goes way back. Like it's built up over the years."

He could be talking about Rafael and me. We've definitely shared plenty of all-consuming, intense feelings over the years. Nothing I would call *romantic.* Not even close.

The warmth and fullness I've felt these last few days, though, would disagree. My gaze gravitates to Rafael's back, the T-shirt clinging to his lean muscles like a second skin. An answering throb in my chest convinces me that this is a symptom of my condition and not being fully myself these days.

As if he can feel my gaze, Rafael's eyes drift to me. My stomach somersaults at the way he checks in—like to make sure I'm okay. I swallow past the embarrassment at having been caught staring and shoot him a thumbs-up. *Everything is fine,* it says. Totally and completely fine.

"Lots of good energy here, and that energy is strong enough to keep her here." Doug's eyes snap open. "In other words, don't lose hope, fam, because she's hanging on."

Lupe drops her hand from Rafael's arm. "Good! Did you hear that, primo?"

"When I can think past the pain," Rafael says, rubbing his arm.

"All will be well, my man," Doug offers, beginning to blow out the candles. He tosses them back into his backpack as he goes. "Sometimes, if you believe it'll happen, it will."

"I believe this was a mistake," Rafael hisses in his cousin's ear.

"Don't be a cranky pendejo, Raffi," Lupe chides. A vein throbs along the length of Rafael's neck.

When he turns to me, his grin is apologetic. "I'm sorry for putting you through that. Lupe is going to pay for it," he assures me.

I think of how she gets under his skin, and I shrug. "Lupe's doing great."

Rafael's eyes widen. "Were you not here for the last ten minutes?"

"Technically, no."

"That's not what—"

"It's cool that you're talking to her, my man," Doug says, appearing beside Rafael. Rafael tenses immediately. "Lean into that connection. That bond is special, and it can bring her back."

I bite back another smile as Rafael's jaw clenches. He spins around to face Doug, who is unbothered and unaware that

Rafael has glided into level-seven someone-give-this-man-a-joint territory (which—not to judge a book by its cover—I'm convinced Doug would readily supply Rafael).

Doug holds up a card. "Here, call me anytime."

Rafael eyes the card like it's lit on fire. "You're a *psychic*?"

Lupe snatches it from Doug's hand like she's confiscating contraband. "Thanks, Doug! This was great. Super helpful." She purposely ignores Rafael's death glare as she wedges herself between the two men and begins to rifle through her purse. "Now, let's get this man paid." She tugs out a wallet and hands Doug several bills. "This should do it."

He shoves them into his pocket without counting. "Right on, fam," he says, bringing his hands together. "Thank you for allowing me to be part of your journey." He glances at my shrine. "And hers."

"Thank you, Doug. I'll see you out," Lupe says, escorting him out of my apartment with a pointed look in Rafael's direction. Oblivious, Doug looks back.

I catch his gaze—it snags on mine—and he winks. Right. At. Me.

Lupe tugs him out the door before I can process it. My mouth hangs open as I watch the door shut behind them. *Ohmygod.*

"I didn't think that was going to be such a dumpster fire. I'm sorry," Rafael says, shaking his head in dismay. "Lupe can be so . . . disconnected . . . sometimes, but it's from a good place."

I nod, speechless. I think Doug saw me . . . or maybe I imagined it.

"Hey, you okay?" Rafael asks.

"Uh. Yeah." I shake off the preposterous notion. If Doug saw me, that would mean he isn't a phony, that he wasn't messing around, that he was maybe telling us the truth. I rewind the last fifteen minutes.

What was it he said?

Something about strong energies keeping me here?

Romantic energies—is that what I'm putting out into the energy-verse?

Oh *God*.

Am I into Rafael?

No. I can't be. I mean, am I a little distracted by his dimple and smiles? Yes. Do his hands do something to my imagination? Also yes. Would I like for them to do something to me? Certainly.

Okay, so it's lust. I'm lusting for Rafael, my archnemesis, the person I've imagined in various states of begging on his knees for my forgiveness and for my help. And now, when I imagine him on his knees—

"Evie." Rafael's concerned voice jerks my attention from the deepest recesses of hell.

Fire licks up my face, and I press a hand to a cheek.

His features crinkle in concern. "You sure you're okay?"

I nod, my throat too parched to talk.

"Are you sure? You look a little flushed," he says, and his hand moves through the air as if he wants to make sure. It stalls between us. I stare at his hand, the one that could easily knead away all kinds of aches.

"Oh," I croak. "Must be all the candles."

His frown remains as his hand drops.

I find myself missing a touch that hasn't happened.

Rafael sighs. "I'm sorry about Doug. I'll make sure to leave a review." He digs his hands into his pockets. "But enough about Doug. Let's get to that bucket list, shall we?"

"I thought you'd never ask," I say, my voice a little breathy.

CHAPTER TWENTY-ONE
ELEVEN DAYS AFTER, PART II

To be Vela'd is to fall victim to Rafael's charm. I've seen everyone, from the stalwart CEO of a billion-dollar pharmaceutical company to a shy DoorDash delivery boy, go googly-eyes for Rafael, and all it took was a flash of The Dimple or one of those husky chuckles.

Rafael knows exactly what weapons he has in his charm arsenal—*charmsenal*—and he's not afraid to use them.

Which is how we're standing inside the gym of the Norwood Park Senior Center, waiting for the 1:30 PM Latin dancing class with Alma Cabal to start. Bucket list item #14: *Take professional dance lessons* (and not one of those I discovered on YouTube).

It would take most people at least twenty-four hours to plan it, but not Rafael. In less than an hour, he managed to get the name of a friend from his grandmother and drive us twenty minutes north of downtown (minimal car sickness included).

Not long after stepping into the gym, he was greeted by the dance instructor. Alma, a lithe sixty-something Puerto Rican woman, whose big hair is pulled up into a ponytail and whose eye makeup is something out of a TikTok tutorial, didn't blink when Rafael walked into the center and told her he wanted to try one of her classes.

And here we are in a dance studio that—between peeling walls and a water-stained ceiling—has seen better days, but none of the students filling the room seem to mind. They're chattering excitedly as they find their places around the room, their energy palpable. Something I wouldn't have imagined, given everyone is over the age of sixty-five. Everyone except Rafael.

I'm standing off to the side, beneath an open window, catching bits of conversations about grandchildren and recitals, retirement trips and bridge clubs. Rafael hasn't moved from where a group of ladies swarmed him upon entering. They've been pinching and patting him since, oohing and aahing at whatever he's been telling them. And I bet it has nothing to do with grandchildren or bridge games.

He tried to extricate himself from their manicured hands, which only resulted in them holding on even longer and tighter. So he's offered me several apologetic smiles and shrugs, but I've been enjoying every minute of it, and we haven't even started the class.

"All right, everybody!" Alma's voice echoes off the yellowing walls. She claps her hands, then raises her voice. "We're going to start!" Some seniors snap to attention; others continue to chat away until they're nudged by their friends, who shush them and point in Alma's direction.

Alma sashays across the room in her spandex-and-lace ensemble, headed for Rafael. The chittering ladies part around him, reluctant to give Alma the space. She swats at a grabby hand and tugs Rafael to her side. "We have a guest with us today."

"And what a handsome guest," chimes one of the women, teetering on shiny kitten heels despite her body being curved by age. She squeezes Rafael's bicep with a waggle of her silver eyebrows, and I almost snort-laugh out loud. Rafael smiles between the two women.

"Martha, you wouldn't want to make Horace jealous," Alma says, shooing Martha toward an older man who's dozing and drooling on a bench in the corner. This time the laugh snorts out of me, and I cover my mouth, catching Rafael's attention. He winks. My heart spins and dips in response.

Alma, undeterred by her unruly audience, continues. "This is Rafael, and he is here for a lesson because he is trying to impress a lady."

"*Oo-oo-ooh.*"

"*Aaaah.*"

Rafael looks meaningfully at me, and because I left my better judgment at the hospital, I blush and glance from him to Alma, who is a head shorter but no less imposing with her arched posture and intense gaze. Must be something in their Latin blood, I'm sure.

"And because of that, mis amigos, we are going to do one of my favorite dances today . . ." She pauses for effect. The room goes quiet for a moment, save for the whirring of the ancient fans hanging from the equally ancient ceiling tiles. "The tango!"

"*Oo-oo-ooh.*"

"*Aaaah.*"

Hands clap loudly. Horace startles awake.

"Now, everyone, partner up!" At her command, the swarm of seniors detach from Rafael and listen to their instructor. They find their partners, some in walkers and others in orthopedic footwear, leaving him alone at the center of the room. Unbothered by the fact that he's on his own, that his doting fans have abandoned him, Rafael brushes his unruly hair off his forehead and straightens his shoulders.

Even in jeans and a tee, Rafael's allure defies clothing. It's unfair, really. Worse yet, I've seen him without it, and it's the *last* thing I should be thinking about, because Rafael is staring at me.

And beckoning me with the crook of his finger.

Mortified, I shake my head. No. Absolutely not. There's no way I can be near him now, not when my chest feels like a furnace burning at max temp.

Come here, he mouths.

I shake my head again and snap my gaze elsewhere. To safer things. Like the couple in the corner, their matching outfits enough to make me believe in love eternal. The wife leans her head on her partner's chest, and he begins to sway, dancing to some silent song.

A clap of Alma's hands breaks the moment. Music starts, swelling through the room, and I chance a look back . . .

Alma and Rafael stand at the center of the room. Everyone else has paired up.

"It's time to get started," Alma announces. "Rafael will join those of you practicing the leader's parts, and I will partner with him as soon as I make sure you are all doing what you are supposed to be doing." She pats his back and begins to wind through the group, adjusting couples' limbs. A hand here. A foot there. Heads tilted just so.

"The tango is a dance about love . . ." she says, instructing a couple to lock eyes. "And intimacy." She encourages another pair to pull closer. "And it is my favorite, because it is muy sensual!" She nudges a couple closer together until their bodies touch.

The tempo picks up.

Martha leans into Horace, who wraps her in his arms. She peers up at him, murmuring something that makes him stroke slow, soothing circles along her back. My chest tightens, squeezing out the air and any illusion that I'm fine. Because I may never have that.

"You're a terrible listener, E." The whisper is warm against my skin, sending a jolt down my spine.

I turn sharply, my pulse skyrocketing. Rafael is right beside me, close enough that I can almost feel his breath ghosting across my cheek, the heat of his body seeping into mine. A trick of the mind. Because I can't feel *him*. Not in any way that matters.

And yet . . . I imagine I could—the way his palm would settle at my lower back. The way his fingers might graze my arm. The way his body would line up along mine. The way our bodies might fall into rhythm, step for step. I know it's impossible—

"Evie?"

I blink the terrible fantasy away. Like I said, I left my better judgment elsewhere.

"Rafael?" I fold my arms, needing protection. "I'm not doing this," I add.

He quirks a brow.

I take a tentative step backward. He follows.

The music turns up, the beat thrumming along to my erratic pulse. Around us, couples start moving to Alma's instruction. "Slow, slow, quick quick slow." Some listen; some dance to their own beat and rhythm, holding on to their partners.

"I'm not dancing," I repeat, eyeing the dancers.

"You are," he says.

I catch myself swaying and stop. Meet his gaze. Frown. "You're breaking the conditions by talking to me."

Rafael leans in slightly, a ridiculously thin sliver of space between us. "Coward."

I grind my teeth, willing myself to resist the bait, to ignore the buildup of pressure that's making it hard to do things like breathe and make sound decisions. I should refuse. But his gaze is a dare—and whatever hold I typically had in my *human* form has . . . disappeared.

"Fine," I breathe, closing the space between us.

Rafael's lips pull apart into a smug grin as his left arm moves up and his other curves around my hip, close enough he's almost touching me. Almost. And somehow, the *almost* is worse.

"Ready?" he asks.

I nod, because I think speaking would betray my new yet undiagnosed heart condition.

Following his lead, I move with him. Three steps backward, one to the left—and repeat. The steps are simple. Nothing else is.

With only a sliver of space separating us, I can feel the heat of him everywhere, his hand on my back, along the length of my body, in places he doesn't need to touch. It's hard to not think about the way he might feel. Warm and solid.

Rafael smiles at the couples around us without missing a beat or a step, effortless in his ability to be with them *and* me.

"I didn't know you could dance," I say as we spin and transition into the basic steps of the tango, needing to distract myself from my fantasies.

"You didn't ask." Rafael's intent gaze turns to me. I become waffle batter beneath his dark gaze.

"Any other secret talents?" We turn, dancing toward a corner, his back to the room. His eyes trace the lines of my face, which only succeeds in making me feel like I've been smushed inside a life-size waffle maker.

"I know the words to most Disney songs. I flunked tenth-grade chemistry." Rafael moves like he idolized Patrick Swayze growing up while I'm torn between counting steps and the beauty marks along the length of his neck. "And I can talk to spirits," he adds.

I roll my eyes. "Sweet-talking others isn't making the list?"

"You said *secret* talents." He winks. My heart staccatos, matching the thumping beat of the song.

"Bravo, Rafael! You are a natural, even on your own!" Alma appears beside Rafael, clapping loudly.

I jump away as she replaces me, her hands curving around his shoulders. His arm wraps around her waist, pulling her close, making me feel a pang of an emotion I refuse to acknowledge. Rafael's gaze connects with mine, his lips move, but Alma whips him away before I can decipher whatever he's mouthing. They move to the other side of the room as she projects her voice. "Now, for the next part of the dance, we are going to focus on spinning our partners."

I stare in awe as Rafael turns, then dips her in one smooth movement. Martha clutches her pearls. Alma smiles with pride. The audience oohs and aahs and claps. I join them, smiling from my corner of the dance floor. There's clearly more in his charmsenal than even I know about.

The lesson continues, and I stick to my corner, where I dance on my own.

But for once in a *really* long time, I don't feel quite so lonely.

* * *

Not for the first time, I think I made a mistake asking Rafael to do the bucket list. Even though I had more fun than I've had in a while, I'm not so sure it's working . . . but it is succeeding in making me feel even more desperate to figure this out.

The lesson was far from what I imagined when I penned *take professional dance lessons*, but in the best way. There was something special about being surrounded by couples who were so wholly absorbed in one another instead of their phones and social media accounts. There was so much life in that room that for the span of sixty minutes, I felt almost alive again.

All because of Rafael, who forced me to practice along with Alma and snuck in another dance between wicked winks and secret smiles. Who roped his cousin into this whole chaotic mission to "fix" me. Who Vela'd me into tackling more of the bucket list, including beginner Spanish lessons. We covered numbers, colors, and basic greetings. He praised my pronunciation. I asked him to repeat the words where he rolls his *r*'s. *Tres. Miercoles. Yo quiero.*

And then he left me to get takeout.

I'm sitting at his dining table, alone for the first time in days—and the quiet taunts me, giving my thoughts space to play a game of tug-of-war. Part of me can't stop thinking about today, and the other can't stop thinking about two days from now, when I'll be moved to a care facility. One of the best days of my life pitted against what will arguably be one of the worst . . . if I even make it that long. The dull pain at the base of my skull doesn't make me feel warm and fuzzy about my prospects, which only makes me question if the bucket list is the answer. If I'm focusing on the right *unfinished business.*

The not-knowing sharpens the pain, sends it shooting down into my chest.

With a groan, I drop my head into my hands, my eyes locking in on the chaos atop Rafael's table.

A familiar image stares up at me. The skull with the finger to its lips, the words *La Clandestina* written beneath it. The logo is plastered on more of the documents on the table. Presentations. Budgets. Sketches of blueprints.

I recognize the chicken-scratch writing as Rafael's. Squinting, I try to make sense of it. The words take shape. *The Secret's Inside. Take this secret to your grave.* Taglines.

The physical pain twists into something much worse. I don't need to scan more of the documents to know these are part of a business plan. The marketing proposal. Social media plans. Even local ad placements. I recognize the templates he's using because they happen to be ones I created for Media Lab. This is one of Rafael's accounts.

My headache turns dizzying.

He said he hadn't been to work, but that doesn't mean he hasn't been working. I know that game; I perfected it. Working on weekends and days off, like a virus I couldn't kick, and it looks like I wasn't the only one infected. I'd be lying if I said I wasn't surprised. One, because Rafael doesn't go out of his way to bring work home. And two, because he fooled me again when he said he wasn't working.

Pre-Coma Evie would be shifting through the papers, trying to figure out if the account is up for grabs, if I can snatch it from his hands. But Coma Evie, this ghost me who has seen a different side of Rafael, who has blush-inducing, heart-stopping thoughts of his fingers trailing against my skin, caressing and lighting me on fire—well, that version of me is unsure how to feel about him hiding this.

I shouldn't care.

I *don't* care.

In fact, I promised to help him with Dana and the promotion when this all started, and we haven't even talked about it. I know I should be grateful, but if Rafael hasn't brought it up, it means he might not actually need me to help him, and while he's not entirely wrong, it can only mean he doesn't trust me. And if he doesn't trust me, it can only mean nothing's changed for him.

I feel like I'm going to be sick.

What if it's only me feeling these strange symptoms? The pressure. The inability to stay focused and in control and in rival mode. What if this is only one sided and I've been spilling my guts to him while he's been . . . *Vela*-ing me?

Oh God.

I'm a walking bundle of anxiousness when Rafael returns twelve minutes later, a plastic bag of Tham's Thai in one hand—a very late lunch—and a six-pack of beer in the other. "What's wrong?" he asks, his brow creasing as he sets the beers on the table and runs into the kitchen to wash his hands.

"Nothing," I say, the tightness in my chest disagreeing. "I mean, besides the obvious."

Rafael watches me as he returns to the dining table, shoves the papers aside, and begins to remove the food containers from the bag, enough to feed an entire family. He opens the lids, licking the sauce from his fingers as he goes. While I haven't felt hungry in as long as I've been a spirit, I feel pangs for something that has nothing to do with the noodles and everything to do with the man eating them.

"Something's bugging you." He settles into his chair, choosing one of the containers.

"Is it?" I ask, clearing my throat. My anxiety crackles.

"You tell me." Rafael twists a fork into his carton of pad thai and takes a bite, sighing with pleasure.

I stall my pacing, long enough to watch him lick the sauce from his lips.

"Evie?"

I mentally kick myself for getting distracted, which is precisely my problem. I'm getting distracted by *him* when I should be getting answers.

"I know about La Clandestina," I say, a little too forcefully. Rafael chokes on his food. "You don't have to lie or hide or anything. It's all there . . . in my templates." I gesture to the paperwork he shoved to the end of the table. "I realize you don't have any reason to trust me, but you don't have to hide your accounts. I mean, would it have pissed me off before? Sure. But now . . . we've spent the last few days basically connected to one another, so I thought that perhaps you would maybe . . ." I didn't think I would do such a terrible job of getting everything out, but I'm surprising even myself. "What I mean is that as reformed rivals, you could've felt comfortable telling me about it."

Rafael sets his fork back in the carton. "Is that right?"

I shrug, increasingly unsure about going down this path, maybe discovering that he's still very firmly planted in Evie vs. Rafael territory when I'm . . . *not.*

Somehow—terrifyingly—he's managed to throw me so far off familiar ground these last few days that my checklists will need checklists to get me back on track. But Rafael? He seems *fine*—more than fine.

I can't dwell on it. I won't.

"I mean, I get it—why you didn't want to say anything—but I can't steal an account from you like this, Raf." I gesture helplessly to plasma me, chuckle awkwardly, and wish I could disappear when he doesn't respond.

The chairs scrapes against the floor as Rafael pushes from the table, circles around it, and stands so close we're sharing the same air. I swallow, peering up into his too-intense eyes.

"Evie," he says, my name on his lips like the roll of thunder on a summer night.

I need to hold on to something, because the way he's looking at me makes me feel even more unsteady.

I press my hands together instead. "Rafael."

"It's not a secret, and it's not what you think."

I don't even know what I think . . . because my *thinking* glitches. I *think* he's beautiful, especially up close. I *think* he makes me *feel* too many things—and forget how to *think*. And mostly, I *think* I regret not taking him up on the promise of that kiss when I had the chance.

Rafael continues, "La Clandestina has nothing to do with Media Lab."

"Oh." I blink, feeling a blush creep up my neck, feeling like I'm doing a shitty job of not letting him be my distraction. His nearness is to blame. I find myself inching closer.

"It's a family business, and I'm working on the marketing plan for it. For the launch," Rafael says a little sheepishly, burying his hands into his pockets, looking at me like he's expecting me to tear into him at any moment—and I want to, just not in any of the usual Evie vs. Rafael ways.

I swallow past the lump in my throat and nod.

"I was using your templates because they're fucking helpful and have made my life easier since Media Lab shared them. Also, I wasn't keeping anything from you—not on purpose, at least. It wasn't relevant to this." He gestures between us.

I still don't trust myself to speak.

He wasn't hiding anything, and while it's relief I should feel, the urge to ask the *other* questions barrels into my throat, onto the tip of my tongue. Does he feel this thing I'm feeling? Has it shoved itself somewhere between his ribs and his lungs, and is it making it impossibly difficult for him to breathe and think? Is he distracted too? Is it just me?

I feel breathless—and a little lightheaded—with the need to know, and this plasma me might be brave enough to ask, because if I've learned anything, it's that I might not have tomorrow. And if tomorrow isn't guaranteed, I need to do the brave and stupid things I didn't do before, things I penned on my bucket list and things I've only begun thinking about, and asking my question feels like the brave and stupid thing I need to do right now.

My heart thumping so loudly I can barely hear past it, I take a deep breath and tangle my fingers to keep them from shaking. "Rafael?"

His name is barely a whisper on my lips, which feel parched. I lick my lips.

As if tethered to them, his gaze drops to my mouth and lingers there, long enough that my lips part.

I attempt to drag in a breath of air.

"Evie," he says, his voice warm and husky. He's so close I can push up on my feet and relieve my lips of the curiosity of what his mouth might taste and feel like.

He leans in closer.

I imagine I'm physical me, who can feel the press of his body against mine, warm and hard and wanting something I haven't asked for. Yet.

The intensity in his dark gaze is a dare. *Ask, ask, ask,* it implores.

I breathe in a shaky breath.

"I think—" I start, heart thundering so loudly I stall.

The room tilts.

"Catch me," I say, feeling myself fall.

CHAPTER TWENTY-TWO
ELEVEN DAYS (AND AN ALMOST-KISS) AFTER

A drum solo is taking place inside my head—and I need it to stop.

I blink my eyes open, groaning as a ringing phone wakes me.

The pounding intensifies.

Nausea pushes into my throat.

I might be dead.

"You're here." Rafael's warm voice anchors me.

I blink past the fogginess.

His face solidifies in my line of vision, his brows creasing with concern. "Thank fuck you're here," I think he says, but I can't be sure because I can't hear past *thump, thump, thump* in my head.

Grinding my teeth, I push up and force myself to sit, resting my elbows on my knees and trying really hard not to be sick. The world blurs and tilts around me until finally it settles into place.

Good news is I'm not dead.

Bad news is I'm not *alive* either.

I'm back in Rafael's loft, my dress and shoes disappointingly the same as the first morning I woke up here, although it's evening, judging by the waning light. Desperation—tears and all—crawls into my throat, and I bury my face in my palms, attempting to push it back and get a hold of myself.

The couch dips beneath Rafael's weight. "Are you okay, E? What happened?" His voice is cautious. I'd meet his gaze if I weren't one blink away from emotional combustion—and possibly passing out again.

I shrug, swallowing tears. "I'm not sure. Everything went dark and hot," I say, throat burning with the sting of disappointment. As everything faded to black, I thought perhaps I'd get my second chance. That the prayers had worked. That our efforts were paying off. That I was being sucked back into my body so I could get back to my life.

Wishful thinking.

Rafael's hands are in my periphery. He stretches his fingers, then balls his hands. "You . . . just disappeared for an hour," he says, his voice tired. "I called the hospital, thinking that maybe you . . ." He trails off, and I'm still too much of a coward to look at him. "But they said everything was the same. A slight spike in temperature but nothing to worry about. All normal." I feel his eyes on me. "Is it?"

The concern on his face might be enough to knock me out again. "Is it what?"

"Normal? Do you feel the same?" He scans me, his eyes roaming over my body like a torch that burns wherever it touches. Probably why my temperature spiked. "Evie?"

His question.

"Do I feel the same?" I repeat, pressing a shaking hand to the base of my head. The throbbing, the pain, the dizziness. The symptoms are more intense than a few days ago—I definitely don't feel normal, or anywhere in the vicinity.

"I feel . . . fine." I'm not sure why I lie. Maybe it's the concern in his eyes—or the flicker of vulnerability. For once, I'm not lying to win at work or bring him down. I'm lying to make him feel better.

The realization makes me bolt from the sofa, too fast.

The room spins.

I blink it away, focusing on the poster of us. It feels like years ago that we took that photo . . . that I hated him.

Hat*ed.* Past tense. Not present.

Oh God.

"Evie?" Rafael is beside me, so close his breath would feather my hair and caress my skin if I were physically here. The desire to figure all this out is so all-consuming I may pass out again.

"Yes?" I whisper, retreating a step, needing a moment to collect myself.

Rafael's gaze scans me with concern. "Are you sure you're okay? Because we can put this all on hold if it's making it worse."

I'm not sure what "this" is for him, but for me it's becoming the inability to stop the inevitable, to slow time so I can separate my daydreams of Rafael and his hands from the ones where I should be doing everything possible to get my spirit back into my body—before I'm moved to the care facility, before it's too late to do anything, before I can't go back to my life.

And I need to get it together, because something *is* happening. The pain. The dizziness. The incessant pounding in my head. It's worsening by the day, and it scares me.

"I'm fine, I promise." I force a small smile with the lie.

"Fine enough you can tackle more of the bucket list?"

I nod, because the bucket list means taking action, trying to figure this out. "If you're up for it, I've always wanted to learn how to cook but haven't had time for it. I physically can't do many things on the list, but I think . . . I think that would be fun," I say, a little uncertain about admitting another weakness. Most adults know how to cook . . . or rather, most adults who haven't spent their time chasing clients and promotions would have found the time to learn.

Rafael grins like it's Christmas. "Cooking?"

"Yes."

"Anything specific in mind?"

"Anything you're really good at?"

His grin turns wicked. "No Vela would speak this out loud, but we all know that my cooking is second only to Abuela's."

I feign surprise, because I knew this already. "You don't say."

He rubs the back of his neck, his shirt lifting, revealing a strip of tanned skin beneath.

Catching on fire, I snap my attention to his face—his stupidly handsome face that doesn't lessen the temperature.

"I mean, my primo Jorge Luis thinks he's really the best chef in the family, but that's because he hasn't tried my pozole rojo," Rafael says.

"Pozole rojo?"

"Don't tell me you haven't had it."

"I haven't even heard of it."

Rafael's eyes bulge dramatically. "Damn, E. You've sat beside me for years and haven't realized it's only one of my favorite Mexican dishes?" He shakes his head. "Slacking."

I snort. "I actually worked. I wasn't only planning your demise."

Now *he* snorts. "Tell yourself that."

"You're delusional."

"I think you mean delectable."

The denial catches in my throat.

He's not wrong.

"Tell yourself that," I say, already walking toward the door and outside (really hoping I'll find my senses along the way). "Also, you might want to get that." I gesture toward his phone, which has buzzed and dinged for as long as I've been awake.

* * *

"Like with most dishes, making good pozole rojo is all about the ingredients," Rafael says, pushing a shopping cart down the aisle of Mexico Lindo Supermercado, a quaint Latin produce store a few blocks from his apartment. "Hominy and pork are the main characters, but I like to focus on the side characters."

"Hmmm. Tell me more, oh master chef." I walk beside him, abandoning my self-imposed task of trying to decipher the contents of containers lining the walls only to discover Rafael's attention is entirely elsewhere.

"The trick to making it *delectable* is in the chilis." His eyes scan a dried- and pickled-veggie-laden shelf as his finger runs along the packages of dried peppers. Muttering beneath his breath, he slows over a package and holds it up to me. "Ancho chilis." He tosses it into the cart. We move along the aisle. "Guajillo chilis . . . and . . ." He holds up another package of peppers. "Since I know you like a little extra kick: chiles de arbol."

I shouldn't be surprised he knows this other thing about me, but not many people know I love it when my food fights back. "Looks like I wasn't the only one spying . . ."

Rafael shrugs casually. "Needed to know what I was up against."

His words spark an image—me, pinned to the shelves, his mouth trailing fire down my skin, my fingers tangled in his hair, legs locked around him like live wire.

I forget to breathe.

"What's wrong?" Rafael stalls in the aisle, watching me with panicked concern, the humor gone.

"Erm. Nothing." I press a hand to my cheek.

"Are you sure?"

"Tell me more about the peppers," I say, a little too breathlessly, and gesture at the cart for him to move.

His all-knowing eyes linger.

Feeling like I've just downed a bag of chilis, I turn away, hiding my face. I pretend to be consumed by the containers of dried and pickled vegetables, even though soup making is the farthest thing from my mind.

Seconds later, Rafael is pushing the cart again and explaining the magic of fresh produce and perfect ingredients as we wind our way through the market, which isn't very busy so late in the day, which makes it easier for Rafael to talk to his invisible friend (me).

We arrive at the cash register, where Rafael speaks to the middle-aged cashier in Spanish. I don't need to understand what she's saying to know she's being Vela'd. While her hands pick up and scan the produce, her eyes never stray from Rafael. It's fascinating to see him in his element, making people feel seen and important regardless of who they are. Meeting them at their level. Smiling without reserve.

If he were an ingredient, Rafael would most certainly be a hot pepper. The Vela chili.

"Thinking about me again?" He casts me a devilish grin as the doors slide open. An older couple eye him curiously.

I scoff, marching out the door and straight for his truck. "You're very full of yourself, Rafael. It can't be healthy."

The shopping cart squeals behind me. "So you're not going to tell me?"

"I was not thinking about you!" I throw my hands up in feigned frustration.

"Right." He opens the truck's trunk and begins to load in the groceries. I purposely avoid his curious gaze. "You think you're a good liar."

"I can be when it serves my purpose," I say, crossing my arms.

"Is that so?" He tosses in the last bag and closes the space between us, scanning my face for the truth with such intensity I'm surprised I don't melt onto the pavement. He's like a furnace . . . or maybe I am.

"Yes."

"Then tell me what you were thinking . . ."

Your hands gripping my thighs. "Peppers."

His brow shoots up, a dare sparking in his eyes. "Really?"

"Holy shit, if it ain't Raf Vela!" The voice bellows from our right, and any bit of me that's been burning is doused in cold, cold water. Freezing, in fact.

I don't move or breathe as Art Betton, owner of Betton Sporting Goods, saunters across the parking lot toward Rafael and me—toward Rafael, because Art can't see me. For the first time, I really wish Rafael couldn't see me either, because right now, with Art heading toward us, the past—Rafael's betrayal—hits me like a semitruck, painful and completely unexpected.

"Art." Rafael takes Art's proffered hand and shakes it once before dropping it.

Art, who is somewhere in his mid-fifties, is short, stocky, and chock-full of cockiness. "It's been a while," Art says. "What—two years?"

Rafael nods, but he's tense.

I wonder if he's remembering his betrayal—the epic fallout that happened soon after. The day I learned I was kicked off the account, I pulled him into an office and let him have it with enough fire it would put his chilis to shame. I didn't hold back, and the rest is history.

"I hope there were no hard feelings." Art grins, his stained teeth broadly displayed. I can almost smell his cigar-tainted breath.

"None," Rafael says, his tone as rigid as his posture. He shuts the trunk with a thunk that matches the one in my chest.

"It was nothing personal. I simply had something else in mind for Betton Sporting Goods."

"I understand." Rafael, his discomfort palpable, walks to the driver's side. Art follows.

I can't help watching and listening and thinking about how much I cried that night. It had nothing to do with losing the account but everything to do with how much it hurt to have seen Rafael's true colors, to have had my friend betray me after we'd spent years working alongside each other, getting to know each other and leaning on each other to learn the ropes.

"Whatever happened to your coworker? Evie, was it?"

Rafael goes whiter than I've ever seen him. "Yes."

"Would have probably stayed at Media Lab if she was on my account, though." Art's sly chuckle sends a shiver of disgust through me. "Had to keep her for yourself. Can't say I blame you."

His words are so shocking I'm surprised I haven't been catapulted back into my body. I watch in disbelief as he pats Rafael's shoulder.

"Please don't touch me," Rafael says.

Art drops his hand with a confused chuckle. "Didn't mean to offend."

"I have to go." Rafael opens the truck door, his eyes finally connecting with mine. There's an apology in them as he climbs into the truck. I follow, sitting rigidly in the seat. Art mutters a goodbye, but Rafael has already closed the door.

We sit quietly for the span of several seconds.

"What was that?" I ask, attempting to keep my tone even and unaffected.

Rafael shifts so he can face me, the leather creaking beneath his weight. He scrubs a hand down his face and takes a deep breath. On the inside, my thoughts are so erratic no amount of ABBA will help.

"I wasn't completely honest with you, Evie," he says, making me feel like I've been hit by a car all over again.

Whereas a few days ago I could have handled the hurt, I don't know how to now. I've been too busy wanting him—aching for things I swear I didn't need—to hold on to his betrayal. I let my guard down.

And I'm paying for it.

"Clearly." I swallow, unprepared for any of this—the last five minutes and the next.

Rafael's face contorts like he's eaten a package of chilis. "The truth is that Art Betton wanted you on his account because you were hot. *A hot piece of ass,* to phrase it his way." Rafael winces and his throat bobs. My stomach bottoms out. "He saw you as a conquest, and I just couldn't let him think he was entitled to that kind of behavior, so I told Dana that I didn't need you on the account. That I could handle it myself."

I stare at him, feeling like I've had the rug ripped from beneath me. Again and again.

One Mamma Mia.

Two Mamma Mia.

When I catch my breath, I ask, "Why not tell me the truth?"

"Because I knew how much you'd thrown yourself into getting the account, and I didn't want you to think it had anything to do with you. You were . . . amazing, and Art was—*is*—a dirty scumbag, who was going to bring Media Lab a lot of money, but I couldn't let him near you like that." Rafael's tone is thick with emotion. "I'm sorry I made that call for you, and I'm sorry I lied about it after. I thought I was protecting you . . . and I fucked up."

It's hard to think of words I can string together in response.

He didn't steal the account with the intent to *beat* me.

He did it to protect me.

Do I believe him? When he's pretended for so long? *No,* Pre-Coma Evie shouts at me. This is Rafael Vela, the person I've spent the last two years trying to thwart and beat. I know more about Rafael than I know about most other people, including Gemma and my mother. This new information is paradigm-shifting.

"Evie?" His tone is low, tentative.

I release a shaky breath. "This entire time, you kept that to yourself?" My voice comes out even and hard, even though my heart is engaging in emotional acrobatics. I don't let him answer. "It made me hate you."

There's an almost imperceptible sag to his shoulders. "You can keep hating me. I wouldn't blame you for it. It shouldn't have been my decision to make, but I couldn't fathom the thought of you being in meetings or at dinners with him when I knew what he wanted. And I could have—should have—gone to Dana, but I thought I was making the right choice for Media Lab and for you. All I can say is . . . I'm sorry." He sighs. "Lo siento."

My chest aches and I can't talk yet, not when I feel like roadkill all over again.

I spent so many years believing a lie and feeling betrayed. I invested so much of my energy in hating him when I could have spent it . . . not hating him, feeling more of what I've been feeling these last few days.

My throat closes up to the point where all I can say is, "We can go now."

CHAPTER TWENTY-THREE
ELEVEN DAYS (AND A MAJOR REVELATION) AFTER

By the time we're back in Rafael's apartment, his phone has buzzed four more times, but he's answered none of the calls.

I've processed a thousand thoughts, but I've voiced none of them.

It's hard to chat when everything I thought to be real—the entire foundation of our rivalry—was shattered in the span of a few minutes and nothing looks the same.

I sense him wanting to say something, but he doesn't fill the silence either. He simply watches me in a way that makes me question everything I know all over again, but mostly it makes me want to forgive him. It makes me want to admit that it was me who was an oblivious idiot, who should have been sharp enough to see Art Betton for who he was: a sleazy, entitled weasel.

It's not that I didn't notice his lingering gazes or too-lengthy handshakes. Sure, I wanted to shake it off and shower for hours afterward, but I let it go because I was naive and didn't want to jeopardize a client who would bring Media Lab a good chunk of change . . . and me a commission that could help me put a down payment on an apartment. I also didn't want to disappoint Rafael after we'd worked so hard researching the account and preparing our pitch. There were countless reasons I excused Art's inappropriate-adjacent behaviors when I should have known to question them or talk to Dana about it.

In the end, we both messed up.

Rafael had me removed from the account, and I didn't bother to question how it didn't match up with the person who'd become my friend. Instead, I invited him to a one-on-one meeting, during which I called him a "backstabbing asshole with no moral compass or humanity" who would "perish alone and miserable like he deserved," after which I swore to him that he would pay one day.

It wasn't one of my finer moments. I was in an emotional and vulnerable place, because my plans fell apart right after, and I'd barely pieced myself together after losing Annie, running away from home, and trying to survive on my own. Every day those first couple of years I'd been in survival mode, trying to make ends meet, and Rafael had jeopardized that by taking the account from me and a huge chunk of my cut—and he didn't even know if Media Lab was for him. It was unfathomable and unforgivable.

I held it against him for so long, and he let me.

I'm not sure which has been worse.

I haven't been able to figure it out the entire ride back to his place, and he hasn't spoken a word either.

Rafael is quietly unpacking the groceries from their paper bags and putting them into the fridge, stopping every now and then to throw furtive glances in my direction, across the kitchen, where I've paced an invisible track into his floor and gnawed on another fingernail (but fortunately for me, one of the very tiny, very few perks of my predicament is waking up with a new manicure each day).

We've let silence do the talking too many times—and look where a got us. So I break it. "Why are you putting the groceries away?"

His eyes snap to me, the fridge door partly closed. "I assumed you weren't going to be in the mood for cooking lessons," he says, somewhat sheepishly.

I've given him no reason to believe otherwise—and the way he looks like a pup getting the feel for his legs is enough to make me tell him I've forgiven him. Almost. I step from the dining space into the kitchen, allowing the island to remain a much-needed buffer between us. "I think that a lot could have been different if you didn't *assume* what it was that I wanted or needed," I say quietly.

He nods, letting the fridge door close, and tucks his hands beneath his elbows as he leans against the fridge. When he sighs, his shoulders sag. "I know."

In all these years, I've never seen Rafael so . . . defeated—and I experience none of the joy I always imagined. Which only reaffirms what I've been wanting to say.

"I don't think you should have made a decision about Art and his account for me."

Rafael sags further, but he doesn't look away.

"But I get why you did it, and I'm not mad . . . not that I haven't spent the last two or so years being furious." I huff out a mirthless chuckle, glancing down at my hands as if I can find the fortification I need there. "Only I *am* mad at you for letting me believe that you were a backstabber all this time." I lift my gaze back up to his, knowing I'm holding nothing back, and say the last part in an almost-whisper. "For letting me hate you for so long."

Rafael looks at me, shocked. He silences his buzzing phone. "Mierda."

"*Shit* is all you have to say?" I aim for levity, but it comes out flat, almost angry, and his features contort in alarm.

"No! It's just this damn—it doesn't matter," he says, tucking the phone into his pocket. Rafael pushes from the fridge, lays his palms flat on the counter, and levels a serious gaze at me. I try not to stare at the way his muscles bunch as he leans on his forearms. "Trust me, I regret letting you believe that, more than a lot of things. When I realized how much my decision hurt you, I wanted to fix it, but there was no going back, not without you thinking I was making up another lie."

"You mean I wouldn't listen when you wanted to talk?"

"That, and—"

"I wanted to sabotage you at every turn?"

The corner of his mouth lifts slightly. "I hadn't noticed."

I mirror his half smile. "I guess I didn't try hard enough."

"Could have fooled me." He holds up his hand, the one with a pale scar across his pointer finger. I wince at the memory of locking him in a janitorial closet before a meeting with the executive team. He cut his finger trying to get out using paper clips and scissors.

"You could have waited." I attempt to defend the outcome of that day.

"And miss the meeting?" He stares at me with incredulity. "Or your reaction?"

Guilt sends a rush of blood up my neck and into my face at the memory. He walked into the meeting, half out of breath and sheets of paper towel around his bleeding finger. It wasn't long until the blood seeped through, the sight of it making me faint atop the conference room table. Rafael and I spent the next couple of hours at urgent care. Together.

We both missed the meeting.

"Like I said, it could have all been avoided if you had told me the truth," I say, going back to Rafael's (nonexistent) betrayal.

"I'm sorry I didn't tell you." His gaze is so open and honest it draws me toward him like a rope, a tug-of-war I'm losing. I take slow steps around the counter, stopping shy of touching him. "Just don't do it again."

"Okay," he says.

"Okay." The momentary silence thickens as our gazes remain locked, each second liquifying any sort of wall I've ever built to keep him out. I find myself inexplicably drawn to him, like a moth to a flame, a flower to the sun, a bewitched human to a vampire. It makes me want to forgive him for just about anything when his eyes devour me like I'm his favorite meal.

"How about that pozole rojo?" I croak as the yawning crevice in the ground between us begins to close. And when it does—when we're no longer rivals—what will we be?

You'll still be a ghost, Evie.

* * *

It takes a few hours for Rafael to walk me through his pozole rojo recipe. And if I thought I'd seen Rafael at his best—charming and disarming—I simply hadn't seen him in a kitchen. His movements are confident and smooth as he navigates pans and bowls, knives and blenders. He tastes as he goes, humming and muttering beneath his breath, explaining each step of the process. I ask questions, but mostly I watch . . . and admire.

The way his forearms flex as he maneuvers his way around the kitchen. The way his brow crinkles with focus, his lips moving as he measures ingredients aloud.

When it's finally ready, I've never despised not being a living, breathing human more. I want to inhale what I imagine is its decadent scent. I want to taste its rich flavor, chilis and all.

Steam rises from the Instagram-worthy bowl of soup—of which I've made him take several photos as proof I was part of making it, even if purely in an observational, ghost-mode role.

"Aren't you going to try it already?" I prod, admiring his handiwork from my perch on a stool.

Rafael's gaze connects with mine as he tosses the kitchen towel over his left shoulder and picks up a spoon from the counter, holding it in the air like he's toasting with it. "I'm trying this for both of us."

"You could always take some to the hospital." I struggle to keep a straight face. "Hook up a bowl of it to the feeding tube."

The spoon halts halfway to his lips, which twitch with displeasure. "You're a very disturbed person, E."

I suck on the inside of my cheek to keep from smiling and offer a one-shoulder shrug. "Perhaps the chilis will shock me back to life."

He shakes his head. "I stand by my statement," he mumbles, downing the first bite of soup and holding the spoon between his lips as he savors his concoction. I've never been more jealous of a spoon.

Oh God.

I *am* a disturbed person.

"How is it?" I ignore the spoon and his lips as he takes another bite.

Rafael smacks his lips. "Picante, but good. Cousin Jorge Luis couldn't deny it if he wanted to." He takes a few more bites of the soup, and I could be content watching him cook and eat for the rest of what could possibly be a very short existence.

I blink away the inception of a Rafael-and-food fantasy and clear my throat. "Are you two close?"

Rafael swallows before he answers. "Me and Jorge Luis?" I nod. "He's ten years older than me and Lupe's brother, but she and I have always been closest of the three. He was the good kid. Knew what he wanted his entire life. Went to culinary school, moved to Michigan, opened a restaurant in Grand Rapids, and has been doing that since. I see him when he visits, and the rest I get from social media." He holds another spoonful of soup to his lips. "What about you? Do you have any family you're close to?" His tone turns tentative when he asks this last part. I've never talked about family, and he's never pushed.

"No," I say, also tentatively. "My mother was—*is*—complicated. Annie and I were nuisances to her more than anything, baggage she couldn't get rid of, especially after Annie's diagnosis. Some days she forgot we existed. Other days we were in her way." I glance at Rafael, expecting pity or discomfort, but his expression is unreadable. "She was always chasing something—*someone*. She never told us who our father was or if he was even alive. I wonder if she even knew." I used to be embarrassed by this truth, but telling Rafael is easier than I expected. Maybe because he's not judging me or my past, one I've tried so hard to outrun. "She didn't take care of Annie like she should have, and Annie died when I think she could have been saved." I take a deep breath, the ache of talking about it duller now but still there. "The last time I spoke to her was almost fifteen years ago."

I exhale, forcing my voice to stay steady. "Beyond that, I had my mother's aunt—Julia—and Annie, and it was enough. For as long as I had them, it was enough," I add. "But I lost them both."

Rafael leans forward slightly, as if hanging on each word. "I'm sorry."

"Thank you," I say, smiling to myself. "Time makes it hurt less. And Annie used to tell me that when someone we love dies, they become teeny-tiny so they can go and live in our hearts." I rub the place over my chest where Annie once said the dad we never got to meet had gone to live. She assumed the only reason he wasn't in our lives was because he'd died. I didn't argue. I didn't know the truth—because our mother refused to tell us. Because according to her, our dad didn't want us.

That was Margot's bedtime story—the one she'd tell when she was drunk enough to be honest but bitter enough to twist it. Our dad, some nameless, faceless man, had stolen her dreams.

Tricked her into a life of diapers and screaming kids. He had promised her the world and then abandoned her in a trailer park, saddled with two daughters and no way out. She told us we should be grateful she kept us. That plenty of women would have dumped us on the side of the road.

I used to believe her. Annie never did.

I swallow past the old bitterness. "So, when I could finally accept that Annie wasn't here anymore, I started thinking of her as living in my heart and began talking to her again. It helped me get through a lot—like living in a basement with Roger the Rat."

"You had a pet rat?" Rafael's eyebrows shoot up, spoon clattering into the bowl.

I laugh, glad to shake off the memory of Margot. "No! He just came with my first 'apartment,' if you can call a dingy basement an apartment." I shudder at the memory of falling asleep with my blanket wrapped around me and a baseball bat strapped across my chest. "I never actually saw him, but I knew he was there because of holes in clothing and the less savory evidence he left behind, but I didn't have much of a choice."

"No doubt you made it work, E."

My cheeks warm at the honesty in his voice. I glance down at my hands. "I don't know why I'm sharing this. It's . . ."

"Okay to share," he finishes for me. "I've sat next to you for so many years. I know so much about you but so little about *you*."

"What does that even mean?" I laugh to keep things light and airy, because I'm nervous about going down the path of personal and intimate. *Chicken,* one of the Evies says.

"I mean—I know you prefer spicy food and green teas, have run at least four marathons, would choose stiletto heels to most other shoe types, hate tardiness, disorganization, and phones that aren't silenced, and you have a weird fascination with ABBA." Rafael pops up a finger for each item as he goes down his list.

"It's not weird!" I chirp, straightening.

"Poor word choice. I meant *unique*."

"ABBA *is* one of a kind."

He raises his arms in surrender. "I can be converted."

I narrow my eyes. "You just wait."

"Happily." His tone turns serious, and the one word—the promise there—sends a kiss of goose bumps across my skin. My ghost skin. Plasma. Whatever it is.

The reminder douses the heat and fills my chest with other things. Despair. Hopelessness. Sadness. I take a deep, deep breath and push it out. "What is it that you *don't* know, then?"

"Things about your life outside of work—friends and family. Your past. Your life before Media Lab. Where you used to rush to on Wednesday evenings. There's a lot I haven't been able to learn from the sidelines."

"I wasn't going to give you more ammo," I huff dramatically. "Clearly, you had more than enough." More than I could ever imagine.

Rafael shakes his head. "I wasn't going to use it against you, you know. Despite what you might have thought."

I arch an eyebrow. "Am I supposed to believe you when not three seconds ago you made fun of my choice in music?"

Rafael chuckles. "'Mamma Mia'? 'Super Trouper'? Really?"

"They're musical geniuses, and I will not be dissuaded!"

"I wouldn't dare, E." He begins to wipe down the countertop, humming "Mamma Mia" beneath his breath.

"You're the worst," I grumble, wishing I could throw a towel or a mug at his smug face.

"Am I?"

My smile slips at the heat in his eyes, daring me to answer.

Pounding on the door saves me from having to confront my increasingly complicated feelings.

We both turn toward the door.

"Another one of your jilted lovers?"

Rafael marches past me, flicking his towel in my direction. "Funny."

The knocking is incessant, and Rafael wrenches open the door.

I hold my breath, half expecting Violet to have returned for her phone . . . or a SWAT team ready to knock down the door.

Lupe glowers in the doorway, one hand on her hip and her phone in the other. She assaults Rafael with rapid-fire Spanish before she advances, swatting in the direction of his head.

"*Sorry!*" Rafael shouts, ducking.

Lupe follows. "You better be! You can't do that to me!"

"I said I'm sorry!" He holds up his hands to defend himself.

"I have no choice but to forgive you, but it'll take a moment," she says before she flicks his head once more.

"For what?" I can't help asking.

"I didn't pick up her call." Rafael smooths down his hair.

Lupe glances across the dining room in my direction, a few feet from where I'm sitting. "Hi, Evie!" She waves. "It wasn't *one* call; it was several. I thought something happened."

"He's horrible like that," I add, hating that we can't commiserate over all things Rafael together. He levels an almost scathing glare my way.

"What's so important you couldn't wait for me to call you back?"

Her gaze turns accusatory again. "Two things. One, Rabbi Steve came by the hospital, and he sends his regards."

"Oh," Rafael and I both say at the same time. I've been so distracted I forgot to ask.

"The second thing?" Rafael asks, rolling his shoulders.

She slides her eyes across the room to me, then back to Rafael. "I know she's here, but . . ."

My curiosity piqued, I lean in.

"Out with it, Lupe." Rafael's impatient.

"There's a problem . . . at the bar."

"Can it wait?"

"No. Not anymore," she says, a little less patiently. The glare she shoots him makes me want to cower in a corner.

"Fine." Rafael brushes past her and grabs his keys from the table. "This better be worth it."

CHAPTER TWENTY-FOUR
ELEVEN DAYS AFTER (LATE NIGHT)

We arrive at La Clandestina, parking in the same alley as before. Mr. Sasquatch stands guard at the door, his bearded face cast in strange shadows from the lone light hanging above his bald head.

"I'm not waiting in here," I say as Rafael turns off the engine.

"Even with Owen guarding the door there?" Smirking, he gestures to the security guard.

Before I can respond, Lupe taps on the window, startling both of us. "Let's go!" she commands impatiently, peering into the truck and hooking her finger toward the door.

"I hope the building's on fire," Rafael grumbles, pushing open the door. I exit the truck and follow after them, staying close to their heels as they walk past Owen into the building and down the dimly lit hallway.

Rafael walks beside me, irritation pulsing off of him. "And here I thought you didn't have 'rough' days," I say, attempting my best Vela-esque smile. His frown smooths out, but I can tell he's still annoyed about whatever his cousin wants.

"She can be a real pain in my ass," he mutters as we turn the corner into the bar.

Lupe stops abruptly, earning another curse from Rafael. She grins and flips a switch.

Lights flicker to life.

"SURPRISE!"

I startle, squeaking as the shouts wash over us.

A group of people manifest from the shadows, blowing on colorful horns and waving shiny streamers. Some wear cone hats with *HAPPY BIRTHDAY* written across them. Silver and white balloons dance atop the ceiling.

"Shit," Rafael mumbles, clutching his chest.

Lupe throws her arms around his shoulder with a laugh. "¡Feliz cumpleaños, primo!" Eyes bright, she squeezes him, and he tucks her beneath the crook of his arm. "I know you're on a mission that's *life and death*, but I figured a couple hours of celebrating *life* won't hurt."

"I really hate you." He plants a kiss on her cheek. Lupe playfully shoves him away as a rowdy group of people move in on Rafael from all directions. Their eager voices become muffled as music starts, getting louder and louder. Other bodies begin to move throughout the bar, waitstaff bearing food-laden trays and guests boasting gifts and bottles.

It's his birthday. June 18. A date on which I religiously made it a point to send gifts one might buy for (very) old family members: a yearly subscription to *Senior Living Magazine*, boxes of Poligrip, and on occasion, adult diapers. I've been so distracted I haven't paid attention to the dates. They've bled into one another, and now it's mid-June. The unexpected—and potent—surge of panic makes me stumble.

Blinking it away, I force myself to focus on the birthday boy. People swarm him, hugging and kissing. He fields at least a dozen people's well wishes before he's ushered to the bar and given a shot of tequila, followed by another and another.

Many are strangers, but I recognize two of Rafael's sisters, who join him—Gloria, the oldest, and Graciela, the pregnant one. Another one, who looks like the female version of Rafael, squeezes between them and wraps her arm around his waist. Gianna, the youngest Vela sibling. I know her from his lock screen photo—and the ones at his abuela's house. Rafael beams as he talks animatedly to her.

Beside her, Rafael's best friend, Harry Hughes, whom I met every time he popped in to take Rafael to lunch, sips on a drink. He's Rafael's foil in every way, rugged and blond and very Australian. Harry's a head taller than Rafael, and while he looks like a long-lost Hemsworth brother, Harry's shy, reserved, and not at all into women.

Rafael and Harry laugh at something Gianna says. The lights dim further, the music gets louder, and the drinks flow freely.

And I soak it all in.

I don't need flesh and bones to feel the Vela effect. It's around me. In smiles and laughter. In hugs and comforting touches. And it draws me from my shadowy corner, steering around people dancing as a DJ spins from a booth. Strobe lights move in rhythm to the music. Waitstaff pass around trays of appetizers—mini assorted tacos, ceviche, pastries. Another waiter serves drinks with skeleton bones as stir sticks.

I move closer, gravitating toward Rafael, needing to know what's making him seem like he's been lit up from the inside, so unlike the Rafael I saw when I woke up on his sofa days ago. It tugs me toward him, like mind compulsion.

Pieces of conversations make me slow and lean in.

"The vision really came to life!"

"The food—best I've had."

"Anything he touches is gold."

Eyeing an empty place around the circular bar, I plant myself on the side opposite Rafael and his squad. He catches my gaze, smiles—deep enough The Dimple says hola—and winks before he leans across the bar to talk to Lupe, who is in full bartender mode.

She sashays behind the counter, clad in leather shorts and a black tee, shouting over the music to another bartender. I should go home, or better yet, go back to the hospital and force this plasma back into the body until it sticks.

But I stay. Because I'm curious about Rafael's life in ways I can't explain. I want to be a part of his day without waiting for him to unwrap a year's supply of Just for Men because of the sick joy it brought me. I want to be here with him and his people, wearing a sexy dress and stealing his time and attention. I imagine finding a quiet moment, wrapping my arms around him, and breathing him in. I'd curl my fingers into his unfairly thick hair and rise up on my toes to whisper *Happy birthday* in his ear before letting someone else take my spot. We'd separate, reluctant to let go, but with the promise of more.

Daydreams and wishful thinking are going to be my actual demise. They knife into parts of me I didn't know existed—namely, the fullness in my chest that continues to take up real estate.

"Rafael said you were by the empty seat. Says he's sorry he can't keep you company." I startle at the sound of Lupe's voice. She's gazing to my right, talking to no one.

One of the bartenders narrows his eyes in question, but Lupe points to an AirPod in her ear and tells him to go pour drinks. He listens, pumping the shaker in his hands. Her bossiness makes me smile.

"Rafael hates celebrating his birthday, but this year has been a hard one for him, and he's done so much for me. I figured this was the least I could do." She pours gin, champagne, and juice into a crystal tumbler. "This place wouldn't exist without him. I mean, it's his baby." Lupe grins as she stirs the drink, her cheek dipping into a dimple. I want to ask her what she means.

Desperately trying to hear every word over the music, I lean in. "It only took years to drag him away from Media Lab. No offense, but it sounds like literal hell having to go into an office and be in meetings and shit all day. Don't get me wrong, but it seems like you were a little bit of a cabrona." Lupe winces. "If you're here, sorry, but that's the truth. Yet for some reason he stayed there longer than anyone expected—and that includes him. Neither of us stuck to anything we didn't like for too long, so him choosing office life for so many years was crazy and made it hard to get him to leave. And when I finally succeeded in convincing him to jump ship, your accident happened, and it was all put on hold. Again."

Lupe tosses a lemon slice into the drink and slides it across the bar to a woman whose pink lips curl into a smile almost as big as her teased hair. Alma from tango lessons at the senior center.

Dressed in a fitted magenta outfit, she lifts the glass up in a toast and sashays to the dance floor with swinging hips.

"I know I said I didn't want to help you, but he's better now that he's around you—or your spirit," Lupe adds. "It's gotten him out of the dark place he was in this past week. For a minute, I didn't think I'd get him back, so if you can hear me, please, try to stick around. Yeah?" She slaps the bar. "Now, I've got a party to rile up!"

She leaves me for a group of women who shout at her to come and take a selfie. Lupe obliges, ducking beneath the bar to join them and leaving me to make sense of her words.

I stare after her, questions buzzing louder than the music.

Rafael leaving Media Lab? The accident changing his plans? Maybe because of me? These bits of information have me wanting to ask *so* many questions, needing to know more and more, at the worst possible time.

I peer up at the ceiling. *If you're up there, I'm seriously ready to come back.*

Nothing happens. Except for Pitbull's singing splitting my eardrums as he encourages the crowd to *give him everything tonight.*

Wistfully, I eye the dance floor, where everyone from Alma to Rafael's pregnant sister shakes and grooves to the beat. Rafael's spinning his mom. Harry and Gianna bump hips and laugh.

Tucking the questions and my desperation away, I separate from the bar and find a semi-empty corner to watch from, hating the music for the way it sharpens the pain at the base of my skull. I pretend it's not there.

Guests continue to fill the bar. Rafael is animated as he talks to them. Charm mode engaged—and it makes me smile, because being Vela'd isn't the crime I thought it was. Far from it.

Rafael scans the crowd, and I know he's looking for me. His grin is almost blinding (another vampiric trait?), and he picks up a shot glass. I toast with an invisible glass.

A "Cheers!" booms from the crowd around him as they down their shots. I shudder.

The last time I drank . . . was the last time I was physically with Rafael. The memory is still hazy, but I remember being so angry at him for breaking Dana's Doctrine, because we had an account to win. Cyril and OhLaLove had consumed so much of the past year, but none of it has mattered these past few days . . . because none of it is important. Not to the extent I thought for so long. Too long.

And everything else that was actually important and worth my blood, sweat, and checklists? I put off or ignored—and I might never have a chance to remedy things.

The notion hits me like a jab to the throat, knocking the air out of me. Making me feel like I can't suck in a steady breath. I know I need to get out of here before I ruin Rafael's special day with my impromptu pity party.

"And now, honored guests, we invite our birthday boy to the stage for cake and speeches," the DJ announces. The crowd cheers. I startle.

Rafael shouts, "No speeches! Please!"

Harry nudges Rafael to the front of the dance floor, and Lupe comes to finish the deed, threading her arm through his and pulling him through the parting crowd.

The DJ hands Lupe the mic. She beams at the crowd, waiting for everyone to quiet. "One speech only. Only one that matters!" The crowd laughs. "I'll keep things short and sweet so we can get back to the party."

She pumps her fist in the air; someone agrees with an enthusiastic "Whoop!"

"For those of you who live in a hole or under a rock, Raffi is like the brother I never had. Just kidding. I have a bigger brother," she says, peering into the crowd. "He's the chef tonight, so make sure to tell him how terrible the food is." Again the crowd laughs. "All joking aside, Raffi is one of the coolest dudes, family or no family, and I wouldn't be here without him. Literally. He was there at my lowest, and I'm celebrating with him at my best." She laughs along with everyone, but emotions strain her voice. "When he said he'd be down with my idea of starting a tequilería-slash-bar, I didn't believe him, but then he showed up and helped me bring it together, not only as a cousin but as a business partner."

My jaw unhinges from its sockets as more puzzle pieces click into place.

"So . . . tonight isn't only his birthday, it's also the soft launch of La Clandestina. Enjoy the party. Try the tequila. And let's have fun celebrating my favorite human!"

CHAPTER TWENTY-FIVE

ELEVEN DAYS AFTER (LATE, LATE NIGHT)

This is Rafael's bar and Rafael's tequila.

I repeat this several times, and it still doesn't make sense.

I watch him maneuver through more hugs. He's laughing and talking with his entire body, charming people as he goes. Too late, I realize he's made his way toward me. He gestures toward the hallway with the crook of his finger, and I follow after him, like a puppet on a string, zinging with the energy of the evening.

"Here," he says, pushing into a room with a PRIVATE sign attached to the door. Cheeks flushed and eyes brighter than usual, he's smiling at me like it's *my* birthday.

Feeling too many new things, I step tentatively into the room—an office crammed with boxes and crates. Rafael leans against a desk while I stick to the comfort of the wall. Only the space doesn't steady me as I'd hoped.

"I didn't know about tonight. I'm sorry," Rafael says, a little breathless as he brushes back his hair. Curls stick to his neck.

"Don't be." I knot my fingers to still the onset of the shakes. "It's your birthday! Why didn't you say anything?"

He lifts a shoulder. "Not important."

"Everyone out there would disagree."

"And the person in here?" The way his voice dips makes me hot all over.

"*Everyone*'s birthday is important."

Rafael chuckles warmly. "You always have an answer for everything."

The penetrating look in his eyes kindles a fire that's already raging. I'm surprised I don't breathe smoke when I talk. "Not everything. Why didn't you tell me this was your business? That you planned on leaving?"

"Didn't want you to die from joy." He winces. "Shit choice of words, E. Sorry."

"I'll forgive you if you answer. The real answer."

Rafael's lips twitch. "It's . . . it's been something I've been working on for years, and it only became something that needed my full attention this past year. It all happened really fast. I wanted to say something, but there was never a right time to bring it up, so I planned on doing it the night of the OhLaLove dinner . . ." His voice trails off. "And when you showed up again, it wasn't a priority to talk about me and my plans. Helping you was so much more important. It *is* the most important."

The naked truth darkens his gaze, and awareness zings through me. *Me*—I've been his priority. I swallow past the knot in my throat. "So, when's your last day?"

"The day of the accident. I wanted to come there for the dinner. Help out," he says, his voice trailing off.

"You quit already?" I squeak, torn between focusing on his words and on his lips.

Rafael nods, looking sheepish. "Weeks before the accident, actually."

I try to do the math—to add it all up—but shock makes it impossible to compute. "You could have told me."

"I could have," he says, his throat bobbing. "But we were working on OhLaLove, and I wanted us to do the pitch before I told you." He hesitates. "It was one last . . . rodeo. With you."

I swallow hard, uncertain what to make of the way he says *you*. Like I was someone he'd miss instead of someone who'd made his life hell.

"But—you loved Media Lab."

Rafael pushes from the desk, closing the distance between us in two strides. One hand lands on the wall beside my head, his body so close my pulse trips, then stalls. The room shrinks, the air going with it. I think about his scent—sandalwood and soap—because I've memorized it over the years, and it takes everything not to lean in.

"I never did," he murmurs. "I meant it when I said it was a job, nothing more." His voice is low and husky, making my thoughts short-circuit.

I lick my lips. "But—why stay for so long?"

Rafael's gaze dips to my mouth. "I thought it was obvious—"

"Raffi!" The door bursts open, Gianna's head poking in. "What the hell are you doing here on your own?" She frowns as she takes in his posture and motions for him to follow.

Rafael lithely pushes from the wall and rolls his shoulders. "Can't a birthday boy get some air, G?"

"Air? In here? It smells like an armpit," she says, lacing her fingers through his and tugging him out of the room. He mouths *later* as he disappears, leaving me to assess the damage. His truths. Mine.

He quit Media Lab, and I should be celebrating, not feeling a dull ache at the thought of Media Lab without him. I want to call him back, to ask him questions, to understand why he stayed as long as he did if it was just "a job." I follow after him instead.

The bar is more crowded than before, and the dance floor moves to the flow of bodies and beats.

I try to find an undisturbed corner to observe from and find myself beside a table with three tequila bottles. I peer down at them, squinting in the scant light to make out the design. It's a skeleton with a bony finger to its lips. *La Clandestina—Tequila Añejo* is written beneath it. Another says *Tequila Reposado*, the last *Tequila Blanco*. Rafael's tequila.

It's hard to believe it. Rafael left Media Lab to start his own business. All those documents at his place? Those were for him—for *his* new venture. It's the secret he's been hiding, and I would never have guessed. I thought I knew most things about Rafael, yet I missed this very major, very important thing.

As I watch him among the crowd, I can't help but wonder what else I might have missed.

The only answer is Bad Bunny rapping on the speakers.

Burning questions aside, I inch toward the crowd, toward Rafael, his family and friends.

If the last few days have taught me anything, it's that I've spent too long living life with checklists for the sake of playing it safe. I'm tired of watching from the sidelines, especially when tomorrow isn't guaranteed. Not for anyone. Especially not for me.

As I go, I kick off my shoes and dance around the others, forgetting about hospitals, unfinished business, and the chance of no tomorrows. The dance floor is crowded, but it's easy to find Rafael. He spots me—with a wink and a smile that hits dead center. He circles around me when he can, close enough to almost touch. I go with it, allowing myself to be Vela'd.

And on the dark dance floor, where anything is possible, so is dancing with a ghost.

We dance around each other until the crowd thins and the remaining guests are buzzed enough to have kicked off their heels and loosened their ties. Until people canoodle in the booths and others are almost half asleep by the bar.

"We have a special request!" The DJ speaks into the mic. "This one goes out from the birthday boy to a special someone." My chest constricts as a familiar melody blasts through the speakers. "Dancing Queen."

I can't help but laugh as Rafael begins to shake his hips. The other dancers move to the beat, even if the song is unlike the other club hits that have played all night. Some begin to sing along. Rafael's oldest sister, Gloria, commands the dance floor with her moves, and everyone claps along as she throws her hands into the air and lives the classic song with her entire body.

"It appears at least one Vela has been converted," Rafael shouts over the music as he dances beside me.

"Appears so!" I shout back, shimmying to the beat. I sing along, and I notice Rafael's lips moving to the words as well. "Aha! Busted!"

He shrugs. "I guess it's contagious."

If anyone sees him talking to himself, no one says anything. My lips itch to remind him of his conditions, which he's broken considerably more often than me.

"Thanks!" I shout instead. "I'm honored to be your special someone."

"Who said it was you?" Rafael frowns.

I clutch my chest. "What? I thought I was your only rival!"

"Is that what we are? Rivals?"

I dance around him, pondering his question as ABBA wraps up one of their greatest hits.

"Evie!" Rafael nudges when I haven't answered.

The song comes to an end, leaving me breathless and without a cover. "Rafael," is my only answer.

CHAPTER TWENTY-SIX
TWELVE DAYS AFTER (EARLY, EARLY MORNING)

Rafael says we have one stop to make before we go home, but he doesn't tell me where the Uber is headed.

We're dropped off near the Adler Planetarium. Rafael guides us right past it. Past the food stand not too far from it. He continues walking, to the beach, across the sand, motioning for me to follow—and because I haven't had a rational thought since I've been knocked out of my body, I do.

"Where are we going?" I shout, following him like we're tethered together. In some divine, inexplicable way, we are. How else do I explain waking up at his place each morning? Or him being the only one able to see me? Or the way I internally combust from the way he looks at me?

"You ask too many questions!" He laughs, the sound caught by the wind and the waves and carried into the night.

I roll my eyes and rush after him. "Rafael!"

I almost barrel into him as he slows to a stop, hands on his hips. The wind ruffles his hair, and the moonlight makes him seem younger than his (newly) thirty-five years.

A blush creeping up my face, I turn my attention to the water. Lake Michigan is beautiful in daytime, but at nighttime, there's something almost frightening about its enormity. Unlike Rafael, I love the water, the way it makes me feel, like I'm connected to all the other people who stand in it. Big and small, all at once. Now I wish I could dip into it, will its cool depths to soothe me.

"What are we doing here?" I ask.

Rafael turns a positively wicked gaze in my direction. He rubs his palms together. The wind attempts to braid his hair into knots. And yes, I'm also jealous of the wind.

"For someone who's devoted her life to obsessing over me, I'm surprised you haven't caught on," he says.

"Obsessed with you?" I balk.

"I won't tell a soul." He winks, standing oh-so-close to me, and my breath hitches in my throat. His lips lift to one side, and the feeling of imploding spreads.

"You're ridiculous when you drink."

He leans closer, his eyes dark orbs. "I think you mean ravenous."

"I—no," I begin to say, but his hands move to the hem of his shirt and begin to pull upward, revealing bits of tanned skin.

Alarm makes me stumble backward, and I'm not sure if he's talking about him or me being ravenous.

I gawk at him, mouth dry.

"What are you doing?" My voice rises in pitch as he tugs the shirt over his head and tosses it onto the sand.

"Undressing." He begins to unfasten the belt at his waist. His *bare* waist.

"Undressing?"

"Sí."

I'm feeling hot and cold, confused and aroused. Someone's pulled my hormonal fire alarm, and it's going haywire. I hold a hand to my head and breathe in and out. It sounds like wheezing. "Why?"

He stops midway through unzipping his pants and considers me like I'm the one who's undressing on a beach in the middle of the night. "Your bucket list." He holds my gaze as if willing the list to telepathically transfer to my brain. It's hard to think about all the items on the exhaustive list when all I can focus on is the lean muscles of his torso. The sugar skull tattoo wrapping around his toned bicep. The tanned skin stretched taut over his thighs (and all the way to the other side of them).

And then it hits me, like being knocked over by a powerful wave or a lightning bolt, either of which would be much appreciated at this moment.

Bucket list item #72.

Skinny-dipping in Lake Michigan.

A bucket list item born of too much cabernet sauvignon and originated by the perpetrator of all troublesome ideas: Gemma.

"No, no, no," I say, stumbling backward with my arms thrown out, needing him to stop from going further.

His pants drop to the ground.

Oh. God.

If there's ever been a moment for me to finish dying, it's now.

Or maybe in a minute.

I assess the length of his body, trailing my gaze over the lines of his lean muscles because my conscience has joined my body on that hospital bed. I force my eyes to focus on his face. His smug face.

Rafael's hands are on his hips, on which his boxer briefs hang very, very low. He watches me expectantly. "Well?"

"Please . . . put your clothes on," I choke out, past the fiery knot in my throat, while Rafael's standing in the sand like one of Michelangelo's *David*s.

His left eyebrow arches. "Evie." I hear the challenge in his voice, which is rolled up with amusement and something dark and molten. Rafael—even when sober—barely has a poker face, doesn't bother to conceal his emotions or to mince his words. But left wholly unfiltered—thanks to tequila and the aftermath of celebrating his birthday—he's an open book with the pages fluttering in the wind. Pick a page and read your heart out.

I'm trying to grasp at my traitorous (high-definition, palpitation-inducing) thoughts and shove them back into their compartments. Close the Evie Pope book firmly shut, lock it in a chest, and toss it into the lake.

No way we're doing this.

No. Way.

"We can keep our underwear on." He tugs on the elastic band of his boxers as if to reassure me. I don't know why I look, because looking makes me flustered, and feeling flustered doesn't line up with making sound, safe decisions.

I'm a grown woman, who is going to turn away while he puts his clothes back on.

I'm a ghost, who might not wake up tomorrow.

I toe the line between doing one of the most impulsive things I've done in my entire life . . . and regretting not doing it.

Not dropping my gaze from his, I suck in a deep breath and begin to unzip my dress. "Consider this your birthday gift."

Rafael's eyes spark with surprise, even in the moonlight, and I shiver despite not feeling a bit of the breeze that's kissed his skin in goose bumps. His eyes follow my movements without an ounce of shame, and though I never dreamed I'd be stripping in front of Rafael Vela, I shrug off the dress and let it fall into a pile of cotton and rayon at my feet.

With only the cover of moonlight, I'm standing in my dust-pink bra and satin hipsters on the beach, in the middle of the night, with the person I've often dreamed of holding underwater until the bubbles stopped. It's insane. I want to throw my hands over the bare parts of my skin, which tingle and burn as Rafael's eyes take stock, roaming over every dip and curve of my body.

I'd be a hypocrite to deny him when I was doing much of the same a minute ago.

"It's my favorite one yet," he says, his voice a husky purr.

"Favorite one?"

"Gift."

"Oh," I breathe, very much wanting to cover at least my midsection or my cleavage, because I feel exposed. I curl my hands into fists and straighten, mimicking Rafael's nonchalant, non-self-aware stance.

"Don't you even think about covering up, E. You're breathtaking."

"I—"

He steps nearer. "No argument."

My heart skips like a stone across water. I swallow, knowing it's a bad idea to participate in this very dangerous challenge of his. "I wasn't going to argue."

His dark brow arches. "Oh?"

"I was going to tell you that you're not so bad yourself," I say from low in my throat. "But I don't want it to go to your head."

Rafael throws his head back with a warm laugh. "Thanks for your relentless commitment to keeping me humble." His words make me smile, but his eyes make my toes curl as his gaze inches downward. "It does look like a wing."

My hand moves to my right thigh. His gaze sears my skin. Feeling about to combust from his attention, I face the lake. "Are we going to do this or what?"

I don't wait for his answer as I rush for the water with a squeal, stopping where it laps at my feet. Rafael slows beside me. He shivers. "Cold?" I ask, glancing sidelong at him.

"No." He shakes his head.

"Afraid?"

"A little."

"I guess we're both crossing something off our bucket list, then." Taking a deep breath, I cross the water's edge and wade into the lake, arms at my side. The sensation can only be described as having a paintbrush dipped in oil paint dragged across my flesh. It's not unpleasant. It's not familiar.

The water splashes as Rafael walks in after me, taking slow, tentative steps into the lake; he stops where the water reaches his knees, but I wade deeper into the lake until it covers my hips, then most of my chest. "There aren't sharks in the lake, if that's why you're spooked," I say over my shoulder.

He scowls, gliding through the water until he's beside me, the water hugging his hips.

"Such a baby."

Rafael stands rigidly. "I almost drowned on a fishing trip when I was thirteen."

My smile slips. "Oh. I'm sorry." I cringe inwardly at my idiot mouth. "We can go back."

"No need. If you can be so brave about everything you've done these past few days, I can get this far into the water." His tense shoulders tell another story. "You can't be the only one getting over her fears."

"I wouldn't call it getting over my fears. It's more like succumbing to them and hoping for the best."

He chuckles, his hand very tentatively dragging through the water. "That's very Evie of you."

I snort. "Very Evie of me?"

"Taking everything—goals, plans, fears—dissecting them, taking them apart, and making them less indomitable than they actually are. It's what you do. Your ambition is . . . infectious." It's not my body I want to cover but my face as a flush creeps up my neck. He continues, "It's fascinating. Nothing seems like too big of a challenge."

"Except for you," I say. "Haven't figured you out yet."

His hands draw circles in the dark water. "I'm an open book." With lots and lots of chapters.

"If you say so." I slip deeper into the water, letting it come up to my neck, wishing it could cool my burning skin. Rafael follows suit, slowly submerging himself to my level. We're close enough we could touch.

Behind us, the city glows and twinkles against a velvet black sky, the stars barely visible. If someone had told me I'd be crossing off bucket list item #72 with Rafael Vela, I would've laughed in their face and immediately gone to erase the ridiculous item from my list. That and #44.

We listen to the waves in silence, Rafael gradually relaxing beside me.

"Truth or dare?" I ask, surprising myself. And Rafael, whose eyes widen.

He pretends to think about it. "Truth."

I consider all the questions I've collected in the last twenty-four hours. I consider the answer I want to know the most. The question comes easily. "What happened with Charlene?"

Amusement flickers, disrupting the intensity in his gaze. "Can I get a pass?"

"No," I say. "The truth and nothing but the truth."

His throat bobs. "I met her for the first time when I dropped off the files for the Dalton account a year ago." He'd dropped them off because Dana had trusted no one else and I was out with a virus that had me feeling like I'd been chewed up and spit out. I opened the door with the hope it was highly contagious (it wasn't). "We took the elevator together. She asked me out for coffee, and because she seemed like someone I'd enjoy having coffee with, I said yes."

"You've been known to wear a person down." I grin.

"I was a gentleman through and through." He dips lower into the water. "She wanted something more than I could give her, so I didn't pursue it."

"Too serious for you?" I try to keep my tone light, even though I feel relief that it was never more. I'm a terrible person, I think.

"Not what I was looking for," he says. A wave hits the side of his neck, drenching his hair. He pushes the hair from his face, slicking it back. A rivulet of water snakes down the side of his face, and I have the urge to wipe it away. Wishful thinking and all.

"Your turn, Pope. Truth or dare?" His eyes tell me *dare*. I think about what I'd be willing to do in the middle of the night. About him daring me to take off the rest of my clothes (and me not completely hating him for it).

"Truth," I croak.

"Coward." His eyes glint, and I know I would've been right. I've played *WWRD* plenty of times.

"*You* took the easy route first," I say pointedly.

"I got into the water, didn't I?"

"Ask before I change my mind."

He turns thoughtful. "Why Stevie?"

"*Ohmygod,*" I groan into my palms, feeling like memory lane is the last place I want to go down.

"It's so not *you*."

I drop my hands to glare at him. "It isn't *me*. Not anymore." I make a face, and Rafael's amusement flickers. I refuse to let my past kill the moment. "I don't think you deserve to know." I feign indignation, crossing my arms over my chest.

He narrows his eyes. "Backing out of the game?"

"Never," I say, but really thinking we should stop. "My mother was obsessed with music. Stevie Nicks was one of her faves, right after Annie Lennox. That's the Stevie *and* Annie story." Or the very short, nighttime-swim-appropriate version, because my mother and past don't have room out here. "Truth or dare?" I go next.

"Truth."

I peer up at him. He's watching me the way I want to touch him—with intent, with care, like I'm breakable and burning all at once. "Do you still hate me?"

Rafael laughs with his entire body—and for a moment I falter, wondering if I've wasted a truth. I swallow, resisting the urge to take it back. "Raf."

He stills. "I never hated you, not for a single moment."

The weight of his words sinks in, sending a hot shiver through me. Drawing me nearer and nearer. I'm close enough I can count water droplets on his skin and watch them slide down the lean planes and dips of his muscles. One droplet pools in the hollow of his neck. Another sits atop his upper lip. I find myself feeling jealous of them . . . their ability to caress his skin so openly and intimately. If I could, I'd touch him in all the places the water's touched. I'd be bold and brave, and I'd snake my arms and legs around him, like a jellyfish.

I hate this ghost thing.

"Do you? Still hate me?" he asks. The shift in his tone catches me off guard. The lightness gone. The game paused.

I swallow. "I do . . ." His eyes shutter for the briefest moment, but they remain dark and intense, as if he's peering into my soul. Seeing beneath the defenses, the games and the fake truths. "I hate you for making me want something I can't have," I whisper, feeling bold enough to lift my finger to his collarbone, to bring it to his skin. Rafael's muscle shudders beneath my almost-touch.

"That's cheating," he rasps. I trace up along his neck and the lines of his face.

"Not being able to experience this is cheating." I hate that I can't feel the softness of his skin and taste the lake on his lips. Mostly, I hate myself for not seeing him—and the truth—sooner.

Because I don't think I ever hated Rafael.

My fingers stilling their path along his chin, I shove the frightening, world-shifting realization deep down for examination another time.

"No," I answer honestly. "I don't hate you. Not even a little bit."

"Good. Because I need to tell you something," he says. Something tentative lurks beneath his words, and it has a sobering effect.

I search his eyes for a clue. "Is it a good something or a bad something?"

"I hope it's a *good* something."

I want to know and not know. I imagine his good something has to do with another crazy solution for fixing me, and while I know I should be doing everything in my power to get me back to my life, nothing about Evie's Second-Chance Checklist has a place in this moment—this beautiful, perfect moment.

Almost perfect.

"The thing is, E," Rafael begins.

Before I can overthink it, I hold a finger up to his lips, shushing him. "Save it for tomorrow. We need to save a few good somethings for tomorrow," I say. His lips part to speak. "I have a good something too."

Only my good something hinges on him not seeing us as rivals when tonight's over, so I silently will the moon and stars to hang out for a few hours longer, just in case.

CHAPTER TWENTY-SEVEN
TWELVE DAYS AFTER, PART I

For the first time since I've started waking up on Rafael's sofa, I don't completely resent it. Except, perhaps, for the fact that I didn't wake up next to him, like the way we fell asleep after we spent the rest of the night watching *Bridgerton*, because while it's not on my bucket list, reading more books is, and this was close enough (also, Regé-Jean Page).

While I made it through two episodes, it took Rafael all of five minutes to pass out after his birthday festivities and our (very courageous and soul-baring) late-night swim.

I put off falling asleep as long as I could, half reluctant to end a night so full of surprises and revelations and half afraid I might not wake up at all. When I finally fell asleep, it was staring at Rafael's profile, the lines of his familiar face—fine laugh lines I've come to adore. In the time since the accident, he hasn't shaved, and the scruff has grown on me. So have his smirks and sidelong glances. My favorite, though, has been The Dimple, which hides when he's not Vela-ing some poor, unassuming soul (i.e., his former mortal enemy).

Falling asleep next to Rafael Vela was the second-most reckless thing I did last night.

Falling for him was the first.

Waking up with this shocking and mildly terrifying secret makes me want to float out of his apartment and find a dark, quiet corner of the universe so I can examine its validity.

I fell for Rafael Vela.

Rafael. Vela.

Someone on whom I've bestowed several titles over the years—coworker, friend, public enemy number one—but about whom I've never, not in all this time, thought *potential soulmate.*

Fall for the enemy. How's that for a bucket list line item?

I want to bury my face in a pillow and scream into it until the world rights itself. I want to call Gemma and tell her that I think I've lost my mind (in addition to my body). But mostly, I want to run into his bedroom—to touch him, kiss him, lose myself in him—until I feel brave enough to tell him the truth.

The truth doesn't scare me. His potential reaction to it does.

Because what if he doesn't feel the same? Could I have misinterpreted his lingering gazes—the desire in them? Or the way he drank in my almost-naked body last night? Or touched my almost-flesh?

No, I don't think I'm wrong to think he might return my feelings. I *know* Rafael (*WWRD* and all).

But I've also misjudged him and his actions in the past. I thought he was a backstabber. A cheater. A competitor with no qualms. I ignored any and all actions to the contrary. For years.

Which part of me do I trust now?

Which part of him?

Morning sunlight filters through the windows. It's been several minutes of listening for movement, but I've heard nothing from his room. Nothing save for the sound of traffic along the street below. A police siren in the distance. And the incessant *thump, thump, thump* in my head.

Will any of these feelings matter if I don't figure out how to get back into my body? Even if I tell Rafael about my feelings doing a full 180, what happens then? I'm a ghost. A spirit. An apparition (depending on the Google search of choice).

To the world, I'm nothing more than a figment of Rafael's imagination. A hallucination, as he referred to me that first morning.

But, if I really want to change—to get back to my life—I need to try harder. I need to *refocus*—on my mission, the checklist, the bucket list. I've allowed myself to get distracted by my feelings. And by Rafael and his stupid dimples and searing gazes and the way he's giving this his all, like it's the most important thing in the world.

And none of it will matter if I don't get back into my body.

A sharp, shooting pain lances through my skull. Nausea follows. The room tilts.

It takes fifteen breaths for it to pass, and when it does, I know with certainty that something is very wrong. Dread settles in.

This doesn't feel like healing or progress.

It feels like a countdown.

Like if I don't find a way back *soon*, there won't be anything to come back to.

No checklist. No bucket list. No Rafael. No me.

Tentatively, I stand on weak legs. I need to find him. We need to find Lupe and Gemma. We need to figure this out. Soon.

I go to his room and stop at the open doors, nerves tangling with nausea. "Raf?"

No answer. No movement. I step into the room. He isn't in his bed. Not in the living room or the kitchen. I end up in the dining room, searching the table for a sign of his wallet or his keys, but nothing. Except for my planner . . . and a note with his writing.

Ran to the hospital. Lupe says she found a real shaman. I don't believe her, but I'm going to check it out. Don't work yourself up about not coming. I can handle it.
Won't be long. Feel free to snoop.

—Your favorite taffy

My first thought is to go to the hospital. The second is to trust him to handle it. I can't do anything anyway, and I'd rather not induce another fainting spell by seeing my comatose body.

Rafael has this, I remind myself. Some of the anxious edge dulls. But the panic—and pain—is there. Sharp and impossible to ignore.

And while he's on shaman duty, trying to figure out how to fix me, I need to think of a way to tell him about my feelings. I'm not sure which seems like the more impossible of the two.

Figuring yourself out, the Evies say.

* * *

An hour into pacing the length of Rafael's apartment, I still don't have a plan. Not for telling him about my feelings, not for what happens if I ever get back. But I do know I need to find Rafael.

To tell him about the pain—to tell him that we need to speed things up. Whatever it takes. I'll try all the crazy ideas Lupe has. I'll be open to whatever plan.

Even if it takes another Vela.

Determined and more than a bit nauseous, I head for the hospital.

It takes entirely too long to get there. My head pulses with every step.

By the time I enter Northwestern Memorial, the dull throbbing has intensified. The fluorescent lights feel like searchlights.

The white walls blur. Even the floor seems to wobble beneath me. I have the strongest urge to lie down on the concrete until the nausea passes.

I push forward, up the stairwell. Past patients. Past nurses. Past doors.

With each step, I feel worse. What if it's not just my body rebelling? What if this is *it*? The end? Goodbye?

Panic knifes at my resolve.

No. Not yet.

Not when there are ninety-two reasons on my bucket list. Not when I haven't lived or loved. Not when I haven't told Rafael the truth.

Please don't take me yet. I send the prayer out as the lights glare brighter and the floor lurches with each step. I really need Rafael . . . and a place to lie down.

I force my legs to move.

And then he's there—pacing outside my room, talking animatedly on his phone. Relief pushes past the other symptoms, and I almost throw myself at him, wishing so desperately he could sweep me into his arms and just hold me.

I don't. I pull on a mask of composure and go to him.

He sees me. Surprise flits across his face, followed by concern. "Evie," he says, as breathless as I feel. He ends the call without a glance at his phone.

"Hi." I smile even though I feel like I'm in the late stages of food poisoning.

Rafael's smile doesn't reach his eyes, not even close. Some of my calm facade cracks.

"What's wrong?" I ask.

"Nothing." His phone buzzes in his hand, but he ignores it. "I—you didn't have to come," he says, his voice edged with something I can't name. Something sharp and strange and not at all like anything from last night.

A nasty feeling twists my stomach. "I know, but I wanted to help." I glance behind him at the door. "Is Lupe in there? The shaman?"

Rafael's jaw ticks. "No. She didn't come."

I nod slowly. "Okay. That's okay, right?" I ask, even though his signals tell me otherwise.

He scrubs a hand through his hair. "Yeah, it's okay." His words sound wrong, like they've been dragged from somewhere he didn't want to go.

"What—what's wrong?" I move instinctively closer, feeling cold and hot. Hospital staff move past us. Rafael is oblivious to them, to The Conditions™.

He opens his mouth. Closes it. "I—I'm sorry," he says, looking like he may actually want to be farther away from here than even me. The apology—the pain in it—sends a wave of panic rolling through me. Then another.

"What's happening? Tell me." I'm almost begging. A beeping noise cuts through the pounding in my head. I need someone to turn it off.

Rafael sighs as his body curves ever so slightly inward. "I thought we had more time." Those six words make my ghost plasma run cold.

"What is it?" I whisper. "Did they taper off the sedation? Is time up?" The nausea spikes again, hard and fast, battling for control of my (not) body. The edges of the hallway start to blur.

"That's not it, E," he says. I don't know if I should be confused or scared or both, judging by the way he looks utterly lost. "I should've tried harder to figure out how to bring you back. I should've found other doctors. Specialists." He swallows. "Instead, I let myself think I could help you figure it out."

"You have been helping," I say quickly, firmly. "You've done more than anyone else."

Rafael sighs shakily. "Did I?"

I don't answer, because he's not asking me. He's asking himself.

"What happened, Raf?"

His eyes meet mine. "Gemma—"

Confused, I blink at Rafael. "What about her? Is she okay?" A different kind of worry blooms—tight and cold. Because if something happened to Gemma . . . I can't fathom . . .

"No—she's fine," he says quickly, but his restlessness gives him away as he shifts from one leg to another, like he's trying to dodge the weight of what comes next. "It's just . . . she went looking for your family." A pause. "For your mom."

The words sink in, digging their teeth deep, deep down. My breath catches. My knees wobble. I stumble, surprised I haven't disintegrated into a pool of plasma already. "No," I whisper, shaking my head.

"She left for Michigan the other day." Rafael darts a look to the room, then back to me. "To find Margot."

My mother's name unlocks something I've long buried. "And?" I ask, swallowing past the rush of emotions. Gemma knew about Margot—I've shared bits and pieces without allowing my mother to own too much of my present, my relationships, my life.

"She went looking for her because she didn't know if you'd recover . . . and thought your mom should know," Rafael says. "And she found her."

I let out a short, bitter laugh. Hollow and humorless. "I can't imagine how *that* went." Margot—with her rehearsed tears and rotating boyfriends. If she even remembered me at all, it would've been for how inconvenient I made her life.

"Not well," Rafael says.

Relief prickles through me, chased quickly by hurt. I nod. Of course it didn't go well. Margot doesn't care. Fifteen years didn't change her stripes.

"I—that's okay," I manage, feeling the need to reassure Rafael that it's better that way.

But then I hear them. Muffled voices. From inside the room. My stomach drops. I glance past Rafael's shoulder, then back to him. And that's when I see it. He's not just standing in front of the door; he's blocking it. "Who's in there?"

Rafael meets my gaze, and I instantly know.

"No," I breathe. The hallway tilts again. "No, no, no."

CHAPTER TWENTY-EIGHT
TWELVE DAYS AFTER, PART II

Margot is here. At the hospital.

She's feet away.

I feel unsteady.

"Evie?" Rafael's voice is laced with concern. He leans in, his eyes scanning my face.

I take a deep breath, then another.

"Why is she here?" I ask, breathless. Rafael pales. Stalls. "Rafael?"

His throat bobs. "She—she wanted to see you."

I cackle, feeling unhinged. Feeling torn between the need to march in there and tell her to leave and the need to run far, far from here. "Why would she want—" The rest of the question burns my throat. "No," I breathe. I move forward on autopilot.

Rafael steps forward, blocking my path.

I stop short, startled. "What . . . what are you doing?"

"Gemma's in there with Margot," he says. "She can't do anything."

I gape up at Rafael. "She can do *everything*," I say, desperate to make him understand—to let me pass. "If Margot is here . . . if she made an actual effort to come here, it's because she wants to stop the sedation. Feeding tube. Whatever medical intervention." Air becomes scarce. "Haven't you been listening to *anything* I said?"

"She can't do that," Rafael says.

"She can," I glance past him, to the door, to where Margot is at. "She's my next of kin. She can do whatever she pleases on my behalf."

Rafael pales, like he's finally seeing what I'm seeing. Because if she's here, the decision for what happens next falls to my mother. The same mother who doesn't stay sober for anything other than putting in for another disability check or some sort of government aid to sustain her while she screws around. And now she's sorting it out with Gemma—making decisions for me.

She's on the other side of the door. Margot, her bleached-blond hair and her overdone makeup, arriving at the hospital and making it about herself. How it's *her* daughter on the bed. How much it hurts *her* that I'm suffering. How unfair life has been to *her* to have taken not one but two of *her* girls.

She's here to bask in the attention, soak up the sympathy, and see if she can make a free buck out of the situation. Then she'll have the doctors turn off the machines because of Jacob Moses, one of her loser boyfriends, who convinced her modern medicine is a conspiracy. It's why we weren't vaccinated and why we didn't see doctors. It's why Annie didn't get the proper treatment, why she's gone.

I want to scream until my throat's raw, until the world shifts back into something that makes sense.

No matter how far I've run to get away from her, she's the one who's going to end it.

I rub my chest, begging my lungs to draw in air.

"When did you know?" I ask Rafael. It hurts everywhere, almost as bad as it hurts to look at him. An hour ago, I was ready to give him my Big Secret, and now . . . I don't remember what I wanted to say. "How long have you known Gemma was looking for my mother?"

Rafael swallows, then shrugs. "She started looking a few days after the accident, but her searches yielded nothing."

I stare at him. "So you've known for *days*? And you didn't think to mention that Gemma was out there looking for my mother?" I can't control the sharp edge of accusation in my voice or the hurt slipping through. "Why didn't you tell me Gemma wanted to find her? Why didn't you stop her?"

"I didn't know about your mom—your history—a few days ago," Rafael says. "And once you showed up? I was distracted, okay? You were here, and we were going to figure out how to get you back. I didn't check in with Gemma to see if she'd found your mom."

I clutch my midsection, feeling ready to throw up. "So at no point between tango lessons and midnight swims did you think *Hey, maybe I should mention this very important thing to Evie, with whom I've been spending almost every minute of my day? Maybe she would care about something like her best friend seeking out a mother she barely even mentioned?*'" My voice is a rasp. "How very Rafael Vela of you!"

His stance stiffens. "What does that even mean?"

I step toward him, emboldened by how anger numbs everything. "It means that you can't be bothered to take a step back and think things through. You never have. I mean, why would you? Everything is rainbows and butterflies in your world! You smile and the world parts for you." He flinches now. "The worst part is that I let myself be Vela'd, and I can't blame anyone but myself. I've sat beside you for years—I've seen you in action. I should have known better than to drop my guard and focus on anything but figuring out how to fix myself." I take a deep breath, feeling like I'm being picked apart molecule by molecule. "I was nothing but one of those girls who forgets how to use her brain because of some guy with dimples and a tattoo." Another molecule has been picked off, and another. "And now? Now I'm going to die because I didn't plan when it counted most. How's that for sticking to every checklist except the one that was literally a matter of life or death?"

The muscle in his cheek jerks. "Are you mad at me or yourself?"

I blink at him, furious. "I should have never thought we could work together again. I should have done this on my own, without all this"—I gesture toward his body, which has somehow moved closer to mine—"distracting me and making me feel like I can't catch a breath." His eyes. Lips. Hands. All the parts of him that have been making me forget about my plans. It's a low blow, one that leaves a bitter taste in my mouth, but I can't stop my hurt from pouring out. "I should have never trusted this to work. It was doomed from the start."

Hurt flashes in his eyes. "If that's how you feel," he says.

I sniff, angry and devastated, and I hate that he's just taking it. "What do you care about how I feel?" I laugh through tears, because I can feel this ghost-form becoming undone—molecules separating in bigger pieces now—and it makes me desperate enough to say things I shouldn't.

"If you had cared, you wouldn't have kept so many secrets from me. Quitting Media Lab. Gemma being your friend. The Art Betton thing. And I thought you were a *bad* liar!"

"Evie." His one word has me halting.

"Rafael," I parry, not caring that he's telling me it's enough. A point of no return. But I've always liked a challenge—and it's not like I have anything else to lose, because it's all gone. Or—at best—dangling by a thread.

I draw in another shaky breath. "Do you know that Margot couldn't be bothered to fill Annie's scripts on time? Or that the night Annie died, my mother threatened us with foster care if we didn't shut up about her feeling unwell?" I'm huffing through tears. "This is the same mother who didn't call or text, not once in fifteen years—the one who is *here*."

"Evie, I'm so—" His gaze softens, as if none of the hurtful things I've said matter.

It pisses me off.

He can't Vela me now.

"Don't apologize. Don't pity me," I whisper as pain, physical and emotional and foundational, explodes everywhere. The hospital corridor flashes around me on all sides.

I blink, willing it all to still.

Only it feels like I'm suffocating.

I turn away from him, needing to steady myself.

I stare right at the door. I need to go in and find a way to stop her.

Another flare of pain sends bursts of white flashing behind my eyes. I gasp, almost doubling over.

I think I'm dying.

"Evie?"

I press the heels of my palms into my eyes, where the pressure threatens to burst, and grind my teeth against it.

I thought I'd be more prepared.

"Talk to me," Rafael pleads.

"Please. Go, Rafael," I say hoarsely. "There's nothing you can do."

Rafael closes in. "I'm not going anywhere."

His refusal reverberates through me, making me feel even more unhinged.

I glare at him. "It's not a request, Rafael!" I swipe furiously at the tears running down my cheeks.

"I'm not leaving you alone." His voice is steady, resolute.

I drop my palms to my sides and curl them into my dress. He's bullheaded until the bitter end, but so am I.

I breathe past the hurricane of pain sweeping through, separating me molecule by molecule, and meet his gaze as I say, "It's better on my own, because I can count on myself more than I could ever count on you."

He opens his mouth, but I don't hear what he says, because an invisible force slams into my middle, deep and hard, knocking me backward.

And I'm falling down, down, down into nothingness, hoping Rafael didn't believe a single word of my lies.

CHAPTER TWENTY-NINE
NOW(ISH)

I'm with Annie.

We're sitting on a bench overlooking Lake Michigan. It's a warm day, and the sun glimmers across the lake. A breeze tugs at our hair. Hers is the same pale yellow I remember, tied into a ponytail. Mine hangs around my shoulders in dyed light-brown strands.

"Isn't this amazing?" Annie's voice is a balm. I stare at her, unsure if I should hug her or kiss her or both.

"It's the *most* amazing," I say, wondering if this is a dream or something more permanent.

A gust of summer-scented wind breezes over us. Annie laughs as she clutches her daisy dress between her knees to keep it against her. I curl my hair behind my ears, failing miserably to keep it from flying everywhere.

"You and that dress." I shake my head, not at all surprised that she still wears it.

"It's the best, isn't it?" Annie smiles so big it crinkles her face as she leans back onto the bench with a sigh. The beach is empty save for an old couple strolling down the boardwalk. A man walking his dog in the distance. And a woman sitting on the bench beside ours, her face buried in a book.

"Where are we?" I ask, my throat tight.

Annie tilts her head in my direction. "You know you're my favorite person."

Unsure about her completely ignoring my question, I nod. "Uh-huh."

"And I want you to be happy."

"I'm happy, Annie."

"You're a terrible liar," she says, and it makes me think of Rafael. My heart somersaults.

"I know. I need to work on that," I drawl. "Just don't tell Great-Aunt Julia."

Annie laughs as her fingers thread through mine. Her hands are smaller than mine now, and the realization makes my chest constrict tightly. "You also forgot about our big dreams."

I stare at her, shocked. "I did not."

"You did. You carried that list everywhere, but you stopped trying to do the things on there because you stopped dreaming," she says. I open my mouth to argue. "I know why you did it, though, and I'm sorry you were so alone, Steves." She squeezes my hand, and the old nickname squeezes my Annie-deprived heart. "But you're not anymore."

I stare at her, swallowing tears, unsure what to say. "Is that why this happened?" I face her, needing to know why I wound up here, wherever *here* is. "Because I was too lonely?"

Annie laughs, leaning into me. "You're silly! Of course not."

I have a hundred questions I want to ask, all fighting to be first. I don't know which one to choose, so I land on the one that scares me most. "So, what's next?"

"That's up to you to decide when you wake up."

I blink, relief making my limbs weak. "I'm not dead?"

"Maybe a little on the inside, but you're going to fix that."

I sniff back tears. "Am I?"

"Your new bucket list item number one," she says. "You need to start living a little. Or else." She narrows her eyes in a poor attempt to threaten me, and we both burst into laughter.

"So scary," I say.

Annie smirks. "I have to get through somehow."

"Message received. Loud and clear. I'll go out there, get tattoos. Some piercings. Hell, I might even ride a motorcycle."

"Can't back down now."

"I won't."

Huge grins on our faces, we sit in silence, watching the waves and feeling so at peace. I startle when Annie nudges my shoulder. "I'll be there watching." Her words sober me, because she won't be with me. "I'm always with you, silly." She taps my chest.

Tears press into my nose and throat. "But . . ."

"Shhh. Close your eyes a minute."

I shake my head, but she elbows me again. I'm reluctant as I do what she says. "Still so bossy . . ."

Annie chuckles. "Big-sis stuff." She sighs, her hand warm against mine. "Isn't it wonderful?"

The sun is warm against my face, but I can't relax. "Annie . . ."

"Come on, Steves."

Feeling uncertain about whatever she's got planned, I breathe in and out, tilting my head up to the sun. After a moment of apprehension, I relax a little, feeling like I've missed its warmth on my face. I take in another big breath. The scent of the beach mixed with sunshine fills me with a sense of calm I haven't felt in so long. Maybe ever.

"It's the best, isn't it?" Annie asks.

"Nothing compares," I whisper, squeezing her hand tight, wanting to hold on forever.

We sit like that, eyes closed, faces tilted up to the sun. Birds chirp. Waves crash. The wind sighs.

Annie takes a deep breath. "I love you. Always."

"I love you—"

CHAPTER THIRTY
NOW

I didn't die.

The thought weasels through the outrageous headache making my head feel like it's being torn apart by piranhas. This is followed by a wave of nausea creeping into my throat.

Groaning—as one does when they wake up from dying—I blink my eyes open. Muted light sends a pang of pain vibrating through my brain. I feel as if I've downed a bottle of tequila and topped it off with two bottles of merlot, so I turn to breathing exercises.

One Mamma Mia.

Two Mamma Mia.

The sensation sinks its razor-sharp teeth in again, and I close my eyes, forcing my brain to focus. A staccato beeping cuts through my brain fog, and I snap my eyes open, then narrow them to slits when the light in the room makes my stomach crawl its way into my throat. I clamp my lips together and grind my teeth.

I will not throw—

"Oh my God, she's about to throw up."

Cold hands touch my skin and hold back my hair as I heave into a plastic tub, my throat burning like the nine circles of hell. I'm heaving and crying, but the cold hands stay with me as it passes. I lie back down, and Gemma's face comes into focus.

Her hair is tied into a messy bun, and her eyes are puffy and red. Her cool fingers move to my hand and squeeze. "Hey," she says, then sobs. Such a baby. "You're back. You're here."

I take in a deep breath. Pain follows, settling deep into my bones and making it hard to make sense of Gemma's words.

"Back?" I croak. The throbbing in my head lobs from the base of my skull to the forefront. Gemma's face contorts in confusion, but I don't know if it's my imagination . . . or reality.

Her hold tightens. "You've been . . . out for a while." She smiles, her teeth straight and white . . . and too bright? I close my eyes and sink back into the pillows with a groan. A wave of weakness swamps me.

Everything goes black.

* * *

When I open my eyes, it feels like someone's anchored them to iron weights, and it takes legitimate effort to blink them open. The room's darker than before, so I let my eyes adjust.

I'm in a hospital bed, and I'm attached to IVs and monitors, which hinder my already feeble movements. I feel like I'm an anchor that's been tossed off the side of a ship and gotten stuck at the bottom of the ocean. Most days I can name at least three deep-sea species of fish on the brink of extinction; now I simply feel like one of them.

Taking a deep breath, I push myself upward, wincing at all the parts that hurt. But another groan joins mine, then the scraping of a chair and a male "Hold on!"

As I will my synapses to fire and for coherent thoughts to form, Ollie appears above me, a phone in his hand. "Evie! You're awake!"

"I'll be right there!" Gemma squeals from the other end of the phone.

"Hi, I'm Ollie," he shouts, like I've forgotten who he is . . . or gone deaf. He holds the phone up to my face, where it has the uncanny power to make more of the nausea climb into my throat.

"Too bright," I croak, attempting to lift my hand to ward off the brightness.

"Sorry!" Ollie drops the phone as Gemma shouts into it. "I'll get the doctor." Ollie trips over his legs as he scrambles for the door, Gemma's voice bidding him to do her will.

The door closes and I lean back, breathing in and out.

I'm in a hospital. I'm attached to tubes. And I have no idea how the hell I got here.

CHAPTER THIRTY-ONE
A WEEK LATER

Recovery for coma patients can take several weeks, says Dr. Wagner, neurologist at Northwestern Memorial Hospital. She's on the bossy side, but she seems capable and answers my questions, and what more can I ask for?

Will I recover? Yes.

When can I go home? Depends on me.

Will I regain my memory from the night of the accident? Maybe.

Well, they're half answers, but I understand. Brain injuries are complicated, and I'm lucky to be alive. Waking up after almost two weeks in a coma without significant disabilities is rare. She doesn't use the word *miracle*, but her implication is clear.

Gemma does use the word *miracle*, and she hasn't left my room in three days, save to go home and shower and sleep. She alternates between asking me if I need anything else (I don't) and frantically typing into her phone.

I want to know about work—about what's happened at Media Lab in the time I've been gone—but I'm afraid to know about what's changed. It doesn't take a wild imagination to guess. Rafael got the promotion, and he's probably made himself comfortable in the corner office.

I don't think too long on it, but it's likely I'll have to find a new job, because there's no way I'm working for Rafael Vela. Even if he did send me a bouquet of beautiful hydrangeas and a Kate Spade planner with a note that said *Glad you're back, E.*

I wanted to toss the planner across the room, but it was too nice to do something so atrocious to it. Instead, I had Gemma disinfect it and set it with my things.

"All right, Evie, do you have other questions for me?" Dr. Wagner asks.

"When do I go home?"

Her smile is kind, professional, and devoid of annoyance, even though I've asked the question several times. "When you can walk from one end of the hallway to the other three times without needing to stop."

I return her smile, checklists of how I get to that point coming together. "Perfect."

When she's gone, Gemma replaces her beside my bed. "How do you feel?"

"Tired. Frustrated."

"Be patient with yourself and the process."

I think of Rafael making himself at home in what was going to be my office. "Not among my greatest traits."

Gemma laughs, her hand taking mine. "Work is right where you left it."

"Is it?"

"We said we're not talking about anything that can stress you out."

"Did we?"

She squeezes. "Yep. Work, recovery plan, and Rafael—all off the table."

I crinkle my nose. "Can I get clues?"

"Nope."

"Not even one?"

"Not even one. We need you to get out of here, and that means taking it easy."

I bury my face in the pillow, groaning in frustration. "This is going to be awful, isn't it?"

"I think it's going to be just what the doctor ordered."

CHAPTER THIRTY-TWO
TWO WEEKS LATER

I'm finally home and alone.

It took all of another week—six days, to be exact—to walk the length of the corridor for Dr. Wagner and to pass a few other tests before she signed my discharge papers, telling me I'd need to give it another week before I resumed normal activities, like work, which I still haven't inquired about, even when Dana and a few of my team members texted to check in. The temptation to know about the status of OhLaLove and Rafael made my fingers itch, but I was too "frail" (cowardly) to ask, so I updated them on my health and progress instead.

I'll face the music on Monday—thirty-one days since I was last there—when I meet with Dana and see what's next for me.

But I promised the doc I wouldn't stress. Yet.

I have an entire weekend to settle back into my life without the incessant mothering of Gemma, who unsurprisingly roped Cristina into a twenty-four-hour-a-day mission to keep me comfortable and relaxed. I was *one* of those things in the last week of being coddled and fed (and almost bathed, which only my vehement opposition prevented). *It's from a good place,* I had to remind myself every time they popped their heads into my bedroom with another bowl of soup or a cup of tea. Still, I nearly hugged my door when it closed behind them earlier.

It's finally quiet. No monitors or beeping. No medical staff or hospital noises. No Gemma or Cristina. Just silence. I soak it in as I settle at my kitchen counter, which is now cluttered with bouquets of flowers and boxes of chocolate and cookies—gifts from friends and coworkers. A beautiful orchid from Charlene. A homemade card from Cristina's granddaughter. And to my shock, another gift from Rafael.

Mildly curious, I carefully unfold the note attached to it. *#8—From Yours Truly.* It's nonsense in his scrawl. I crinkle my nose at his choice of sign-off. *As if.*

Reluctant, I open the package to discover *Madrigal's Magic Key to Spanish.* I flip through the pages, hoping another note will explain the meaning behind the gift. I've tried to learn Spanish several times, and most of those times it was an attempt to start deciphering Rafael's rapid-fire Spanish conversations. If his "gift" is meant to taunt me, I'm only mildly annoyed by it (because I'm not allowed to feel anything but super *relaxed*). When—and if—I decide to learn Spanish, I'll do it on my own terms, thank you very much.

I ball up his note and drag myself to my bedroom, where I practically melt into my bed, into the down comforter and pillows, because—between a near-death experience, two weeks of being in a coma, and two more weeks in recovery—the post-coma exhaustion is real, and not that I'd admit it, I don't think I'm completely fixed.

I press a hand to my chest.

Even though it wasn't my heart that was hurt, it's the part that feels the sorest, like it was pulled out of me, altered in a substantial way, and shoved back into my chest, where it doesn't quite fit the same.

Like I lost a part of me I might never recover.

Nothing a good sleep won't fix.

* * *

I wake up in a panic, my heart skittering against my rib cage. My phone tells me I've slept for six hours, yet somehow I feel worse than before I napped.

The gnawing sensation that was contained to my chest seems to have spread while I slept. I try to rub the sensation away. To breathe and relax.

When it doesn't immediately happen, I go to the kitchen for a glass of water. I gulp it down, pour another, and lean against the marble counter, nudging Rafael's crumpled note with my elbow. I set the glass down and smooth down the paper, imagining his tanned fingers and hand moving across the paper. Him smiling his insufferable smirk.

#8. Yours Truly.

He's not the best with words, but this means *nothing.* A bunch of nonsense. A joke only he understands.

Number eight? What in the hell does that have to do with anything?

The Spanish guide stares at me from beside the note.

And it hits me, like a wrecking ball to the brain.

#8: Learn Spanish.

My bucket list. One that Rafael apparently knows about.

Taking a deep, deep breath, I try to *think, think, think* about how he could have gotten his backstabbing hands on it. Sure, I've crossed some boundaries in our rivalry, but my *planner*?

God! I could just . . . tear out his hair. He doesn't even deserve those luscious locks. And when he runs his hands through his hair . . . watching me from across a dance floor, senior citizens around us, a tango playing in the background and my heart thumping to the beat . . .

I blink, confused by the images.

But there are others.

A man in a poncho lights candles in my living room. People and food and music fill a backyard. Rafael and I are standing oh-so-close in my guest bath. In his apartment, pots and pans on the stove, Rafael is tasting soup while explaining the magic of chilis. We're wading in the lake in the middle of the night, playing truth or dare. My breathing stops. And *ohmygod.*

I sink to the kitchen floor with a thump.

I don't think I hate Rafael Vela.

I'm glad for the ground beneath my ass, because my heart's engaging in emotional Olympics.

Closing my eyes, I force my breathing to *get it together.*

One Mamma Mia.

I was a ghost (or a spirit—I never quite figured it out).

Two Mamma Mia.

I spent all those days with Rafael.

Three Mamma Mia.

And I fell for him.

Leaning my head against the island, I mentally pick apart each of the memories, or was it a dream? But I wouldn't have *dreamt* those days with Rafael. Vivid nightmares in which he's torturing me or sweet dreams where I torture him? Yes. But imagining a reality where I wake up with him each day? Most certainly not my idea of a dream.

It was real, and I spent those days with him. Up until . . .

"I can count on myself more than I could ever count on you." The words—*my words*—right before it ended, before I pushed him away.

I feel sick.

I went for the kill, and he wants nothing to do with me. No emails, no texts—not even ones to taunt me. The evidence is all there.

And can I blame him? Not even a little. I was cruel and selfish. If he never wants to see me again, I deserve it. If we're back to being rivals, I earned that.

Liar! My heart snaps. I could never hate him again. I never hated him to begin with. And I can't let him think I meant any of it. I wish I could get a do-over and take it all back (just kidding, Great-Aunt Julia!).

All I know is I can't live with Rafael cutting me out of his life. Because turns out, I want to be in his. Not as a coworker. Not as a ghost with unresolved feelings. But as me, flesh and flaws and all.

The threads of a plan—the craziest, most reckless one—begin to weave together. My checklists until now were written with a specific goal in mind: moving ahead in the world. I was ensuring my future, ensuring that I never went back to survival mode. That I never felt vulnerable again.

My next checklist doesn't guarantee any of that. Because I'm going to tell him.

Teetering on the verge of passing out or doing a dance, I push from the floor and find my phone. My fingers wobble as I unlock it and tap on Gemma's name.

She's beaten me to the texting game.

Gemma: *Are you okay?* (Sent 9:18 PM)

Gemma: *I hope you're not answering because you're sleeping.* (Sent 9:20 PM)

Gemma: *You have ten minutes to text me before I head over.* (Sent 9:25 PM)

I groan aloud.

Me: *I was sleeping. I'm alive and well and fed. I promise.*

Three dots dance on the screen, but the text never comes because Gemma's face pops up on the screen as it buzzes. Steeling myself, I answer.

"Are you okay?" She sounds breathless.

"I'm fine." A lie. I'm the opposite of fine until I find Rafael and talk to him, after which I might permanently reside in the *opposite of fine* zip code.

"You know I've known you too long to believe that."

I start pacing. "Physically, I'm fine," I amend. "But I need you to tell me about the day before I woke up . . . or the day I did. What happened?"

"Hard to explain," Gemma says carefully. "One moment you were burning up, and the next, the doctors came in. There was chaos—alarms and scrambling. They kicked me out of there . . . and then, after what seemed like ages, you started stabilizing."

I try to think back to that moment. "Margot was there," I breathe, piecing it together.

Gemma's quiet. "Yes," she says reluctantly, like's she's not quite sure how I know . . . and one day, when I process it all, I'll tell her. "I went looking for her," she adds quickly. "And I know you're going to hate me for it, because I should have known better, but I thought she should know. That if . . ." Gemma hesitates. "If you didn't make it, she should know. But she decided she was going to come along because she was your mother, and that's when I knew I had fucked up."

"I don't hate you," I interject. "And you did what you thought was right."

"Still, I felt like a turd. A big turd," Gemma says. "Especially when she showed up, acting like a doting mother, demanding the doctors take you off all the medication because it was *unnatural*—that it was prolonging the inevitable."

I stop pacing, needing to know. "And?"

"She tried to strong-arm the team, started screaming about being next of kin, about not wanting you to live like that,"

Gemma says. "It was bad. So bad that eventually the doctors told her to step back, but she only kept escalating, so they asked her to leave, and when she refused, they had her removed. And during all that, all your vitals were through the roof."

"And that's it?" I ask, not connecting the dots.

"I mean, that's the summary of it," she says. "In the end, your vitals—they stabilized. Quickly. Unnaturally, almost." She has no idea. "They tapered the sedation, and you did well on your own." There's a smile and relief in her voice. "And that improved until you could be weaned off of it entirely. Until you could come back."

I have so many questions. I ask the loudest one. "And Rafael?"

All I hear is the hum of the road in the background. "Are you sure it's a good time to talk about Raf? You know Dr. Wagner said you need to—"

"Relax. I got it, Mama Bear. I promise this has nothing to do with work or anything stress inducing."

"Raf? Not stress inducing?"

"Gem!"

"Okay, I'll bite. He's fine. He's doing his thing."

"His thing?" I hope *thing* isn't code for a person.

"Well, I don't know if this is a big ol' secret or not, but he quit Media Lab. He's making tequila now." La Clandestina! The bar. His business with Lupe. More memories click into place. "Anyway, he's good. In fact, tonight is the launch of La Cla—his bar."

A knot tightens in my belly. Of course it's the night of his launch. Of course he's moved on with his life. Of course I'm here being a fool who thinks she can track him down and explain everything.

"Evie?" Gemma's tone turns panicky.

"Yes, I'm here." But I'm thinking about Rafael and where to go from here. I could schedule a time to chat, like normal people who have lives and friends and people who love them. Or not.

The thought of waiting makes me restless, and I stride into my closet and flip on the light. Rows of color-coded clothing and shoes line each of the walls. "Gem?"

"Yes?"

"I want to go to the launch." A surge of adrenaline makes me dizzy.

"Um. Do you—"

"And I'm going to need you to be a little less Mama Bear Gemma and a lot more Ladies' Night at the Club Gem. Okay?" My tone leaves little room for her to argue.

"I don't think . . ."

"No thinking involved," I say to the both of us. "Not tonight."

CHAPTER THIRTY-THREE
A MONTH SINCE THE ACCIDENT (THE HARD PART)

The line around La Clandestina wraps around the building.

Jitters make me wobble on my stilettos—Stuart Weitzman pumps that complement the red bandage dress I'm wearing.

Beside me, Gemma's dressed in a black, flowy minidress. Gemma's one of those women who make beauty effortless. I, on the other hand, needed Gemma's magic touch to make me appear like I didn't spend the last month in a hospital. Another miracle.

Gazes from curious to heated follow us as we march to the front of the line, where a security guard—Owen!—keeps the crowd at bay. Behind him, music thumps over the din of chatter. Even so, my blood thunders between my ears, and syncope might be both my best friend and my worst enemy right now.

Gemma's shrewd eyes zone in on me, so I flash her a thumbs-up. "This is amazing!" My voice sounds like I've sucked in a balloon's worth of helium. Her eyes turn to slits. "*Ladies' Night*

Gem!" I remind her, directing her to Owen, still somewhat intimidated by his girth and tattoos.

"We're on the list," Gemma says, flashing her phone in front of his nose. "Personal guests of Rafael's."

Owen's eyes slide from Gemma to me, and I mimic Gemma's confident posture. A little part of me hopes he'll think I'm awkward and turn us away.

His bald head jerks toward the door. Gemma's cool fingers thread through my clammy ones, and she drags me into La Clandestina. It's dim inside the bar. The massive skull glows faintly on the wall, lit from underneath. Music thrums through the space—steady and upbeat—blending with the low hum of the conversation. The place is full but not crowded, just enough to give it a pulse. And somewhere in the midst of it all . . . is Rafael.

I retreat a small step, Gemma's shoulder brushing against mine, eyes boring into me. "Ladies' Night Gem wants to know if you really want to be here," she says over the music.

"Yes!" I say, but it comes out too enthusiastically.

"Then why aren't we going in?"

Rafael turning me away seems like a good answer. "Taking it all in."

"Let's take it in from inside, because I'm not sure the line behind us appreciates being kept from the bar." Gemma pulls me forward, leading the way as we cross the space toward an empty high-top at the same time that another group of women, looking like they've come from a *Vogue* photo shoot, encroaches on it as well.

Gemma decides we can share the table, and she's already introducing the two of us. Before we slip into small talk and I lose my courage, I cut in, "I'm grabbing a drink. Want anything?"

"I can come with."

"Stay and make friends. I'll be right back." I force a smile to reassure her that *I got this*.

"A skinny marg," Gemma concedes. I slip away before she can Mama Bear me some more.

People crowd around the bar, which makes it more difficult to reach the counter . . . and to discern which person might be Rafael.

I circle around until I find an empty stool, nerves pulsing along to The Weeknd on the speakers. Crystal skull candleholders line the length of the counter. La Clandestina tequila lines the shelves. And everyone seems to be enjoying themselves.

"What can I get you?" someone shouts from the other side of the bar. She smiles, her white teeth contrasting with her burgundy lips.

"Lupe!" I squeal before I can catch myself, because we never actually met. Her smile falters, and mine wavers too. "I'm Evie." I jut my hand out to shake hers. Her eyes bounce from my face to my hands and back. I want to forget the last five seconds, but her cat eyes narrow and focus.

"Evie Pope?" I add. "Or does *cabrona* ring a bell?"

Her features transition from confusion to recognition in the span of a blink. She throws her head back and laughs, a deep throaty laugh. Then she's ducking underneath the bar and wrapping her arms around me in a tight hug. "Holy shiiiit! You're here!" She pulls away, her head shaking in disbelief. "And you remember that? Damn! I mean, I thought Raffi was losing it or something, but—mierda—wow!" She pulls me into another hug.

"Yeah," I mumble into her shoulder. She pulls away. "Congrats! On everything. It's great!" I gesture at the space.

"Thanks. It was mostly Raffi," she says with a wide grin. "But enough about me and him. We have so much to talk about!"

"Lupe!" someone shouts from down the bar, waving her over.

"Uh, people." She rolls her eyes.

"Go, you're needed. Plus we can chat another time," I say, wondering if she'll still want drinks if Rafael decides he wants nothing to do with me. She waffles, indecision warring in her bright eyes. "Seriously, go!"

"Okay! Can't wait!" She smacks a kiss onto my cheek and begins to walk away before she spins on a scuffed boot. "I'm sorry about the *cabrona* thing," she shouts, then winks, grabbing glasses and a bottle as she heads to her guests. "Your drinks are right here!"

A drink. Something I never ordered. A little of my energy drains at the prospect of calling for another bartender or doing this entire thing without some liquid courage. Maybe I'm *not* ready. Maybe I should have stayed home. Maybe—

"Evie." His husky voice makes my knees give.

My insides set afire, I turn to him, digging my fingers into my clutch to keep them from shaking.

Rafael is within touching distance, one elbow leaning against the bar, the other hand at his side. He's dressed sharply—dress pants and a dark navy shirt rolled up to his elbows. Unlike the last time I saw him, his hair's trimmed, but he's kept his facial hair.

I want to feel it. Feel him.

"Are you okay?" He leans in, his nearness a magnetic pull I have to resist. His familiar eyes scan me, hypnotize me, and make me forget words.

"Um. Yes," I say, my voice a croak. "Really great." I smile too wide, because he frowns.

"Are you sure you're supposed to be out?" His question stops me from burying my face in his chest. "I'm glad you're here, but should you be?"

He's looking at me like we're the only two people here. Thoughts become obsolete. I should be saying all the things I came here to say, but all I want to do is touch him. My fingers zap with the urge.

I lean into him, as if tugged nearer by an invisible thread. "Yes," I respond, sounding a little too breathless to prove I'm indeed okay. "Don't listen to Gemma."

"Never." Rafael smiles, a shadow of The Dimple in his cheek. Everything about him is so heartachingly familiar. I want to thread my fingers into his hair and pull his face to mine. I want to press my lips to his and finally see what he tastes like.

The music's beat changes, and its erratic thumping transfers to my chest. My heart shimmies.

"You . . . forgot your pen." I dig into my clutch, holding up a pen from the day of Doug's séance.

Rafael looks at me with concern as he takes it. His fingers brush against mine, sending a jolt through me, and I wish I had more pens to give him. "E—"

"Can we talk?" The words rush out without preamble. No number of pens is going to do what I came here to do. He looks past me for a second, and I immediately regret asking, because he's going to say no. He's going to send me away. He's going to—

Rafael jerks his head to the back of the bar. "Come on." His hand drops to his side, and I feel the insane urge to take it and hold on to it as he cuts a path through the throng of people. Others shake his hand or touch him without a second thought, but for me, it's all I can think about. I dig my nails into my palm.

Gemma catches my gaze. Her face furrows with a question as she begins to pull away from her table. I shake my head, mouthing *stay*, when I should be begging her to come save me from doing something stupid. The crease in her usually smooth forehead deepens, like she can see my nerves beneath the surface, but she listens and halts. And I follow the man I cannot touch.

Always a sliver of space between us, we squeeze through the crowd around the bar and past the DJ booth into a hallway, where it's darker and cooler. Yet somehow my temperature spikes.

Rafael slows in front of the room with the PRIVATE sign and turns to me, his face inscrutable as he opens the door, pushing into it with a shoulder.

"After you," he says, waiting for me to pass.

Taking a deep and not-at-all-helpful breath, I do the bravest thing I've done since waking up and enter.

CHAPTER THIRTY-FOUR
A MONTH SINCE THE ACCIDENT (THE HARDER PART)

I don't know what I'm doing.

It's all I can think as I step into the room, which feels much, much smaller and more furnished than the last time we were in here. Between the desk, chair, two-person sofa, and *him*, it feels too snug. Another frisson of heat licks down and up and everywhere, scorching as it goes. I press my thighs together.

My back to the desk, I face Rafael, who leans against the door. Muffled music thumps from the other side, mirroring a lot of the thumping happening in my chest.

I can do this.

I'm Evie Pope.

"Nice party," I say, a slight hitch to my voice. "It's really nice." I inwardly cringe. *Nice*?

Rafael's lips quirk to one side. "Thanks, though it's mostly Lupe's doing."

"That's what she said about you."

"She thinks too highly of me, and she shouldn't. I'm sure you can agree with the sentiment."

It takes a second for his words to sink in. This is the moment when Pre-Coma Evie would have said something harsh and biting. When I would have said the opposite of what comes out of my mouth. "I don't agree with that sentiment at all. In fact, that's why I'm here."

Rafael's gaze turns quizzical. "Are you sure you're okay?"

Far from it, I should say. Instead, I nod. "Yeah, totally fine." The pressure in my chest would disagree. "I . . . there's some things I wanted to talk about, and I know this is probably not the best time, given . . ." I gesture to the door behind him. "But I couldn't wait." I shake my head. "But it could, I guess. If you have to go back."

Any amusement flickers out of his gaze, replaced by concern. "What's wrong?"

"Nothing. It's just . . ." *That I have no clue what the hell I'm doing.* But maybe I do? Because this may be scarier and bigger than any dream or goal I've ever pursued. Or any account I've prepared for. Years of research have gone into this moment—into learning about and understanding Rafael. This pitch has been hundreds of hours in the making. It all comes down to me—to this moment, to my delivery—to bring it home.

I dig my fingers into my clutch as if I'm siphoning the courage I need for this next part.

"I'm not good at this part, Raf, but I am good at making plans and checklists. It makes me feel in control in a world where very little actually is. Those plans keep me focused and offer me stability, because checking off the boxes means forward motion, and that's what I've done for years, moving forward and running. From my mother and past, from nightmares and heartache." I breathe out shakily, then smile the way you would if you were chewing glass. "Running brought me to Media Lab, where I could make money to ensure my future, and this made my job *everything.* So maybe you can understand that I saw you as a threat after the Betton situation." Saying the name no longer makes me angry or hurt. "But I was so wrong, because while I saw you as a threat, you were also a constant. You were always there, pushing me, even if you knew it or not. Helping me move forward."

Rafael's features are inscrutable. My heart stutters.

This is a pitch meeting, I remind myself, and keep plowing ahead. "I would never have admitted this out loud to a living soul—including myself—but I looked forward to seeing you—the back-and-forth, our stupid contests, the way you always questioned whether I had some secret agenda before a big client meeting or outing."

I huff a laugh when I think of all the times Rafael skipped office meals in advance of client meetings in case I had messed with his food or checked his golf clubs to make sure I hadn't swapped his for others.

"You were also the last person I saw in the office a lot of those nights. In some strange way, there was comfort—security—in knowing you were there, and I didn't realize how much that meant until I spent those days with you and everything suddenly came into focus. How you could pull me out of my head and make me slow down. How you could calm me down or make me laugh. You were there in more ways than I knew I needed. Even at the end, you—" My voice wavers, but I keep going.

"You were comforting me, taking care of me, and making me *live*, and the worst part is I didn't realize until that night in the lake that I had it all wrong. You'd never been a threat to anything. You were *it*—somehow you'd become stability and survival." Tears burn the backs of my eyes and throat. I sniff. "The realization scared the shit out of me . . . because the last time someone was stability and survival for me, they were taken from me, and it hurt for a really long time." I flick a tear away. "I realized too late you'd been there all along, and I only had to stop running long enough to see it. I would call myself smart, but clearly, I haven't been very smart at all."

Rafael watches me with his dark eyes, giving me no indication of whether the pitch is working or if he thinks I've permanently messed up my head. But it's too late to turn back.

"That morning at the hospital, I came to tell you how I felt, but when you told me Margot was there, it threatened *everything.* And I was so hurt that it was easier to go back to how it all was before. To see it as another betrayal. To push you away and hurt you back."

Another tear escapes. Rafael's eyes shutter, like he's closing up, like I should probably leave.

Be brave, Post-Coma Evie whispers.

I continue, "When I woke up at the hospital, I didn't remember any of those days as a spirit, or whatever the hell I was, but I felt different—altered in some inexplicable way—and it took a couple weeks for me to put it together and understand this fullness in my chest." I huff a tearful laugh. "Sure, I lost my memory, but I couldn't shake the feeling that something was missing. *Someone* was missing. So here I am, on this incredibly special night for you, doing an incredibly stupid thing, because that's this new version of Evie Pope."

Post-Coma Evie cheers.

My cheeks flush with embarrassment when he's quiet a second too long. But then he pushes from the door, taking a step toward me. My heart throws itself against my rib cage when he draws near and stops inches away. "To be clear, I'm the someone?"

"I thought it was obvious."

"Making sure it wasn't Rabbi Steve or something," he says, his hands in his pockets. Depriving me of them.

I chuckle, swiping at my face. "If anything, it was Doug. All that hair."

Rafael grins, then takes a measured breath. "I have to say some things to you too—things I've wanted to say for a long time but never found the time for." There's an unsteady edge in his voice, beneath all his confidence, that makes my chest go tight.

"Okay," I say, barely above a whisper.

"This is going to sound insane," he mutters, dragging a hand through his hair. "But I think . . . I think this was all my fault."

"What do you mean?" I gape at him, surprised. Confused.

"The accident."

I blink, unsure if I've heard him. "Raf—that's ridiculous."

His gaze locks with mine, and there's something unguarded in his expression, something that makes my breath hitch and halt. "That night . . . we had an argument. You were furious I didn't follow the plan, and I was frustrated because you were fixated on that instead of us winning the account . . . and you wouldn't stop to listen. And I tried to stop you, but not hard enough. I let you go, thinking we'd pick things up tomorrow, thinking you'd be there." His jaw clenches. "And then you weren't."

My chest feels too small for my lungs and heart.

"I didn't sleep for days," he admits. "I ran through that night on repeat, thinking about how I could have done it all differently, wishing I could take it all back. *All* of it." Tears blur my vision. I blink them away. "And the worst part? I still couldn't let you go. Even after the doctors said there wasn't much they could do, even when I sat there, looking at you, knowing I'd have to say goodbye, I just couldn't."

I press a shaky hand to my chest, unsure if my heart's stopped altogether.

"I begged," he says. "I *prayed* for you to stay. Even if you hated me, even if you never spoke to me again. I just needed you *here*." His throat bobs. "And then . . . you were."

I don't think I'm breathing.

"That morning when you showed up in my apartment, I thought I was losing my mind. It was impossible that you were there . . . a *ghost*. And when I realized you weren't, I felt . . . relief. Like maybe I had another chance to fix it."

His confession knocks the air out of me.

Rafael *blamed* himself for the accident. "Raf . . ."

"One more thing, E." His expression softens. "That's not the only reason I couldn't let you go."

I swallow hard, really needing to reach out and reassure him that it's *not* his fault.

"I've loved you for as long as I've known you," he says, his voice steady, certain. "And I couldn't let you go until you knew."

Ohmygod.

"I came to Media Lab on a whim," he continues, oblivious to the fact that I might be experiencing an actual heart condition. "Harry knew someone there and thought I might learn to like it. The first month I couldn't stop thinking about how I should have stuck to law school, because nothing clicked. Nothing kept my attention too long or made me feel like I could be good at it." A small smile splits his face. "Not until you started, not until you made me realize that I had to *want* to be good at something long enough to *become* good at it. I had to try. Plan. *Commit.*"

I choke out a laugh through the lump in my throat.

"But I ruined it with the Betton shit. I felt lost . . . and I knew I had to find a way back to being your friend, and I didn't know how. Didn't realize what I was up against." He levels a pointed look at me, and I huff out another laugh, even as a stray tear betrays me. "Truth is, despite your anger and your vengefulness, you made me want to be better. You made me want to work harder, to fight for what I wanted." His voice is hoarse. "And in the end, it was you."

I squeeze my eyes shut for a beat, overwhelmed by emotions and the need to touch him.

"When the accident happened, the thought of a world without you was unfathomable. So having your spirit around made it okay, made me feel like I had my chance to tell you how I felt, like I've wanted to tell you every day since the first day, especially on the days I knew you hated me most and thought I returned the favor." Rafael chuckles like he's barely holding himself together. "I didn't understand any of it until we talked to Abuela and Helene and Doug." He shakes his head. "You didn't have unfinished business, E." He lifts his gaze to mine, eyes full of something so fierce and devastating it makes my knees buckle.

"You were *mine*," he says.

I feel myself swaying.

"*Mamma Mia*," I breathe shakily.

"*Mamma Mia*," he echoes. "You don't have to process it all at once, E. I'll repeat it again for you tomorrow . . . and the day after. For as long as you need." He leans in, his forehead pressing against mine. "If you'll let me."

My pulse riots. "I just—I can't believe—"

Rafael's mouth captures mine, cutting off the rest. Thoughts. Words. Air.

I lean into him, into his lips. It's not urgent, not desperate. It's steady and certain, like he's meant to be kissing me. Like he's *waited* to. And all the yearning—the last few weeks, maybe years of it—feed the moment.

His full, warm lips press into mine with a tenderness that makes something deep in me sigh in relief. His hands cup my face, his thumbs caressing my cheekbones. I flatten my hands against his flat, hard chest and press into him, curling my fingers into the fabric of his shirt, needing more of him, of *this*.

I tug him closer still, and he deepens the kiss. His breath is minty, with a hint of tequila. I don't think I can have enough of him. Yet I want more.

I want him.

I shift, arching into him with a soft moan. Rafael groans. And the heat that's been simmering between us since day one ignites, a warm pool of lava and desire, churning and burning and making me want to tear off his clothes. I tug him even closer.

Rafael chuckles against my mouth, guiding me back until the desk edge digs into my thighs and his body presses in. I drag my hands over all the parts of him I've wanted to touch for so long. His kisses move over all the parts of me that have needed his touch for so long.

Rafael braces his hands on either side of my hips, caging me in as he leans into me. I tilt my head, giving his lips access to my neck. His breath ghosts over my skin, coaxing a shiver. Slowly, torturously, he trails lower . . . down the column of my neck, pressing soft kisses in a path of slow, seductive sabotage . . .

I press my thighs together, resisting the urge to wrap them around him, to pull him to me and live out fantasies I've only dared imagine. I thread my fingers into his hair—soft and thick—and he exhales like my touch alone is undoing him.

"Dios," he mutters into my skin, his voice raspy, reverent. "You taste like heaven."

"Must be my close call with it," I breathe, earning a chuckle that rumbles through both of us.

His hand drags down my thigh, gathering the material of my dress, fingers trailing fire over bare skin. The sensation sears itself into my flesh, my bones, my DNA.

The deep ache coiled low in my core threatens to overcome me. A shaky breath shudders out of me as my legs part slightly, instinct and desire overriding logic, reaching for—

A knock on the door snaps us out of the moment.

We still. Rafael's lips hover against my neck, my fingers tangled in his hair, his hands gripping my thighs.

He scowls at the door.

"Who is it?" His voice is a raspy bark.

"Can you open the door?" a woman asks.

Rafael groans. "What is it, Gracie?"

"Mama wants to leave, and she'd like to say bye. Also, there's like a million people out there looking for you, so whatever you're doing right now better be more important than *your* launch party."

Rafael drops his head with a shake, his hair disheveled and his shirt untucked. His hand doesn't so much as twitch against my thigh. In fact, he caresses the skin there with the pad of his thumb, his eyes glazed with desire as he turns his head toward the door. "I'll be right there."

"Two minutes!" she commands before her footsteps retreat.

Sighing, he leans his head against mine and groans again. "Mierda."

"Mierda," I echo, breathless.

For a second, we just exist in the wreckage of what almost was. I'm buzzing—frustrated, flustered, and way too aware of every inch of space (or lack thereof) between us. Because almost isn't enough. Not anymore.

Rafael pulls away, reluctant, disheveled. He watches me as he tucks the shirt into his pants and attempts to fix his hair. It refuses to stay in place. "Good?"

I run my gaze over his (still unfairly attractive) form and crinkle my nose. "I liked the sweatpants better."

He smirks, thumb brushing my lower lip like he's memorizing the feel of me. "I need ten minutes." Everywhere we touch, my skin burns. "If you want to stay."

"I . . . should probably go. You have your party, and I shouldn't have come and—"

Rafael drops his hand to my waist and tugs me to him. "I wouldn't have cared if you were the only one who showed up. In fact, I hate it didn't go that way."

I flatten my hands against his chest, smoothing down his now-rumpled shirt.

"Too bad for you, everyone loves you."

"Is that so?"

I push up to my feet and meet him at eye level. "More than can possibly be healthy." I feel his smile as I press my lips to his, leaning into him, breathing him in and committing his scent to memory.

Another knock rattles the door, and Rafael curses.

I nudge him away. "Go."

"I'm sorry." He opens the door, blocking his older sister from view. Her eyes snag on me, widening with shock, before the door shuts.

Rafael's gone—and it takes all of my willpower not to follow.

CHAPTER THIRTY-FIVE
THAT NIGHT (THE HARDEST PART)

I fix my hair, recover my clutch, and check my phone. Ten texts from Gemma.

Where are you?

Are you ok?

Do I need to come bury Rafael's body?

I laugh, inclined to text her that the only crime that's happened here tonight is that I've been left to burn and that the perpetrator continues to scorch all the places he's touched, especially the ones I've only imagined him touching.

But to be fair, it is Rafael's night. I shouldn't be feeling any sort of way about him having to go back to his family and friends and business.

Fighting the urge to go out there and yell at everyone to go home already, I text Gemma that I'm totally fine and that I'll find her soon.

I take a deep breath and curl my hands around the doorknob.

It moves before I can twist it, and the door opens.

Rafael stands in the doorway, his gaze so intense it makes my knees knock together. Without looking away, he closes the door and locks it. Prowls forward.

"What—" I don't finish because his mouth is on mine, swallowing the rest of the question. He moves so fast I grip his shirt to steady myself, and he's pushing us back into the small office, his hands cradling my face as he guides me backward, his lips searing a promise into mine.

My ass hits the edge of the desk.

I don't think or question or doubt.

Dress hiking up around my hips, I hook my legs around his waist and draw him to me. Rafael leans forward, one arm braced on the desk, another one curling around my neck, holding me to him. I lift up, into him, his hardness pressing into my core, taunting me through the thin material of my panties. I moan into his mouth as he mutters against my skin, kissing as he goes. His breath hot against my neck, I lean my head to the side, hands braced on the desk, to give him unobstructed access. His lips singe my skin, sending sparks of heat low into my belly (and lower), leaving me wet and wanting more. His hungry lips drift to my collarbone, licking the dip there, and my legs clench in response.

"Wait . . ." I groan, pulsing with desire. Rafael peels his face away, and the ravenousness in his gaze makes me want to be his feast. Legs weak, I drop them from around his waist and push from the desk. Rafael watches, his breathing hitched and stilted, but I need to even the playing field . . . so I start with his shirt, my fingers surprisingly agile and adept as they begin to unbutton the very frustrating and inconvenient row of buttons. Rafael growls impatiently and dips his face to my neck, where his tongue flicks against my skin, making me stumble.

"Cheater," I breathe. He chuckles into my ear, a husky laugh that has me tearing through the last of the buttons. "Take it off."

When he pulls away, his eyes are glazed with want. "Bossy," he says, peeling the shirt off and tossing it onto the sofa.

His chest is tanned and toned, and I want to give in to the fantasies his bare chest (and other parts) inspired that morning in his bed. So I hook my finger into his pants and tug him back into me, kissing the length of his neck, along his collarbone, letting my lips taste and nip and lick, enjoying the way he tenses as I go. My fingers explore his chest, lingering as I caress the dips of his muscles, moving downward.

His hands capture mine before I can reach for his belt. "We need to even the score," he rasps, ragged and breathless.

I lift my gaze from his hips to his eyes, which hypnotize me long enough that his fingers hook beneath the strap of my dress and tug it down. He does the same to the other side, until the top of my dress falls to my waist. His eyes shutter as his fingers graze the bare skin of my abdomen. I shiver at the contact, leaning into him. His hand moves upward, along my stomach, his fingers plucking on invisible strings and making my insides sing in want.

"You're fucking incredible," he says, cupping my breasts.

"You're a terrible tease." I twist my head into the crook of his neck and bite.

Rafael lets out a low, tortured sound as his hands slip from my chest to my hips, spinning me around in one fluid move. My hands anchor me to the desk as his body molds to mine from behind, his bare chest pressed to my spine.

My breath hitches into my throat as liquid heat soaks through my panties. He drops a kiss into the crook of my neck, and I shiver and tighten everywhere. His hand skims along the length of my abdomen, grazing my ribs, then my hips, until he reaches the hem of my dress, where he grips onto my thigh. The promise in that grip makes my nipples harden, and his lips on my shoulder—his tongue against my skin—make me want to dig my nails into the desk.

I almost combust into a pile of ash as Rafael lifts the hem of my dress upward, leaving my skin exposed. His fingers and lips tease and torture, and when I think I can't possibly break apart even further, his hand slides from the hot flesh of my thigh to my panties. I arch into him, into his hardness, gasping when his fingers slide beneath the lace. The heat in my body collects in the place where his fingers touch and stroke, and it takes only seconds to convince me the clit is most certainly an organ, with the vital function of making me feel like I'm alive for the first time in so long.

Rafael's fingers plunge in and out of me, creating a friction that makes me press into him.

"I—please—" I gasp, pressing into the hard length of him. Rafael bites the place between my shoulder and neck, and I buck into him when his finger turns into two. I tighten around him, gasping, "Please."

"Since you asked nicely . . ." He nips at my ear. I barely register his movements, so focused on not dissolving into a pile of molten lava on the floor. "Now, stay." Rafael's fingers slip out of me, and I throb, needing him back.

I twist so I can see him. He's in his boxer briefs, which hide none of his erection, but he's not taking them off . . . and he's taking so long.

"What?" I breathe, turning fully to face him.

"I don't have any condoms."

"I have an IUD," I say, low and impatient, watching as he removes the rest of his clothing. Rafael dressed is a sight to behold; undressed, he's a sight to drink in, over and over again.

He watches me like he's the one who's thirsty, and he closes the space between us.

"Raf." I tug him impatiently, needing him to ruin me already. He lifts my hips, wrapping my legs around him, the heat of him pressed against me making me feel like an endangered—soon-to-be-extinct—species. When I feel like I'll combust from the buildup of pressure and heat, I growl at him hurry up already.

"So impatient, Ms. Pope." His hands grip my thighs as he braces my ass against the desk.

"Raf—"

He pushes into me before I can say anything more. I moan as my walls clench around him, wet and wanting. He pauses, breathing hard and ragged. "Fuck." He pushes into me again, and the room blurs. And again. And again. Rafael grips my hips as he drives into and out of me, increasing the tempo as he goes. My breasts move against his chest while my breaths come out in ragged puffs. I find myself chanting his name, and I wonder if I begged this hard when it came to getting back into my body.

The friction of his skin on mine, him inside me, makes me think no. I've never wanted anything as badly as I want this, right now. Right. Now.

"Raf, I . . ." I pant, digging my nails into the wood of the desk. "Please."

His moves harder and faster, everything coming to a crescendo. "Now," he growls. All at once, my pulse quickens. My vision fades. My muscles tighten. And I come like it's the first and last time, shuddering with him.

He groans, dropping his forehead against mine.

We're both breathing hard.

But I'm extinct.

* * *

Dressing feels like a crime when all I want to do is push Rafael onto the sofa, straddle him, and return the favor of making him feel like he doesn't have a choice, any control. I'm fixing my dress while Rafael is buttoning his shirt. He smiles when he reaches the two holes without the buttons.

I bite my lip. "Sorry."

He tucks the shirt into his pants. "No, you're not."

"You're right, I'm not." I drag my fingers through my tousled hair. Rafael approaches, his hands gripping my hips. I heat all over as he tugs me to him. "You're going to miss your party."

"There's so much tequila flowing, no one will notice."

I think about Gemma pacing the length of the club, Mama Bear on the prowl. "You might have to explain yourself to a person or two."

Rafael presses a searing kiss to my lips, setting me aflame anew. I push upward on my toes and press into him, running my hands up his torso. When he groans, I bury my fingers into his hair, pulling his head to mine while our tongues explore. His hands move up my back, hot and desperate against the material of my dress.

"Raf—" I rasp after a minute, unable to pull myself away. If only there weren't an entire crowd waiting for him. "We need to go."

He nods, his forehead against mine, his breathing heavy. His thumb brushes against my cheek, then my bottom lip. "What do you call rivals who fall for each other?"

I smile, circling his waist. "Unprepared?"

Rafael chuckles. "Smartass."

I drop my hands to his ass. "Firm ass," I say, and squeeze, surprising him. "Although I'm not sure how your diet makes this possible."

"Part of the Vela package."

I roll my eyes and playfully shove him away. "You're incorrigible."

"I think you mean irresistible."

"I hope you're better at your new job than at your old one, Raffy Taffy."

He brushes back his hair and smooths down his shirt. "Better? Probably not. But I do have an office now, so I'm looking forward to taking full advantage of it."

EPILOGUE
THREE MONTHS LATER

Back in a Media Lab conference room, I'm about to make my first pitch meeting since returning to work—a return that took longer than expected thanks to an extended out-of-office. A time during which a lot happened, but to keep things short and sweet—I was promoted.

It happened the Monday after I spent the rest of the weekend holed up in Rafael's apartment (because I missed it, and admitting that is *not* a symptom of a terminal fever; extra perk—Gemma couldn't make surprise visits there). Upon my return, Dana promoted me, minimal questions asked. The promotion came with a raise, an office, and ten account managers, including Gemma, who had taken on several of my clients while I was gone.

Today she's with me in this very important pitch meeting, dressed in a navy jumpsuit that makes her auburn ponytail pop. She's on her third cup of coffee while I haven't even touched mine. Coffee makes me jittery . . . and jitters are the last thing I need when there's a fifty-page presentation and a ten-item checklist I need to get through during this meeting.

If we land this account, it could bring Media Lab a few million dollars over the next five years, possibly more as the business scales. *Crucial* doesn't begin to cover what this means for me.

Dressed in pale pink and plum, I'm standing at the head of the massive conference table, a wall-sized TV monitor at my back. An assortment of fruit and pastries graces the center of the table, water bottles and glasses at each of the six seats around it. Gemma and her assistant, Finn, sit on one side, while Dana taps furiously at her phone on the other. Her jet-black hair matches her blazer, and her equally inky nails swipe furiously at her phone. "You might want to stop chewing those pretty nails, Pope," she says, not bothering to glance up.

I drop my hand from between my lips, embarrassed I've been called out.

Truth is—I'm nervous AF. I've been in this conference room countless times, pitching numerous clients, strategizing marketing plans for several accounts, and contemplating Rafael's downfall. We spent hours collaborating on accounts and sharing late-night takeout. After our fallout, we sat across from each other, holding silent staring contests or vying to share the most input. We've been chided for our behavior, and we've been celebrated for our successes. There's so much history inside the walls of this conference room that it makes me unreasonably emotional. On top of it, this pitch meeting is the first one after my accident, but it may as well be my first one ever. My throat's dry, my hands clammy, and I think I need another layer of deodorant.

Eager for a diversion, I turn my gaze from Dana's fervent swiping to the floor-to-ceiling windows. It's a sunny day, even for late September, and the trees in the park below are changing color. Through the gaps in the buildings ahead of us, I catch glimpses of the lake. Not long after we decided we had a lot of lost time to recover, Rafael and I went back to the beach to recheck item #72 off my bucket list—only this time we followed the rules and *skinny*-dipped. We spent hours enjoying the lake, and while it was a few degrees above chilly, I'm still partly shocked the water wasn't boiling by the time we got out. Heat licks along my neck at the memory, and my thighs clench in response.

"They're here!" The office assistant's perky voice snaps my attention to the door. I instinctively straighten and smooth down my outfit as nerves skate along my back. I press a cold hand to my cheeks as everyone stands. Gemma frowns at me, and I mouth *I'm okay* before she can engage Mama Bear, who is still very much a thing. I catch Dana's gaze next, but hers is the opposite of Mama Bear, which, I suppose, is a determined hunter, because it tells me to *not screw up or else*. I give her and Gemma a thumbs-up.

Nothing to worry about.

Nothing.

Lupe walks in first, her caramel curls bouncing as she struts into the room. Her megawatt smile is hard to resist. Even Dana's lips quirk in response as she holds her hand out for an intro.

I watch the door, waiting. Rafael strolls in, his eyes finding mine like magnets. The brief gaze makes me grip the edge of the table. "Hi," he says, grinning. The Dimple makes an appearance.

"Hi," I respond, my voice a little more strangled than firm. "Welcome back."

"Yes, welcome back, Rafael." Dana smiles brightly (and authentically) as she shakes his hand. "It's nice to see you." While Dana hasn't been into men in at least three decades, genuine joy creases her face when Rafael pulls her into a hug.

"You can miss people, Dana. It's a normal reaction," he says, his eyes locking with mine, his gaze searing and doing things to me that scream NSFW. I blink away the thoughts.

Dana allows herself to be held for all of two seconds before she pulls away and fixes her hair.

"You rascal," she chides, sliding back into her seat. Rafael makes the rounds until he reaches me. He takes my hand, his touch warm and grounding. My toes curl. My breath stutters. And my cheeks blaze like I've sprinted. I want to tug him closer—but I don't because I'm the consummate professional . . . and because Gemma and Lupe are the only ones who know there's an *us*.

"Can't wait to see what you have planned for La Clandestina, Ms. Pope," Rafael says. His thumb brushes the inside of my wrist.

My breath catches, goosebumps trailing up my arm. "It won't disappoint."

His eyes spark with heat and mischief. "Is that a promise?"

"It's a guarantee," I say, so breathless it sounds like my words are clipped.

"Please, I thought we were past this," Dana intones from her seat. "Let's play nice, Pope. We're trying to *win* the account, for hell's sake."

Rafael and I exchange knowing glances. "I aim to please," I respond, my voice sweet and sunny, with just enough edge to tease out Rafael's smirk.

And because I can't help myself—and everyone seems temporarily distracted—I swipe my planner off the table. As expected, Rafael reaches down for it. I follow, crouching beside him.

His eyes crash into mine at the same time my lips press against his—soft and fast, but enough to knock the air out of both of us. I feel his surprise in the stillness of his hands, the way his breath catches. And then I pull away.

"Magnets in the floor," I say with a wink, reaching for my planner.

"Evie."

"Rafael."

I straighten, heart pounding.

Item #100: *Live a little. Each day.*

Check.

ACKNOWLEDGMENTS

Hey there—

You made it. All the way to the end. Which means you've either just read the last page of Evie's story or (no judgment) flipped here first to see the mushy stuff. Either way, I'm so glad you're here.

This part of a book—tucked right at the end—is magic. It's more than a rite of passage; it's the summation of the journey. I think of acknowledgements as a kind of bucket list in reverse—not the dreams we're chasing, but the people who made them possible. Books aren't born in isolation—they're long, winding journeys, and so many hands and hearts are part of the making.

So if you're here—thank you. Thank you, dear reader, for picking up Evie's story. I hope it made you laugh, maybe pause a moment, and most of all, inspired you to stop saving your "someday" lists for someday and start crossing them off now.

This book was my big bucket list item—the one at the very top: *Write a book.* Closely followed by *Publish a book.* I couldn't tell you which was harder, but both stretched me (in more ways than one), made me question my life's choices, and brought me the care of so many others.

My writing journey began long before this story (think: when I first held a pencil), and it really gained steam with the Instagram writing community, where I met people who became part of my bucket list of gratitude. Amanda Munro was there for the clunky first draft of a fantasy romance (I'm so sorry). Hillary Sames, Anca Demeter, Camille Le Baron, Jessica Parra, and Alexandra Kiley—thank you for your part in this journey. Sari and Rosalie—thank you for guiding me through Pitch Wars and beyond, for helping me grow as a writer, and for showing me what came next. To those who were there in big and small ways—even if it was just to tell me, "You're doing great"—I appreciate you. And to my beloved Manifestors of Swoon—Jenn, Monique, and Nirmaliz—what a privilege to have you along for this ride, long before publishing was even on the horizon! (P.S.—We're due for a writing retreat.)

The publishing journey wouldn't have happened without my amazing agent, Aurora Fernandez, who took a chance on Evie and Rafael and helped turn my biggest bucket list dream into a reality. You've gone above and beyond in championing this story, and I'm endlessly grateful (and indebted to you). I also had the privilege of working with two incredible editors—Holly Ingraham, who saw a place for *Dead Set on You* in bookstores and took the bet, and Jess Verdi, who adopted Evie, Raf, and me later on with such enthusiasm and care. Holly and Jess, your encouragement and belief in this story mean the world, and I value you both deeply.

To the entire Alcove Press team—Thai Fantauzzi Pérez, Julia Abbott, Rebecca Nelson, Dulce Botello, Mikaela Bender, Stephanie Manova, Lexi Baker, and Megan Matti—thank you for the talent, time, and heart you brought to every step. Each of you had a hand in shaping this book and shepherding it into the world, and I'm so grateful. And to Mallory Heyer—thank you for creating a cover that was its own little bucket list dream.

To my village—my squad, my fam—you're the real reason this book exists. Lori—you're more than a BFF; you're my truest champion. Thank you for reading every draft of everything, every time. I could dedicate this whole section to you (and one day I will). Chloe—you're the kind of friend who makes "thank you" feel too small. Your excitement for this book and characters kept me going, you celebrated every milestone, and you made the journey all the more worth it. I'm so glad you're part of my (and this) story.

To my other amazing readers and supporters—Casi, Marie, Miha, and Iulia—thank you for reading this story in its infancy and cheering me on. The Baddest Bs—thank you for your enthusiasm along the way.

To my family—my parents, for making it possible to dream at all. Alex, for keeping two little vamplings fed and happy so I could write. Julian and Luca, for inspiring me to show you that the biggest, scariest dreams are worth chasing—and possible.

And last—but always first—I'm endlessly grateful to my constant in every storm, plot hole, and writing block: God. Thank You for making every bucket list possible.

I wish there were better ways to thank you all—but these words on these last few pages are the best I've got. So if being in someone's acknowledgements was ever on your own bucket list, consider it officially crossed off.

Acknowledgements may come at the end, but they're really the beginning—of the next story, the next dream, the next thing to cross off the list. Let's get started.